T0265892

PRAISE FOR *CONFESSIONS*
BY CATHERINE AIREY

'*Confessions* is a remarkable debut. A complex and compulsive read that unravels the intricate twists and revelations among three generations of women with elegance and urgency.'
—Miranda Cowley Heller, author of *The Paper Palace*

'*Confessions* is a beating heart of a novel, intricate both in its weaving and its unspooling. An irresistible read.'
—Yael van der Wouden, author of *The Safekeep*

'Brilliantly conceived and magnificently executed, I truly could not put it down. I haven't come across as honest, truthful, compelling and gripping a writer for decades. The work of a debut novelist that feels like the work of a seasoned and highly accomplished author.'
—Anna Fitzgerald, author of *Girl in the Making*

'I was mesmerized from the very first pages of Catherine Airey's startling debut, *Confessions*. The story of Máire and Róisín, two Irish sisters living an ocean apart, proceeds with an almost hypnotic power and grace – it has the certainty of fable and the true originality of a powerful new voice in fiction.'
—Tara Conklin, author of *The Last Romantics*

'*Confessions* is a tender and bitingly original work that effortlessly weaves the parochial weight of Irish family history with the mendacious allure of Manhattan's seedy streets. Catherine Airey reads like a natural successor to Maeve Brennan, a chronicler of the pain and peril of self-determination.'
—Darragh McKeon, author of *Remembrance Sunday*

'Exciting, expansive and transporting storytelling. It's hard to believe *Confessions* is a debut novel.'
—Roxy Dunn, author of *As Young as This*

'*Confessions* is a remarkable debut. With fearless ambition and phenomenal poise, Catherine Airey weaves an intricate and far-reaching tale that is both compelling and heartbreaking.'

–Ben Hinshaw, author of *Exactly What You Mean*

'A sweeping story that spans both generations and continents, Catherine Airey's *Confessions* is, at its heart, about the desire to know ourselves and those who came before us as well as an exploration of the mystery that lies at the heart of love. A bold and ambitious debut from a remarkable new writer.'

–Daisy Alpert Florin, author of *My Last Innocent Year*

'Catherine Airey's *Confessions* is a wonderfully moreish feast of family drama, flowing prose and psychologically compelling characters. I devoured this remarkable debut that charts the lives of three generations of women and their intense interior lives. Gracefully plotted with sentences that glide along, it's a book that rollercoasters with secrets and revelations, exploring love and desire, longing and belonging. Airey's novel has the complex yet deeply human undertones and poetry of Anne Enright combined with the effortless flow and vim of Louise Kennedy. I absolutely adored this novel and will be reading all future books by this immensely talented author.'

–Rupert Dastur, author of *Cloudless*

'One of 2025's most exciting literary debuts.'

–*Service95*

'An absolute triumph that deserves to be read widely.'

–*Bookseller*

Confessions

CATHERINE AIREY

MARINER BOOKS

New York   Boston

CONFESSIONS. Copyright © 2025 by Catherine Airey. All rights reserved. Printed in the United States of America. No part of this book may be used or reproduced in any manner whatsoever without written permission except in the case of brief quotations embodied in critical articles and reviews. For information, address HarperCollins Publishers, 195 Broadway, New York, NY 10007.

The Mariner flag design is a registered trademark of HarperCollins Publishers LLC.

HarperCollins books may be purchased for educational, business, or sales promotional use. For information, please email the Special Markets Department at SPsales@harpercollins.com.

Originally published as *Confessions* in the United Kingdom in 2025 by Viking.

FIRST U.S. EDITION

Library of Congress Cataloging-in-Publication Data has been applied for.

ISBN 978-0-06-338013-4

24 25 26 27 28 LBC 5 4 3 2 1

For everyone I've loved but left

She herself is a haunted house. She does not
possess herself; her ancestors sometimes come and
peer out of the windows of her eyes
and that is very frightening.

Angela Carter,
The Bloody Chamber and Other Stories

Contents

The Game

Scream School is a text-based choose-your-own-adventure video game. It puts you, the player, right at the centre of the story. You get to decide how it unfolds.

In this adventure, sisters Magnolia and Rosemary have been sent away to boarding school in Burtonport, County Donegal.

Not long after they arrive, students start to disappear.

Your task is to help the sisters set aside their differences, so they can work together to unearth the school's secrets and save the students.

But tread carefully. Your efforts must not be discovered — if they are you risk grave peril.

Cora Brady

New York

2001

I

Two days after she disappeared, most of my mother's body washed up in Flushing Creek. The morgue had comfy armchairs in the lobby, and I can remember being annoyed that it didn't take longer for my father to identify the body. I was reading *Little Women* and would have quite happily sat there all day. I was eight.

Almost exactly eight years later, my father jumped from the 104th floor of the World Trade Center, North Tower. I don't know that he jumped for sure, but it's the story I've told myself.

I saw the photo of the Falling Man the next morning in the *New York Times*, along with everyone else left in the world. As well as that famous one, the photographer captured eleven others of the same man falling. Years later, when it became possible for a person to do such a thing, I inspected each photo, then pieced them together like a kineograph to see the man in motion, tumbling over and over.

For a while it was accepted that the man had been a pastry chef working in the Windows on the World restaurant. Later they said he was a sound engineer, brother to a singer who had been in Village People. They never said it was my father. I never told anyone that I thought it could be him – not just because the chances of it being true were next to none, but because I knew I wouldn't have been able to handle being proved wrong.

If someone were to somehow *not* know what had happened that day, and simply seen that photo, they'd be forgiven for thinking it must be showing some kind of stunt.

In 1974, a man had walked between the tops of the two towers on a wire tightrope. The following year, a different man dressed up as a construction worker made his way to the roof of the North Tower and jumped off, attached to a parachute. Two years after that, a third man scaled the side of the South Tower. It took him less than four hours to reach the top. None of these men were harmed.

I knew all about these stunts because I'd done a homeroom presentation on the towers once in elementary school. I remember asking my parents (my mother was still alive at the time) if they remembered any of this happening, but they told me that they weren't even living in New York at that point. The main thing they seemed to recall about coming to the city was the garbage strikes – piles of trash, eight feet high along the sidewalks. But what did I care about trash?

· · ·

When the first plane hit, I was waiting for Kyle to come over. We'd spent the summer taking drugs and having sex in my apartment while my father was at work. I was supposed to be going into Junior Year, but in the week since Labor Day I'd stayed at home deleting voicemails left by the school.

Mr Brady, this is Principal Green calling from Our Lady of

Perpetual Help. Cora wasn't in roll call today, again. Could you please call back.

By the time I got up, my father had already left for work. I showered, brushed my teeth and put on a dress I didn't think Kyle had seen yet. It was navy with little lady-bug dots on it. The weather was perfect, the sky such a fearless blue. I was going to try to persuade Kyle to walk as far as Coney Island. But I could already imagine him calling it 'Phoney Island'. I liked it there – the playground of the world. My favourite film at the time was *Annie Hall* and they'd recently taken down the roller coaster that had been featured in it. I wanted to see what kind of presence its absence had created. I liked the fact that Coney Island was always changing and yet somehow felt the same. I wanted to walk along Surf Avenue and for Kyle to see me sparkling in the sunlight. I wanted summer to never end. I wanted to pretend.

I checked the time on the microwave. Kyle was late. I hated waiting for things, because I was always on time or early. So was my father. He said it was an incurable illness I'd inherited from him.

There was a bowl of dry oatmeal on the kitchen island. My father prepared it each morning to encourage me to eat breakfast, as if the effort of pouring out the oats from the packet was the thing stopping me from eating. I added what was left of the milk to the bowl and put it in the microwave, set the timer for two minutes and stared at the bowl spinning round and round through the darkened glass.

I was pissed at Kyle. He didn't have a cell phone and used this as an excuse to show up well after we'd agreed.

I would remind him that people did manage to be on time before they were invented and that, actually, if he did have one he'd at least be able to let me know how late he was going to be. But he thought cell phones were going to rot everyone's brains and make them impotent, that they were invented to control the world's population which was getting out of control. The anticlimax that had been Y2K was still a sore point for him.

The timer on the microwave went off. I stirred the oatmeal and put it on for another minute, then looked around for the remote so I could watch TV while I waited. Kyle had been four hours late once, with some excuse about the subway being down and after that being searched by the cops. He said I didn't live in the real world. Sometimes he called me 'princess' and I didn't know if he was saying it because he cared about me or because he didn't. He liked the fact that I had money and an apartment that was empty most of the time, the fact that the refrigerator was usually full and that I had my own room. He said he liked my body and the way that I smiled and the smell of my hair. But if I asked him how many girls he'd slept with before me or if he saw any of them still, he would get mad and say I was such a kid and I wouldn't see him for a while. He'd show up in the end pretending nothing had happened and I'd pretend like nothing had happened too because I'd been going crazy for three days wondering if I'd ever see him again.

Once he yelled that nothing bad had ever happened to me and that made me cry. He told me to 'turn off the waterworks' and I realized I could play my mother like a trump card, my get-out-of-jail-free, the ace up my sleeve. It worked. I knew that I had used her death for my advantage, and wondered if doing so would come back to bite me. I suppose it did.

Call it fate, call it karma, call it cosmic justice keeping the universe in balance. Belief in whatever it was would leave me making stupid bargains in my head. If I could just do X then maybe Y would happen. If I went out and walked for an hour and didn't step on any of the cracks then maybe Kyle would be waiting outside when I got back. If I fasted for a day then I'd hear from him the next morning. Often these bargains didn't work out, or I wouldn't stick to my end of them, but I'd still make them with myself – with God or whatever.

My mother had been a Catholic and took me to mass when I was growing up. I found it hard to breathe there. Perhaps it was the incense. When I told her this she started crying so I didn't mention it again. When I got older, I assumed she'd been upset because she thought I had asthma or something, but she never took me to a doctor to get my lungs checked out. I still get the same breathlessness whenever I am feeling anxious. I know now that it's just my body reacting to feeling out of control, but at the time I took it as a sign that God was there, sitting on my chest. Those were the moments when He might be bargained with, I thought.

As I got older, the nature of these bargains began to change. Instead of promising to do a good thing in exchange for something I wanted, I would do a bad thing on purpose. I don't know what the rationale behind this was. Perhaps I wanted to prove that God wasn't real rather than to trust in His existence. How many bad things could a person do, I wondered, before the universe would seek them out in some way? I suppose I just wanted to be seen – for something, or someone, to intervene.

The remote was between the cushions on the couch, where Kyle had taken my virginity and I'd had to soak the cushion cover in the sink to try and get the bloodstain out after. I forgot you were supposed to use cold water, not hot. When my father got home that evening I told him it was tomato sauce. He probably thought I was on my period, so he didn't question it. Sometimes when I lied to him I'd hope that he would question it, but he never did.

The timer had gone off on the microwave again. I wasn't hungry. I was angry. There was still time for me to go to school, to cut Kyle off and turn my life around. I know now that it was too late for my father to survive, that it had already happened. But I still blame myself for what I did next, still believe that if I'd made a different decision it might have changed everything, stopped everything.

I did it because I wanted to feel different to how I felt then, waiting. I went to where I'd stashed the acid tabs, between pages 100 and 101 in my copy of *Beloved*. I took one out and put it in my mouth. I held it underneath my tongue like Kyle had told me to the first time I had taken it.

'Hold it there for ten minutes, princess,' he had said.

I shut the book and put it down on the coffee table. I turned on the TV and went to get my oatmeal from the microwave, even though I knew I wasn't going to eat it. I heard the news reporter before I saw the footage.

Witnesses at the scene said they heard an explosion. We are still waiting to confirm exactly what the cause of that explosion was. As you can see, there is currently a lot of smoke coming out of the World Trade Center, North Tower.

2

Worrying about my father is one of my clearest child-hood memories. Well, actually, witnessing my mother worrying about my father after the World Trade Center bombings in 1993. He was fine, obviously, but my mother was frantic waiting for him to call. The memory is specific not because I really understood what was going on, but because it was the first time I was fully conscious of trying to stay calm for the sake of my mother, as she paced up and down beside the phone in our apartment. I stood, still as a statue, out of her way, staring at the hour hand on the clock in the kitchen, trying to catch it moving.

My mother suffered from agoraphobia, hypochondria, paranoia – and many other ia's. Because she didn't like to leave the apartment much, my father and I would go off on trips – just the two of us, walking. She'd fret that it wasn't safe. He'd insist it was important that I didn't become one of those city kids with no experience of surviving in the open. We'd sleep up in mountains in a tent and cook canned food on a Primus stove. I wasn't afraid of bears or cougars. I knew what I should do if I came across a rattlesnake: *stay calm, don't panic*. There's a photo of me with my arms wide trying to stretch around a giant tree trunk during Redwood Summer. Another of me lying on my front at the edge of the Grand Canyon, looking down, a New York Giants cap backwards on my head.

. . .

As I turned to face the TV, a line I'd rehearsed from that homeroom presentation, about the Twin Towers stunts, started playing in my head.

The Twin Towers are taller than the highest redwood, but no way near as deep as the Grand Canyon.

I thought that if I didn't move the phone might ring. Or perhaps if I didn't breathe? As I watched the second plane slice into the South Tower, I remembered what I'd done, put my finger under my tongue. The yin-yang symbol had blurred into a black hole on my fingertip. The paper had pretty much dissolved.

I figured I had about an hour before I'd really feel the acid – an hour for my father to call, for Kyle to show up. I grabbed my cell phone, left the door on the latch and headed for the stairs. When I got out on to the roof I could see smoke trailing from the towers, seemingly straight over the East River to Brooklyn. It smelt like burning wire. There were other people up there too, all of us staring at the same thing, like we'd been hypnotized.

I tried calling my father's office number. Then his cell. Both played back arpeggios that sounded like the end of the world.

Dum di dah. Dum di dah.

I waited. Tried again.

Dum di dah.

I closed my eyes and counted. I made all kinds of

promises. But I knew they wouldn't work this time, that I couldn't undo what I had done, unsee what I had seen.

'There must be hundreds dead,' someone said.

'Thousands,' said someone else.

'Do you think anyone can get out from above where the planes went in?'

'Man, I wouldn't even believe a movie where this happened.'

I began to panic like my mother did on the day of the bombing. My breath caught in my chest. I was burning up. Even my arms began to bead with sweat. When the South Tower collapsed I thought I must finally be hallucinating. The cloud of dust and debris was alive, breathing, colour streaming from what I could see of the North Tower like a rainbow, then all the colours turning red, the red spreading, filling up the sky, closing in on me. I turned and ran back through the fire door, hoping I could shut the red out behind me. But I was too late. It followed me down the stairs and into the apartment. I was gasping for breath. I held my hands over my face but I could feel it entering my mouth through the gaps between my fingers, possessing me. My ears began to ring. My vision was static, like bad-quality video. The grains of red were shuddering and each had its own high-frequency voice, like they were all whispering, laughing. The picture on the TV had turned red too and when I closed my eyes the insides were like fireballs.

The voices became screams when the North Tower fell too. I turned off the TV and closed my eyes, covered my ears with my hands and thought about how ostriches bury their heads in the sand.

I crawled over to the answering machine, on my hands and knees. Nothing. I unplugged the phone and sat in the corner of the room, knees pulled into my chest. I pleaded with the Devil for some kind of grim trade. But I knew I couldn't stay in hell for ever. I wasn't strong enough.

I remembered the pills Kyle had given me to look after, how he'd said people would pay a fortune for just one to help them sleep after festivals and raves.

'Sweet, dreamless, sleep,' he would say when people asked him what they did.

We'd never taken them together because I didn't want to sleep when I was around Kyle. What I liked about getting high together was that it would keep us both awake. I wanted to stay up with Kyle for ever.

I was hiding the bottles behind where I kept my sanitary pads, which I never used and knew my father would never touch. I found the pills, poured three into my hand and swallowed them at the sink, being careful not to look in the mirror.

I thought about the way my father helped me fall asleep when I was little. We would play what he called the alphabet game. First, we would come up with a category, then take turns going through the alphabet, thinking of something in that category that began with each letter.

American Cities, I thought. *Anchorage, Boston, Chicago . . .*

I went to my room.

Denver, El Paso, Fargo . . .

I hardly made it any further.

3

When I woke it was light. White, not red. The colour of my ceiling. When I blinked, the insides of my eyes were basically black. Outside my window, the sky was blue, but only at the edges, either side of the trail of smoke still blowing over from the city.

My cell phone had run out of battery. I must have slept through the rest of the day. The whole night, too. I didn't bother plugging it in. I didn't turn on the TV. I knew that what I'd seen was both real and not real, that I'd tripped into a hellscape from the shock of something that had really happened. I knew my father must be dead, along with countless others. I knew there wasn't anything that I could do, but I needed to get out of the apartment, to get closer to where it had happened.

As I headed for the Brooklyn Bridge, along Flatbush Avenue, I kept closing my eyes then opening them again to check the towers were still gone. It was like I was pretending my eyelids were the shutter in a camera, and I needed to capture enough images to categorically prove the towers were no longer there. I was sure I could still make out their outline. I wondered if this was what it was like to lose a limb and still feel it.

There were NYPD officers stopping people from crossing the bridge into the city. A woman was pleading with them, saying that her son had been there. She was fighting them, punching at them, crying and yelling until she was exhausted. The officers took the beating. They comforted her afterwards. She fell down on to the concrete and the officer she'd just been hitting crouched to put his arm around her shoulder.

I turned back the way I had come, this time taking Sixth Avenue instead of Fifth. That's when I saw it: the photo of the Falling Man on the front page of the *New York Times*. I picked a copy up and handed it to the man behind the kiosk, then realized I hadn't brought any money out with me. I was still wearing the ladybug dress. I tapped its sides as if hoping it might have grown pockets overnight.

'Take it,' the vendor said. 'I'm not gonna make money outta that poor man's final moments. People falling from the sky. In New York City!'

I thought about saying thank you, but I couldn't work out how to do it. It was like a wire had been cut that prevented the physical act of making words come out of my mouth.

'Here. Take this, too. You look as if you need it, ladybug.'

He had handed me a Twix.

. . .

Back in the apartment I sat down at the table and read the paper from cover to cover before I allowed myself to go back and look at the picture. Reading had always helped me to stay calm, to escape my thoughts when they began to gain momentum. Pictures rarely worked on me in the same way. But I couldn't tell you what I read that day. It could have all been in a foreign language and I wouldn't have noticed. I was reading the words but thinking about the picture, and trying to remember what my father's last words to me had been, or what mine had been to him.

I know that we had Chinese takeout Monday night, that we watched two episodes of *Everybody Loves Raymond* before the New York Giants game, during which I fell asleep.

I realized I hadn't eaten anything since that meal, remembered there were leftovers of beef and black bean noodles in the fridge. My bowl of oatmeal was still on the coffee table in front of the couch, congealing beside *Beloved*. I found myself gagging when I scraped the oats into the trashcan. I gagged some more when I opened up the plastic tub the noodles were in. I knew I wouldn't be able to eat them but I couldn't bring myself to throw them away. I put the lid back on and placed the tub back in the refrigerator. The shiny wrapper of the Twix was poking out from under where I'd put down the paper. Had the man at the kiosk given me a chocolate bar that looked like the towers on purpose? I took both bars out and bit into one, then the other. I demolished them in ten seconds flat.

4

They reopened the bridges into the city and I somehow made it past the downtown checkpoints. There was still dust in the air, everywhere. The smell reminded me of using a soldering iron to make a circuit board in middle school. Some people were wearing surgical masks, or pressing wet dishcloths to their faces. It was like being on set for a movie about the apocalypse. I could feel the dust getting into my chest, but I hadn't brought anything to cover my face with. It was the same feeling as I got during mass. I walked through the discomfort. I walked not knowing what else to do.

It was quiet. Hardly any cars. As I got closer to where the towers had been I heard sirens. Fire engines and ambulances drove right down the middle of the street. There were papers that had been blown out of the wreckage swirling down the sidewalk, getting stuck in trees.

The National Guard were patrolling roadblocks, stopping civilians from getting closer. The first time a fighter jet flew by I thought it was happening all over again. I cowered in a doorway, not knowing if I should go inside or run away, which way to turn. I froze. I could feel the panic building in my chest, the world distorting, like the acid was still in my system, the red coming for me again. I started counting as I slid down the side of the doorway on to the ground, holding myself around my waist.

'Hey girl, you OK?'

I opened my eyes. A man had crouched down beside me. Big, probably in his mid-to-late thirties. He was wearing sunglasses but he pushed them up on to his head so I could see his eyes. I realized I was crying and I couldn't stop, the fear streaming through me, pushing its way out. I couldn't take a breath.

'It's all right. You're having a panic attack. It's going to be OK. I know first aid. What's your name?'

I couldn't speak, shook my head.

'My name's Gary. Those planes are scary, huh? They got me too the first time. They're fighters, patrolling. You're safe. What you doing down here, hey?'

I didn't know if he meant downtown or down on the ground. I didn't know how to explain. I didn't want to have to.

'It's all right. You don't have to talk. Just breathe, OK? Breathe with me.'

I don't know how long I stayed there, looking into Gary's dark eyes and trying to follow the pattern of his breathing. At first I couldn't. A sob would jump out of my chest and stop me from inhaling or I'd cough and feel my lungs burn and think of what must have happened to my father, in the inferno of the blast zone. Then I realized I was breathing, in and out, in time. My tears had stopped.

'Do you think you can get up?' Gary asked.

I nodded.

'OK, let's get you home, shall we? Your parents know you're here?'

I shook my head, started crying again.

'Do you want to try and call them, let them know you're

safe? My cell hasn't really been working, but it's worth a shot. Or I'll take you to a payphone.'

I shook my head again.

'I bet they're worried about you. You wanna just tell me your address? I'll make sure you get back there.'

The panic had receded enough for my thoughts to start spiralling again. I didn't want to think about what I was going to do now. I didn't want to have to tell anyone about my father, to admit I was an orphan now. Something about the care that Gary was showing me was making me want to hide. I knew I needed comforting, but I didn't want to believe that I did. I had spent all summer pretending to be an adult. But it was obvious to Gary that I wasn't, that I hadn't been fooling anyone, that I was just a child.

'What about a friend?' Gary said. 'If you just put a number in my cell.' He was holding his phone out to me.

I ran. I ran even when I could tell Gary had given up following me. He wasn't in good shape. I had been on the track team. But I was running out of energy, running on only the sugar content of a Twix bar. I stopped, out of breath, my calf muscles like jelly. I didn't know where I was and couldn't see any street signs. The sun was falling between the buildings like an egg yolk about to burst. The movie theater I was outside had a paper sign Blu-tacked in the door.

All movies will be free today. Stop for a soda and popcorn.

. . .

It was a relief to smell popcorn, to suck up Sprite through a straw and for it to taste the same as it ever did – not like the stuff you got in the store, but watered down, the cup half-full with ice. It was cool inside the theater, mostly empty. Nothing inside suggested that the world had changed. None of the actors in any of the trailers knew what was going to happen.

The movie was about two siblings who were at college together, driving home for spring break. It was set on the other side of the country on the other side of the year. It worked as an escape, put me into a meditative state. I was hardly following what was happening until the final frame, which showed the brother's disfigured head, his eyes gouged out. It didn't affect me.

I stayed sitting until they'd finished playing all the credits. The lights went on and I realized I was cold. There were goosebumps on my arms. I got up and left.

. . .

That day I had learnt that in a crisis I would freeze, and flee when offered help. Not a great combination. Perhaps that had happened to my father, too. Perhaps that's why he didn't call.

The missing-people posters had already started to appear, stuck to store windows, lamp posts, trashcans, later covering whole walls like they were trying to plaster over what had happened, or make it so nobody could forget. At first they really did seem hopeful. Just like everyone waiting in line outside hospitals to give blood that was never needed, the people who put up the posters really believed there would be more survivors turning up, that perhaps people had been concussed and were unable to find their way home or to a hospital.

When I got back to the apartment it was late. I had been walking for hours. The dust on the soles of my shoes left marks on the white carpet. When I took my socks off there were blisters on my feet, red and raw. I swallowed more pills, took a shower, went to bed and slept, dreamlessly.

5

Over the days that followed I didn't plug the phone back in and I hardly watched the news. What I did was walk.

. . .

When I was twelve, my father and I planned a hike that he liked to call the Brady Bridges Tour. It involved walking over every bridge around Manhattan Island.

I can remember the two of us sitting down with the big map spread over the table, plotting out the route. I drew arrows over each bridge, pointing in the direction that we would cross it in. Then I highlighted the whole route in yellow. The plan was to start at the New Jersey side of the George Washington Bridge, walk up through Fort Tryon and Inwood Hill to the Henry Hudson Bridge, then along to Broadway Bridge, snaking back and forth until we got to Brooklyn.

'We'll cross that bridge when we get to it,' my father had joked about a hundred times, and I had rolled my eyes, almost too old to want to go on these adventures. The reason he had come up with this idea was because he knew I wouldn't want to spend the whole of spring break out of state. In fairness, I was excited to walk over all the bridges. As a child, I had loved books about explorers and adventurers, daredevils and record-setters. I knew that in 1928 a female pilot called Elinor Smith had flown under the four bridges that were then along the East River – Queensboro, Williamsburg, Manhattan and Brooklyn – when she was only seventeen, and all because a friend of hers (a man) had said that she couldn't. I liked walking with my father, and walking was all I could think to do now that he was gone.

. . .

I blew away the dust that had settled on my Pentax camera. I checked that it still worked and wore it round my neck. I took photos of the missing-people posters – not each poster, but every time I saw a different missing person. Some people must have had thousands of the same poster printed. You could follow the route they had taken, stopping every fifty steps or so to put another up. Perhaps they were telling themselves that if they covered every corner of the city with their loved one's face then they'd be waiting outside the door when they got home. Perhaps there was a magic spot, and if they could only find it and put a poster on it, they'd discover they had the power to turn back time. I understood this sort of logic, even if I didn't believe in it any more. At least putting up the posters gave them something to do instead of waiting at home for a miracle that would never happen. Walking helped, even when you didn't have a destination.

Whenever I saw a poster where the person had worked for Cantor Fitzgerald (there were so many of them), I wondered if they had known my father, if they had been with him when it happened. I wanted to call the numbers listed on the posters, but knew the call wouldn't go through to the people who were missing, just the people who were missing them.

The funeral processions went on for weeks. Bagpipe music on the streets. Fire brigades standing to attention, some of their uniforms chalky white from working on the Pile, gas masks round their necks. At the end of each day people stood out on the sidewalks to clap for the emergency service workers and volunteers as they were driven away from the wreckage on the backs of trucks. I only watched this happen once. The workers kept their heads down and stayed silent.

I didn't go to any vigils. Burning a candle wouldn't bring my father back. Instead, every evening I went to a different movie theater and watched whatever was showing.

The routine of this left me comfortably numb. I thought I'd find it difficult to sleep or be disturbed by nightmares. But every morning I would wake, a little disconcerted by how blank my brain was, how I wasn't really thinking about anything at all.

I know that other kids my age were glued to computer screens, trying to find refuge in chat rooms that came up with conspiracy theories or planned how to take revenge. We had a computer in the apartment but I didn't turn it on. I was worried that if I did the authorities would somehow figure out that I was on my own and I'd be picked up by social services. As long as I didn't talk to anyone and didn't spend too much time in the apartment and carried on walking, then I might remain undetected.

Walking also stopped me from thinking too much about the fact that Kyle had totally abandoned me. I could tell myself that perhaps he had come by while I was out walking. Perhaps he thought I'd left the city – a lot of people were simply leaving New York, too traumatized to stay. Perhaps he thought I was the kind of 'princess' who'd be sent off to boarding school upstate, or in Vermont. Then I realized that Kyle *had* known where my dad worked. Of course he had. That was where we had met, after all. I was just waiting for the hurt of this to sink in – Kyle knowing where my dad had worked and knowing what had probably happened to him, yet still leaving me alone that day, and the next, and the next – when the buzzer rang. It was the mailman.

6

Kyle and I had met on New Year's Eve, 2000. Every year there was a party in the Windows on the World restaurant and every year my dad would enter into the staff ballot for tickets. I'd been invited to a party at Madison Brooke's summer house in Montauk. I wanted to go to that party so bad, but then my dad came home one night just before Christmas holding out these tickets and I knew it would break his heart if I didn't go with him.

. . .

I'd been to my dad's office before, a few years earlier – at the end of our bridges walk, in fact. We were crossing the Brooklyn Bridge (almost home), when my dad told me to stop and turn around.

'Right up there,' he said, holding his long arm out, finger pointed. 'You see it? One hundred and fourth floor, North Tower.'

I'd seen this view before, but it never got old. The towers were so much taller than any of the others, but it was hard to get a sense of all the storeys. It almost didn't look like there were windows, just long vertical stripes of glass and metal, kind of like piped icing on a cake, melting in the sun.

I took a photo, then asked my father if he'd take my

camera into work one day and take a photo of the Brook-lyn Bridge from his office.

'Don't you want one facing the other way, towards Central Park, the Chrysler?' he asked.

'No. I want it so that I remember this,' I said.

He stared at me in that way parents gaze at their children when they're growing up, like they're looking at two versions of the same person, in a kind of mournful wonder.

'Well,' he said, 'how about we see if you can take that photo now?'

'OK,' I said, and we walked back the way we had come, back into the city.

There was music playing in the World Trade Center Plaza, like at an amusement park. The wind caught between the buildings, almost lifting me off my feet as we walked past the huge fountain with the big bronze sphere in the middle.

'Look up,' my dad said when we were standing right between the two towers.

When I turned my face up to the sky, it looked as if the towers were bending towards each other, like they were curved, not straight. It made me feel dizzy, like when you stop still after spinning round on the spot.

I was speechless, and a little scared about going up there.

At first, it didn't seem like Security were going to let us in. My father had his building pass on him, but visitors were supposed to be approved a day in advance and children weren't usually allowed in.

'She's not a child,' my father argued. 'She's twelve. And this is for her school project.' This last bit was a lie; I loved him for it, fiercely.

My father explained that you had to take two elevators to get up to his office floor, a bit like changing trains on the subway. First, you got the express elevator up to what was called the sky lobby, on the seventy-eighth floor. Then you got another elevator from the sky lobby up to the higher floors. There were ninety-nine elevators in each tower, and each elevator could hold fifty-five people.

'Easy to remember, huh?' my father said, clearly buzzed. In another life, he would have been an engineer or an explorer. He knew just as many facts about cities as he did about mountains. He said the towers were safe, and I believed him, because he was right about everything.

In the express elevator, my ears popped as we whooshed up. When we got out, I followed my father across the lobby, where we waited below a sign that said 101–107, mirror lettering on the marble wall. There were no windows in the sky lobby, much to my disappointment. I wanted to know what seventy-eight storeys high looked like so I could compare it to the top. I was at the age where I needed to experience everything very directly to believe it.

Both elevators had mirrors in the ceiling. In the second one I took a photo looking up, but the camera flashed and it came out totally over-exposed. Then the doors were opening. The 104th floor.

My father introduced me to his co-workers and I forgot their names immediately. I wanted to get to the windows, to find the right spot for me to take my photo. It wasn't like being on the observation deck of the Empire State Building, where as soon as you get out you're conscious of being in the sky. This was just a regular office space, like on TV. Commercial carpet and suspended ceiling, partition walls and panel lighting. A man was talking on the phone while leaning back on his desk chair, his head popping out of his cubicle like he was a tortoise. A woman walked past, seemingly in a hurry, but only able to take short steps because her skirt was narrow and she was wearing high heels. People had Post-it notes stuck around their computer monitors, family photos pinned up on noticeboards. It was like nobody knew how high up they were, like they had all forgotten.

My father's desk wasn't by a window, but he asked one of his co-workers – Bill or Barry or Harry or whoever – if I could stand over by his desk to take a photo. To get a good view down, I had to climb on top of a heater and press my head against the window. Earlier on, when we were walking, it had been a clear calm day, but the wind had picked up and clouds were gathering. I could feel the tower move, I swear, with my head against the glass.

'It's moving, Dad,' I said, turning around, genuinely frightened.

'It's made of iron, sweetie. It rocks a bit, up here, but it would actually be unsafe if it was rigid. Sometimes, if it's really windy, the water in the toilet bowls isn't level.'

I took my photo. It didn't come out properly. The office lighting reflected in the glass was easier to capture than the world beyond the window.

. . .

I didn't bring my camera with me to the New Year's party. I no longer thought it would be cool, taking photos of the view. And none of my friends were going to be there.

It turned out there weren't even any other teenagers at the party. This was really a relief. If there had been, we'd have been thrown together and expected to get on.

It was an awkward venue for a party. The Windows on the World restaurant had these built-in divider things that separated all the tables and doubled up as seat booths. They couldn't be removed, so everyone was standing in the space between the tables. My dad was talking to a tall blonde woman who was wearing a full-on evening gown. I think she said her name was Franny, and that she worked for some law firm in the South Tower. She was trying to involve me in the conversation but I was feeling claustrophobic, standing there, sort of behind my dad because there wasn't space for the three of us to make a proper circle. I felt sorry for the servers who were supposed to be going round with canapes and champagne. One of them was valiantly squeezing through the maze, sucking in her stomach and holding the tray high to avoid bumping into the guests, who would make sudden movements with their elbows, almost sending the contents of the tray flying. When she passed by, I followed behind her like a suckerfish so I could get out to the edge of the restaurant, then pushed my way through a fire door.

There wasn't a spectacular view. It was just a small internal courtyard where the bins were kept. But the biting winter air was such a sweet relief after the closeness of the restaurant. I turned my head up to the sky and gulped at what was left of the last hour of the year 2000. It tasted almost medicinal.

'You all right there?'

I spun around. He was sitting on the floor against the

wall, dressed like a server. He was smoking, and it took a while for my eyes to focus on his face instead of the end of the cigarette. I suppose I looked suspicious, staring down at him, not saying anything.

'Well sure, I was here first, lady,' he said, holding the cigarette between his thumb and forefinger, like men did in movies.

Nobody had ever called me 'lady' before. I wasn't sure what it meant. Did he think I was older than I was, or was it just a thing he said? I couldn't work out if it was polite or a slight. I couldn't work out his age, either. Definitely older than I was. Perhaps a college student earning money in the evenings.

'Don't talk much, do you?' He stood up. 'Here, you want some of this?'

He was holding the cigarette out to me. I only realized when I took it from him, between my forefinger and middle finger, that it was weed. I put it to my mouth, sucked the smoke inside. It tasted dry and sticky, catching in my throat and making me cough.

'Easy,' he said, not unkindly, but taking the joint back all the same, as if I'd proved I wasn't cool or mature enough to be trusted with it.

I was still coughing, my eyes watering. 'Sorry,' I managed to squeak.

'You're all right.'

But I wasn't. It took ages for me to stop coughing. I was embarrassed. I'd never smoked weed before.

He thumped me on the back, and when that didn't work he told me that he *could* go to get some water but that a) it would take ages – 'It's like Times Square in there' – and b) someone would realize that he was meant to be working so he wouldn't be able to come back out again. 'Which means I'd be leaving you out here, coughing yourself to death all on your own. And I can't be doing that now, can I?'

I shook my head, laughing now, which seemed to counteract the coughing. Then it felt like I wouldn't ever be able to stop laughing. I wasn't properly high (not yet), but that was the first time I felt that feeling – the edges of things softening, my senses sharpening. I wanted more of it.

'Thank the Lord,' he said, laughing too. He sounded crystal clear but distant. 'Thought I was gonna have to go and find whoever it is you're here with and explain that you'd dropped dead. Who are you with, by the way?'

'Just my dad,' I explained, lamely. 'He works here.'

'Lah-di-dah,' he said, looking me up and down. 'Daddy Warbucks.'

I smiled, almost apologetically.

'I'm Kyle, by the way.' He put the joint back in his mouth to free up his hand. When I shook it, he held on tight and winked as we made eye contact.

'Cora,' I said.

'Glad you found the trash, Cora. Nice dress, by the way.'

I didn't know what to say. The dress had been my mother's. It was black and tight, but really nothing special. Kyle had dropped the end of the joint on to the ground between us and I looked down at it, as if it might say something and break the silence.

'Well, I should probably go back in there. Got a bit of business going on with some of your daddy's esteemed colleagues, if you know what I mean?' He winked again and tapped the side of his nose with his little finger.

I didn't know what he meant at all.

He was about to open the door to go back inside when he turned to me and said, 'Say, Cora, if I grabbed a bottle of something do you think you could get away from Daddy Warbucks again, for the countdown?'

'I can try,' I said, feeling that heady rush of anticipation that I soon came to associate with waiting to see Kyle, waiting for that feeling.

'Try hard, princess,' he said, and I knew that nothing was going to stop me from being kissed by him at midnight.

7

'Hey,' the mailman said, through the intercom. 'Mr Brady? Miss Brady? Your mailbox is full. Can you come down and get your mail, or I won't be able to fit any more in?'

I ran downstairs to catch him.

There was a ton of mail. I used my chin to hold the pile steady as I went up the stairs. Still, a few envelopes flew out, so I had to make another trip to go back for them. I dumped everything on top of the *New York Times*, which was still on the table, and started sorting.

I used my arm to brush the magazines and junk right off the table, sending them flying to the floor. Of the letters that remained, only two were addressed to me – both used my full name. I saved them till last.

Most of the envelopes addressed to my father contained bills – for our cell phones, water and waste, power, cable, health insurance. There was also a letter from my school.

We regret to inform you that, given Cora's non-attendance this term, she will not be able to continue her studies at Our Lady of Perpetual Help. We would welcome meeting with you and Cora in the future if you decide she should return. Cora was a good student and it would be a great shame were she not to gain her high school diploma. We hope you are both well and enjoying your extended summer vacation.

I gave it the same treatment as the junk mail.

Then there were the letters of condolence, some of these addressed to a 'Mrs Brady'. At first I thought these were meant to be for me, then realized they were from people who didn't know my father was widowed. Most of them were from clients who had worked with my father. They must have heard the news that everyone who worked for Cantor Fitzgerald was dead. I didn't read the letters properly, but they were full of platitudes.

Words cannot express how sorry I am for your loss . . .

What happened that day was simply unimaginable . . .

Among the kindest people I have had the privilege to meet . . .

Finally I picked up my letters. One was official-looking, my name and the address typed, a New York postmark. The other was handwritten, and the envelope had lots of stamps on it. It was slightly heavier.

I opened the official-looking one first.

Miss Brady,

I am writing to inform you that, under Mr Michael Brady's life insurance policy with A. C. Clements, you are entitled to a lump-sum payment, as well as monthly installments amounting to the estimated worth of Mr Brady under his projected life expectancy. To receive these payments, we will need to be provided with Mr Brady's death certificate, along with your bank details.

As your personal representative at the firm, I invite you to send any questions you might have direct to me. At your convenience, we can arrange a meeting at our offices to discuss the plan. As you are a minor we can provide you with legal representation free of charge.

I have enclosed my business card. My secretary would be happy to arrange a meeting.

Yours sincerely,
Richard O'Sullivan
Policy Payments Manager
A. C. Clements

I was going to be rich.

. . .

I had been spending very little in however many days or weeks it had been since the attacks. I had a debit card connected to an account my father kept topped up. I was only supposed to use it for emergencies – if I needed to get a cab, or to get takeout if my father was going to be home late and I was on my own. I had an actual allowance I got in cash each week as well. I spent this on clothes and make-up and dumb stuff other girls in school had. Since I'd been seeing Kyle, I'd been spending quite a lot of my allowance, and the occasional debit card spend, on him.

Kyle did earn money, but erratically. Some weeks he'd be acting like he'd won the lottery, buying me expensive gifts, taking me out for fancy meals and paying for hotel rooms. But the work he did, by its nature, wasn't stable, and he obviously wasn't good with money. He tended to use euphemisms when talking about his work, though it hadn't taken long for me to figure out what it was he did. For example, he'd say he was having to make some 'investments', which meant he'd just bought a shitload of drugs to sell and so wouldn't have any money for a while.

I didn't think it was cool that Kyle was a drug dealer, but I wasn't too worried by it, either. He told me that he would never involve me, and he mostly didn't – or not in any way that felt dangerous to me. Looking back now, I just don't know how he did it without a cell phone. How did it work? I knew that he had 'contacts' in all kinds of industries. He wasn't just standing around on street corners selling weed. He could shift serious money sometimes, when he got his act together, but that money always seemed to disappear.

It's clear to me now that Kyle's paranoia was through the roof from all the weed he smoked. But I didn't know that weed could do that, then; I thought the whole point of it was that it made you more relaxed. Kyle appeared to be one of those really chill people, but he was always on the verge of totally flipping. It didn't help that he was often carrying drugs on his person. If he was ever caught, he'd remind me often, he'd be given some crazy-ass life sentence that would be about twice his actual life expectancy.

'One-hundred-fifty years in jail,' he would say, almost dreamily, as if he thought he would live for ever.

I, on the other hand, was able to walk the streets of New York without attracting suspicion. I mostly felt invisible during those days after the attacks. I must have looked worn out and thin, though. The only people who did seem to pay me any attention were the street vendors. Most days, someone would offer me free food, as if they could sense just by looking at me that I wouldn't eat all day unless they gave me something there and then. So I was basically living off pretzels and hot dogs, slices of pizza, bagels and hot nuts, sometimes slush puppies or tortilla chips covered in melted cheese.

As soon as I got my hands on any of this food I realized how hungry I was and would stand there on the spot in a kind of trance, getting the calories into me as quickly as I could. More often than not, the vendor would try to press a second pretzel or whatever on me, but then I'd get embarrassed and worry that they'd want to talk so I'd refuse to take it and run away down the block.

I'll admit I found it satisfying, seeing how long I could stay on my feet with my stomach completely empty. It gave me a certain strength, like the starving saints we learnt about at school, around the time of my confirmation.

. . .

I made myself a coffee before I opened the final envelope. I was trying not to think too much about the letters I had already opened, all the admin that I would have to deal with now my father was no longer alive. Up until that day, I hadn't been thinking about all the things a person has to do to live in the world – the constant bills and paperwork, remembering to feed yourself. I could understand why the saints wanted to get away from it all, why a person would choose to become a nun. Submitting to an order must give a person so much space.

The coffee burnt my tongue. I went back to the table

and held the final envelope in my hand. I cut my finger opening it, waited for the blood to appear and licked it. There were three sheets of plain paper inside the envelope. The handwriting was neat and narrow. It had an elegance to it, like it had stayed the same for decades.

Dear Coraline,

I have spent a few days now trying to decide how to begin this letter. Not knowing where to start, not quite believing it when I calculate how old you must be now – sixteen. I am so sorry to have missed all of your childhood, to be writing to you now as a stranger.

I'll try to keep this as simple as I can. I am your mother's younger sister. My name is Róisín.

I do not presume to know how this letter will find you, and I cannot be sure that it will find you at all. But I wanted to write to tell you, before you find out through the authorities that be, that your father's will appoints me as your legal guardian.

Your mother and I were not close when she died. I regret this deeply. I would have liked to have attended her funeral, but circumstances prevented me from flying. Your father wrote to tell me about her death and to say that it was his wish that, should anything happen to him, I would be the one to take care of you.

Though I have my own experience of loss and bereavement, I cannot imagine what you are going through. I never thought the day would come when I'd have to write you this letter. But I am glad to be writing to you – whether or not you write back, whether or not I ever get to meet you. I'm glad that you will know now that I exist, and that I am here for you.

I know you are old enough to take care of yourself, that you have a life in New York that you will be reluctant to leave, and friends who are probably looking after you right now better than I will be able to. But I wanted to honour your father's wish by offering you a place to stay, with me. Even if it's just for a holiday.

Where I live is about as different from New York as a place can be — a small village called Burtonport, in County Donegal, Ireland. I do not have a phone or a computer, and I understand that my way of living may not be to your liking. But the offer stands, whenever you might want or need it. We are family.

I'm sure you will have questions, questions you may want answering before you even think about coming to stay with a strange woman in Ireland. You can write to me, and I will respond as well as I can.

I hope I get the opportunity to fill in some of the gaps I know this letter will have left. And I hope I get the opportunity to meet and know you, Cora.

Your Aunt Ró

8

I knew my mother had been Irish. And my father. But it wasn't something I had thought a great deal about. Partly because neither of them *sounded* Irish to me. I couldn't hear that they had accents, because they were just my parents. Also, because I went to a convent school, a lot of my classmates had Irish parents.

There was one time, in my elementary school, which hadn't been Catholic, when two of my classmates asked if I was a Gypsy. I didn't know what a Gypsy was but I could tell it wasn't a good thing. I told them that of course I wasn't and they said that my mother surely was, because of her accent. When I went home that afternoon I made a conscious effort to try and listen for this accent. I had to pretend that I was someone different to hear it. If I imagined I was one of those boys, instead of myself, Cora, then it was true: she did sound different. I felt betrayed, like she'd been lying to me, like I didn't know her at all, like she wasn't even my mother. I think I was worried that maybe she actually was a Gypsy. And if she was, then I didn't want to know. I couldn't let those boys be right.

. . .

After I had finished reading Róisín's letter I felt oddly calm. I threw away the junk mail. I dealt with the gone-off items in the refrigerator. I took the trash out. I went to the bodega down the street and bought some milk. I prepared oatmeal for myself and put it in the microwave. I plugged in the TV and watched the news while I was eating.

Yesterday had been a bad day for Wall Street but the finance reporter was insisting 'Nothing has changed.' The commercial real estate market had apparently not been broken, despite all the displaced tenants. 'The terrorists picked the wrong skyline to mess with,' the male anchor said, almost manically. Toddlers who had frequent temper tantrums were more likely to have criminal convictions later in life, a new study had found. US troops were arriving in the countries bordering Afghanistan. The Board of Education was upgrading its evacuation plans for schools. A teenager in the Bronx had been shot in the face by another teenager. The city was described as 'a hotbed of insomnia'. A specialist interviewed was telling New Yorkers not to hesitate to ask their doctors for a sleep remedy. Addiction, they were saying, was a 'very, very remote possibility'. Broadway box office sales were up from the week before, but still down 50–60 per cent compared to normal levels. President Bush had been going into high schools to urge teenagers not to give in to terrorism. 'They cannot win unless you give them permission,' he was saying, in the footage. This was one of the dumbest things I had ever heard.

Though I had kept the TV switched off until then, I had been listening to music stations on the radio on and off, before I went out walking and after I got back from whatever movie theater I had ended up at. I wanted to drown out my own silence. The two songs that seemed always to be playing were 'Fallin'' by Alicia Keys and 'Hanging by a

Moment' by Lifehouse. Once, someone called in to the radio station to point out the grim significance of these song titles. The DJ quickly ended the call, then played 'It Wasn't Me' by Shaggy.

It felt good to listen to hit music stations. When we had been together, Kyle had taken it upon himself to 'educate' me, which meant we listened to a lot of rap music. Kyle was *obsessed* with Tupac. Everything about Tupac's life to him seemed noble, heroic. Getting sent to prison, getting shot. At the time we were dating, Kyle was twenty-three, and he'd often joke he only had two years left to live, because Tupac had died at twenty-five.

When Tupac was shot (the time that actually killed him), he had been on his way to a nightclub called Death Row. This, Kyle said, couldn't just be a coincidence. Kyle liked to say that every person on this planet was just sitting on death row, waiting for their time to be up. That, I didn't disagree with.

· · ·

Humans see patterns in everything, my father used to say when he was trying to make me more enthusiastic about math. It didn't work, but I could see his point.

When I had just started middle school, a couple of kids in my grade went down to Florida at Christmas to see the Virgin Mary who had appeared in rainbow swirls on the window of an office building. I was still getting used to being at a Catholic school. My father wasn't religious, but there was, I think, an unspoken agreement that it was what my mother would have wanted.

'You know that's nonsense, right?' I remember him saying as he watched me watching the footage of the rainbow Virgin Mary on our boxy television.

I wasn't sure about it all being nonsense, though, if I was honest. I found the way the people were reacting to the swirls compelling. Falling to their knees, crying, praying. They interviewed one woman who seemed both overjoyed and terrified at the prospect of meeting our 'soon-coming King'. They got experts to pitch in on both sides of the debate. Scientists struggled to explain how the shape had occurred through water deposits and chemical reactions. Architects who'd been designing buildings for decades said they'd never seen such a thing. It was hard to know who to believe.

The same thing would happen with the towers. The complicated reasons scientists were giving to explain why they fell the way they did were less compelling than the people who were so sure it had been a demolition, controlled by the government.

9

I washed up my bowl before I plugged the phone back in. Richard O'Sullivan had called, three times, repeating more of what had been said in the letter – that he needed my father's death certificate to process the insurance payments. I didn't care about the money, but I knew my father had taken the insurance out to make sure I'd be all right without him. He had always been sensible. That's why he was an accountant. My mother had been an artist. They couldn't have been more different, or so it seemed to me. But they had grown up together. High school sweethearts (or whatever the term for that is in Ireland).

The story was that my mother had come to America to attend this brand new art school. It was the school's first year of teaching, and she was one of only a handful of students. She had been awarded a full scholarship, but the school didn't really have any money. The teaching took place in the basement of a church. It was freezing cold and my mother didn't get on with the other students, so she dropped out. At some point, my dad came to New York, too. They waded through piles of trash on the streets. They made ends meet. My dad worked a load of menial jobs while also taking accountancy classes and studying for his exams. My mother became fairly well known in certain experimental art circles. Then they had me.

I never really asked either of them much about their

lives before all that, though, hardly wondered about who and what they might have left behind. I suppose my lack of questioning had something to do with my mother's fragile mental state. By the time I was old enough to start wondering where my parents had come from, where I had come from, my energy was centred on trying to keep my mother stable in the present. This was practically a full-time job. And perhaps my subconscious knew that asking about her family, about her childhood in Ireland, wasn't going to help matters. Then, after she had killed herself, I was worried that my dad might fall apart if I reminded him of her at all.

I'd seen my mother's art, though. When she was alive, she went through phases of being extremely productive, dragging me along to whatever studio space she was working in after she picked me up from school. But sometimes she'd lose track of time and forget to pick me up and the principal would have to call my father. Other times she'd forget to pick me up because she wasn't doing anything at all. My father and I would get home and she'd just be staring at the wall, like she was waiting for something. It reminded me of that optical illusion – you know the one where if you stare at the black blobs for long enough, let the outlines blur into your retinas, then blink at a white wall, Jesus's face would appear on it. Her art was like that. Difficult and abstract. Towards the end she didn't finish anything she started.

For a bit after she died I went to see a child psychiatrist. The first time he showed me those cards with the splodges I thought he was showing me my mother's art. A lot of the 'techniques' the therapist used reminded me of what it was like to be her daughter. He asked me to draw my feelings, to write down my dreams. But thinking like that hadn't helped my mother – if anything it had made her worse.

Usually I came out of the therapy session more upset than I had been when I went in. Eventually, my father said that I could take a break and I never went back. During the break, I had been determined to demonstrate that I was better off without the therapy. If I felt my mother's absence pressing into my consciousness, I pushed her out again. It helped that we had moved to a new apartment. It helped that I had started a new school where the other kids didn't know what had happened. It helped that I was approaching the age where every child wants to cast off their parents' influence and define who they might be without them.

Occasionally, though, one of my mother's pieces would be included in an exhibition somewhere in the city and my father and I would go to see it. The paintings were always attributed to her artist name. The fact that she had worked under a pseudonym and refused to do any publicity added a layer of mystery to the work she left behind. Or so I once heard someone say. But seeing or hearing this fake name always left me feeling like I wasn't supposed to be there.

I knew my father didn't enjoy going to the galleries, either. We would stand there, looking at the art, not speaking, for not very long. Then we'd find the nearest diner. I wouldn't even look at the menu, but my father always ordered something for himself that came with fries because he knew that I would dip them in my vanilla milkshake.

There was one painting that stuck with me. From a distance it looked like it could just be newspaper print pasted on to a huge canvas. But when I got closer I could see the black marks were all tiny figures, linked together. They were almost photographic, with distinct faces and features, but they didn't look exactly like people. The description printed on the wall said that it had been painted at the peak of the Aids crisis. It was about connection at a time when people were afraid to touch each other. But it made me think about the paper-doll chains my mother and I used to cut out and string around the apartment together when I was little. And every time we did she would remind me that the two of us had been a part of Hands Across America in 1986. I had no memory of this day, when I was only one, but it felt like I was being forced to face things I had forgotten, standing in front of that painting. I didn't like it.

. . .

After I had finished going through all the messages on the phone, I went back to the letter. I read it lying down on the sofa. Of course, the obvious question came to mind: Why hadn't I known about this aunt? But the thing I kept returning to was the bit where she had written where she lived: *Burtonport, in County Donegal, Ireland.* I was sure I had heard about this place before. Perhaps my parents had spoken about it. But that wasn't it. It was a more specific memory – something tangible, tactile.

I was actually rubbing my fingers and thumbs together, trying to spark my subconscious, when I realized I was going to be sick. I ran to the bathroom and just made it to the toilet. And it was after – in the clarity that comes from emptying yourself, that sweaty resurrection – when

I realized that I hadn't heard about Burtonport in County Donegal at all. I had seen those words in print.

'*Scream School*,' I said out loud, feeling something like excitement. For I could remember it all clearly. Not so much the game itself, which I had quickly got bored of, but the cassette tape insert which I read from cover to cover, over and over, in secret. I must have been about seven or eight.

'Don't tell your mother,' my father had said, when he came home with the game after work one day. 'You know she's funny about technology.'

I wasn't able to play the game straight away, because we didn't have the right kind of console. But I was delighted with the insert – how it opened up. The instructions explained that the game was about two sisters, sent away to boarding school. The older sister has the power to see and speak to the dead. The younger sister has fainting spells where she is able to tap into the minds of the living. They have to work together to solve the quest and stop the other students from getting murdered.

I read the instruction insert under the covers, after I'd been put to bed, using a torch I had that was shaped like a little girl. I wasn't allowed to play with Barbie dolls, but I had this creepy torch. To get it to light up you had to squeeze the girl's plastic legs together which opened up her mouth. If I released my grip, even a bit, the girl's mouth would close and the torch would go out. So my hand would end up aching as I read about the sisters at the school, in Burtonport, County Donegal. I had always wanted a sister.

. . .

That evening, I ransacked the apartment. I listened to my father's CDs – Marvin Gaye and the Pointer Sisters and Odyssey – and drank two bottles of expensive-looking red wine. I emptied every closet and drawer looking for that tape. I turned the place upside down, wanting to go back, to burrow through to some other place, like Alice in Wonderland.

My mother had loved those books. I found Alice's adventures terrifying, but I would still let her read them to me, whenever she had the urge. I would have nightmares after, every time, but it was worth it to have her behaving like a normal mother, lying next to me on my bed. She would let me stroke her hair while she was reading. It was blonde and curly and coarse. I liked to wrap the curls around my fingers, or try to pull them apart from each other. I loved the way they always bounced back into place around her face. I could do this with my own hair, too, but it didn't feel the same as doing it to hers. It must have hurt, but she let me do it anyway, while she was reading.

Eventually, we moved on to the second volume, which was even more frightening than the first. The bit that troubled me the most was the Red Queen's race, where 'it takes all the running you can do, to stay in the same place'. To be trapped like that. Even as I got older I continued to have nightmares that seemed to have stemmed from this. I'd be trying to get away from something, and no matter how hard I tried I wouldn't be able to move a muscle.

. . .

I finally gave up looking for the cassette, after hours of searching. I leant against the wall in the hall, my head spinning and my mouth dry from all the wine. I thought about how Alice is always surprised that, despite all her adventures, everything remains just as it was when she gets home. In my home, there was stuff all over the floor, on every surface, in every room, but no cassette tape. It must have been among the many possessions that we simply left behind when we moved, after my mother had died. A fresh start, my father had said, would be best for both of us. I hadn't thought too much about the stuff I never saw again. It was hard to be sentimental when I knew my mother wouldn't be coming back. But now it was driving me crazy, remembering the cassette and not being able to hold it in my hand.

If I closed my eyes, I could almost see it. The drawing of the boarding school on the cover, with its two sets of chimneys and the steps going up to the front door.

IO

The letter I sent back to Róisín was about three lines long, just saying that I'd bought a plane ticket and informing her of the flight number. Of course there were questions I could have asked. But I needed change more than I needed answers.

There was one thing I felt I had to do, though, before I left. I couldn't just disappear, without a trace.

I turned on the computer and went to the albums I had put together – all the photos I had taken with my digital camera. It killed me, as I went through the albums in reverse chronological order, that I hadn't taken *any* photos of my dad – not even on our bridges tour. I didn't have any photos of Kyle either, because he thought people who were into photography were 'precious'. The photos in the albums were all of school friends who I never spoke to any more, or painfully embarrassing pictures of myself, posing in my bedroom, the camera set to self-timer. There I was at fourteen, wearing a new push-up bra I had bought from Victoria's Secret. And at twelve, with choppy bangs that covered half my face, my hair straightened. And ten, looking small and lost in the middle of my double bed in my new bedroom after we had moved to Park Slope.

I was sure there must be a photo, that one would appear. The perfect portrait I had never taken. 'Damn,' I shouted, after I'd gone through all the albums, picking up the mouse and throwing it back down on the desk, like a cat playing with its prey. I didn't cry, though. I don't think I was capable of crying then.

Instead, I went over to where we kept a couple of actual family albums – in a cabinet by the front door. I had already emptied this cabinet looking for the cassette tape the night before. But I hadn't opened up the albums then. I hadn't looked through them in years. It always made me feel weird, seeing my mother in photos, because she always looked so . . . not sad exactly, but vacant, lost. On the floor, next to the albums, was a paper packet of photos which hadn't been sorted into a proper album. I flipped open the packet, and recognized the photos as the first I'd taken with my Pentax, on my eighth birthday. I had spent the whole day taking photos, getting used to the way the camera worked. I had obviously gone through a whole roll of film that day. There were photos of Gus the polar bear at Central Park Zoo. And of the birthday cake my mother had made – a giant toadstool with fairy figurines around it, made from marzipan. There were my new Nike Air Max sneakers, on my little feet. About a third of the photos were too blurred for me to make out what they were meant to be of. Then, finally, there it was.

A photo of the three of us, all standing together, me in the middle, pressed between my parents. My father, beaming. My mother, blinking. My own face looks quizzical – I must have still been searching for the 'little birdy' my father told me was inside the camera lens. My father's arm is around my mother's shoulders. I'm reaching up, holding my mother's hand. She's wearing a plain vest so you can see the tattoo that went right up her arm. Puzzle pieces, connected together. Like a jigsaw without a picture.

I loved that tattoo. When my mother was low, and needed to spend a lot of time sleeping, I'd go into my parents' room and lie there next to her on the bed, running my finger over the pieces, then delving the same finger into one of her corkscrew curls.

. . .

I took the photo to the closest internet café and asked if they had a scanner. I paid for thirty minutes of computer access, and did my best to crop myself and my mother out of the photograph using the eraser on Microsoft Paint. It was easy to remove myself, but I found it difficult to erase my mother. I was missing her as well. I kept using the undo button to see her face next to my father's one more time. My father's head had little chunks missing at the edges, because my hand was wobbly on the mouse. I could still see a strand or two of my mother's hair, blowing over his face. I left them there.

MISSING, I typed at the top. MICHAEL BRADY, CANTOR FITZGERALD, 104TH FLOOR, NORTH TOWER. FATHER.

I didn't know what else to put, so I left it at that. I printed off a copy then took it to the Xerox. I'd meant to print fifty but the copier ran out of paper only a quarter of the way through and I didn't want to have to ask the man behind the counter if he had more.

. . .

I spent the day before I left depositing the posters in places I would miss. I said goodbye to Gus the polar bear and stuck a poster to the bars of his enclosure. I walked to the middle of the Brooklyn Bridge and wrapped a poster round one of the suspender cables, securing it with coils of Scotch Tape. I even got the subway to Coney Island, which was pretty much shut down for winter.

It must have been raining while I was on the train. The water on the asphalt was shining in the afternoon light as I tried to work out where that roller coaster had been – the Thunderbolt. But its absence was unremarkable. The towers were the only part of the city that would be for ever missing.

I was walking around, feeling like I wanted to evaporate, when I saw the tattoo parlour. I went in and explained what I wanted, already pulling up my sleeve. I looked away and hardly felt a thing. When the machine stopped, I turned my head and watched the tattoo artist wipe away the blood and excess ink. He wrapped my arm so tenderly, the Saran Wrap going round and round, protecting my lonely puzzle piece.

. . .

Back at the apartment, I packed basically nothing. At the last minute, when the cab I'd booked to take me to the airport was waiting outside, I went over to the kitchen table where I'd left the photograph of the three of us on top of the *New York Times*. I put the photo in my jacket pocket, and looked down at the Falling Man for just a moment. I left him there, for ever falling.

. . .

On the plane, the woman beside me was agitated. She'd never been keen on flying, 'Even before,' she said. 'And hadn't it been chilling in the airport, everyone on high alert, and dead quiet? Though they say it's safer now than ever.'

I mimed a yawn, then closed my eyes for take-off. I had swallowed four pills before boarding. I missed whatever movie was showing, only waking up when the plane was over Ireland and the pilot was warning passengers that the seat belt sign would shortly be turned back on.

'You slept like a lamb,' the woman said, while I massaged my strained neck. 'I've been wide awake. Not a wink.' There were two cans of tonic water and an empty plastic cup on her fold-down table.

When my suitcase failed to appear on the conveyor belt in Dublin airport, I didn't care. I walked through the door that said 'Nothing to declare' with only the slightest awareness of why I was there. Róisín had red curly hair. I knew it was her because she was holding a sign with my name on it. It was the same handwriting as in the letter. I hadn't expected her to sound exactly like my mother. I hadn't arrived with any expectations at all.

The car journey was laden with the throbbing of my arm, where the tattoo was. I put pressure on it, with my right hand, and tried to think about anything else. But the blur of passing fields was making me feel sick. At one point, Róisín had to pull over so I could throw up on the side of the road. I remembered then, when I clicked my seat belt back into the buckle, that the rest of the pills had been in my suitcase.

I started shivering, and Róisín explained that the heating

in the car was broken. She uncoiled the scarf around her neck and told me I could use it as a blanket.

The scarf was striped like Joseph's Technicolor Dreamcoat. I ran through the colours in my head. *Red and yellow and green and brown and blue.*

I felt all right, focusing on that. I hardly noticed when the car stopped and Róisín turned off the engine.

'Here we are,' she said. 'You must be wrecked.'

I looked up from the scarf and peered through the window. We were parked outside the Scream School.

The Wild World

A hundred years before the Easter Rising,
Ireland . . .

A volcano erupts on the other side of the
world.

The sky goes dark. It is the year without
a summer, the sun pale in the ashen sky.

Crops fail. Disease spreads. The poor die.

Your father drinks and shouts. Your
mother coughs and coughs, leaving spots
of blood on her handkerchief.

'Stay close,' she tells you both, before
she dies. 'Hold on to each other.'

Your father is sending you away to school.

Before you go, you must decide which sister
you will play as, Magnolia or Rosemary?

(A or B?)

Róisín Dooley

Burtonport

1974–77

July 1974

The old school house is up for sale. I watch them put the sign up, two men trying to slide the stake into the lumpy earth.

I run up the hill, all the way home to tell my sister, Máire. I can imagine what she'll say, though: 'So?'

She'll pretend she doesn't care, though I know there was a time when she thought about the house even more than I did.

. . .

She had said it was symmetrical and striking, those big words so forceful, coming out of Máire's mouth. She had drawn pictures of it, over and over again, when we were younger. I watched her pencil strokes take shape from across the kitchen table, so in my head the building's always upside down. She drew it accurately at first, with its two sets of chimneys and the wide steps up to the front door. But then she started to distort the things she saw. She put the chimneys underground and turned them into secret tunnels. She drew doors coming out of the roof, opening up on to carpets of cloud in the sky. She added staircases that led to nowhere. I thought her drawings were amazing. It was like she had this whole other world in her head. She didn't do them for me, though. They were always for our father. He stuck each one of them up inside the milking shed. Sometimes they would fall down and he'd have to reinforce them with more sticky tape. They were faded and dirty and a little bit torn, but they had survived when our father had not.

I remembered the pictures on the evening of our last night in the farmhouse. We were moving to the Atlan estate. What was left of our stuff was packed up into boxes. Mammy hadn't helped with any of the sorting. She'd taken to bed, the day after the funeral, and hadn't spoken a word since. Dr Hughes had diagnosed the problem, prescribing pills that might alleviate the symptoms. I asked him to spell the words out to me, so I could write them down.

Catatonic Melancholia.

Máire had been the one to organize the house sale, then the auction to sell off all the furniture we couldn't keep. The O'Mahonys, who were buying the farm, wanted to knock the house down, build a new one from scratch. I was there when they came to look around, hiding in the outside toilet. I heard Mrs O'Mahony saying to her husband, in the garden, that the whole house was damp, that it had a stench to it. She wanted the new house to have two inside toilets, one of them an en-suite. She said it wrong though – 'suit' instead of 'sweet'. I wanted to barge out and correct her, to have one over on her. But that was the sort of thing Máire would do, not me. I was quiet as a mouse, shivering on the toilet seat, wishing I had worn gloves.

The only person who had been going into the milking shed since Daddy's heart attack was Michael. He'd said he would help out with the milking until the farm was sold. He was doing all of it himself. I think he was hoping the

O'Mahonys might keep him on, once they took over, but they have four sons.

I was in bed, reading, when the pictures came into my head. I do all my best thinking while I'm reading. Maybe it's because it actually stops me from thinking too much. If I'm relaxed, following someone else's story, my own fresh thoughts pop up like snowdrops. It happens with writing, too. Most of the time it feels like I have nothing to say, but then sentences come out, filling up the page like someone else is writing them. I like it when that happens. Máire hates it though, when I'm reading or writing. Because although she hardly ever wants to actually do things with me, she doesn't like me being in my own world, either. I can remember, clearly, the covers of the library books she wrenched out of my hands and tore to pieces. But it was more painful watching her destroy my notebooks, after she'd spat my words back at me, gleefully, making me ashamed of everything I'd ever thought to put to paper.

So I didn't write about what I saw, that last night at the farm, after I remembered the pictures and got out of bed. It felt too much like a secret, even to admit it to myself. And if I wrote it down, Máire would find out I knew. But I've a good hiding place now: inside last Christmas's USA biscuit tin, which Máire knows full well is empty.

Daddy brought home those biscuits every year, a few days before Christmas. Mammy would then ask if we remembered how the tin had got its name. I could remember, but would pretend I had forgotten because I knew she liked to tell us: 'They were made to celebrate the Americans joining the Great War, a year after the Easter Rising.' Máire and I were allowed to choose a biscuit every evening, so long as

we'd eaten all our dinner. But we were forbidden from starting on the second tier until the biscuits in the first were gone.
Máire couldn't help herself, though, and blamed me when
the second tier was officially revealed, the chocolate-coated
rounds already gone.

By the time the decorations came down, even the Nice
biscuits had been eaten, the least-nice ones. So we knew
the tin was empty when we found it, going through everything before the move. Máire said the tin was 'junk' but I
wanted to keep it.

The tin was packed up in one of the boxes downstairs, which I had to make my way through to get to the
back door. I put on my boots, remembering Máire doing
the same thing the night that Daddy died, on Shrove
Tuesday. I remember, because Mammy was making pancakes and Daddy was late coming back from the milking.
Mammy had asked Máire to run out to hurry him along,
and Máire had tried to make me go instead, but it was my
pancake next. Máire had just finished hers, and Mammy
said she couldn't have another unless she went. Máire
pulled on my plaits before she left in protest. I didn't give
out. I knew not to.

Though I was well able to cross the field in the pitch
black, I was grateful for the moon that night – not when
Máire found Daddy in the milking shed, but when I went
to get her pictures. I climbed over the gate into the field,
the one Máire and I used to swing on like there was no
better fun to be had in the whole wild world. That was how
she said it – wild instead of wide.

I was halfway across the field before I started to feel
scared, before I got the sense that the milking shed might

now be haunted, because Daddy had died in there. I slowed my steps. I thought about turning back but I knew I had to get those pictures.

The pumps were still running, which was strange because the cows were back in the field and I could see that they'd been milked, their udders no longer bursting. The noise of the machine must have meant they didn't hear me approach – Máire and Michael. She had her overalls pulled down to her waist, like she was about to get out of them. He was holding something in his hands. It looked like a bundle of papers, tied together with string. He was trying to hand the bundle over to her. I couldn't hear what they were saying to each other but I could tell it was some sort of disagreement. She took the bundle from him and pulled one end of the string so the bow came undone. She shook the contents so that the papers started to swirl around in the air before they hit the ground. It was only then that I realized they were all her pictures, falling down on to the wet concrete. I wanted to run out and save them but I was frozen to the spot. Michael made an effort to grab some of the sheets around him, but my sister stopped him. She took both his hands in hers then moved them up underneath her top – high up, over her chest. Nothing else happened. They just stood there like that for a while – I don't know how long for – until eventually my sister removed his hands and started stepping out of her overalls, leaving them empty on the floor, the ghost of herself still giving them a slightly human form. Then she walked away, right past where I was standing, like I was invisible.

After she had gone, Michael started scrambling to save whatever he could of the pictures, and when I realized what he was doing I ran over to help him. He didn't ask why I was there. We just set about salvaging what we could in silence. After we had finished, I handed the ones that I had saved back over to him. I wanted to keep them for myself, but he had been the one to get to them first. I imagined him climbing up on the stepladder and using his fingernails to remove the sticky tape, carefully peeling it off so the pictures wouldn't tear, collecting them all and securing them together with a length of string, tying the ends off in a bow, like I had planned on doing as well.

. . .

When I do tell Máire, about the for-sale sign, she says she already knows – though how can she? I'm hanging out the laundry on the line. Máire's lying on her front in the scraggy patch of grass we have for a garden now at Atlan, propping herself up on her elbows, out of the sun. She's caught a ladybird on a stick. When it tries to crawl back to the grass, Máire turns the stick over in her hand, so it has to walk the length of the stick again. I wonder is she trying to get it to fly, waiting for it to remember it has wings?

'Who do you think might buy it then, the house?' I ask, rearranging some of the wet clothes because there aren't enough pegs.

'I don't know, Ró,' Máire says, languidly.

'Maybe they'll turn it into a school again,' I suggest.

'I doubt it.'

I want to ask if she ever misses the ghost stories, or the game the stories became. I wonder if she ever plays the game at the senior school. For a few weeks, last September, the girls in the class above mine tried to keep the game going. But it didn't work properly, without Máire. And the thought of bringing up the stories now, so many months later, makes my bones turn to jelly.

. . .

I didn't invent them entirely, the stories. People in the village talked about the abandoned house. It had once been a boarding school for the daughters of rich landowners – prim, Protestant girls. But it was shut down when the English were finally chucked out, after the Irish War of Independence.

There had been other owners, since. But nobody had stayed for long. It was said the house was haunted by a student who must have died there once, in terrible pain.

That was what the stories were about. This student who was now a ghost, trapped inside the house.

Even though I was the one making the stories up, they would scare me more than Máire. She delighted in maintaining her coolness, encouraging me to make the stories darker and more gruesome. As the plots progressed, I crept closer to Máire for comfort, underneath the covers. She'd trace a finger up and down my arm, because she knew how much I loved that – being stroked so lightly, like her finger was a feather.

I soon found out that Máire was telling my stories to the girls in her class. I wasn't hurt she was pretending they were hers. I felt proud she wanted to claim something of mine. The stories turned into a game everyone could play at lunchtime. Máire pretending to be the ghost, the other students trying to avoid being turned into ghosts too. At the beginning, everyone would be trying to get away from the ghosts, but increasingly it became difficult to know who was still alive and who had gone over to Máire's side. It was more complicated than simply being caught. More psychological than physical. You couldn't kill anyone during class time, but there would be a lot of veiled discussion about who the ghosts were. The teachers soon banned the game so we had to be secretive about it. There was a lot of pretending involved, girls tricking each other into thinking that they hadn't been killed yet. In the end, everyone would want to be a ghost. The girls still alive would be desperate, begging the ghosts to take them to the other side.

Each game could last the length of a school week. They were always slightly different. In our bedroom, Máire would press me to come up with new developments and twists. When my words failed to please Máire – or even when they did – I'd feel her strokes get harder, sometimes turning into scratches. 'More,' she'd demand, never satisfied.

If I tried to move my arm away she'd grip hold of it with both hands, like a cat toying with a mouse. I'd go limp, then, but still she'd twist her wrists in opposite directions, burning my skin. My eyes would smart and start to water, but I wouldn't shout out. That was always how the stories ended.

October 1976

Máire has said we can carve turnips for All Hallows. But she won't come with me to the grocer's. It's a dazzling day, the tarmac glossy with iridescence and reflection, sun after rain. Even Atlan looks quite cheery, the four rows of houses facing the sun like open flowers. The peeling paint over the pebbledash reminds me of my nose being sunburnt, of summer, swimming. Then a cloud covers the sun and the estate darkens.

Once, Daddy brought me along to a meeting about the plans for the estate. I must have only been seven or eight. I can remember being upset because I hadn't known we were going to this meeting, and I didn't have a book with me in the truck to bring into the village hall. But I was pleased to be up past my bedtime, to be doing something grown-up. So I listened to the adults discussing the building plans. On the one hand it was good that they were being built cheaply, because it was taxpayers' money funding the project. On the other, the estate would bring the 'wrong sort' to Burtonport. It was said the houses would probably be blown down as fast as they were being put up, which at the time made me think of the three little pigs, and that foolish man in the Bible who built his house on the sand. I wished I had something to read, other than the handout I'd taken from Daddy that mapped out the architectural proposal from the council. The handout didn't say what material the houses would be made from, but I could see where they were going to be built – as far away from the sea as it was possible for them to be, on the outskirts of the village.

Then Daddy surprised me by standing up and speaking. He wasn't an outspoken man. 'With everything going on across the border,' he said, 'we should be proud to be able to offer housing to the needy. Who's to say when some of us might get into trouble and need state housing, God forbid? Isn't that what taxes are for?'

I didn't really understand him. But I knew that I was proud, that he'd said a bold thing. Of course, there was also the fact that more households in Burtonport would mean more milk would be needed, more business for him.

He wouldn't have expected his own family to have ended up living on the Atlan estate, though. He'd have been ashamed. I can't help but feel that way sometimes, too.

. . .

I stop outside the Screamers' house, move the wicker basket to my other shoulder. Everyone does it – stops outside the gate on their way into the village. Children run ahead of their mothers, bend to tie their shoelaces with their ears angled to the door. Women suddenly remember to check their shopping lists. Fishermen pause to relight their pipes.

When the rumours of the screaming started my theory was that they were witches, that the screaming was some sort of ceremony, like at the beginning of *Macbeth*. I was

74

obsessed with witches then – all the women burnt at the stake or thrown into rivers with their wrists and ankles tied together. This wasn't long after they'd moved in, the Screamers. I don't know how the rumours started (no one seems to have actually heard the screaming first hand), but everyone was calling them the Screamers long before that journalist came knocking and the article was published in the *Sunday World*. It ruined the magic for me a bit, the article, but it did confirm the screaming.

They had given themselves an official name, the Atlantis Primal Therapy Commune, but who was going to call them that?

'What a mouthful,' Máire had interjected when I read the article out loud to her and Michael at the breakfast table.

The idea was that you could release demons from your past by screaming. But, more than the screaming, the thing in the article the adults all seemed horrified by was the fact that anyone wanting to join the commune would have to give up drinking and smoking. That *had* to be some kind of witchcraft.

The summer after they moved in, the house was painted cornflower blue, then decorated with strange symbols. For days I could watch them outside the house when I walked past. There was usually at least one of them singing or playing a guitar. One time somebody was giving out back rubs to whoever's shoulders were aching from the painting. As it got hotter, they revealed more skin. Some of them even had tattoos, though I never got close enough to see these in any detail. Occasionally, one of them would wave at me but I'd pretend I hadn't seen and carry on walking, almost running away from them. Eventually they stopped trying to say hello to any of us.

The symbols were the signs of the zodiac. I found them in a book at the library. *Linda Goodman's Sun Signs*, the book was called.

I took the book home and learnt that there were twelve signs, but they didn't correspond to the months of the calendar year exactly. My sign was the last one: Pisces. Máire was a Gemini. Michael was a Libra. I read that book from cover to cover at least a dozen times, renewing it every other week at the library. I read the descriptions of Gemini and Libra out loud to Máire and Michael. Máire said it was all rubbish but Michael listened to the nonsense as if he wanted to make sense of it. I was sure the sun signs really did make sense of everything, like they were a code to crack the whole wild world. I could see why Máire could be so volatile, why there seemed to be two sides of her. It made sense that Michael was so drawn to her, because he was always seeking equilibrium. And me, I was always absorbing everything, remembering things.

It made me remember what Mammy used to say about us, before she stopped speaking. She said that Máire had been born kicking and screaming, and that I'd come out silent. She told us that we'd had a brother too, her first-born. He had the cord caught around his neck and never took a breath. Declan, she'd been going to name him.

'We thought you'd never stop crying,' Mammy used to say, about Máire. 'The only thing that would shut her up was when your father was able to bring back a jug of bee-stings. And you,' she had said, looking at me now. 'You came during a snowstorm. The midwife said you must have been simply stunned by the cold. And though you didn't make a sound, your eyes, they were so wide.'

Máire did always make a scene out of everything, when we were small. That was how Mammy used to put it – 'Don't go making a scene now,' she'd say. I can remember our father carrying her, screaming, out of mass. For months once she'd tried to argue that she couldn't breathe in there. 'How convenient,' our mother would say, but Máire swore she wasn't lying and even now she seems to fidget the whole way through mass. She's stopped saying that the statues move, at least. I must have spent years trying to catch them, upset that they only seemed to move for her.

I was obsessed with that sun signs book for a while. It helped me understand everyone and everything that was going on. But eventually I started picking holes in it. Sometimes absolutely nothing would happen, even when all the signs were pointing towards change. And it didn't make sense that everyone born at a specific time would have the same kind of personality. People surprised me all the time, failing to stick within their sign.

They must believe in them, though, to have painted the signs around the house.

On the wall out the front, the Screamers have put out pumpkins instead of turnips. There are apples, too, from the orchard in their garden. I heard Mrs O'Mally say the other day that they'll have spiked the sweets with acid. When I asked Máire what acid was she said it was a drug that made people go loopy. A piece of cardboard has been attached to the gate with fishing twine. APPLES FREE, it says. I can already imagine what people will be saying later at the parade, that the apples have been poisoned. And so to prove them wrong I remove one from the wall on my way home. I savour the acidic sweetness of each bite in my mouth and run through a list of the things I have heard people say about the Screamers in my head.

You'll be kidnapped by the Screamers and made to cry like that for ever.

All those unrelated adults living under one roof.

And not one of them comes to mass.

You know they don't even eat meat.

They'll come after our husbands.

They'll corrupt our children.

. . .

We're getting ready for the parade, the three of us in the kitchen. Máire's turnip has a wide-open mouth. Michael is helping me fashion a witch's hat out of black paper, rolling it into a cone and trying to staple it together. I start to tell him the story of Petronilla de Meath, but Máire says, 'Oh, spare me about poor Petronilla, please,' so I stop with the story and think about how our father used to call us 'little horrors' when we put our costumes on for All Hallows. I want to ask Máire if she remembers this too but she'd just say something about the past being a pestilence. The first time that she said this it sounded like a line straight out of the Bible, but I couldn't find it in mine anywhere.

'I still think my skin's too dark to be a vampire,' Michael says, holding up the cloak I've stitched for him. I want him to be Dracula.

'Says who?' I ask.

'Vampires are always pale, white.'

'I could paint your face,' Máire offers.

'All right,' Michael says.

I watch as Máire paints his whole face a deathly white, even his lips, his eyelids. He keeps saying that it tickles, trying to keep his eyes closed. When she's finished with the white she washes her brush in the glass of water I brought over for them. There's a snowstorm in the glass in the seconds before the liquid turns opaquely white. She covers the brush in red, adds a trickle of blood to the corner of Michael's mouth.

'OK, done,' she says. 'I'll go and get the mirror.'

'How do I look?' Michael asks, turning to face me.

'Strange.'

'Sure, vampires are supposed to be strange,' Máire says, returning with the mirror from the hall.

'But you don't look like you any more,' I say to Michael.

'That's the whole point of All Hallows, Ró,' Máire says as if I am stupid. 'Disguising yourself.' She holds the mirror out in front of Michael, blocking my view. But I can hear him laughing.

'The state of me,' he says.

'Don't laugh,' Máire tells him. 'You'll ruin the white around your eyes.'

'And what will you be, Máire?' he asks.

'A banshee, of course.'

. . .

The main feature in the parade is a big crow puppet, a shapeshifter. I'm one of the rotating wing bearers. We've been practising the transitions for weeks, after school. During the procession the crow will transform into a beautiful young woman, who will in turn become a terrifying old hag.

It's freezing out. I'm shivering, waiting for the procession to start, even though I am covered from head to toe. Everyone helping with the puppets is wearing black, including gloves and balaclavas. This is so the audience might think the puppets are moving of their own accord, not simply being manipulated. We are supposed to blend into the background. It's busy on the road, people lining the streets down to the harbour, where the procession will finish. There's a sense of excitement, anticipation. The drummers lift their sticks and everyone gets into place, faces the same direction down the hill. I lift the painted-black pole that moves the crow's left wing. We descend into the village.

I only have to carry the wing as far as the shops. As we approach Casey's I switch places with Joanne O'Donovan. The bits of the crow's body break apart and the next team assembles the puppet of the beautiful woman. The crowd is thick, the air so cold you can see everyone's breath, lit up by the street lamps. I slide through the crowd like a black eel. It is strange to even have my hair covered. I am usually someone who is easy to find, because of the colour of my hair. I have a sense of déjà vu as I leave the shops behind and get closer to the harbour. Like knowing something's going to happen before it actually does.

Michael is standing next to Laura Cotter. She's in my sister's class. He's laughing at something she's said. His face looks even more ridiculous now the white paint is coming off. She's wearing cat ears. Michael reaches around to touch

Laura's tail – a stocking stuffed with tissue paper, pinned to the back of her coat. She's laughing now, looking over her shoulder, their faces close.

Then I see my sister, Máire. More than her bloodied costume, I recognize the way she holds herself, so surely. She walks up to Laura and Michael and begins to talk to them. This is odd, because Máire has never liked Laura. I think it's actually because the two of them are quite alike. They have the same colour hair and Laura's tall too and even their names sound sort of similar. Then there's the fact that Laura's good at drawing. Seriously good. In a different way to Máire, but undeniably talented. She even makes money out of it. If you bring her a photo and 50p she'll do a realistic little portrait. It's a skill that's made her popular. Once I asked Máire whether she'd ever thought of doing the same – selling drawings of people's houses – but she just told me not to be ridiculous.

I watch Laura's face turn from cordial to confounded. Michael's has also changed to deadly serious. He really does look like he could be a vampire now, in the smoky harbour light.

Then he moves towards my sister, goes straight for her neck and bites it.

. . .

Everyone knows that Michael's always been in love with Máire. Right from the moment he first saw her. I think I could tell then, even though I was only nine at the time.

Our father had a new delivery boy. When he talked about this boy his eyes lit up in the same way as they did when he bought a new bull at market. He'd invited the boy and his mother for Sunday lunch, he explained. 'They've come from Finner Camp, and they don't know anyone in the village. You're to play nicely with him.' He said this last bit looking at Máire.

'What's Finner Camp?' I asked.

'It's a place where people who have lost their homes in the North have been living,' Mammy explained. 'Isn't it in Bundoran?' She looked over at our father, who was shovelling the food on his plate into his mouth. 'I met your father in Bundoran,' Mammy continued. 'At the Astoria Ballroom, on the night it first opened.'

'Yuck,' Máire said.

Mammy used to like telling stories. I have a clear picture of her past, even though she never speaks now in the present – not since Daddy died. She would talk about that night at the Astoria Ballroom with a glassy look in her eyes. I could smell the polish on the shiny new sprung dance floor, the paint only just dry on the walls. I could see the electric candelabras and the mineral bar. I could hear the band playing: Chick Smith and his orchestra. I imagined the frost glittering on the grass when she stepped outside to get some air with my father, her coral lipstick coating the end of his cigarette. She could describe places with such vivid detail then.

. . .

Michael's mother was young and glamorous. Even her name was. Georgina. No one in Burtonport had names with three syllables.

That Sunday, she was wearing a fur muffler at the door. 'It's mink,' she said, when she caught Máire staring. 'Do you want to stroke it?' At the table, she spoke endlessly about the job she'd found at the fish factory. How the cold got into her bones but you were able to forget about the smell after a while. One of the other girls there had said her boy should ask about work with Brendan Dooley, the milkman. Michael had helped his mother on the assembly line in the school holidays in Belfast, folding linen. He was a hard worker, even if he'd never seen a cow before.

'He never spills a drop or breaks a bottle,' our father agreed. He had always wanted a son, must have been disappointed to have had two girls after our dead brother, but he'd never taken a shining to any of his boys before Michael. Not like this. It must have been something to do with Michael himself being fatherless, or to do with how pretty his mother was.

Michael hardly said a word at the table, but he had very expressive eyes. I was examining him. I'd never seen someone with dark skin before. Our father hadn't warned us about this. I couldn't keep my eyes off him. And he couldn't keep his eyes off my sister.

Máire must have sensed him staring, too, because she was acting differently to usual. She was holding her knife and fork properly, and sitting still in her chair, chewing with her mouth closed. It was as if she wanted to seem like someone else entirely. It made me nervous. This other Máire wasn't bothered by me at all, when usually she'd have been kicking me under the table, or trying to shift her unwanted food on to my plate.

After the meal, the three of us went off to play in the

lower field. It was September. The leaves of the willow tree were already starting to turn from green to gold, and the sun was low in the sky. Máire was holding up her hands to shade her eyes, still oddly silent, so I asked Michael if he wanted to climb the tree with me.

'I've not climbed many trees before,' he admitted.

'It's easy. Just do what I do.'

I went first, showing Michael where to step on the willow trunk to get up to the lowest branches, like how Máire used to do for me. It took him a few attempts to get it right. Máire followed up behind. She hadn't climbed the tree with me in ages, but she didn't like to be shown up. It didn't take long for us all to get to the best branch – the one I liked to bring my books up to so I could sit there, reading. It was difficult to get much higher, but Michael was enthused. Máire followed him up to the next branch. It sagged under their weight.

'I don't know if that's safe,' I said, worried.

'Don't be such a baby,' Máire said. 'Follow the leader.'

This was a reference to a game we used to play, where Máire tolerated my presence so long as I did everything she did. This game had only really worked when we were younger. When I couldn't jump as far or reach as high or think as fast.

I craned my neck to see where they were sitting. Máire appeared to be whispering something into Michael's ear. I felt so envious, wanted desperately to be up there with them.

There was no room on their branch, so I took a different route. If I wasn't going to be included, then I wanted to go even higher, to show them that I was as able as they were, just as grown up. Somehow, I did it. I was almost at the very top. Their heads were now below me, looking up. Máire was furious. It felt fantastic.

'How about we tell Michael the stories, since he's new to the village?' I suggested, enlivened by my daring. This was around the time the game was in full swing at school. Máire and I had spent pretty much all summer thinking up developments for the stories.

'What stories?' Michael asked, looking up.

I started to explain, but Máire said the stories were stupid. She explained the basic premise of the game, not putting in any of the context. She didn't make either of our roles clear – the fact that I had invented the stories and she was the lead ghost in the game. She made it sound boring.

'There's more to it than that,' I said, hurt. I felt exposed, left out. I started looking for a way down. That was when I lost my footing. I felt myself falling, but Máire somehow grabbed my hand. She held on so tight. I don't know how she moved so fast. She was yelling at me to find somewhere to put my feet, but I was too scared to look down, in case there was nowhere for my feet to go. Then I heard the crack, saw the branch Máire and Michael were on shudder. I closed my eyes.

Máire didn't let go of my hand, even though that might have saved the branch and stopped her from falling with me. Luckily, the grass below was soft.

Michael was the first to laugh, once we'd realized none of us was hurt. It was the first time I properly saw him smile. His eyes completely crinkled shut.

'What's so funny?' Máire asked. She was still holding my hand.

'Just what you said,' he explained. 'Pussy willow.'

This must have been what Máire had whispered to him. I didn't understand why it was so funny, but the way he said it made me laugh, too. Then we were all laughing, pulling the hanging trails of leaves from the lower branches and chasing each other round the field with them. 'Pussy willow, pussy willow,' we all shouted, over and over, until we had exhausted all our energy.

On the way back to the house, when it was nearly dark, it felt like we were now firm friends, the three of us. I wanted to know about Michael's life, and asked what it had been like, living at the camp.

'You can't ask questions like that,' Máire barked. I felt her fist come into contact with my shoulder. I tripped over. When I got back up, Michael was standing still, his eyes wide in concern. He wasn't used to siblings, I supposed.

'I just mean, it's rude,' Máire said. She must have noticed Michael's face, too, for she seemed embarrassed, keen to excuse herself. 'Ró's always putting her nose into my business. Don't go telling her anything. She'll be after writing down your secrets in her stupid diary.'

. . .

I know the story now, though.

At Finner Camp, Michael had slept in a canvas tepee. When they left Belfast, he was ten — not quite young enough to find the whole thing an adventure, though there were other boys at the camp who acted like they were on holiday, running round pretending they were in the Wild West, that they'd taken over an Indian tribe.

'Bang bang, you're dead,' they shouted at him with their arms outstretched, jumping out from around the toilet hut.

They called him Chief at first, trying to get him to join in with their games. But the games always ended up with chants of 'Kill the Redskin.' Michael being hunted down, hiding.

At night he dreamt of smoke, thick and black, coming at him from under the door in his old house. He dreamt of being backed into corners, men calling his mother a whore. He knew it was his fault, somehow, their house being torched. It was to do with the colour of his skin, which was darker than his mother's. It was to do with his father, who Michael had never known.

When Michael first asked Georgina who his father was, she said he was an African prince. 'He had to go back to rule over his tribe,' she explained, reasonably.

'Why didn't we go, too?' Michael remembers asking, imagining his father in an opulent palace somewhere in the desert, or the jungle.

She had paused before saying that it wouldn't have been safe for him, growing up there.

But it wasn't safe in Belfast, either. Perhaps nowhere was.

By the time they arrived at Finner Camp, Michael was old enough to know his father probably wasn't a prince, but he couldn't help but ask his mother, after that first night, if they could go and stay with him in Africa instead. His mother began to cry, and Michael swore to himself he'd never ask anything about his father again.

Sometimes Georgina went out in the evenings, to the

Astoria Ballroom. Sometimes she came back with a soldier and Michael would pretend to be asleep, playing a game he made up in his head. What you did was think of a category – countries, animals, fruit, colours, sports players, whatever. Then you went through the alphabet trying to think of something in the category that starts with each letter.

Argentina, Bulgaria, Canada, Denmark, Egypt . . .

They stayed living at the camp for over a year. It was quieter in the winter, when people took their chances over the border, where they had solid walls and storage heaters. But in the summer newcomers descended on the camp, hoping for a seaside resort. Whenever Michael made a new friend he reminded himself that they would probably leave soon, that nothing lasts for ever.

But when he first saw my sister, something inside him felt fixed, like a puzzle piece falling into place.

Those were his exact words.

. . .

Because our father was taken with Michael, and because Michael was taken with Máire, he spent more and more time at the farm. 'A fine runner, up and down the lanes,' our father said. 'Nervous around the cows, though.'

He persevered, inching closer to the cows, turning up early in the morning to watch the milking, listening to the steady thrum of the pumps. He'd always been interested in processes and patterns. Sometimes the pumping synced up to the music our father played from the radio strung up inside the shed, the milk flooding into the glass vat in timely bursts. Before long, Michael was helping with the milking, no longer just a delivery boy. He knew which composers the cows liked best – Haydn and Mozart. And the ones they didn't like at all – Stravinsky and Messiaen. Sometimes he imagined taking over the farm, introducing the cows to genres other than classical – Motown, jazz, soul. He had a suspicion they might really like punk, though he wouldn't dare take charge of the radio.

Our father must have thought about the possibility that Michael would end up marrying Máire. Perhaps he'd even hoped for this, so he could pass the farm down to them one day. But he hadn't prepared for a heart attack. It turned out he'd made some risky investments, so the farm had to be sold, along with almost everything in it. Máire and I packed up what was left. Mammy didn't say a word.

The only silver lining was that the house we were moving to, on the Atlan estate, had central heating. And it was right next door to Michael's. A mirror image of it, in fact.

. . .

Máire hardly speaks on the walk back to Atlan, after the parade. She doesn't even say goodnight to Michael, just walks straight up to the front door. She's already upstairs by the time I get inside, taking off her make-up at the sink.

I change into my pyjamas and get into bed. Next door, I can hear Michael climbing the stairs. Máire comes into our room, turns off the light, and clambers over me to her side of the bed, against the wall. She gets under the covers.

'I'm cold,' I tell her, moving towards her, reaching out with my toes until they touch her leg. 'I can't feel my feet.'

'For feck's sake,' she says, kicking me. 'I'll warm you in a bit. Will you just give me a moment to myself to think.'

'What are you thinking about?'

'Shush.'

Then I hear the knocks. Three of them, coming through our wall.

'Did you tell him to do that?' I whisper.

'Shut up,' Máire mutters, her back completely turned to me now. She waits, composed, then knocks on the wall twice.

He knocks again, just once this time, as if this is a thing they've rehearsed, like it's all part of a plan.

August 1977

I run to get the paper. It didn't make the cover, but on page 5 is a photo of the launch of *Voyager 2*.

Last year, a crater on Mercury was named after W. B. Yeats. Since then, I've always gone to Mammy whenever there's any space news. Not because she was ever particularly interested in space, but because I knew she was fond of Yeats. She used to be able to recite the third verse of 'Easter 1916' by heart. A party trick, devised by her father. His four children would be able to perform the poem. And they did. Until one of my grandfather's friends pointed out that Yeats wasn't even a Catholic. There were no more poetry recitals after that. Then a mine washed up on the beach at Carrickfinn.

'I was peeling a swede at the sink,' is how Mammy used to start the story. 'The house started shaking and I knew something terrible had happened. I thought perhaps the Germans had invaded Ireland after all.'

The bit that always chilled me was when she talked about the scattered body bits, collected up from the beach and taken to the town hall to be identified. 'Some families were lucky,' Mammy said, 'taking home a leg, a wrist, a foot, a finger. But we stayed in that hall for hours – me and my mother – searching for bits of my brothers, our clothes covered in dust.' When she brought up the body bits it made me think about the paper-doll chains Máire and I used to make together, how when they were finished Máire always cut the figures up – severing their hands with the scissors, chopping off their heads. I'd stick them back together, afterwards, in secret, because of those body bits.

Mammy used to recite that third verse to herself around the farmhouse – when she was cooking or cleaning or darning socks – as if to remember what she'd lost. I loved it when she said, 'From cloud to tumbling cloud.' It made me imagine myself falling through the sky, buffeted by benevolent blankets.

So when I saw the story about the Yeats crater, I was sure it might perk Mammy up. I imagined her reciting the verse again, imagined myself reading the rest of the poem to her (for I've learnt the whole thing by heart myself). It didn't work. She stayed silent while I told her about the crater. I should have felt defeated, could have given up trying to get any kind of response out of Mammy. But for whatever reason I went back to her the next time there was anything in the paper to do with space.

I read to her about the *Vikings* and rejoiced when the first one landed on Mars. I kept her updated about the new space shuttles that were in development in California. I showed her the photo of *Enterprise*, the shuttle taking a ride on the back of a Boeing 747. I'm sure she almost smiled.

I look at the photo of *Voyager 2* – smoke pooling from the bottom of the rocket like a mushroom cloud, like the rocket itself could be a bomb, coming into contact with the Earth instead of taking off from it.

The article is short, but enough for me to read out loud to Mammy. I go up to her room. She's sitting in bed. Her skin is pale and thin like paper and starting to sag round the edges of her features. Her eyes are the same pale blue as Máire's. There's something unearthly about them. I open up the curtains to let in the light, try to remember if I washed the bedspread last weekend. I notice a few bread-crumbs in the lacework when I sit down on the edge of the bed.

'Morning, Mammy,' I say. 'How are you today?'

'Mmm,' she manages, not really looking at me, wringing her hands in that way that she does, turning them over and over.

'I've an article for you. The *Voyager* took off yesterday.'

I read the article out loud. It explains that the launch took place without incident, and provides a bit of back-ground to the mission. Eventually, the writer of the article gets to the bit I am interested in. 'Both spacecrafts carry the golden record,' I read, with added enthusiasm. 'One hundred and fifteen images and a variety of natural sounds, music from different cultures and eras and spoken greet-ings from Earth-people in fifty-five languages.'

I look up. Mammy is still examining her hands. Her breathing, though, seems to be shallower than it usually is, like she might actually be listening.

'They're real phonograph records,' I explain, though I've told her about the golden record before. 'Like a time capsule for other forms of life to discover. And they're actually gold.'

I wonder what the sounds are, the ones they've included on the record. Ocean surf, birdcalls, whale song, the wind whistling. Logs cracking in a fire, rain falling on a roof, autumn leaves underfoot. Mammy doesn't look at me, so

I flip through the rest of the paper. I think about the golden tickets in *Charlie and the Chocolate Factory*, and Mammy stuck in bed like Charlie's grandparents. When I first read that book I kept thinking about those grandparents who hadn't been out of bed in twenty years. I was still thinking of them, as Charlie followed Willy Wonka through the freaky factory and one by one the greedy children met their fitting fates. 'No,' I wanted to shout at the end when Willy Wonka crashes the great glass lift into Charlie's house. Four years now, Mammy's been in bed. And that's when I see it, while I'm having that thought, in the ad section.

ARTIST IN RESIDENCE NEEDED

We are looking for an artist to help document the work we do here at the Atlantis Primal Therapy Commune. Your time will be mostly self-directed, with a small number of specific tasks e.g. helping to make placards for protests. Bed and board will be provided, including materials and studio space.

Please send in a recent example of your work, along with a few words about who you are.

Deadline: 20 September

September 1977

I find a sheet of paper scrunched into a ball beneath our bed. I smooth it flat and see the startings of a sketch. The man in the moon, trapped inside a crater. Proof that Máire has been thinking about the advert.

'If I wanted to join that cult, I'd just walk up to the front door,' she'd said, when I showed her the advert, covering the newspaper with her breakfast plate on the table, spreading butter on her toast.

She wasn't wrong. Any of us could walk up to the Screamers' house and ring the doorbell, get invited inside like that journalist was. But none of us does. No one from Burtonport, at least.

But I know the advert was meant to be for Máire. It's a sign, I'm sure. I still secretly believe in the signs, some of the time.

Laura Cotter thinks it's a sign, too. She's making Burtonport in miniature, to submit to the Screamers. Everyone knows, though she's told the teachers she's making it for the school.

After classes, I linger outside the art room where Laura's working, pretend I'm looking through my bag. I cough, and she looks up, beckons me in.

Laura's always been nice to me. She only has much older sisters. I remember one time, when we were all in primary school, Laura was having a birthday party and I got an

95

invitation. Máire was furious, ripped up my invite and said I couldn't go because I wasn't in their class. So I stayed at home. The next day, Laura brought in a piece of cake she'd saved for me, as well as a complete set of *The Twins at St Clare's*. She'd received the books from her grandparents, who hadn't remembered they'd given her the same ones the year before. I still read them sometimes, imagine I've a twin sister and that we go to boarding school together.

. . .

Laura's miniature village is made from papier mâché. Up close, I can see that Laura's recreated almost every building – except the Screamers' house, which she's saving till last.

'I wanted to make sure I was really good at making the houses look right before I started theirs. Because it's so different to the work I usually do.'

'You mean your portraits?' I ask.

'Yes,' she says, sighing. 'People keep telling me I should become a courtroom artist. Or, you know, be the person who draws those suspect portraits they put on the news.'

'You'd be so good at that,' I tell her. 'Can you study that at college?'

'But I want to be a *serious* artist. I didn't even realize how much until I saw the advert. I don't want to be stuck doing portraits for ever. I want more. So I need to reinvent myself. I know it's a long shot, though. I'm sure there will be professional artists applying.'

'Sure,' I say, walking round the table.

'Did you ever think about entering yourself?' Laura asks, glue stick in her hand.

'Oh, I'm awful at art,' I say.

'Writing's art,' she tells me. 'I always knew you were the one who came up with the ghost game. You know. Back in primary.'

I'm touched that she remembers. It makes my body go all warm. I don't know what to say, though. Can only look down at Laura's project. 'This is really good,' I tell her, even as I notice the miniature village doesn't go up as far as Atlan. The edge of it is right where the turning to the estate is. There's always something that has to be left out, I suppose. That's the thing with art.

But when I'm walking home, I start to think maybe that's not true. What I used to love about Máire's drawings was the way she was able to add things in, not leave them out.

'The grass is always greener for our Máire,' Mammy used to say, which would confuse me because Máire never drew grass green. She made it red or orange or blue. Perhaps what Mammy meant was that Máire could always see more than the rest of us. Further, into the future even. Because while Laura was only just getting started on her version of the Screamers' house, Máire had perfected hers years ago. She didn't need to reinvent herself like Laura did.

This is what I'm thinking all afternoon and evening. By the time Máire and Michael do their knocking thing before bed, I've it all planned out in my head.

. . .

It's a spectacular morning, the sun throwing itself at the windows, as if to say it won't stay like this much longer.

Michael must have had a similar thought, because the next thing I know he's let himself in through the back door.

'I'm going to the beach,' he announces.

Máire is in her pyjamas, waiting for the kettle to boil. She still has the imprint of the pillow on one side of her face. I watch as Michael comes up beside her, kisses her there. I feel that flutter in my stomach – not like a butterfly, but as if there's a fish flapping about inside me, gasping.

'Will you come?' Michael asks, turning to me, because he knows Máire will say no. She hates the water.

'Let me just get my togs,' I tell him.

. . .

Walking to the beach we play the alphabet game – colours, this time. I don't know if he does it with Máire too, but I know he played it with me first. It was the thing I was most fascinated by when he told me the story of his life – that little detail that's not strictly part of the plot, but the thing that brings it to life all the same. When he told me about Finner Camp, I asked if he still played the game, and he said he did all the time. 'Wherever you are, whatever the situation, you can always play it in your head,' he had said.

'You ever played it with another person?' I had asked.

'How would that work?'

'We take turns, of course. So if the category's animals I start with . . .' I paused, not able to think of an animal beginning with A.

'Antelope,' he said.

'Hey, it was my turn.'

'Well, it's your turn now.'

'OK . . . beaver.'

What I love about the game is that it's always different, even if you reuse the categories. There are always animals that come into your head, as if from nowhere, animals you didn't even know you knew. Emus and fireflies, geckos and hornets.

Usually I'm so focused that I have my next three turns lined up ready. But this time I am distracted. I have to get Michael to repeat his answers several times so I know what letter I'm supposed to be turning into a colour. This is because I'm practising what I want to say in my head. I know he'll still have the pictures, but I'm nervous about bringing them up. Sometimes it feels like I made up that whole scene in my head – the drawings swirling to the ground and Michael's hands under Máire's overalls.

'I can't think of anything for E,' he says, after a silence.

'Emerald,' I say, surprised how quickly this comes to me.

. . .

Michael's really good at swimming. A soldier taught him in Bundoran, at Finner Camp. He glides through the water and only needs to take a breath on every fifth stroke.

He's been giving me lessons, when the sea's calm enough, holding my middle and letting me use his goggles.

'The most important thing,' he says, 'is to keep your head down. It will keep the rest of your body up. Your toes should be kicking along the surface, just tickling it.'

I'm improving. It's the only time I've felt better than Máire at anything and I know she doesn't like it. She hasn't been back in the sea since the time when we got caught in a rip tide and I was the one who calmed her down, remembered that the way to get out of it was to swim sideways, rather than to struggle to the shore.

After swimming, Michael stands there in the sand with his towel in his hand, soaking up every droplet until his skin is matte again. I like to let myself dry in the sun, lying down on my towel, feeling the water slowly evaporate from my skin. I try not to look at him too much, pretend I'm reading my book. I think about the noises I've heard through the wall from Michael's room when Máire is over there. The sound of his bed frame, knocking against the wall.

When Michael only has his feet left to dry he stops totally still, crouching with his towel in his hand, looking at the water.

'In or out?' he often asks about the tide. Another game we play together. The first few times, he was amazed by my talent. 'How do you do it?' he asked, like there was a secret.

'I've been here all my life,' I said, simply.

But he doesn't ask about the tide. It's as though he's been reading my mind.

'So you know this residency thing?' he says, still looking at the sea, as if we're continuing a conversation we've already been having, not starting a new one.

'I found a screwed-up start to a drawing,' I tell him.

'You did?' he asks, standing up and spinning round to face me.

'I have it here. It was under the bed.' I flip through my book to find the page where I've been keeping the crumpled bit of paper.

Michael sits down beside me on my towel, takes the bit of paper from me when I pass it to him. 'It's just the moon,' he says, clearly disappointed.

'There's a bit more to it than that,' I say. 'I don't think she's taking it seriously, though. Or she's not letting herself take it seriously.'

'No,' Michael agrees. 'She doesn't want to try in case she fails.'

I'm about to ask him about the pictures, to finally bring them up to someone who's not myself. But he's already speaking.

'I've been thinking,' he says, his voice rehearsed, like I had meant mine to be. 'We could apply for her.'

'We?' I ask.

'Well, I need someone to help write the words, don't I?'

I watch him reach into his own bag. He pulls out an envelope. It's the pictures.

'It's as if I always knew I was keeping them for some-thing, you know?' Michael is saying. 'Is that crazy?'

'It's not crazy at all,' I say, looking through the pictures. They're even better than in my memories. And they're real, here in my hands. The windows that look like eyes and a tongue coming out of the door.

'So you'll help me?' Michael asks.

'I will, sure.'

November 1977

It's lashing, the day that Máire disappears inside the Screamers' house. Biblical. The three of us are standing outside the
gate under Mammy's old umbrella. Michael in the middle,
holding the handle.

. . .

It had taken some persuading, getting Máire to agree to go.
She was furious that we'd applied on her behalf. I hadn't
seen that kind of fire in her since before Daddy died. She
was screaming like she used to and it felt like home to be
hated by her, like we were little again. She said she wouldn't
go, that she didn't want to, that she would have applied
herself if she *had* wanted to and submitted something
better. 'Not this kid shite,' she said, for they had returned
her drawings. I looked over at Michael, and he was just
staring at the drawings in her hand, his eyes moving with
them as she waved them about. Perhaps he was thinking
that as long as he kept his eyes on them then she wouldn't
be able to do anything extreme – like rip them up or throw
them in the fire. He had been right to save the drawings the
first time. They had served a purpose. But I knew the drawings really mattered to Michael. It was like they were a part
of Máire. If she were to destroy them, then she'd be attack-
ing part of herself, which he would not be able to bear.

'Did they return the letter, too?' I asked.

'What letter?'

'The one I wrote saying why you should be the artist in residence.'

'Jaysus,' she said, dramatically. 'And what exactly did you say in this letter, Ró?'

'Just that you'd always admired the house. I used the words "symmetrical" and "striking".' I had written far more than that. I had been quite pleased with the letter, and was disappointed that I wouldn't get to keep it.

'I could murder the both of ye,' she yelled. But her anger was burning out. Beneath its fiery surface was something else entirely. Pride had always made her seem to glow. She would go to the Screamers.

. . .

Máire takes out a pack of Player's and lights one, almost ceremonially. The smoke is caught inside the umbrella, adding to the atmosphere. Then she steps out into the rain and opens the gate. She takes a final drag on the path up to the steps and flicks the butt into the grass. As she climbs the steps, the smoke she's blown clears in her wake. Seven steps, getting narrower as they go up, just like in her pictures. Her hair is plastered to her head now – darker and straighter than it is when it's dry. I watch, waiting for her to ring the bell, one of those old-fashioned ones that you pull down like a handle. But she keeps her hands by her sides, standing straight.

Then she screams. Her voice pierces the rain. It's chilling, going on and on. Until the door opens. Then she's gone.

I wonder if Michael senses the gravity of what we've done – securing Máire a future that mightn't include either of us in it. He must, for we're still standing under the umbrella, not speaking, even though it's been minutes since Máire went through the door. She's someplace else now – like Alice down the rabbit hole, and Lucy through the wardrobe into Narnia, and Dorothy in Technicolor Oz – and neither of us knows how to be in this less-wild world without her in it.

The Dormitory

THE SCHOOL IS SYMMETRICAL AND STRIKING, EVEN IN THE DIM LIGHT. EITHER SIDE, TREES SWAY THEIR BARE BRANCHES. THE TWIN CHIMNEYS PUFF SMOKE INTO THE GREY SKY. THE WINDOWS PEER DOWN AS YOU APPROACH. THE DOOR OPENS WIDE.

YOU ARE SHOWN TO A SMALL, NARROW BED WITH A TRUNK AT THE END OF IT, IN A SEPARATE DORMITORY TO YOUR SISTER, ACROSS THE HALL. BACK HOME, YOU USED TO KNOCK ON THE WALL BETWEEN YOUR BEDROOMS BEFORE YOU WENT TO SLEEP. YOUR SECRET CODE.

THE OTHER GIRLS SEEM PRIM AND PROPER. WHEN THE LIGHTS GO OFF, THEY DO NOT EVEN WHISPER. BUT YOU ARE SURE YOU CAN HEAR SOMETHING LIKE A SCREAM, IN THE DISTANCE. PROBABLY THE WIND.

THE NOISE IS STOPPING YOU FROM SLEEPING, BUT YOU KNOW YOU WILL BE PUNISHED IF YOU'RE CAUGHT WANDERING THE SCHOOL AT NIGHT.

WHAT DO YOU WANT TO DO? SNEAK OUT
AND START EXPLORING OR WAIT UNTIL MORN-
ING?

(A OR B?)

Máire Dooley

New York

1979–81

August 1979

The aircraft seems flimsy in the sky, everything rattling, rain running down the windows. The pilot makes an announcement and the passengers fasten their seat belts. The hostesses calmly take their seats, their neckties all angled in the same direction. The turbulence passes.

In the immigration queue, you hold on tightly to your passport. It's new, the golden harp embossed on the green cover. You keep looking at the photo inside, the one you went into a special booth to have taken. You'd put the coins into the slot and kept your eyes wide open. But there must have been something wrong with the machine, or the mix of chemicals inside it, the man at the passport office said. For the photo had come out over-exposed, and you didn't have the money to try again. You look like a ghost – pale and confused. Like you don't know why you're there, what you're supposed to be doing.

You're worried, also, about the stamp inside, issued at the US Embassy in Dublin. The word 'INDEFI-NITELY'. At first you thought this meant you'd been rejected. It didn't sound definite at all. Your sister had been the one who'd explained it meant for ever.

The border protection officer takes your passport, looks at your photo, then the stamp. She stamps the opposite page, passes the passport back, says, 'Welcome to the United States.'

You collect your luggage from the conveyor belt of bags.

It's dark outside Arrivals. Raindrops obscure the view from inside the taxicab. The drops light up with colour as you edge through traffic. Red, white, orange, blue, like if you squint your eyes at a lit-up Christmas tree.

It feels like you're inside a film, the yellow taxi going over one of the bridges into the city. But even when you roll down the window you cannot see the skyscrapers through the fog.

The taxi stops beside a green awning and the driver goes to get your suitcase. You open up the door from the inside, and the driver runs to hold it open for you, nods as you step out under the awning. You pay him, remembering to tip, then pick up your case and fit yourself and it inside a segment of the revolving door.

The lobby floor is like a chessboard. Shiny black and white squares, polished marble. Like pieces, girls are strewn across the board, gathered in groups. There are white girls and black girls – girls of every colour, making moves. From the edges, parents' eyes follow their daughters, reluctant to let them out of sight. When you look down you notice your left foot is straddled between black and white. You move it in, keep yourself inside a single square of white, frozen to the spot.

'Hello and welcome to NYU!' A girl with a high ponytail and arched eyebrows has appeared, as if out of nowhere. She is wearing an oversized white T-shirt, the sleeves rolled up to her shoulders. You cannot read what is written on the shirt, because the girl is holding a clipboard to her chest. 'My name is Holly and I'm one of the Freshman reps here at Rubin Hall. If you give me your name we'll have you settled into your room right away.'

Holly does not take a breath until she has finished speaking. You can see all the way back into her throat when she opens her mouth to take oxygen in. Her voice is high and loud and so American. You are not sure you will be able to answer in a way she understands, though you speak the same language.

'That accent. Where are you from?' Holly asks when you tell her your name. When you say you are from Ireland, Holly says, 'You never!' like she can't believe it.

There will be times when you won't believe it either, where it will seem like you were never here at all. Not now, though. Not yet.

. . .

Ask me anything, Holly's shirt says, on the back.

Your room is on the seventh floor, which is higher up than you have ever been, except when you were flying in the sky. You squeeze inside the elevator with Holly. It has carpeted walls which you want to hold on to as you feel the lift whoosh up.

Rubin Hall Rep '79, Holly's shirt says, on the front.

'It used to be a hotel,' Holly explains, when you step out into the corridor, which is lined with doors as far as you can see. 'It's a great spot. You're just down here, room seven o six.'

Holly knocks on the door of room 706 then pushes it open. You can see a big window, straight ahead. A bed either side of it, desks at the end of each bed, two dressers. Everything a mirror image except for the girl standing with her back to you on the bed on the right, putting up a poster of The Beach Boys. She is wearing knee-high socks and a pleated skirt. Her hair is almost as blonde as yours, but sleek and swishy.

'I have your room-mate,' Holly shouts out, excitedly.

The girl on the bed spins around. She is wearing a head-set over her head and ears. It is connected by a wire to some kind of machine, which is clipped to the waistline of the girl's skirt. She uses one hand to remove the band, the other to unclip the machine, letting them land on the bed as she bounces off it. This all in a single movement, like it's some kind of magic trick. She bounds over the carpet and pulls you into a hug. You are still holding your suitcase, your right hand clenched around its handle. It's the same suitcase your father used to take to England when you were small, before he became the milkman.

'I was worried I'd be paired with someone lousy,' the girl says, her arms still pulling at your neck.

'How do you know I'm not?' you ask, when the girl finally lets go.

'What?' she says.

'Lousy.'

'Oh.' She narrows her eyes, tilts her head. 'You don't look like you will be.'

'Looks can be deceiving,' you say.

'Can they, though?' she asks.

. . .

Your room-mate's name is Franny. Her looks are not at all deceiving. She is exactly how she looks. Peppy and preppy, pretty and popular. She is from Minnesota. You have never heard of Minnesota, but you like the sound of the word, the length of it in your mouth.

'It's the land of ten thousand lakes,' Franny tells you. 'What's it like in Ireland?'

You have never been asked this question before. You try to imagine ten thousand lakes and say that Ireland is small.

There are more people in New York than in all of Ireland, you will find out. The room you share with Franny is twice the size of the one you shared with your sister back home. Rubin Hall is a Gothic, red-brick building. From the outside, you count the floors, top to bottom. Twelve. Not even that high by New York standards.

New York is 'crazy dangerous', Franny tells you. 'My father was against me coming here, but the university is supposed to be going to *great* lengths to protect the students and make sure everyone's safe. I persuaded him to come to an open day. And I have cousins in Long Island, so I can always get away.'

Franny speaks fast. You have to concentrate to keep up. She uses unfamiliar words and phrases which you pretend to understand because she's always moved on to the next thing before you have a chance to ask her what she means.

'Catch you on the flip side,' Franny says before you go to sleep each night. In bed she wears an eye mask with open eyes embroidered on the front. She snores – softly, like the calves you helped to bottle-feed, the ones who had been rejected by their mothers.

There is a yeasty smell to the room, which you don't mind, though Franny is always spraying perfume to try and mask it. During the day, Franny smells like the green apple

LipSmacker she carries around everywhere, which doesn't smell like real apples.

Franny is going to major in Law. She wants to become a lawyer for record companies. 'My real passion is music,' she tells you. 'But I'm not musically talented. I'd like to marry someone in a band, though. It's a way in.'

Franny seems so sure of who she is and what her life will be. There is something relaxing about being around a person like this, you find.

You go with Franny to all the activities she has highlighted on her welcome week flyer, which is pinned to a noticeboard she has hung on the door. The promise of a welcome week was one of the things that sold NYU to her father. Orientation tours and society fairs, student mixers and tasters. You fill your bag with handouts which you won't ever read, though you'll use the blank backs for sketches. Franny picks up friends like garments at a store, other girls who join her table in the cafeteria.

. . .

The Saturday before classes start, after you have both gone to bed, Franny suddenly sits up. She is wearing the eye mask. 'You haven't even really seen New York yet, have you? I'll take you out, tomorrow,' the open eyes say.

She lies back down again, fans her hair out on the pillow.

It's true, you haven't even really seen New York yet.

Franny begins to snore.

At Orientation, the Rubin Hall reps told the Freshmen to be careful and purposeful, taking turns to impart advice. 'Don't just go wandering about.'

'And don't go out alone.'

'Especially if it's dark.'

Franny took notes. *How to stay safe in the city*, she wrote in blue at the top of a new page in her leather-bound academic year planner, then underlined the words in pink.

. . .

Before the two of you head out into the big bad city, Franny prepares her 'mugger money' – a slim stack of notes which she keeps in a wallet in her purse. A purse, you have worked out, is actually a bag. Franny keeps her real money in a belt underneath her skirt. Her mugger money amounts to more than your actual money.

Franny takes you to the Chelsea flea. The whole way on the walk you can see the Empire State Building. You do not know what a 'flea' is. It is not what you would have expected Franny to bring you to. It is like a car boot sale. Other people's junk, displayed like treasure. Vases and lampshades, candlestick holders and ships stuck in bottles. Your eyes follow the dust motes lit up by the sun.

'Now this is proper New York,' Franny says, her smile inexhaustible. 'Daddy used to take me here when I was little.'

You leave the flea with a collection of items that will 'brighten up' your shared room. Everything is picked out and paid for by Franny. She uses her mugger money so people won't see her secret belt. She buys two framed prints, a full-length mirror, a bag of records and a gold-effect mannequin bust. You carry the mirror and the mannequin, your arms feeling like they are about to fall off. By the time you get back to Rubin Hall you've missed lunchtime in the cafeteria.

'We'll get pizza,' Franny tells you.

It is the first pizza you have ever eaten. A revelation.

. . .

You learn that Franny's father is a beef baron. When you tell her that your father was a milkman, she starts referring to you as twins.

'Have you seen *The Parent Trap*?' she asks. 'It was my absolute favourite movie growing up.'

'I haven't,' you say.

'Get out of here!' Franny exclaims. She says this a lot to you, but the way she says it isn't like how people mean it back home. 'It's about these two girls who meet at camp, and they hate each other at first, but then they work out that they're twins. Every year, I would go to camp and I'd be so disappointed when there wasn't anyone there who looked like me. I always wanted to have a twin sister.'

'I don't look like you, though,' you say.

'Yes, but that's mostly your clothes, and your hair. Those things can be changed.'

You know that Franny is an only child. 'Only, not lonely,' she is careful to point out, though there is something lonely about the way she says it. You don't talk about your sister. What would you say? That she was like a shadow you felt the need to sever from yourself. Or perhaps you were the shadow. Ró was always lighter, brighter. Franny would have been a better sister to her than you ever were. In Minnesota, Franny would have brushed Róisín's hair without pulling at it. They'd have played with dolls and skipping ropes for hours.

> *Lady, lady, touch the ground,*
> *Lady, lady, turn around.*
> *Lady, lady, show your shoe,*
> *Lady, lady, run right through.*

You remember playing follow the leader, jumping in the crusty cow pats, the ones that were fully dry. Then you'd select one for your sister, knowing it was only crusted over on the surface, fresh inside. 'That one,' you'd tell her. She knew what you were doing but she fell for it every time, the shit exploding underneath her, splatting up her legs, one time into her eye.

September 1979

The chess-piece students rearrange themselves across the lobby, forming allegiances, trying out new personalities. Everyone is carving out the kind of character they want to be.

You start your classes at the Institute of Fine Art. The Institute is separate from the rest of NYU. It's almost a ninety-minute walk from Rubin Hall. Franny has told you to avoid the subway at all costs. 'You'll surely get mugged there, and worse. Or you'll pick up some sort of disease from the seats,' she says. So you walk.

It is a completely straight line from Rubin Hall to Central Park, as the crow flies. Sometimes you imagine you are a crow flying over the city, following the human you all the way up Fifth Avenue. The roads are flat as a pancake, straight as a poker. Even the sidewalks are wider than the windy roads in Donegal, where you had to press yourself into the hedgerow when you heard a car coming.

Often your eyes hurt in the lectures because you have already worn them out during the morning walk. Street vendors and bodegas, movie theaters and colossal churches, such intricate stonework. Traffic lights strung up in the sky, steam coming out of manhole covers. So many smells and sounds and faces even before you get to the corner of Central Park where there are horses pulling carriages, the rich sweetness of animal dung.

Your course, you soon find out, will not involve doing any actual art at all. The History of Art is what you are studying. You attend lectures in dark rooms where pallid professors show pictures of ancient art on the mimeograph. Your handwriting is often illegible, you find, when you look over your notes in the light.

'The syllabus,' the Institute's president says, on your first day, 'is like a bathtub.' This is the first thing you write in your notebook.

How is it like a bathtub? You never find out.

October 1979

You get a job as an usherette at a movie theater called the Playhouse. Your shifts don't start until seven, and your classes finish at two, which leaves you with hours to kill, most days of the week. Instead of walking all the way back to Rubin Hall and up Fifth Avenue again for your shift, you find a diner that does free coffee refills, not far from the Institute. The day after you get your first pay cheque, you order a stack of pancakes and drown them in maple syrup. They're thicker than the ones your mother used to make back home on Shrove Tuesday, but they still remind you of that February evening when you found your father. You try to stare them down, and when you find you can't, you eat them as quickly as you can.

You stop eating with Franny and her followers at Rubin Hall. In the mornings you pocket bread rolls from the cafeteria. If the staff notice, they don't say anything. Sometimes, seduced by the smells, you buy food from street vendors. Hot dogs and pretzels, slices of pizza and roasted nuts.

Franny has forbidden you from walking home alone at night. So you tell her that you're getting cabs, that you can afford them now because of your job. But you don't ever get cabs. You enjoy the walk. Enjoy isn't the right word. The walk feels necessary to you. Even when you get blisters and it's raining and the straight line ahead goes on for ever. Even when you get catcalled and followed. When you're scared all the time of being mugged or worse. But really, there are far more dangerous places to walk than up and down Fifth Avenue.

When you're in the lecture hall or library, you're really looking forward to going to the diner. You don't fit in with the other students at the Institute. It's as if they don't notice you at all. Most of them are boys. They wear tweed jackets and smoke cigars in the lecture hall. You're supposed to wear black to work at the Playhouse, and you like the way it makes you feel. Like you're invisible, undercover.

'You look . . . cool,' Franny says, suspiciously, squinting at you with her eye mask pulled up on to her forehead. 'This black look.' She draws a square in the air, framing your body. 'It suits you. You look like an actual art student now.'

You haven't told Franny that you're not doing actual art at all. That the course is so different from what you expected. That you find it boring. That you sit there in the dark doing your own sketches.

. . .

You get a letter from your sister. Everyone is stir crazy about the Pope coming to Ireland. She is going with the school to a youth service in Galway. By the time you have the letter in your hands this has already happened and the Pope is flying to Boston. He will soon be in New York.

On Tuesday you get caught in a crowd outside St Patrick's Cathedral. It is pouring with rain and you can't see a thing because of all the umbrellas.

'Of course, you're Catholic,' Franny says, as if being Catholic is something exotic. 'There's something on in Battery Park tomorrow. Elsa told me. She's Catholic, too. Italian Catholic. We should go.'

'I have class,' you tell her.

'You can take one day off, Máire. It may be a moment.'

Franny lives for what she refers to as moments. 'They're the things you will remember when you're old and grey,' she explains. 'Usually a moment will happen when you least expect it. But you can't just sit around expecting one to happen.'

. . .

In the morning, you walk to Battery Park with Franny and Elsa, turning left out of Rubin Hall, the opposite direction to your usual walk in the mornings. It's not as wet as the day before, but still grey. There is a moment, as you approach Washington Square, when the Twin Towers are framed perfectly inside the marble arch. The one on the right slightly higher, slightly closer, with the radio antenna coming out the top. You like that they do not stand side by side, that they're not exactly identical. The whole scene looks like something you could pick up and trap inside a snow globe, hold in the palm of your hand. The towers make you think about the advertisements you have been seeing for a new chocolate bar. *Two for me, none for you*, the slogan says.

You've seen the towers before, of course. On a clear day you can see them if you put your head out of the window of your room in Rubin Hall. But you've never walked towards them like this. It's as if you never stopped to think that there was this whole other side to the city, that the towers were actually a three-dimensional part of it, not just a backdrop.

'One day, I'm going to work in there,' Franny says, not needing to explain where *there* means. 'Right up top.'

'Not me, I'm scared of heights,' Elsa says, shuddering at the thought of it.

'I can't believe they're even real,' you say.

The towers are still new. Built extraordinarily quickly, only a decade ago. Most of the construction finished within two years. The antenna wasn't added to the North Tower until a year ago. Before then, it was hard to tell the two apart.

The three of you walk around Washington Square, instead of through the park. The reps at Orientation told you to keep clear of the square. 'We know it's close,' they said, 'but there are other parks you can go to instead.'

'It's full of junkies,' Franny had whispered into your ear.

You see the coloured vials on the edges of the pavement. The glimmer of a needle even though the sun isn't shining. Or perhaps you just imagine the glimmering.

The streets get narrower past the park. The closeness of the buildings makes the towers disappear. But you know they are still there, getting taller as you get closer to them. When you see them again you feel like you are shrinking, like Alice after falling down the rabbit hole, when she drinks from the bottle and shrinks so small that the tiny door becomes too tall, and she cannot even reach the handle. That was the one book you didn't mind your sister reading out to you. You liked the illustrations – Alice stuck inside the White Rabbit's house, too big to get back out. One arm out the window, one foot up the chimney.

As you hit the financial district, the streets open up again. The buildings get bigger, newer. But all of them dwarves compared to the towers at the edge of the island. Gatekeepers of the city.

From Battery Park you can see the Statue of Liberty, tiny in the distance, a little lady holding up a torch. You wait for what seems like hours for the Pope to arrive, playing I Spy in the drizzle and taking turns to listen to Franny's Sony Walkman. The tape is *Off the Wall* by Michael Jackson. Franny bobs her head and taps her foot to the music. A toddler jumps around in a puddle by your feet.

'I'm sorry,' his mother says, trying to pull the boy up out of the puddle. 'Don't be splashing the poor lady, Donal.' She's Irish.

'You're grand. He's a dote,' you say, wanting her to know that you're not from here either.

Once the rain really gets going, everyone stops trying to stay dry. The water seeps inside your shoes, soaks into your socks. The excitement is palpable as the Pope takes to the stand.

'Isn't this a beautiful city?' he says, in his equivocal accent. Women are holding up their rosaries to the sky. Children sit on their fathers' shoulders. Cameras click and flash.

The Pope speaks about the Statue of Liberty, about freedom, about the city's immigrant history. You feel a part of something. Not really a moment, not in the way that Franny means, but to be pressed up close in a crowd like this. Something about it makes you feel at home, and less alone.

. . .

'Let's get sushi,' Franny says after the Pope's address. 'My dad showed me this place not far from here.'

'I have to get back,' Elsa says. 'I have a quiz tomorrow, and I'm frozen. Thanks for coming to see John Paul the Second with me.' She says the Pope's name like he's a celebrity, which you suppose he is. Or at least he is in Ireland, a framed photo of him adorning practically every hallway in Burtonport.

'You'll come, Máire?' Franny asks, linking her arm through yours as if you have said yes already.

You turn back towards the towers, the rest of the city behind you.

. . .

Grab Sushi, the place is called. Tiny inside, when you walk in. Just a central bar with high stools round it. Men in suits with their backs to you.

'Room for two?' Franny asks the chef behind the bar, holding up two fingers like a peace sign.

Sushi turns out to be raw fish. Tiny bits of pink salmon and yellow tuna, arranged on top of balls of rice, or rolled up with swirls of seaweed. The plates move round the bar on a conveyor belt, like waiting for your luggage at the airport.

'You have to grab the one you want,' Franny explains.

But you don't know what you want. You don't have time to look at what's on each plate before it's gone again, transported to the other side of the bar.

'California rolls,' Franny says, grabbing a plate and putting it down in front of you. It looks like a work of art. You can't believe they're meant to be eaten.

You copy what Franny does, plucking your chopsticks from their paper cover, pulling the points of the sticks apart until the wood splits at the top. You try to hold the sticks in your hand the way that Franny does, but you keep dropping them, have to get off the high stool and bend down to retrieve a stick from the floor.

'Take these ones instead,' Franny says, sliding another pair of freshly wrapped and stuck-together chopsticks over to your plate. 'Let me show you how to hold them.'

You like the fact that Franny doesn't make you feel uncomfortable about all the things you do not know. You wonder if this is the same as liking someone.

. . .

The rain has stopped and night has fallen when you leave the restaurant. Everything looks different in the dark. All the coloured lights shocking life into the city. Your eyes can't see as far, but what you do see you see more clearly, closely.

When you see a stall selling postcards you ask Franny to stop a second. You flip through the different images. Times Square, Central Park, Empire State Building, Statue of Liberty. You find a postcard of the towers. You root around in your wallet, find a dime and pay the vendor.

When you sit down to write to your sister, you let yourself miss Michael for a minute. The last time you spoke, it was to agree not to speak to each other. You were barely seeing each other, before that. You'd been avoiding him, ever since you went to the Screamers. The way he looked at you was suffocating. You had to lock yourself away to feel free. Find out who you might be without being loved like that.

. . .

You like working at the Playhouse. You show people to their seats and stand at the back while the movie is playing. You learn to draw in the dark, standing, without anything hard to steady your sketchbook against.

When you were first offered the position, there was a poster for the film *Alien* up in the lobby. *In space no one can hear you scream*, the poster said. In New York no one can hear you scream either, you think. Though you have not screamed since you have been here. The loudness of New York has made you quiet.

You think about the Screamers, how they didn't scream much really, after all. Not in the way that people thought they did, anyway. At first, that had been disappointing. Though you had been full of rage about Róisín and Michael sending in your pictures, you were secretly excited about going inside the house. You were proud to have been chosen. You imagined all kinds of things. A torture chamber full of whips and leather. Maybe a man, tied up, who the women had their way with. Perhaps there really was a ghost the Screamers had somehow brought back to life, like in your sister's stories.

But they were just women, being anything they wanted to be. Being free. All of them different ages, from all sorts of places. You came to know their stories – the homes they had grown up in, the husbands they had left, the hurt they still carried. Most of them told you that they hadn't ever fitted in before. That, until they'd found the Screamers, it had felt like they were playing an elaborate game, trying to follow its rules. Now, they didn't have to do that. They could express themselves, be the people they were supposed to be.

This did involve a lot of shouting. Nell said it was important for people to let their emotions out. Especially women, who tended to let things bubble up inside, because they had been socially conditioned to be agreeable. So there were often blazing arguments, which tended to blow over just as quickly as they started. Chores were shared, and everyone had to attend both group and individual 'healing' sessions. Men could stay the night, but not consecutive nights. Other than that, there weren't any rules.

You were quiet, in the Screamers' house. At first you thought it was just because you were younger than everyone else. But you were able to recognize, through the sessions you had with Nell, that making a scene had been your way of coping – a gut response to feeling stifled. Art was a better way to deal with these kinds of feelings, you learnt. You had known that, somehow, as a child.

In your first session, Nell taught you how to breathe. She said there was no point talking, let alone screaming, until a person could be still with themselves. She taught you how to let your thoughts go free, instead of holding on to them.

It was difficult, to begin with. You noticed that you were always reaching for something to do with your hands, or shaking your leg up and down. Chewing on your lip or sucking the ends of your hair. Grinding your teeth together or crossing your arms over your chest. You learnt to relax, to open yourself up.

Every day, before you picked up a pencil or paintbrush, you would hold your breath. Then you let everything inside you out. The voices in your head went so quiet. Sometimes you forgot they were even there.

Before they received the bomb threat, supposedly from the IRA, you had been working on a painting for them. *Scream School*, you titled it. A painting of the house, with its door turned into an open mouth.

You watch the alien emerge from Kane's chest, dozens of times. You can feel the audience's shock horror. You want to be able to see their faces and capture every one.

When they go out, into the light, they'll leave behind their fright, relieved that none of it was real. They'll feel better for their screaming, in the dark. But your fear is rearing, bucking itself inside you, keeping you awake at night. You've been hearing your father's voice again. *It's just your head*, you tell yourself. You hold the lid of yourself tightly, like a manhole cover about to explode.

You're fine, you think. *Just fine.*

November 1979

The leaves fall, seemingly overnight. So many shades of red and yellow and green and brown. They swirl up on the streets, then turn to mush after a heavy rainfall.

At the weekends, you explore different fleas. At one in the Bowery you find a heavy green wool coat which falls almost to the floor. Having it on makes you feel like you're being held, and when you put your hands inside the pockets you find a scrap of paper there, a handwritten note inside, the writing neat with all the letters in proportion, joined together.

She herself is a haunted house.

You keep it in the pocket and hold it between your fingers when you're walking.

· · ·

'You're coming to Thanksgiving,' Franny announces the day before she's setting off for Minnesota. Her father has insisted on paying for the flights, she tells you. When you try to protest she says, 'He doesn't want me travelling alone. And, besides, I never see you these days. I can't have you staying in Rubin Hall alone for the holidays, so you'd best get packing.'

· · ·

At Minneapolis airport, you're picked up by Franny's family driver, Arun. He's dressed immaculately – white gloves and a soft-crown hat. Franny sits in the back with you, but talks over the seat to Arun, tells him everything about New York and her classes while he makes eye contact with her through the mirror and never stops grinning. You look out the window at all the snow. Endless fields of it where you can't work out where the sky starts. You look out for signs to lakes – Peal Lake, Pleasant Lake, Long Lake, Lake Lakota, Lobster Lake. One big long road for two hours, the light fading.

Finally, Arun takes the turning to Elbow Lake. A few minutes later the car passes a sign. *Welcome to Elbow Lake. Platted in 1886.* Arun takes a left up a smaller road, up to a big entrance gate. He presses a button attached to the sun visor, and the gate begins to open. The driveway is lined with young pine trees. Hundreds of them before a big stone fountain comes into view, the water switched off for winter. Room for the car to drive right round the fountain. The house is big and brick – larger even than the Screamers' house – three storeys high with a turret coming out of one corner. Gables and chimneys and a porch wrapped around the outside. Some of the windows lit up, golden.

'Home sweet home,' Franny says, actually reaching forward and squeezing Arun's shoulders in excitement. 'Thank you, Arun.'

'You're welcome, Miss Franny, Miss Franny's friend.'

As you get out of the car, the house's front door is opened by a middle-aged woman. Grey hair, pulled tightly back. She is wearing a smart black dress. Her lips are thin, her eyes narrow.

'Miss Franny,' she says from the door. 'Come in out of the cold now.'

'Mrs Scott,' Franny cries, running up on to the porch and pulling the woman towards her, into an awkward hug.

'It's good to see you too. We've missed you,' Mrs Scott says, almost smiling after Franny's let her go.

'This is my friend Máire,' Franny says. She turns back and ushers you in.

The hall is cavernous. You feel your mouth open when you see the stairs that split in two directions at the top. A stag's head mounted on the wall.

'Your father's in his study,' Mrs Scott says to Franny.

. . .

Franny's father's hand is huge, a ring on every finger. He is a handsome man – broad and tall. His hair is white, but still thick, full. He is wearing a dark grey wool suit with a green tie, different shades woven together – sage and jade. You look into his eyes – ice blue – then notice three guns hung up on the wall, getting larger in size.

'Call me Alfred,' he says, before turning to his daughter, still shaking your hand.

'Daddy,' Franny says, almost impatiently.

Alfred lets go of your hand. 'My buttercup,' he says to Franny, stepping out from behind his desk. He kisses his daughter on both cheeks then holds her face in his hands. 'It feels like for ever.'

'But here I am,' Franny says, putting her own hand over one of his, like she could be trying to hold his there or urge him to remove it.

'Here you most certainly are. A little earlier than I thought you would be as well. What a treat. I'm afraid I've a few bits of business to flourish off here. Why don't you show your friend—'

He said 'flourish' instead of 'finish', you are thinking, before you realize he is waiting for you to say your name.

'And Mama?' Franny says into the silence.

Alfred turns his eyes back to his daughter. 'Your mother's in her room. She'll be down for dinner.'

. . .

'Mama's delicate,' Franny explains. 'She gets migraines, can't have too much light or noise.'

You've followed Franny to her room, so she can select a dress for you to wear. The room is papered with a pattern of daisy heads that match the embroidered flowers on the bed sheets. On top of the dressing table is one of those winged mirrors where, if you get the angle right, you can create identical versions of yourself, on and on to infinity. There are teddy bears sitting together on an armchair. Trophies lined up on top of a bookshelf – figurines of ice skaters in silver and bronze. Horse-riding rosettes, red and yellow and blue, framed and hung up on the walls.

Franny emerges from the closet, which is big enough to walk inside. She sits beside you on the bed, takes a deep breath.

'When I was five,' Franny says, 'my mother lost a baby, my little sister. She wasn't the same after that.'

'I'm sorry,' you say, not knowing if you should share that your mother lost a baby too.

'It's OK.' She takes another deep breath and stands up from the bed. 'It was a long time ago. Now what was I doing again?'

. . .

The dress Franny has picked out for you is navy blue with a Peter Pan collar, knot-shank buttons down the middle. It's not the kind of thing Franny would ever wear in New York. It reminds you of the outfits your mother used to wear to mass. Demure, you would call it. It hangs a little loose on you.

Your room is in its own wing, at the back of the house. 'It has the best view,' Franny told you, 'but you'll have to wait till tomorrow when it's light.' Above the bed is a bell built into the wall, that connects through to the kitchen. 'Ring the bell if you need anything,' Franny had said. 'It goes through to Mrs Scott.'

At seven, you walk along the corridor to the top of the stairs. Franny is waiting, wearing a coral pink dress with a matching jacket.

She links your arm in hers before you descend the stairs.

. . .

The dining room is dim, lit only by candles. There are portraits hanging on the walls. Some of them have lights mounted above them, but they're either not switched on or not working. You want to look at the paintings, to go right up close and examine the brushstrokes, but Franny's parents are already seated at the table, at either end. You sit facing Franny. Her father to your left, her mother to your right.

'Mama,' Franny says, 'this is my friend Máire from NYU.'

'It's nice to meet you, Mrs Jorgensen,' you say.

'Yes, yes,' Franny's mother says, softly, slowly, gazing past you, as if remembering something from long ago. Her eyes are small and sad. She is thin and frail. Your own mother would look solid in comparison, even though she doesn't speak.

'Máire's going to be an artist,' Franny adds, enthusiastically.

'An artist!' Franny's father bellows. 'What do you want to be an artist for, then?'

'Oh, I don't know if I want to be an artist for sure,' you say, crossing your ankles under the table, then crossing them the other way. 'But I like art. Drawing and painting. It's the only thing I've ever felt really good at.'

'You'll have to do a drawing for us, in case you're ever famous.' Franny's father stands up from the table, making the silverware clatter, and walks over to a side table, returns with a decanter. 'And do you know much about wine?'

'Nothing.'

'This is an Australian blend. Rich, oaky, a long flourish. See what you think.' He moves round the table, pours a drop into your glass. 'Go on.'

You lift the glass to your mouth, tip it back and swallow.

'Well, didn't that go down fast?' you hear him say from behind you, laughing.

'Daddy, don't tease her,' Franny says. 'Máire told you she doesn't know a thing about wine.'

'I apologize. Here, let me pour you a glass, Mona.'

'I'm going to take Máire to the lake tomorrow, if that's OK with you?' Franny says, after Alfred has finished pouring out the wine. He has sat back down, and is swirling the ruby liquid around in his glass, gazing into it, longingly.

'By all means,' Alfred says. 'It's your holiday. I have to go to the ranch, anyway, though I'd love to see you skate, buttercup.'

'Oh, I don't know if we'll skate,' Franny says. 'You know, Máire comes from a farming background too, Daddy. Dairy.'

'Oh, you do?' Alfred asks, looking back at you, his blue eyes bulging. 'How large is your family's herd?'

'Small,' you say, not explaining that your family don't have cows at all now, that they haven't for nearly seven years.

Alfred doesn't ask how small 'small' is, seems satisfied with knowing his operation is larger.

'So, where in Ireland are you from?' he asks.

'Donegal. On the north-west coast.'

'Oh, so you're from Northern Ireland.' He doesn't say it like a question.

'Well—' you say.

'Terrible business going on there. Not a wonder you wanted to come to America. You know it was my great-great-grandfather – you see him on the wall there – who came here just after the Civil War. Settled right here, in Elbow Lake.' He knocks a fist on the dining table.

You turn around, try to make out the person in the portrait Alfred nodded at, but it's too dark to discern much of the man. Just a pale face on a dark background.

'What do you think of the portrait then?' Alfred asks. 'Seeing as you're an artist?'

'It's very . . . accomplished,' you tell him, arriving at the word just in time.

'He read, in the paper, back in Copenhagen, that a man could obtain land if he was willing to clear it, out here in Minnesota.'

'I don't think Máire needs to hear the whole story, Daddy,' Franny says, reaching for her wine glass.

You can sense a change in the room, a stiffness. Alfred's neck is turning red.

'I don't mind,' you say to him. 'Please, tell me.'

'As I was saying,' Alfred continues, loosening his tie. 'It was called the Homestead Act, a policy of President Lincoln's after the war. So my great-great-grandfather – Victor, he was called – bought himself a one-way ticket on a steamer ship. Left his family behind. He was a young man, barely twenty. He'd asked his sweetheart to marry him, but she didn't want to leave Denmark. She died of influenza a year or two later, I was told. Anyway, my great-great-grandfather Victor arrived and vowed fidelity to the United States. Never returned. Cleared his acre of land and made it fruitful.'

The door opens and Mrs Scott comes in with a trolley. Alfred removes his napkin from its silver ring, tucks it into his collar, takes another gulp of wine.

'I don't suppose you've had lutefisk before, have you, Mona?' he asks, as Mrs Scott places a plate in front of you.

The fish is white. Cod, it looks like. Bacon bits on top. Three pale peeled potatoes. A small mound of crushed peas. White sauce artfully zigzagged over it all.

'I grew up in a fishing village,' you tell him, still looking at your plate. You can't work out if the food is meant to be hot or not.

'I thought you said your father was a farmer.'

'Well, he supplied milk, just for the village really.'

'There will be turkey tomorrow, of course. This is just a small tribute to my ancestors. But Franny hates turkey, always has done.'

'I don't *hate* it, Daddy,' Franny argues. 'I just don't see why we have to keep up the tradition, when there are so many other nicer meats we could be eating. I just think turkey's bland.'

'See what you think, Mona. Tradition's important, wouldn't you say? Go on.'

You poke the lutefisk with your fork. It is dry and flaky at the top, gluey at the bottom.

Alfred continues telling his story, while at the same time mashing his potatoes, loading up his fork and swallowing down chunks of the food all mixed together, washing it back with glugs of wine.

'When he arrived in Elbow Lake, my great-great-grandfather, there were barely fifty people living here. Just a saloon and a boarding house, not even a general store. But it was a smart move, to settle somewhere that was just beginning. He built a house and got a wife. Got himself some cattle. Reared six sons, some daughters too. The rail-way came to Elbow and that's when the town really got going. Not only a general store but a schoolhouse, a court-house, a church, even a library. Everything you need, right here in Elbow Lake, that's what my father always said.'

The potatoes are lukewarm, the peas overcooked, and there is something off-putting about the sauce. The fish has gone dry in your mouth and you don't know if you should carry on chewing or try to swallow. It's tasteless, at least.

Alfred has changed the subject. 'Franny here seems to think New York is the place to be. Now, don't get me wrong, I like New York – fine for a visit – but I'm not convinced it's the right environment for young girls. If you ask me, the place is going downhill. Too many foreigners, living in squalor. It's past it, that's my opinion. You should have seen it in the fifties – now that was something – before they put up all those ugly new skyscrapers. When it was just the Chrysler and the Empire State – fine buildings. But, it's what Franny wanted, and we want our Franny to have a good education, don't we, Brenda?'

He looks down the table at Franny's mother. She has not touched her lutefisk.

'To home and hard work,' Alfred says, lifting his glass.

'To home and hard work,' Franny repeats, eagerly.

You reach for your glass and knock it over. Red wine soaks into the tablecloth.

. . .

The next morning, when you wake, Franny is sitting on the edge of your bed. She is already dressed. You had not realized how tired you were until you lay down on the big bed after dinner and fell asleep without drawing the curtains, your dreams warm and heady from the wine.

'Time to get up,' Franny says, beaming. 'There's so much I want to show you.'

After breakfast – smoked salmon and eggs – Franny takes you to the stables, where you meet the stable boy, Brad. He looks like he's a couple of years younger than you are, maybe your sister's age. Right away, you can see he is in love with Franny. His face turns bright red when she speaks.

'It's good to see you, Brad. You've grown.'

'Miss Franny,' Brad says, then looks down at his boots.

'Well then, how's Cable? I hope you're taking good care of him.'

Franny walks past Brad, round the corner to where the horses are.

'I'm Máire,' you say to Brad, trying to smile. You are more like him than Franny, you want him to know, but you aren't sure how to do this. The boy hardly looks at you, is already turning back to follow Franny.

'My darling, my darling,' Franny is cooing over one of the stable doors. A silver horse's head pops out, the breath coming out of its nose visible in the cold air. The stables smell like straw and manure and something else. Like apples. Real apples, not Franny's LipSmacker. It is nothing like being inside the milking shed, which you remember smelt like chemicals, the iodine you used to wash your hands when you helped out with the calving. The milking shed always seemed so damp, whereas here the air is crisp and dry.

'Cable, this is my friend Máire. Come and say hello.'

Cable is huge and striking. About a foot taller than the horses in Ireland.

'Have you missed me?' Franny is saying, talking in a baby voice. She does not take her eyes off him as she reaches into her jacket pocket, takes out a sugar lump, the corners of the cube slightly rounded.

'Who's a good boy?' Franny asks, feeding Cable the lump. 'Can you ride?' Franny asks, looking at you now.

You shake your head. 'We didn't have horses.'

Franny looks back at Cable. 'What about skating? We've spare skates. You're a six, aren't you?'

'I've never done it before,' you admit.

'Well, it's not that difficult.'

She is still stroking Cable's nose, and you are suddenly overwhelmed. The feeling is dull but all-encompassing. You have to be alone. 'You know, I'm not feeling too well,' you say to Franny. 'Stomach cramps.'

'Your monthly?'

'I think I just need to lie down for a bit.'

'Ask Mrs Scott for cocoa. I find that always helps. Do you mind if I take Cable out for a bit? I'll check in on you when I'm back. And we can go to the lake if you're feeling up for it.'

'I'll be fine,' you tell her. 'I just don't feel up to much physical activity.' *Up to much.* When did you start to speak like Franny?

'You poor thing. If you need anything, remember, just press the bell.' Franny turns back to the stable entrance and shouts out for Brad, who runs inside. 'There you are,' she says. 'Look, do you want to bring Pepper and ride with me and Cable? We'll just go as far as the lake.'

When his face lights up it reminds you of Michael's, though they don't look anything alike.

. . .

On your way back to your room you run into Franny's father, upstairs on the landing. He makes a joke about the wine you spilt last night, how you hadn't spilt enough of it to stop his head from hurting now. You tell him you're not feeling well.

'Rest, my dear girl,' he says, descending the stairs while keeping his head fixed on you. 'Rest well.'

Back in your room, you examine the old map of Elbow Lake, framed on the wall. The lake does indeed look like an elbow. You look out over the garden from the window. There is a square hedge maze beyond the lawn. If you were positioned more directly over it, you'd be able to work out how to get to the middle, like that maze book your sister got out from the library once, the one you couldn't help drawing the solutions inside.

You don't know why you lied to Franny, about being on your period. Franny and her friends all seem to keep track of their cycles, arranging their lives around them, even pretending to be bleeding when they're not, to get out of things. Which you suppose is what you're doing, too. You weren't able to put the way that you were feeling into words, there in front of Franny. You didn't know how to tell her that you know nothing about horses. You didn't want to fall off or for the horse to run off with you on it. And what if you went skating? You have this terrible feeling about skating, a fear the ice would crack and something very bad would happen. You're not scared of you yourself falling into a hole in the freezing water and drowning. But you have a sense that someone else would, and you'd be standing there frozen when you might have saved them, if you'd been a different kind of person.

You don't press the bell above your bed. You take off everything but your underwear, pull the curtains closed and get back into bed, sleep almost as soon as your head hits the pillow. It's the comfiest bed you've ever been in. You feel wrapped up in it, like a caterpillar in a cocoon, before it turns into a butterfly. Your dreams are fluttery. It feels like someone is stroking your hair. It's nice, the stroking, reminds you of being small, before anything bad had happened. It makes you put your thumb inside your mouth, makes you curl your knees up into your chest under the covers. Then the stroking is running along your back, going up and down and letting the cold air in underneath the covers, getting lower. You feel a tingle between your legs, like how you used to feel before you had sex with Michael. It is a slippery, glimmering feeling that you want to slide inside. But when you open your eyes, when you remember where you are – not in Michael's room in Burtonport but in a mansion in Minnesota – you feel your heart thump in your chest, like it is trying to escape through your ribcage. And a hand is coming down over your mouth, the other sturdy on your lower back.

'Shhh,' he says, although you haven't made a sound.

It's as if you're watching it happen in slow motion from the ceiling, then falling back into your body, fast. This falling sensation, over and over. The covers have been pulled back and Franny's father is on top of you, unbuckling his belt and pushing the crotch of your underwear to the side. When you fall into your body, you can feel him inside you. He holds your head to stop you turning away. Your eyes are moving fast, trying to escape his. You can feel them aching. You try to settle on the ceiling, to get back outside your body. But his eyes keep finding yours with every thrust.

When he comes he groans, and you're worried someone will hear, even though you know your room is far away from anyone else's. He falls down on to you, heavy, his skin sweaty. Then you feel his finger push its way inside you before he brings it back up to your mouth. The ring under his knuckle clinks against your teeth as he forces his finger over your tongue, back into your throat.

. . .

You miss Thanksgiving dinner. You have been throwing up, you tell Franny, which is not a lie. You're scared he will come back to your room in the night, full of turkey washed down with port. You stay awake, waiting, as though sleep is not a thing that humans do. You wonder if he's ever done the same thing to any of Franny's other friends, but you know you will never be able to tell Franny, to tell anyone. You think through everything that happened the evening you arrived – what you were wearing, what you said, how you might have come across, the glass of wine you spilt over the table. At what point did he decide what he would do?

'You poor lamb,' Franny says, when she pushes the door open in the morning.

Your heart is still beating in your chest like a rabbit caught in a trap, like a fly hammering itself against a windowpane.

December 1979

For weeks after, months, you feel frightened by things you hardly noticed before. Lights changing at the crosswalk. People walking towards you on the street. Textbooks being slammed shut. Sudden movements on the movie theater screen.

You begin to avoid Franny. You work later at the Playhouse, leave earlier in the morning. Sometimes there are messages for you, written on the noticeboard.

Gone to a party at Weinstein Hall. Come!

Howdy, stranger.

Baby, it's cold outside.

. . .

Franny goes home for Christmas. You stay at Rubin Hall. Your head is playing tricks on you again. You're sure you are being followed on the walk home from work. Footsteps, voices, eyes.

You know you're acting crazy when you buy a pair of kitchen scissors. But you need to be sure that what you do is real. You put them on the floor back in your room, between the twin beds. You sit down on the carpet, legs crossed. Stare at the shiny blades. Seconds, minutes, hours.

It passes, Nell would tell you. *It always passes.*

You pick up the scissors, separate the blades. You hack

at your hair until all of it is gone. Curls all over the carpet. No one will want you now.

. . .

On the walk home from midnight mass you go inside a phone box. Shutting yourself in reminds you of being inside the confessional booth back home. Your first confession, when you wanted to tell Father Peter about Jesus winking at you from the cross over the altar. Your mother had told you this was a false image, that you were imagining things. But it didn't feel fair to count this as a sin when you weren't the one doing the winking. Instead, you said you sometimes wished your sister was dead. This seemed to satisfy the priest, who sent you off to pray the rosary.

Hail, Mary, full of grace, the Lord is with thee.

Blessed art thou amongst women, and blessed is the fruit of thy womb . . .

You drop coins into the slot and dial the area code for Ireland, key in the only phone number you know. You never had a phone at home, but Michael did, does.

His mother answers. You don't know if you're relieved or not.

'Máire,' Georgina cries. 'It's glorious to hear from you. Happy Christmas. Do you want me to get Michael?'

'I haven't much time,' you explain. You feel like you're about to cry. 'Do you think . . . is Ró next door, do you know?'

You wait, gripping the phone like you're trying to strangle it, the tightness holding back your tears. You hope Róisín is out, or that the money will run out, so you won't have to hear her voice. What if Michael picks up instead? You want to put the phone down. You're about to when you hear her. She sounds so far away, and there's a bad delay, but she's the same. Excited, animated.

She begins to ask you questions – where you are, what you've been doing – but you cover the receiver with your hand because you don't want her to know you're crying.

'I can't hear you,' Róisín says.

'What's the weather like?' you ask, through a crack in your fingers.

'Sheets of sleet,' she tells you, without hesitation, like she's been thinking of how to describe the scene outside all day. 'It's below freezing.'

You want to tell her about all of Franny's pairs of gloves, how she matches them with her outfits. But that would require so much speaking. You'd have to hold yourself together and you can't. 'Tell me something else,' you say instead.

Ró went to see *Manhattan* last weekend, at the Century in Letterkenny. 'I couldn't stop myself from hoping that you might somehow appear in it. I was looking for you everywhere. Have you seen it?'

Of course you've seen *Manhattan*. Dozens of times, at work. But the scenes pass right through you, leaving nothing behind, not even an impression.

The phone beeps into your ear. 'Please deposit twenty-five cents to continue this call,' an American voice instructs. But you don't.

You stay there, shaking with the phone still in your hand, until you're jolted by someone knocking on the glass, waiting to make a call. You place the receiver back in the cradle, collect yourself and push open the door.

...

On Stephen's Day, the city glitters in the afternoon, sun dipping between the shiny buildings. You do not cover your shorn head. The cold so sharp you're stupefied. Brain and bone.

You take out the bit of paper in your pocket, which always says the same thing.

She herself is a haunted house.

January 1980

Dear Máire,

Happy new year, pet. I expect you're all settled in there now. How's the course going? We all miss you here, but I'm writing to tell you that here is no longer the house in Burtonport. We received another bomb threat, and decided it was time to move to pastures new. So I'm writing this from windy and rainy Inishfree. We've taken over some of the old cottages here. It was a bit of a rush trying to get the place liveable before it got really cold, but we're doing all right! The fire's going and the place is dry enough! We have the goats for milk and a little boat for when we need to get back to the mainland. We're trying to be as self-sufficient as possible but we have a way to go. I just keep telling myself that by this time next year we'll have made a lot of progress.

We lost a few of the old gang when we moved here – Ethan and Rox went off to India and we haven't heard from them since. And my sister and Ethel have gone back to England for a bit – God knows why! She'll be back, and hopefully you will come and visit when you're home. You're of course welcome any time, though I expect New York is more exciting than hanging out with us old fogeys.

There's a real sense of freedom here, which is nice. And I don't think the neighbours were sad to see us go – though they'll all have to find something else to talk about now.

I think of you often. The time when you first arrived and stood there screaming on the doorstep instead of ringing the bell. I hope you've found your tribe over there and that you're experimenting with everything and everyone. Remember, if you need to scream, scream. But don't forget to breathe.

All my love,
Nell

. . .

You start a new class called 'The Early Masters of Renaissance Painting'. The professor is not really a professor, you hear people complain. He's a famous art dealer.

'You can call me Harold,' he tells the class at the beginning of the first lecture, which he is ten minutes late to. 'I won't learn your names. Don't be offended.'

He is younger than the other lecturers you have had. In his forties, you think. He's attractive. Thick dark hair, tanned skin. Broad shoulders, high cheekbones. This changes the energy in the room. Everyone is holding themselves differently in the dark of the lecture hall. You can feel it, even if you can't see it. Nobody even takes notes.

'I don't want essays from you,' Harold says. 'Why we're getting Freshmen to write essays is beyond me. None of you knows what to think about anything right now, and that's how it should be. But I want us to be able to talk about the things I show you, OK? All I want is a conversation. I want us to learn from each other, to develop our ideas. This isn't about showing off what you know. In fact,

I want you to forget what you know. OK, just pretend you know nothing.' The class laughs. 'I just want you to *Think. For. Yourself.*'

He writes this last bit on the blackboard, a full stop after each word.

February 1980

It doesn't happen right away, but your brain begins to work again, just like your hair starts growing back.

You learn about contortions, figures twisted in impossible shapes – *La Figura Serpentinata*. Harold's voice is thick like treacle. When he speaks he takes his time, pacing back and forth in front of the blackboard, instead of standing at the lectern.

'If you walk around a sculpture from the High Renaissance, the idea was that it could be viewed from every angle, not just a single one. It put art in the very centre, rather than having it as something on the sidelines. Sadly, there are no examples of these sculptures here in New York. Hardly any Renaissance art at all.'

Still, as an assignment, Harold instructs everyone in the class to go to the Metropolitan Museum of Art. 'Just walk around,' he says. 'Go alone. I want you to think about how painters might be able to produce the same effect, but just with two dimensions. Can you see any contorted figures? And do you think they're powerful, or powerless? We can discuss next week.'

They're neither, you think, at the museum. They're twisted out of shape because of love. They're deformed by it, but that itself gives them a kind of strength, a new shape. You feel your stomach turning as you think of this.

You start to draw contorted figures yourself, twisting scenes you see on screen or putting people at the diner into impossible positions on paper.

March 1980

The snow turns black and melts in the rain, which falls endlessly. You are always wet, your socks soaked and shoes squeaking when you walk across the polished floor at the Institute, when you come into the diner. Sometimes your hair drips on to your sketchbook and you like the way the water warps your pen strokes, makes the ink spread. You're adding shading to a sketch you started yesterday – a woman who came into the diner and didn't touch her cup of coffee, just sat there, smoking, gazing blankly ahead of her. She never even glanced at you, all the time you were examining the lines around her lips and the mascara smudged under her eyes. You have imagined her naked, her body bending so she can reach the cigarette, her lips outstretched to get her that inch closer. You are trying to twist the body even more than is possible, actually holding up the paper and wringing it in your hands, when someone slides into the booth across the table. You keep the paper held in front of your face, as if to hide your own eyes. Beneath the bottom edge you take in a man's shirt, no tie. You know it's him before you even see his face.

'Marie, is it?' your professor, Harold, says. 'Hope you don't mind if I join you.' He looks around the diner, as if to say there's nowhere else to sit. But there are several empty tables.

You're stunned. Not because he's said your name

wrong – this happens to you all the time in New York – but because he never calls anyone by their name in class.

'It's Máire,' you say, putting the drawing back down.

Harold twists his body to get menus from the next booth. He places one in front of you, spinning it the right way round for you to read it. 'So, you come here every day?' he asks, reaching into his shirt pocket for his glasses.

'Most days.'

'And you come here to draw? What are you working on?'

You move your hands to cover up the drawing. You watch them scrunch the paper up.

'Don't do that,' Harold says, putting a hand on your wrist.

'It's nothing. I'm not working on anything.'

He looks over his glasses at you, sceptically. There is something too intense about his gaze. You have to look away, and you're relieved to see a waitress walking over to your table.

'What can I get you both?'

'I'll have the poached eggs, please,' Harold says, though you're sure he never looked down at his menu.

'I'm not really hungry,' you say, which isn't true, but you've been putting on weight from all the pancakes, said you'd give them up for Lent.

'You eat eggs?' Harold asks. He looks back at the waitress before you have a chance to answer. 'Two poached eggs. And coffee.'

'Perfect.' The waitress takes the menu back from Harold then walks back towards the bar.

'So, you always screw your work up?' Harold asks.

'They're just drawings,' you say. 'I've time to kill in the afternoons, so—'

'So, you're doing a lot more *actual art* than anyone else at the Institute.' You have noticed a habit he has, of accentuating certain words in his speech. Ones he sees as significant. He does it in class.

'It's hardly—'

'Can I ask you something, Máire?' he says, putting his elbows on the table and leaning in.

'OK.'

'You care about the art world?'

'Em—'

'Are you interested in dealing, in what sells, in running a gallery one day or working in an auction house? Because that's what your *classmates* are here for. It's all going to be a game for them. They want to be near to art because it's *fashionable*. It seems more exciting than, say, working for a bank. But it's no different really. It's buying and selling. It's about *capital*. And I get the sense, Máire, that you're not especially interested in capital.'

'It's not something I've really thought about before,' you admit.

'Well, exactly.'

You want to ask how he's got this impression of you, when you've only ever been together in a darkened hall, when you're just one of fifty students in his class. But you can't ask him. Is this even happening?

'I'm sorry. Can we start again?' he says, as if it's possible to do such a thing. 'I didn't mean to ambush you. I've just seen you here a few times, through the window, on my way to get lunch, and you're always *drawing*. Then I realized you were in my class, so I thought I'd come say hi.'

The eggs arrive. You slip the scrunched-up sketch into your bag so the waitress can put your plate down on the table.

Harold pours coffee into your empty mug. 'Milk?' he asks.

You nod.

'Say when.' He pours a drop of milk into your coffee, then looks up.

'A little more,' you say.

He pours the milk again. 'More than *that*?' he asks.

'I like a lot of milk. I grew up on a dairy farm.'

'I see,' he says, smiling, as if he is already starting to picture it, in his head. 'Tell me about *that*.'

. . .

You do tell him about that. You tell him all about your life in Burtonport, bring it back into focus, the place you left behind. Every day he comes back to the diner, arriving about an hour after you do. You still won't let him look at your sketchbook, put it away in your bag when he sits down in the booth, the scrunched-up sketch of the woman now smoothed out inside the cover. You never see her again, that woman. You only notice Harold now.

You tell him about the day you found your father in the milking shed. How you knew that he was dead, because the cows were so distressed. Steam rising from their bodies, escaping from their mouths as they moaned, eyes rolling, pressed up against each other for too long, unable to get out. You didn't scream right away. You let it all sink in first. The music at full volume on your father's stereo. The rhythmic hiss of the pressure pump. The smell of hot wet shit and piss and excess milk, pooling on to the concrete floor, creeping closer to your father's body, his face twisted to the side, his mouth wide.

You tell him about the Screamers, the little room you had up in the attic, full of books that had been left behind by the last artist. You tell him that you must have sat in that pink armchair reading for a month before you touched any of the materials. It was the first time you had space to breathe, to be quiet. Before then, you hadn't really realized that you liked to be alone, that you need solitude to survive.

You tell him about your sister and Michael, conspiring to get you the residency, sending in your childhood drawings of the house. You didn't speak to either of them for months.

You admit, at last, that you shouldn't really be here, because Nell helped you get the scholarship through a contact she had at NYU – someone she had 'sensational' sex with, once.

'Sensational, was it? That's the word she used?' Harold says, smirking.

It falls into place, like a punch to the stomach. 'It was you. Why didn't you tell me?'

Harold stubs out his cigarette before speaking. 'She was right, Nell, what she said.' You think at first he means about the sex. Then he adds, 'It's like you're not from here, Máire.'

'I'm not from here.'

'That's not what I mean.'

. . .

You don't go back to the diner the next day. You take yourself to the museums – MoMA and the Whitney, the Frick
Collection and the Guggenheim.

I'm not from here, I'm not from here, you repeat to yourself
when you're walking. The more you say it, the more you
think you understand what Harold meant. And on the
morning of his next class, there are buds popping out from
all the branches – tiny, furry things. Pink and white and
green.

He runs after you when you leave the lecture hall. 'I'm
sorry,' he says. 'I should have told you about Nell. I just
wanted to meet you *normally*.'

'I'll be at the diner,' you tell him, trying not to sound
excited.

. . .

He tells you the story, about how he met Nell. He was in
London, for work. He'd just finished a meeting with a gallery owner in Mayfair. And when he came outside the
streets were packed with people.

Peace in Vietnam, the placards had read. *Stop the slaughter.*
There were peace symbols everywhere. He couldn't believe
it, that they were protesting the war here, in London, where
the war hadn't touched.

Harold let himself get carried by the crowd towards

Grosvenor Square, though he didn't know that was where he was. He was there when the fighting started. Mud and stones, firecrackers and smoke bombs. The police high up on their horses, holding batons.

The next thing he knew he was on the ground. His head was pounding. But there she was, this woman leaning over him, her long hair like a waterfall, tickling his cheek.

She took him back to her flat off the Edgware Road. She iced his head and told him that he had to stay awake, in case he had a concussion. That was how it started. He stayed in Nell's flat for a full week and they hardly left the bed. Except for one evening when she was hosting a protest meeting. Her friends crowded into the little flat and they discussed the issues of the Earth. Nuclear weapons and environmental damage. The housing crisis and the establishment. The civil rights movement and the student rights movement. He had never met people like these before. And Nell, she was something else. Clearly a leader, her presence in the room so much brighter than anyone else's. Still, she didn't dominate the discussion. She made everyone feel like what they had to say mattered.

That week he fell in love. But when he told Nell she only smiled. She didn't believe in love, she said. Or at least, not in the way he meant. She wasn't going to give herself to another person. 'Go back to New York,' she told him. 'There's more for you there than I can ever give you.'

So he went back to New York, half-hoping she might end up coming with him, run through the gate at the airport and board the plane just before it was about to take off, out of breath. But he knew she wouldn't. If there had been a chance that she would do such a thing, he'd have never left London at all.

Back in America, they announced the lottery system for the draft. His brother's number was called up. Little Jimmy, only twenty-two years old, just out of college.

'We can find a *way*,' Harold said, on the phone to his brother, who was in California at the time. 'Get you into a master's course, something like that.'

'I'm going, Harold. I have to.'

'What are you talking about?'

'You know it's the poor who are fighting, right?' Jimmy had said, suddenly seeming older. 'It's black people, people who were never going to be able to go to college anyway. And it's people like us who manage to get out of it, who get special dispensations. God knows I don't believe in this war – but my number's come up, and I'm not going to let some other poor soul go and fight in my stead.'

Five months later, he was dead.

You put your hand on Harold's, over the table. His ring hand. The feel of the metal reminds you, instantly and appallingly, of Franny's father. You lift your hand like you've been burnt, pull the hair on the back of your head instead. Harold picks up his mug and gulps down the cold coffee. He continues with his story, smiling.

'I stayed in touch with Nell. We'd meet up, every year or two. Only ever for a few days at a time. She never came to New York, but I'd find a reason to be in London, or she'd come to Rome or Florence.'

It feels like you're being pricked with something when you imagine him in Italy with Nell. The two of them walking round the statues. Or, worse, not going to see the statues at all, never leaving the room. His words are hurting you, but you want more of them, to know everything. He uses the word 'astounding', talking about Nell. He says he grew to respect her so much that he no longer wanted her for himself, to hold on to her at all.

'Nell needs to be *free*. Without freedom, she's nothing.'

He had come to Ireland, once, to see the commune Nell had set up in Burtonport. Since meeting him she'd been collecting books about art history, had set up a nice little library in the room on the top floor. He loved it there, in that house. Most of all he loved that Nell had invited him – men weren't usually allowed to stay for more than a night at a time. He was the one who said they should get an artist to record what they were doing. She even asked if he would stay, if he could be the artist. But he couldn't abandon his life.

His wife, you think. *He couldn't abandon his wife.* You noticed the ring in that first lecture, when he was writing on the blackboard. It's not like he tries to hide it. Still, he never mentions her, his wife. They talk about the past but not their present lives.

'To think, we were in Burtonport at the same time,' Harold says, excitedly. 'I wonder if we passed each other, without realizing. Though I'm sure I would have noticed you – bold, brash fifteen-year-old you, all out of place.'

'I looked different, then,' you say. 'My hair, it was longer. I probably didn't stand out as much.'

'And that was why you cut it?' he asks. 'To stand out?'

You feel your ears begin to burn. You used to pull your curls down over your face, to hide yourself. 'Actually,' you say, 'it was more the opposite. Stupid, I know.'

'It suits you,' he says, not understanding, not really. He reaches for his pack of cigarettes (L&M's), flips the lid before offering them to you. You take one from the pack and put it in your mouth. Harold lights a match and guards the flame across the table. The tip of the cigarette meets the flame and you suck in. The smoke hits the back of your throat and comes out through your nose. Harold lights his own cigarette. He takes a couple of drags before speaking again. 'Your sister did you a favour, you know, sending in your pictures. Anyway, this is all to say that Nell and I haven't been *romantically* involved in a long time. But we exchanged letters. She wrote me about you. Said you were like no one she'd ever met before, but that she thought you might go mad if you stayed in Burtonport. So I pulled a few strings. I'm sorry. I should have told you sooner.'

'It's OK,' you say, and you know it must be for you to carry on seeing him again, like this. 'It just makes me feel like even more of a fraud than I already felt.'

'You can't believe that, Máire.'

'But the only reason I'm here is because—'

'You're here because, out of all the people who applied for the residency, Nell chose *you*. And from drawings you did when you were a kid. You're here because I'm trying to change things, here at NYU. I want there to be more students like you. Kids who don't come from privileged backgrounds, who don't have trust funds. Kids who want to *actually make things*, not just buy and sell them.'

'Is that how you and Nell think of me – that I'm just a poor "kid" from Ireland?'

'That's not what I said, Máire.'

'But is it?'

CATHERINE AIREY

'You're not a poor kid from Ireland, Máire. You're from nowhere, but now *you're here.*'

You're here, but you don't know what you're doing. You remember what he first wrote on the blackboard. *Think. For. Yourself.* But you're not thinking for yourself. You're not even lighting your own cigarettes. You're not even drawing. But you feel alive again. You're feeling.

. . .

You feel yourself relaxing, opening up. You even tell him about the voices, about how you were sure the statues moved in church, but no one believed you. At the same time there's a tightness, a pressure to feel understood.

'I think I always liked drawing because it meant I could fix things in place. Even if the things I draw have out-of-place things in them, if that even makes sense?'

'Of course that makes sense. A lot of artists see things that aren't there, Máire.'

When he says this, it sounds perfectly reasonable.

April 1980

'Are you *seeing* someone?' Franny asks, one evening when you've just got back from work. She wants you to come out with her to a party.

'No,' you tell her. 'Why would you ask that?'

'You seem different,' Franny says, looking through her nightstand and pulling out a pack of Lucky Strikes. She only smokes if she's going to be drinking. She thinks smoking at a party makes a person seem approachable, yet mysterious. 'Luckies', she calls them, as if they might help conjure up a moment. 'Hey,' she says, looking at you seriously now. 'You'd tell me if anything was up, wouldn't you?'

'Nothing's up. I'm just tired, and sick to death of this weather,' you say, as if you're from California.

. . .

'I'm going to give out an end-of-semester assignment tomorrow,' Harold tells you, at the diner. 'A paper on the development of mathematical precision and its effect on emotional response.' He rolls his eyes. 'I know, I know. I don't want to, but I have to, apparently.'

'OK. So what, you're telling me now so I have a day's head start? How gallant of you,' you say, sarcastically.

'No, I'm telling you now because I'm going to give *you* a different assignment. It doesn't matter to me if you're good at writing a paper or not. I know that's not important to you. And, hell, it's not important to me either. You know I couldn't care less about the way the course is graded. What I'd really like you to do for me is to draw me something, show me what all the sketching you've been doing has been adding up to.'

'I'm not sure it's adding up to anything,' you say.

'Then. *Make. It. Add. Up.*'

On every word, he squeezes his hand over yours on the table. Quickly, he removes it, after.

'Don't I need to do the essay to pass the class?' you ask.

'Screw the essay. *I'll* write you the essay. I want you to take this *time* to produce something that's really you, OK?'

'What do you mean, this "time"?'

He looks out the window for a second, then back at you. 'I'm going to be out of town for a week, so I won't be coming here distracting you. I don't want to be a distraction, Máire. I've not been a very good teacher, in that respect.'

. . .

You miss the way he looks at you – deeply, like he's trying to see inside you, like you yourself are a work of art he wants to understand everything about. You miss the way his Adam's apple rolls up and down when he speaks. Him wiping the streaks from his glasses with the diner napkins, drinking his coffee black, the way your feet sometimes touch under the table. You hadn't realized you were lonely, before.

At night you picture what his house in Vermont might be like, what art he might have on the walls. You picture his wife, wonder if she looks anything like you do. You picture his childhood with little Jimmy. Remember how he told you they were bullied at school for being so dark. Their mother's mother had been a freed slave, and though the family tried to hide this shameful secret, everybody knew.

Day after day you tear up page after page. Nothing will take shape. Every line is wrong, every figure lifeless. You feel sick, sitting in the diner after your shift at the Playhouse, trying to add up to something. Your stomach is churning, and your hands are sweating. You run to the bathroom and throw up in the sink. Mostly water and bile, easy to wash down the plughole. You haven't eaten properly in days, the smell in the diner too sweet, sickly. You look at yourself in the mirror. Your hair is limp, your skin pale. Puffy eyes and a breakout of spots on your chin.

No, you think, when you're walking past St Patrick's Cathedral. You stop. You step inside. The priest asks if you've come to make a confession but you shake your head. You'll bargain straight with God. Kneel in the back pew on the hard floor and pray, knowing it won't work.

. . .

The next four days you work from bed in Rubin Hall. You skip your other lectures, call in sick to the Playhouse.

'You poor lamb,' Franny says, like she did when you were at her house. 'Don't work too hard, OK? I tell you, it's all that walking about in the rain. You'd be fine if you had your classes here. It's like you're not even really at NYU.'

Something that's really you, you think when she is gone. And alone in the dorm room, you find focus. It feels almost divine.

You don't dress, don't eat. You get lead and ink on the bed sheets as something takes shape on the paper. It's not like anything you've done before. More classical in style, taking in all you have learnt from Harold's lectures. You know what you are doing is derivative, but isn't all art?

You, of course, are the contorted figure, twisted in the sheets. Half the page is shaded almost black, but if you look closely there's a sliver of another figure. The other side is light, a heavenly aperture through the wallpaper. It is the most detailed drawing you have ever done. Far more technically accomplished than anything you did for the Screamers.

When Franny returns you hide your work, bring your decoy drawing out – the Twin Towers framed in the Washington Square arch. It's not a bad drawing, but it's static, doesn't look alive. Not like the figure in the bed, the picture you perfect until there's only one day left.

. . .

He doesn't look at you in class. He hardly ever does, but it's been more than a week of waiting. At the end of the lecture, you hand over the brown envelope with your drawing inside it. You do not meet his eyes.

In the diner, you try to draw but everything seems trivial after what you've just finished. You keep looking out the window where the sun is shining, waiting for him. You wait for hours.

He doesn't come the next day, or the next. You imagine what he must have thought about your drawing – he must find it repellent, your rawness. You put a finger down your throat and make yourself throw up, over and over again, like if you keep emptying yourself it might all go away.

. . .

'Máire Dooley, can I ask you to stay behind?' he says, after he has run through the names of everyone in the class, returning essays. As the other students filter out, you feel your hands start to sweat. Your heart thumps in time to his feet, climbing the steps to where you're sitting.

'I can hardly bear to give this back to you,' he says, sitting down beside you and pushing the envelope that has your drawing in it across the desk.

'You can keep it,' you say, coldly, pushing it back. 'I meant it to be for you.'

'It's . . .' He pauses, putting his hand on the envelope.

'Don't get it out,' you tell him, placing your hand over his, holding it there, holding it down. You can feel the blood pumping through the veins in his hand – or you imagine that you can.

'It's *extraordinary*, Máire,' he says. 'The style, it reminds me of some of Michelangelo's preparatory drawings. Then the framing of the room, the way you've played with light and dark. And how you've pictured *yourself*. I—'

'I don't think I can talk about it,' you say, feeling as if you're going to be sick. 'You told me to draw something that was really me, and I did that. I thought you were never going to talk to me again.'

'Why would you think that?'

'Because of the picture. Because you haven't been at the diner all week. I thought—'

'I had to go to Vermont again,' he explains. 'I had to mark the other essays. I actually made myself go through all of them first, before I opened your envelope. I can't tell you how difficult that was. But it felt necessary, to *wait* before I opened it.'

'You're married,' you say, simply, as if everything can be said simply now he's seen the drawing, now he's talking to you again. 'And I'm—'

'It's OK,' he says, and you begin to cry.

He puts his arms around you and lets you sob into his chest. He smells like pencil and tobacco and soap and tar, and you want to climb inside his chest and close it up behind you.

'I'm going to take you somewhere private,' he says.

. . .

Harold's apartment is a short cab ride away. On the east side of the city, you think, though you weren't really paying attention in the cab because Harold's hand was resting on your knee. The building is beige brick, tall.

'We're on the sixth floor,' Harold tells you. 'I am, I mean.'

You don't comment on his blunder, take the stairs because you know he doesn't like to be in elevators. He was trapped inside one, once, as a child. He had been all right, but his father had got claustrophobic and panicked. 'He didn't like showing any kind of weakness,' Harold had explained, his voice full of understanding. 'So he lashed out at me. I never felt too great in small spaces after that.' He didn't accentuate any words when he told you this story.

You miss your own father – his steady hands over yours

when he taught you how to pull on a cow's teats. *Gentle, but firm.*

The apartment is spacious. A large central room, the kitchen opening up on to a dining area, with paintings mounted on the walls, canvases waiting to be framed down on the floor.

Harold takes your coat and goes to hang it in the hall while you look at the paintings. Some of them clearly very old, their colours faded. You can't help but imagine something you've created hanging here one day.

'Sit down,' Harold says, when he comes back into the room. There are two steps separating the dining area from the living space, big windows along the length of the far wall, looking out over the river. 'I'll make us some coffee.'

You go down the steps. The carpet is soft and cream-coloured. The sofa almost the same colour, the fabric woven, its texture soothing to your fingers.

'That's Randalls and Wards, across the river,' Harold informs you, from the kitchen. You don't know whether to turn back to look at him or look out at what he's talking about. 'I wanted one of the apartments on the other side of the building. You know, city side. But I couldn't justify how much more expensive they were, just for a better view.'

'What's out there?' you ask, noticing a small blue bridge stretching across the river, a wide white building on the land beyond.

'Nothing of note,' Harold says. 'I think that building's some sort of asylum.'

He brings the coffee over in a tall glass pot. One of those with the plungers you push down to keep the granules at the bottom.

'I don't have any milk, I'm afraid,' he says, pouring the coffee into two plain mugs. 'You should try this maple syrup though, it's from Vermont.'

He unfolds a blanket that's hanging over the end of the couch, places it over your knees. It's made of wool and reminds you of one you have back home. Donegal tweed.

'I want to help you, Máire,' he says, finally, sitting down on the other side of the couch. 'You're pregnant, aren't you?'

Your whole face is hot, top teeth biting down on your bottom lip to stop it from wobbling. You can't look at him.

'Your drawing—'

'It was stupid. I shouldn't have—'

'You're not stupid, Máire. Everyone makes mistakes. And it's going to be OK.'

'How?' you ask, and asking gives you a release, putting the question on someone else.

'It doesn't matter right now.' He shifts over, closer. He reaches out. His hand is on your head, in your hair. The curls are coming back now. He draws one out from behind your ear, straightening it. You tremble, turn your head. Then his lips are on your lips, his hands on the back of your neck, fingers pressing into your flesh. You reach for him, your body burning, trying to pull him down on top of you. But he is resisting, retreating.

'I'm sorry,' he says. 'I shouldn't have.'

'I wanted to.'

'So did I. Of course. But we can't.'

He gets up from the couch, begins to pace around the room. You can see his hardness, through his pants. Then he is saying, seriously, in a way that sounds rehearsed,

'There are some things that I'm going to do for you, and I want you to agree to them.' He's still pacing. 'I want you to move in here. It's not safe for you to be walking back and forth to Washington Square in the cold, or for you to be sitting in the diner for hours. Or standing in the movie theater. You need to let me do this for you. You'll stay here, and I'll figure this out.'

Something like hope swells up inside you, followed by doubt.

'What am I going to say to people?' you ask.

'You don't need to say anything.'

'But my room-mate.'

'You'll say you've found a place to stay, closer to the Institute. That you need to focus on your studies and it's taking too much of a toll on you, the journey. That's all you say for now.'

You nod.

'How far along are you?'

You haven't even worked this out, haven't dared to. You count the months out on your fingers, from the end of November. 'Five months.'

'And does anyone else know?'

'No.'

'You're sure?'

'No one.'

'I'll tell the Institute you're unwell. You can sit the next semester out.'

'What if—?' you say. 'What if I just want it to go away?'

'I'm not sure that would be possible at this stage,' Harold says. 'But if that's what you really want.'

'I don't know what I want. I just don't want—'

'Shhh,' he says, sitting back down on the couch, putting his arm around you. 'You don't have to decide now.' His voice is calming. 'You're just going to stay *here*, and I'll work out a *plan*. It's all going to be OK.'

'Why are you doing this?'

'I care about you. And you want to know the *honest* truth?'

'Yes.'

'Even if you weren't pregnant, even if you'd never done the drawing, this is something I've been thinking about for a *long* time – pretty much since I first came into the diner. Call me a romantic. I feel protective towards you, and when you told me you were doing all that walking, and having to work at the movie theater to make ends meet – I wanted to help you out. I think I was just waiting, maybe, to have a *reason*. So maybe it's *right* that it happened like this. Maybe this was *always* going to happen.'

You lie in his lap and close your eyes. You feel safe, for the first time in a long time. Safe enough to sleep.

You're aware of him carrying you to another room, taking off your shoes but not your clothes, putting you into bed. You sleep like a baby and in your dreams you are one – a floating cherub without a body, like the ones in that painting by Francesco Botticini.

. . .

When you wake it is dark. There is just enough light in the room for you to see the time on your wristwatch – another flea-market find. Five in the morning. The watch face contains an image of the Virgin Mary, the clock hands coming out of her nose. Its strap is made from delicate gold and silver strings, twisted together. You like how small the watch is, how tiny Mary's face – no larger than a pea. Like those miniature portraits people used to send to help arrange a marriage. Harold is very fond of it. The first time you wore it he told you to hold out your wrist. He called it a 'find'.

You push the duvet off you. It is much heavier than the one you sleep under in your dorm room. You find the bathroom down the hall, your bladder bursting. You flush the toilet, avoid looking at yourself in the medicine cabinet mirror as you turn the tap on and bend over the sink, drink.

The note is in the kitchen, a $50 bill beneath it on the counter.

Máire,

> *I thought I'd let you sleep. Please make yourself at home. I should be back tomorrow. Help yourself to anything you need. I got milk, for the dairy queen!*

You hate waiting.

. . .

Inside the medicine cabinet is a tin of hair wax, a herring-bone comb, a razor, Tylenol pills, a tube of lipstick, a bottle of nail polish remover, Elizabeth Arden Eight Hour Cream, a bottle of cologne. You pick up the lipstick tube, careful not to knock anything over. You close the cabinet door and look into the mirror as you put on the lipstick. On the base of the tube is a sticker.

Rich Rosewood, you mouth into the mirror, your lips pouting. It's the first time you've liked the look of yourself in months.

You put the lipstick back, spray the cologne on to your wrists, rub them together and across your neck. *Night Musk*. The smell of him.

The door across the hall from the bathroom is ajar. You push it open, the bottom of it brushing over the thick carpet, making it feel heavy. Inside, the bed is made, the sheets straight and flat. A big painting of a lily over the bed that you could easily get lost in. The carpet is so soft, the bed sheets a burnt orange like autumn leaves. Angled in the corner of the room is a standing full-length mirror and a wicker chair with clothes draped over it, like they've been worn once but aren't yet dirty. A nude mohair cardigan that you pick up and bring to your face, the softness of it tickling your nose. You can tell it's recently been worn, the smell of sweet sweat soaked in, under the arms.

You open the closet, run your hand through his white shirts, rub the woven ties between your thumb and fingers. Behind the next door, dozens of dresses. Linen and cotton and satin and silk. You hold them up in front of the mirror, imagining yourself inside them. The one you like best is black with shoulder pads. Elegant and unadorned. You take off your clothes and step into the dress, like it's that easy to become someone else. You get it on, but the dress is tight against your stomach, and when you turn to the side you can see it – the bump you have been hiding under stretchy clothes.

You feel pretty, in the lipstick and the dress, your hair somehow stylish, bright beside the Rich Rosewood. You pick up the mohair cardigan, slide your arms inside it. It is so soft, so cool, that you are close to tears, spinning around on the carpet until you're dizzy and have to lie down on the bed, the ceiling still moving.

If you'd tried to make him stop instead of waiting for it to be over. If you'd got on to a horse that day or stepped on to the ice. If you hadn't gone to Franny's for Thanksgiving. If you'd never come to New York. If you'd never gone to the Screamers. If you'd destroyed the pictures in the milking shed.

The thoughts fill your head. You wish that you were dead.

. . .

A woman's face is angled over you, like you're an infant in a crib.

'What are you doing in here?'

'I fell asleep. I'm sorry.'

'Did my husband tell you to wear my clothes?' When you don't answer she says, 'Are you OK?'

'I don't know.'

'Does something hurt? Is it the baby?

You sit up on the bed, so fast it makes your head ache. 'He didn't say I could go through your clothes. I just did.'

She looks about forty, maybe a little younger than Harold. Her hair is dark brown, twisted up on the back of her head. A few strands at the front are loose, framing her face, which is symmetrical and striking. A string of pearls around her neck, hanging over a smart camel-coloured skirt suit.

'I'm sorry,' you say.

'It's fine. Here.' She passes you a glass of water, which you hadn't noticed she was holding. As you reach to take it, you see a mark on the sheets. Red. For a second you think it must be blood. Then you see the print your lips have left on the glass rim, remember the Rich Rosewood.

'I'm Isabelle,' the woman says as you swallow. 'Harold's wife.' Her mouth trembles as she says this, but only slightly. 'Did he . . . Did Harold tell you about me?'

'Not exactly. I knew he was married, though. He wore his ring.'

'And you didn't think to ask?' Her eyes narrow. Before, they were wide and round like almonds, but something in them now has cracked.

'We talked about art mostly.'

Her teeth bite down on her bottom lip.

'And – I don't know – stuff about our childhoods.'

'Your childhoods?' she asks. 'Did he tell you about the elevator, what his father did to him? You're not the first, you know?'

You want to tell her that nothing's ever even happened. Nothing really – just a kiss. But you didn't know that there were others, didn't even wonder.

The woman – Isabelle – crouches down, rests her hands on your knees. She looks into your eyes. You look down at her manicured nails. Her hand moves to bring your gaze back up.

'Look at me,' she says. Her face is pink around the edges, her eyes blinking quickly. 'He says he's not the father. I need to know if he's telling the truth.'

'He's not,' you say. 'I mean, he is telling the truth.'

Her hand relaxes on your jaw, her touch almost tender

before she kneels down fully on the floor and rests her head in your lap. When she sits up she removes a tissue from inside her sleeve, dabs beneath her eyes, then gets back on her feet. She has pulled herself together, towers over you again as she speaks quickly, comfortably.

'Of course, in some ways it would have been easier if it were. The baby, I mean. Simpler. It's not like I don't know he's been with other women, girls. But I don't think I'd have been able to handle it – knowing the baby was really his, more than it could be mine. I know they *say* it doesn't matter, but it would feel unequal somehow. I think I'd resent him for it, even if I tried my best not to.'

She seems like a different person now, like she is saying whatever is coming into her head, like you're a friend she's gone out for lunch with. You find that you are nodding to the rhythm of her speech.

'So this is better, really,' she is saying. 'It's almost like it's all been worth it, you know? Like maybe this was supposed to happen. And I can tell just from looking at you that you're not like the others, that there's something different about you. I don't mind that you put on the dress. It looks good on you. And the lipstick. You can wear anything of mine here, though of course we'll have to get you new clothes. They do really quite nice maternity things these days.'

You feel dizzy, like it's taking you a long time to take in what Isabelle is actually saying, to catch up with her.

May 1980

From the window in your room, you can't even see the bridge going over the river, the mental asylum in the distance. But, when you angle your face right down, there's the top of a single tree, planted in the sidewalk. Ash, you think it might be, as you watch its leaves unfurling like a baby's fingers. No, you must not think of babies, though all you can think of is your baby, growing.

Isabelle likes to tell you, cheerily, how big it is each week. She has a book that explains everything, comparing the baby's size to fruit and vegetables.

Heirloom tomato, artichoke.

She prepares special nutritious meals, using recipes from the same book.

'You need *lots* of protein,' she will say. Or 'Roughage, roughage, roughage.' Or 'You need more vitamins. Freshly squeezed orange juice.'

She brings the food into your room, will not let you lift a finger. You eat, you sleep, you take your pills. You look out the window, down at the top of the tree.

The last time you went outside was to see Dr Kneider. 'The best in the business, and very discreet.' Only he wasn't.

'What is your relation to the father?' he had asked. 'When exactly did the intercourse occur?' 'Did you not notice the absence of your monthlies?' This last question while his finger was up inside you, before he inserted the speculum.

'Twenty weeks,' he had declared, more to Isabelle than to you. 'The story does seem to add up.'

There was a map of Elbow Lake hung up on the wall, you wanted to scream at Dr Kneider. *It really does look like an elbow though I never got to see it with my eyes.*

'I'll write out something for your nerves, hmm?' Dr Kneider said, his hand now on your foot, squeezing it.

Klonopin, lithium, folic acid, iron, iodine.

June 1980

Papaya, grapefruit, ear of corn.

'Máire, honey,' Isabelle calls from the hall. She comes into your room, shopping bags hanging all the way up her arms. 'Look what I've got for you.'

Isabelle pulls clothes out of the bags, lays them out on the bed. Maternity slacks with elastic waistbands, wrap-around dresses, special bras.

'And look at these,' Isabelle says, showing you an Alice band, upholstered like a chair, stuffed and covered with flowery fabric. 'I thought you could wear them in your hair, until it grows back out a bit more.' She leans over, pulling the ends of the band wide so she can put it on your head. The movement is tender, like a mother's. She's careful not to catch your ears.

There's a bag Isabelle hasn't emptied, but she keeps peeking inside it.

'What's in that one?' you ask.

'Oh. It's – it's things for the baby,' she admits, holding the bag to her chest.

'Can I see?'

'I suppose one thing can't hurt.' Isabelle pulls out a tiny pair of socks, hardly bigger than her thumb and forefinger.

It does hurt. This one thing. But it's like you can't access the feeling, like it's out of reach. Dull, like the pressure of the Alice band against your skull, pressing just behind your ears. Empty, in your stomach, even when the baby kicks and kicks.

. . .

You stop taking the pills. At first you flush them down the toilet. Then you start hiding them like candy, underneath your bed, in the toe of a shoe. It feels terrible, not taking them, but at least it feels like something. Your heart beating, your legs restless, your mind racing through the night.

The pills were evil, you tell yourself. They wanted to drug you. You can hear them whispering.

Sometimes you get out of bed and sit on the floor with your ear against the wall. The voices are always muffled. Sometimes you hear moans, the bed creaking. The first time this happens you feel devastated. You cry and cry and cry. You thought perhaps they might hear you, that it would make them stop, but it went on and on and on.

. . .

They had tried to have children, Isabelle told you. For the first few weeks she was chatty, and you listened, happy to be confided in, included. They tried for years and years. They went to doctors, took tests. There wasn't anything glaringly wrong with either of them, the doctors said. Harold's sperm was inspected under a microscope. Isabelle was menstruating regularly. They did everything they were supposed to do. She took supplements, went on special diets, even went to see an astrologer who told her which days they should try on. Another doctor said that trying every other day was best. 'Gives the little swimmers a bit of time to recover,' he said, winking at Harold from across the desk. It had been difficult, waiting each month in dread, praying for the blood not to come. And the shame she felt each time, like it was her fault for bleeding. They had talked and talked about adoption, even went to agencies. But something about the idea just didn't feel 'right' to Isabelle. Of course, she reasoned, it was a good thing to do – to give a child a home, a child who wasn't wanted – but she was scared she wouldn't feel invested, that she might not fall in love with the child in the way she knew she would if it were hers. She had found this hard to articulate, though, when they were considering it. She couldn't explain to Harold that she thought she might not morally be 'good' enough to adopt. Wasn't the fact that she couldn't get pregnant a sign she wasn't meant to be a mother, a sign that something was wrong with her?

Isabelle hadn't been brought up in a particularly religious household. Her mother had been Catholic and she took the children to church – Isabelle and her older brothers. But despite this, Isabelle hardly thought about God, growing up. During mass, she went off into her own world, making up stories in her head. She was able to do this while still following the order of service. She had all the responses completely memorized. It was remarkable, really, she reflected. She had really been a gifted child. But the words – the doctrine – must have sunk into her skin. It had all been there inside her, dormant – the sin, the shame. Until it dawned on her that she was being punished, punished for the way she had cheated God as a child, for only pretending to be listening. That was why she could not have a child of her own.

She was thirty-five when she had this revelation. It happened one day after she had touched herself. For some reason, sexual pleasure always made her think of God, of being watched. Harold had been away on business, in London. They had been married for seven years and the novelty of travelling with him for work had long since worn off. Not once in those seven years had she been to mass. Yet she found herself, on Sunday, leaving the apartment as if she was being pulled by a string, straight to St Patrick's Cathedral. She had always known it was there, had thought it beautiful, but she'd never gone inside before. That feeling of being pulled – it felt good. *This* was God, she reasoned. God was about surrender. She imagined Him, a fatherly figure (her own father had died when she was young), a puppeteer high up in heaven, looking down on a tiny New York City like a model village. He was moving her, showing her a path. All she had to do was follow.

The more she thought about it, the more she realized her Catholic upbringing had always found a way to make itself known. When she and Harold had first started dating, when she was working at the Frick Collection, she had found herself telling him about a useless talent she had. She was able to tell from the outside whether a church was Catholic or not. He had chuckled at this, and it became a thing – first just in New York, then whenever they travelled together. 'Catholic?' he would ask, at the wheel of the car. And she would answer either 'Catholic' or 'Not Catholic'. They never stopped to check if she was right. She had demonstrated her ability during their months of courting and walking in New York. That had been how she had proved her worth. Both of them knew that underlying this trick was the fact that she had been brought up a church-goer, but Isabelle wasn't religious. Still, she liked to imagine that, to Harold, being able to identify the Catholic churches implied her goodness, perhaps even her virginity.

It must have been fifteen years between her last confession and her first, real one. When she was a child, confession had just seemed like a not-very-fun game. The knack was to admit to something related to one of the commandments and to say that you were sorry about it. Some of the commandments were just for adults – the ones about adultery and coveting your neighbour's wife – but she could tell the priest in the booth about not honouring her mother. She could even admit to stealing the velvet ribbon in the department store. She told the priest that she had lied about it afterwards, to her mother, then tried to flush the ribbon down the toilet. That was how she had been caught. But she didn't truly feel bad about the things she confessed to. She would say the words 'Forgive me, Father, for I have sinned', but they didn't really mean anything to her. Everyone was a sinner. Wasn't that the whole point of Jesus?

'Forgive me, Father, for I have sinned,' Isabelle said at thirty-five, to the priest at St Patrick's Cathedral. 'It's been fifteen years since my last confession.'

She told the priest everything. It was the true turning point in her life. The point at which she stopped telling herself stories and put trust in God's plan for her instead. She had spent all her life trying to create her own story, exercising her free will. And it was exhausting. It was unholy. It had left her barren.

'Then *you* came along,' Isabelle had told you. 'I'd stopped hoping about having my own child. I'd really come to terms with it. I'd let go of all the judging and the blame. I was even thinking about adoption again. I thought perhaps that I'd be able to do it, now, that I might be "good" enough. But all along, He had *this* plan. It was *you*, Máire. Don't you see?'

. . .

Sometimes you believe it too, the story Isabelle is telling herself now. Her faith that all this is part of some greater plan. Sometimes you feel close to Isabelle. Like when she told you about how her father died. He was out walking the dogs, when one of them came back to the house, barking like crazy. Isabelle's mother had told her to take no notice. 'He's getting old is all,' she said about the dog. But Isabelle had gone outside and followed the dog across the field and into the woods, as it was getting dark. And there he was – her father, on the ground, the other dog licking his face, still trying to wake him up, using its nose to move his head.

This story is so much like your own that sometimes you think you might actually be Isabelle, or that she is a person you have made up entirely in your head. But what if she's imagined you instead, if the reason the voices are always muffled is because you don't really exist?

You think of Franny and her moments. It had felt as though meeting Harold was a moment, but what if all of it was just to get you here, so you could be Isabelle's moment, her angel?

What if you yourself are a work of art? Another one of Harold's pieces, picked up and held on to. Much the same as Franny's father's cattle, waiting to be sold.

. . .

When Harold is around, which isn't very often, the three of you eat together at the table like a family. He avoids looking in your direction.

'Did you hear about the firefighters, Harry?' Isabelle asks, putting down a bowl of salad. 'Just terrible. Two of them, fell from seven storeys high, rescuing people from a tenement fire in Harlem. The rope broke, apparently. One of them had eight kids. Eight. You'd have thought with all this rain there wouldn't be fires like that.'

'I'm not sure that's how it works,' Harold says.

'This rain though, it's not normal this time of year, don't you think? There's no end to it.'

It has been raining all month long, ever since you stopped taking the pills. Pathetic fallacy, this is called in art, you know. Ever since you were small you were sure you could control the weather, that it somehow reflected what was going on inside you. You know it's crazy, to think such a thing. But at times you are sure of it.

'Have some more chicken, Máire, sweetie,' Isabelle is saying. 'The baby really needs protein. It's the best thing for growth.'

You know the rain won't stop until you say something, until you change something. Not taking the pills has made you bolder, braver.

'What's going to happen?' you ask. 'With school. I have a scholarship. I can't just not complete the year. I can't afford to.'

Harold starts to speak but stumbles, like he doesn't know what to say. Isabelle puts her hand over his. He is still holding his fork, a chunk of cucumber speared on its end.

'She needs to know, Isabelle. I told you.'

'What do I need to know?' you ask.

'It's nothing to worry about,' Isabelle says in her best reassuring voice.

'What is it?'

'I'm not going to be teaching at the Institute any more,' Harold tells you, actually looking in your eyes for the first time in months.

'OK,' you say. 'What's that got to do with—?'

'I'm under suspension for enabling plagiarism.'

'Do you know what that means?' Isabelle asks you.

'Yes, I know what plagiarism is. But what—?'

'Don't worry, you haven't been caught. It wasn't *you*,' Harold says.

'I don't understand.'

'Let me explain,' Isabelle says, her hand still on Harold's, gripping it now. 'You know, I'm sure, that Harold doesn't much like the way the course is taught at the Institute. And let's just say he got a little bit too involved with helping certain students fulfil the written requirement. One of the examiners got suspicious, started looking into it.'

'I'm going to step down,' Harold says. 'But I couldn't submit that essay for you, like I said I would. I'm sorry.'

'What?' You can't believe that this is happening, that there were other people he was writing essays for.

'It's OK,' Isabelle says, reaching for your hand now so it looks like the three of you are about to start praying together. 'We've explained to NYU about your . . . medical condition. You're going to be able to re-sit the year in September. A fresh start. Isn't that good?'

'Actually,' Harold says, finally extracting his hand from Isabelle's, 'there might be another opportunity, something more suited to your—' He swallows. 'To your *talents*.'

'Don't go telling her about that now, Harold,' Isabelle says. 'We can't go making any promises. And NYU is a good school, reputable.'

'I just think it might be helpful for Máire to know she has *options*. Dropping out of NYU might actually be the best thing for her, all things considered, if she knew there were *other* schools to explore.'

'What other schools?' you ask. 'You hate the other schools.'

'Nothing's confirmed yet, honey,' Isabelle says. 'And besides, don't you have friends at NYU? Weren't you enjoying it before – before what happened?'

'When were you going to tell me about this – that I'd failed the year? After the baby's born? Did you think you could just keep everything from me until then, wrap me up in cotton wool and drug me so I'd forget I even had a life before?'

You watch Harold mouth to Isabelle: *I told you.*

'I could just leave,' you say. 'You wouldn't be able to stop me. I have rights.'

'You're right,' Isabelle says, softly. 'You could.'

But you don't. You get up from the table and go back to your room, pulling the Alice band off your head, letting it fall on to the carpet. You empty the pills from inside the shoe under your bed and dry-swallow one red, one yellow, one green, one brown, one blue.

A womb in a room, you think to yourself, surrendering to nothingness, letting it wash you away, your hands over your stomach.

July 1980

Cabbage, pineapple, butternut squash, honeydew melon.

August 1980

'No father today?' the midwife asks, when they're taking down your details at the hospital.

'No,' Isabelle answers, on your behalf.

You lie on the bed, fenced in, while Isabelle times your contractions. When they offer you pain relief, Isabelle is the one who nods yes.

Numb, you recall Dr Kneider's bald head, shining underneath a bright lamp, a bead of sweat dropping from the end of his nose, falling down on to your body.

'Forceps,' he says, and you watch, almost disinterested, as he is handed the instrument that will clamp down on the baby's head. It is not so dissimilar from what it was like in the room at Franny's house – how you seemed to leave your body and see things from the ceiling.

You can hear Dr Kneider telling Isabelle that the baby is distressed. 'It needs to come out now,' he says, sounding excited. 'We should take her to theatre.'

'Let me push,' you beg, but Dr Kneider shakes his shiny head. You close your eyes and take a deep breath. You think about the Screamers, how you felt safe inside that house, where there were no secrets. Holding hands with Nell and the others, standing in a circle in the big room off the hall. It was your first time screaming in the house, your initiation. A full moon. You had to be the one to start the screaming, when you were ready, your body bursting with energy, oxygen, your hands hot and sweaty. You opened your mouth, as wide as it could go, the skin around your lips stretching to accommodate the scream, the sound so shrill it was like you couldn't even hear it, like it was silent.

You hate yourself for getting into this situation, for being here with your legs held up in stirrups. The only thing you have left is this fragment of consciousness. You will not let them put you under and cut you open. You take another breath and scream like you did in the house, squeezing Isabelle's hand. You scream until you hear your baby's screams.

. . .

'What will you call her?' you ask Isabelle, exhausted, after you've delivered the placenta and Dr Kneider has put a metal coil inside you, 'To prevent any further mishaps.' He told you it wouldn't hurt, but it did.

'Emily,' Isabelle says. Her voice sounds far away. 'What do you think?'

'Emily's a nice name,' you hear yourself say, tears falling into your ears.

. . .

You're wheeled down to see her: Emily. Isabelle lifts the bundle out of the crib and brings it over, reminding you to support the baby's head. All you can think about is how tiny her fingernails are, how perfectly formed. She is pink and warm and sleepy, and you can't keep hold of her for long. It's too hard, every second stabbing at your heart. You're scared you might see him in her – Franny's father – so you pass her back to Isabelle. You're scared you wouldn't see him in her at all. Then you'd never be able to let her go.

Back in your hospital room, you sign the paperwork that transfers Emily over to Isabelle and Harold. You know that they will love her and look after her. It is better than any other option you can think of, your stitches stinging, organs aching, hand shaking.

. . .

A day later, Harold comes to take you home from the hospital, wheels you to the car even though you wanted to walk.

'Where's Isabelle, and Emily?' you ask, after he's turned on the ignition.

'She's gone back to Vermont,' he says, turning in his seat to reverse.

'Oh,' you say, the passiveness of this not at all in proportion to the pain you feel, even though you've left the hospital with all the pills – the blue ones and the pink ones and the white ones which are supposed to dull sensation.

'She—I mean *we* think it's best for the baby to be there, rather than in New York. It will be easier for all of us, don't you think? Not as hot there this time of year, for a start.'

'Oh,' you say again, looking out the window – a hazy end-of-summer day.

. . .

Harold doesn't take you back to the apartment. He keeps driving downtown, as if he's taking you back to your dorm room. You know it's the summer holidays, that Franny will have moved out of Rubin Hall, but you imagine her being there when you return, imagine her saying something like: 'Four months, Máire. Four months and not a word. Just your professor saying you were moving. No explanation. And you think we can just be friends again?'

You're about to tell Harold that you can't go back to Rubin Hall, when he turns the other direction. East.

'Where are we going?' you ask, finally.

'Well, I have some news for you. Something that might cheer you up.' He is trying to sound light-hearted, looking over at you slumped in the seat. 'So,' he continues. 'I've been helping set up a new school. We're calling it the New York Drawing Association. It's me and some of the people I went to college with, a few other disgruntled professors and the like. And I – I mean, we – want to offer you a place.'

'Next September?' you ask.

'No. Next week. I know it's soon but Isabelle and I – we've rented an apartment for you in the Lower East Side, so you won't have to go far at all for classes. And you don't have to worry about money, OK. The rent's paid, and I've opened a chequing account for you. So there will be money each month for food – or whatever you want, really.' He stops at a red light, looks over at you. 'You've got to *promise* me you'll look after yourself.'

'Like you did,' you say, petulantly.

'I *did* look out for you, Máire,' he says, sounding wounded. 'This is a fresh start. You're going to *love* the course, OK. It's proper art. Back to the basics, you know. And I'll check in on you from time to time, make sure you're doing all right.'

'What do you mean, from time to time? If I go to this school, won't you be teaching me again?'

'No, Máire. My role in the school is more . . . *advisory*. And Isabelle, she doesn't want . . . I need to be in Vermont, with her.'

'And Emily?' you ask.

'Give Isabelle a bit of time, OK? Then I'm sure, some time in the *future*, it might be OK for you to see her and the baby, if she's in New York. You could be like a godmother, something like that. How does that sound? But for now just focus on the schoolwork. You're supposed to be an artist, Máire. Not a mother, or at least not now. You know this.'

. . .

New clothes in the closet. Old post on the table. Four letters from your sister. You run your finger over your name in her neat handwriting, but you can't bring yourself to tear open the envelopes. You ignore the more official-looking letters, too, the ones with stamps to identify the sender. One from NYU. One from the Department of State. Nothing from Nell. You never replied to her last letter. You wonder if Harold has told Nell about all this, or if he's keeping it a secret. She might have been someone you could tell, but you couldn't now you know about her and Harold.

Before he left there was a moment when he looked at

you, his face full of sorrow – like he might say sorry, like he might cross the room and hold you, say it had all got out of hand. You wanted to know that it had hurt him, hurting you. You wanted him to want you, even though you knew there was no way he could want you like that – breasts leaking through your shirt, blood soaking into the pad in your knickers. All of you weak and raw and broken.

September 1980

The apartment Harold and Isabelle are paying for is on Avenue A, near Tompkins Square Park. The building is run-down, cheaply built early in the century. You're on the first floor, which feels low to you now. You can hear the people who walk past, cars honking on the street. There is never much natural light. Beneath you, on the ground floor, is a bodega run by Puerto Ricans.

'Bella,' they say, when you go in to buy milk. 'What you look so sad about, chica? It might never happen.'

It has happened, you want to scream at them. *It has all already happened.*

. . .

The day before your classes start you take a walk round the neighbourhood. No skyscrapers, no landmarks. The streets aren't even numbered. They follow the letters of the alphabet. Avenue A, B, C, D, down to the East River. You remember the game Michael used to play with your sister, how dumb you thought it was. But you find yourself playing it, in your head, replacing the categories with things you can actually see. Alphabet I Spy.

Apple core, bus, cab, diner, East River.

Back in the apartment, you do the same thing.

Ashtray, bookcase, chair, duvet. E. What can you see that begins with E? All you can think of is Emily.

. . .

The New York Drawing Association begins its classes in the basement of a church in the East Village. The church is not Catholic. It is not far from Rubin Hall.

There are just six other students. You're the only girl, the youngest by far. Two are Vietnam vets. One has a wooden leg. Three are black, one Asian. You realize they must have given the places to disadvantaged people, and you experience the same feeling as you did at NYU – that you do not deserve to be here.

You are each given a copy of *Gray's Anatomy* – a huge, heavy thing. Your copy is old, the spine worn and some of the pages loose. The idea is to commit the human body to memory – and to be able to draw each bit of it perfectly. Beginning with the phalanges, ending with the skull. Three years to do what used to take a decade, when apprentices were taught this way during the Renaissance.

Each week you will study a different body part. You will draw endless sketches of bones. You will dissect animals. You will make models.

You sit at an old school desk on a wooden stool. You work under a bright Anglepoise lamp, well into the night. You keep your head down.

October 1980

It gets colder, in the basement. There is never any natural light. Only a couple of electric heaters that do nothing to the damp. You wear fingerless gloves and learn to roll your own cigarettes. You buy thermal leggings, vests. Your feet get cold, so mostly you work standing up, wiggling your toes and walking on the spot. One of the students brings in a boom box, and you enjoy listening to the music. You discover Michael Jackson, Prince, Chic, Sister Sledge and Donna Summer. The other students don't ask you many questions. You are just the quiet Irish girl in the corner, who works later than anyone else.

In the evenings, when you get back to the apartment, you eat eggs and toast and drink glasses of milk. Your fingers are cold and sore and sometimes red raw. The apartment has an old-fashioned bathtub in the kitchen that doubles up as a table or a drying rack. *How is the syllabus like a bathtub?* Twice a week, you heat the water up and fill the tub. At first the water is scalding. You make yourself endure the pain, lowering your body, submerging yourself, inch by inch. Once in, you can almost hear the bits of you thawing. All the bones you know the names of now, for you've been looking ahead in your copy of *Gray's Anatomy*, working your way up the body.

Femur, pelvis, coccyx, sacrum.

Before you go to sleep, you watch TV. It is the first time

you've had a television. You are grateful for its hypnotic colours, the dull noise. Every night there are updates about the upcoming presidential election, Reagan trailing behind Carter in the polls. You watch the death toll rise by the thousand in the wake of the El Asnam earthquake. One thousand, two thousand, three thousand. A man from West Germany crosses the Atlantic on the outside of a plane, walking on its wings. Havana releases thirty-three American prisoners. Turkish troops regain control of a hijacked aeroplane. A million-dollar diamond is stolen. A ship goes missing with thirty-three Americans on board. Irish prisoners are going on hunger strike again.

Whenever the news is about Ireland, you change the channel.

November 1980

Each time the phone rings you think it must be Harold, or Isabelle. Each time you pick up it's a cold caller. One day you walk to their apartment to see if they are there. You wait outside for hours, indifferent to the cold now. No lights go on.

...

Reagan wins the election by a landslide. The phone rings when you're in the bath. You run to answer it, naked, water dripping all over the floor.

'They're saying it's the end of the art world, but it's good news for me, really.' It's Harold, speaking like he's continuing a conversation you've already been having, though you haven't spoken since the day he dropped you off here. 'Máire, you there?'

'Yeah,' you say, trying to stretch the cord so you can reach your towel, but it's too twisted.

'How's school?' he asks.

'How's Emily?'

'She's fine, just fine. Really looking around now, lifting her head up all on her own. She's swell.'

'Swell,' you repeat. There's a pause. 'Can I see her?'

'Well, Isabelle—'

'Please,' you ask, desperately.

'We're actually in New York,' he admits. 'How about we meet? You haven't been to *The Dinner Party* yet, have you? I'm certain it's just a stunt – you know I don't go in for most of this modern stuff – but I'd say it's worth a look. What do you say, a day out?'

. . .

It's the first time you've stepped out of Manhattan since you arrived. You can't believe how high the Brooklyn Bridge is, how long it takes to walk across it. It's a blue-sky day, the sun bringing your body to life, lifting your spirits. You've even put some effort into your appearance. Mascara on your lashes. One of Isabelle's Alice bands pushing back your hair. The same colour as your eyes.

On the other side of the bridge you will see Emily. You'll scoop her up in your arms and cover her in kisses. It's strange, you think, feeling like this, when you hadn't wanted a baby. You're not sure you do now, either. It makes sense for her to be with Isabelle, who you know will love her and look after her. But she's yours. You need to see her.

Harold is waiting outside the museum. There is no sign of Isabelle. No pram. No Emily. Perhaps they have gone inside, you think. Perhaps they will be joining you later. Harold kisses you on both cheeks, steers you into the museum with a hand on your lower back. You don't want to ask where Emily is because you want to still believe she might be in there, at *The Dinner Party*.

You have heard about the exhibit, a huge dinner table with place settings for important women in history. It is in a big dark room, with lights shining down on the table, which is in the shape of a triangle. Each side represents a different era – from prehistory to the women's revolution. You can tell Isabelle isn't in the room, but you begin to walk around the table calmly, slowly, stopping at each place in turn, looking at the embroidered tablecloths and the painted plates – every one of them different.

You don't recognize many of the names from the first side of the triangle. They sound exotic, majestic. *Ishtar*, *Hatshepsut*, *Aspasia*. You can hear Harold's footsteps behind you, but you don't look at him. You turn the corner of the table. *Marcella*, *Saint Bridget*. You stop, looking at the embroidered saint's name. It takes you a while to realize that it must refer to the saint you know as Brigid. Wasn't there a story where a woman came to Brigid, pregnant, and Brigid placed her hands over the woman's belly, made the baby go away? You wonder if Harold knows who Brigid is, if he knows who any of these women are. You keep on walking, the names not really sinking in any more. But there's Petronilla de Meath, that witch your sister used to drone on about. 'She wasn't even a witch,' Róisín would say, delighted by everything she'd read. 'She was just a scapegoat, a maidservant burnt at the stake for her mistress's wrongdoing.'

You feel a pang for her then, your little sister. How she always wanted to hold your hand on the walk to mass. How often you would shake her off, push her away. How you crossed the ocean to put space between you. How huge this space feels now. How empty.

You turn to face Harold. 'Do you know who she is?' you ask, pointing at Petronilla's place at the table.

'Petronilla de Meath?' Harold reads from the placemat. You can tell he's uncomfortable, not used to not-knowing. How quickly tables turn.

Part of you is tempted to explain, to go back to how things were before, when you told Harold stories about your life and he would ask questions that made you feel like what you had to say mattered. Back when you yourself were a work of art. You miss that. But that's not why you're here.

'Where's Emily?' you ask, taking advantage of his ignorance. 'You said you'd bring her here.'

'Well, I didn't promise anything, Máire. You have to understand.'

'I'm her mother,' you say, shocking yourself with the simplicity of the statement.

It takes Harold a while to answer. He's looking at his feet when he speaks. 'Well, legally you're not. And Isabelle—'

'Where is she?' The question comes out in a stifled shout. You watch Harold's eyes dart back and forth, looking to see if anyone else in the room is watching. It's satisfying, seeing him squirm.

'I'm sorry, Máire,' he says, his voice lowered, unconvincingly calm. 'Isabelle thinks it's best for you to have some distance. She thinks it would be confusing, for everyone, if you see Emily. We're not saying never, but I wanted to tell you that it might be best if you *do* think it might be never. That would be best for *everyone*, don't you think?'

'Go to hell, Harold,' you yell, heart hammering. You can hear your own accent, its otherness.

You're not from here. You're not from here.

You sense the other people in the exhibition room, pretending not to look at you. The gallery attendant stiffens in the corner, ready to intervene. You begin to walk away, but Harold grabs your arm. On your radial bone. You know the name of it now.

'Máire,' he says, turning you round.

'Get your hands off me.'

'Don't make a *scene*, Máire. Please. Can we just go somewhere to *talk*? This was a bad idea, coming here.'

'If you don't let go, I'll scream. Is that what you want?'

'Of course that's not what I want.'

'You tricked me. You—'

'We didn't trick you, Máire. We all agreed. You signed the papers.'

'It wasn't that you tricked me about.'

'You mean about Nell? We talked about that.'

'No, I don't mean about Nell. Though you did trick me about that. I mean we were—All that time in the diner.' You're quiet now, practically whispering. 'Then you took me back to your apartment and kissed me and then Isabelle—' You pause, all of it coming back. The power you lost.

'I'm sorry. I was just trying to help. I want to help you.'

'I don't need your help,' you spit, the volume turning up again inside your ears, skin starting to crawl. 'You made everything worse. I wish I'd never met you. I wish I'd never come here.'

'I care about you, Máire. You must know that.'

'Like you cared about the other girls, other students? You think Isabelle didn't tell me?'

He doesn't defend himself, stands there silent, defeated. But it doesn't feel like a victory.

'If you cared about me you'd have left Isabelle. You'd have let me see Emily. You'd have—' You're crying now, the tears falling down your face, running into your mouth. You can see the attendant walking over, shining a flashlight.

'Is everything all right here?' the attendant asks.

'Everything's fine,' Harold says. 'She's just emotional, is all. We were about to leave, weren't we, Máire?'

He reaches for your hand. You yank yours away. Without thinking about it, you grab the chalice from Petronilla's place at the table. You hold it out towards Harold.

'Don't ever touch me again,' you say.

'Put the cup down, ma'am,' the attendant says, shining the light in your eyes.

'Máire,' you hear Harold say. 'Come on now.'

You turn and place the chalice back on the tablecloth, exactly where it was before. 'Don't follow me,' you say to Harold, and he doesn't.

. . .

As you're walking back over the Brooklyn Bridge, the sky turns from blue to white. Pathetic fallacy, you think again, pulling off the Alice band, throwing it over the side of the bridge, not stopping to watch it fall. The air is biting, the wind whistling, the sun struggling to be seen through the clouds as it fades and falls in the distance. The cars turn their headlights on and the windows in the buildings begin to glow. You head straight for the church, go down to the basement.

There's a service going on. You can hear the congregation singing, above your head.

He's got the whole world, in his hands.

He's got the whole wide world, in his hands.

Not Catholic, you think, remembering Isabelle's dumb game. There are no songs at mass in Ireland. You wait for the singing to stop, then heave up the copy of *Gray's Anatomy* from your desk. You climb back up the stairs. From the door you can see the snow swirling outside. You think about going into the church, staying until the end of the service. But it would be better, you think, to feel the snow. There's a bench outside, where you sometimes go when you remember to have lunch. You sit down with the book on your lap and you cry into the sky, getting snow in your mouth, in your eyes. You put your hand into your coat pocket to feel the bit of paper, even though it's torn, the words mushed up beyond recognition.

She herself is a haunted house.

'You a medical student?'

He looks like an angel. Like what you imagine Gabriel must have looked like, appearing to Mary. His clothes are shabby, and he isn't shaved, but there is a brightness about him, the snow sticking to his golden, floppy hair. The same length as yours.

'Sorry?' you say.

'The book – they use it for doctors. So are you a medical student?'

'No.'

'Well, all right. What are you then?'

'I'm not from here,' you tell him.

The corners of his mouth turn up. A couple of his teeth are missing. It doesn't match up with the outside of him.

'I'm an artist,' he says. 'Jac. What's your name?'

You don't want to be yourself. 'Róisín,' you say.

'I don't know if I've seen a person look so sad before. I'd like to paint you.'

'All right.'

'Let's go then, Rosie.'

You take the subway for the first time. Your bodies jumble together as the train stops and starts, all the way to the Bronx.

December 1980

Jac is straightforward about what he wants from you, and what he doesn't think he will be able to give to you. All you have to do is slot yourself around him.

He approaches your body from every angle, arranging it. You find it satisfying, having to stay still, holding yourself in certain positions. Even when it starts to hurt.

'You can move, you know,' he says.

'I don't want to.'

'You're determined, aren't you?'

You don't feel determined, though, the days and nights blending together, becoming brown like when you mixed up all the paints you got for your fourth birthday. 'Must you be so set on spoiling things?' you remember your mother saying, when she had caught you. 'Won't you ever leave them be?'

You don't tell Jac your real name. You don't go back to class in the Village. You don't go back to the apartment on Avenue A. You don't think about Emily.

Jac gets up early in the morning and goes over to his easel. From the mattress on the floor, you watch him work. He smokes endless cigarettes and constantly drinks coffee. His room is filthy. Mug stains on every surface. Overflowing ashtrays.

The first time that he tells you he has to run an 'errand', you set about tidying things up. You wash all the dishes. You put things into piles.

'You're not here to be a maid, Rosie,' Jac says when he returns.

'What am I then, a muse?' you ask.

'No. I don't believe in muses. Just be you.'

You are not cleaning, not drawing, not thinking. You are not Jac's girlfriend. He doesn't believe in ownership. He told you this before you took off any of your clothes. He was clear from the start.

You are not his muse, but you become a kind of canvas, Jac inking your skin. You hold your arm out, let him puncture it. Puzzle pieces. A new square added every day, the past connecting to the present.

. . .

You don't tell him your real name, but you do tell him real things about yourself. Maybe it is because he is not your boyfriend. Maybe this makes it easier. You tell him about Emily, about Harold and Isabelle and those months you spent in their apartment.

'A hostage situation,' Jac says. 'Some crazy rich-people shit.'

You like that he is angry on your behalf.

. . .

You are not his girlfriend, but you spend Christmas together, along with a group of Jac's friends. Other artist types, estranged from their families. You place a candle in the window, and teach the table how to say 'Nollaig Shona Duit': *Null-ig Hun-a Dich.*

You do feel sad about your sister, the real Róisín, spending Christmas with your silent mother. But the way to not feel sad is to not think about these things. You learnt that long ago, long before you stepped inside the Screamers' house.

January 1981

In your head you paint a picture of his past, colouring it in like one of those painting-by-numbers books. His child-hood across the river, in a neighbourhood called Park Slope. His two younger sisters and the brother who died before he was born. Like you, he was brought up Catholic and made to dress up for mass on Sunday. 'I was a mama's boy,' he tells you. His mother would take him to museums, just the two of them. All kinds of poky places, not just the famous ones. Their favourite painting in the city, though, was Van Gogh's *Starry Night*. Both of them could stand and stare at it for ever. The swirling sky, the crescent moon, the stars throbbing like hearts.

He could read and write before he even started school. 'She wanted to give me a head start,' he explained. 'Give me the kind of life she didn't have. We'd walk around Brooklyn getting groceries or whatever and she'd test my spelling. We'd make up rhymes and stuff, to help me remember. I remember one: *Never Eat Cakes Eat Salmon Sandwiches and Remain Young*. Necessary. And I loved read-ing to my sisters – books, or whatever really. Anything there was to read, I was all over it.'

When he was seven, he was hit by a car and nearly died. He was in hospital for a long time. When he was in there, his mother gave him a copy of *Gray's Anatomy*. He pored over that book. 'Knew pretty much every page by heart by the time I got out. Thought I might want to be a doctor.'

But things were different when he got home. His parents, his father informed him, were separating. His mother, his father said, was crazy. She couldn't take care of Jac's little sisters. She wasn't fit. He didn't know what to believe, but it seemed like it would be for the best when his mother went to hospital. Because that was where people got better, like he did. But he wasn't allowed to visit, and whenever he asked his father when she'd be coming home he would get angry and change the subject. Jac didn't even know what hospital she was in, didn't have the first clue how he could find her. He had to give up, after a while.

When his father caught him smoking pot, Jac ran away from home and never went back. He slept on park benches in the city. He took acid in Washington Square Park, three nights in a row. He started painting.

What he liked about graffiti, he explained, was that it was always being covered up. There one day, gone the next, turned into some other artist's vision. Graffiti made the whole city a canvas. One where people could experiment and collaborate. Of course he also liked the fact that it was risky, that you had to be quick about it. But there was something so sensory about the process, too. The metal ball clinking in the canister as he shook it back and forth before he pressed down on the nozzle. The best bit was the hiss.

. . .

Jac's room-mate is a skinny Korean kid called Bernard, a biology grad student. When Bernard does speak it is always softly. He volunteers a few nights a week as a Guardian Angel, a peaceful protector of the subway, returning after sunrise in his red beret.

You wouldn't know Bernard was there, most of the time, except for the stacks of textbooks he leaves on the table. When you open one of them up, the pages look like they're written in another language, the diagrams something only aliens could understand. You're about to shut the book when Jac walks past.

'Would you look at that,' Jac says, picking up the book and holding the pages right up to his eyes. And so it is with him – he will spend the next week copying drawings of chemical compounds from Bernard's textbooks. He will be lost to that.

. . .

You know that Jac sometimes sees other women, even other men. There are days when he goes out and nights when he does not come home. Sometimes you think about going back to the apartment in Alphabet City, just to see if Jac misses you. You think about going to Harold and Isabelle's apartment again, breaking in. You let yourself wonder how big Emily would be now? Like one of those giant pumpkins, perhaps. You imagine Isabelle calling Emily 'my little pumpkin', then stop yourself from thinking such a thought.

February 1981

You take drugs. This becomes your art. You smoke pot, which makes you anxious, makes you think the thoughts you try to keep at bay. But you like the way it makes your arms and legs feel – floaty. You smoke crack, which is kind of the opposite – you soar up and forget everything bad that has ever happened to you, but also everyone you have ever loved. You'd do it more were it not for the crash – that time when Jac had some kind of 'arrangement' in the city and left you there, reeling in bed. But he came back with big black pills and you had sex for seven hours straight. You take smack – once. Feel a soberness like no other as Jac ties elastic round your arm and melts the brownish powder on a silver spoon. It looks like it is happening to someone else's tattooed skin. The bead of liquid coming out the end of the syringe before it plunges in.

You disappear into pitch-black holes, then emerge to find the real world is harsh against your skin. Too bright and too loud.

You cannot bear it, the world's relentless realness.

. . .

Jac disappears for longer. He has been gone for days when you drag Bernard along with you for a night out in the city. Bernard only comes, you think, to make sure you don't get into trouble. 'My guardian angel,' you keep joking. You have to laugh or else you would be crying. You do lines of speed and drink shots of tequila, forcing Bernard to do the same. 'Come on,' you say. 'Don't be queer.'

You know he's not queer, though other people think he must be, wearing that beret. You've seen the way he looks at you, the way he tries not to look at you. You've spent weeks teasing him now, walking through to the bathroom wearing just one of Jac's T-shirts, nothing underneath. Asking Bernard for help with things that you could easily do yourself. Opening jars, catching spiders. You know he's fond of you, fonder than he wants to be. And you like this – his veiled want so opposed to Jac's open aloofness. You want someone to want you, despite themselves.

'We can't,' he says, sweet Bernard, when you lean in to kiss him at a party you end up at, God knows where.

'Oh, come on,' you say, moving your hand over his crotch. 'Jac won't mind.'

He removes it, gently. 'I mind.'

'Nobody owns anyone!' you shout, your voice coming out all wrong. Too loud and laboured. Heads turn.

'You're not thinking straight,' Bernard tells you, his face pleading. 'You're strung out. You have been for days now, Róisín.'

'You don't know me.' You push him as you stand up from the mouldy couch. 'You don't even know my name.'

The room spins around you. You don't recognize it. Still, you manage to find your way out, through all the people. Out on to a stairwell which goes round and round, down and down.

'Róisín!' Bernard is shouting, from above. You ignore him but he shouts again. 'Your coat.'

It lands with a soft thud in front of your feet, just when you reach the bottom of the stairs. You pick it up and put it on.

. . .

You would have frozen without it. The speed is wearing off and the wind is biting, making your nose sting and your ears ache. Your lips are sore and your mouth is dry and your fingers are numb. At first you don't know where you are. You're full of pumped-up rage and hurt, walking blindly in a way that's almost blissful. Then the streets begin to look familiar and you realize you are near your old apartment. Alphabet City. Your hands are balled up into fists in your coat pockets, but you can feel the keys against your knuckles. Still there, miraculously, along with the remains of the paper note.

She herself is a haunted house, you whisper to yourself, over and over, as you walk towards the apartment on Avenue A. *A for attic, B for bathroom, C for . . .*

Someone is selling, outside the building.

'How much?' you ask, reaching into your bra where you keep your money.

'Ten. You need a needle?'

You nod, accept the powder wrapped in plastic.

You're relieved the key still works, that they haven't changed the locks. Everything has been left, just as you left it. This place that has never been a home, but has more of you in it than where you have been living, those escape rooms. There are still packing boxes on the floor, your things from Rubin Hall. Black clothes. Flea-market finds. Diner drawings. The pieces of your life before all this.

You try to get the radiator working but it only hisses at you. You find that you are shaking, crying, hyperventilating, the high from the speed escaping from your body like steam. Usually you can cope with how empty this leaves you, if you're with Jac. When you're both wired and not tired so you smoke weed and have sex until you fall asleep in a heap. You pick up the phone and call his apartment but there's no answer. Bernard must not be back yet. Your mind is racing, and you're pacing, up and down the room, looking at the phone.

What are you doing, what are you doing? you think, over and over.

You find an elastic band and pull it up over your arm, the puzzle pieces. You get a spoon from the cutlery drawer. You light the gas ring. You prepare the smack and hold the needle in the flame.

And you remember how it was with Michael. How he said he'd never leave you – so you left him instead. What if all this was a mistake? What if you were never meant to be here?

You just want to hear his voice, you tell yourself, as you dial his number, as you listen to the line ring and ring and ring and you realize it will be just getting light across the ocean.

'Hello.'

It's your sister.

'Máire,' Róisín says. 'Is that you?'

You put down the phone.

You pick up the needle.

The Bathroom

THE MOON IS FULL THROUGH THE BATHROOM WINDOW. BUT ITS SURFACE DOESN'T LOOK BRIGHT ANY MORE. YOU WANT TO GO BACK TO BEFORE THE ERUPTION, BEFORE YOUR MOTHER GOT SICK, BEFORE YOU AND MAGNOLIA STOPPED SPEAKING. EVERYTHING IS DULLER, DIMMER. EXCEPT THE WALLS, WHICH SEEM TO SHUDDER, THE PIPES THAT SCREECH.

YOU COME IN HERE TO THINK.

THE CISTERN, THE CLOSET, THE SINK.

WHICH PART OF THE ROOM DO YOU WANT TO EXPLORE?

CLOSET

INSIDE THE CLOSET YOU FIND AN OIL LAMP AND A BOX OF MATCHES. YOU GO BACK TO THE DORMITORY AND STASH THE OIL LAMP INSIDE YOUR TRUNK.

Róisín Dooley

Burtonport

1981

February 1981

The entire village comes up to Atlan to see Georgina laid out, the coffin up on the dining table. Michael and I made sure she'd be buried in the outfit she'd selected – that cream lace dress with the full flared skirt, her mink shrug around her shoulders. They did a good job, McGowan & Sons. I brought them a photo of Georgina, the one where she looks like a film star – straight teeth and high cheekbones, not a freckle on her face. I left the photo at the desk, along with some make-up I'd collected from Georgina's dressing table – powder and rouge, matching lipstick and nail polish. I even took in her perfume – Chanel No. 5. They must have sprayed it over the dress and in her hair, but it doesn't quite mask the formaldehyde. I wonder which of the brothers does the embalming, if a different brother does the hair and make-up. Or maybe that's done by their mother. I doubt it, though – to look at Mrs McGowan.

They're polite enough, passing around the table, stopping themselves from peering into the coffin for too long, from getting too close. 'Sorry for your loss,' they say to Michael, holding out their hands. 'Sorry for your loss,' they say again, to me, shaking my hand as well – and I can see them wondering about the two of us.

Back outside, before they're even off the estate, they'll start talking. Sharing all the gossip they ever heard about Georgina and her dark-skinned son, born out of wedlock.

Some of them will actually brush themselves with hand-kerchiefs, as if they might have caught something off Michael. I can imagine them doing it – Mrs Kelly and her daughters, scrubbing themselves clean at the sink when they get home.

We're there for hours, the line unrelenting and the light dimming outside. I need to go to the toilet but I don't get up from my chair. I don't want to leave Michael, and part of me keeps wondering if Máire might walk through the door, even though I know it would have been impossible for her to get back in time, even though I haven't received a reply to the letter I sent, or the one before, or the one before that.

. . .

Máire and Georgina always got on well, back when Máire was going out with Michael, and even before. Georgina was like another mother to Máire – one who talked. She insisted that Máire attend her Debs, even though Michael hadn't officially asked her to go with him. Máire must have known about New York by that point, but she hadn't told me or Michael. She was mostly sleeping in the Screamers' house, but she would come back from time to time, acting like she'd turned into someone else. Reading big hardback books about art, sitting cross-legged on the floor.

On the night of their Debs, Georgina had managed to style Máire's hair so she looked just like Bette Davis – that's what Georgina said, at least. The dress she had picked out looked totally different on Máire. It didn't cling to her body the way it did when Georgina wore it. It showed off Máire's broad shoulders and brought out the colour of her eyes. Though I pretended not to care about my looks, I was envious of Máire then. Her collarbones.

'Doesn't she scrub up well?' Georgina had said, standing in our kitchen. 'Go up and show your mother now. You as well, Michael.'

Georgina and I didn't have anything to say to each other, then, left alone in the kitchen.

We didn't have anything to say to each other for a whole year after Máire left. But I knew that Michael had been taking her to hospital, in Letterkenny. She'd been having pains in her stomach, and I thought perhaps she'd have to have a hysterectomy, like Mammy. But it was worse than that. The cancer had spread from her ovaries into her stomach, Michael told me. There was nothing to be done, the doctor had said. She mightn't see another Christmas.

Michael and I weren't seeing each other that much. He had got work on one of the trawlers before Máire even went to New York, perhaps in the hope that she might start to miss him and ask him to go with her. He stuck with it, after she left. What else was he to do?

'I can help,' I said to Michael, when he told me about Georgina.

'I can't ask you to do that,' Michael said.

'You didn't ask. I'm offering.'

She began to waste away. The clothes that had once hugged Georgina's hips and breasts now hung off her. She lost her appetite, except for sweet treats, which I was happy to help her indulge in. I brought her Opal Fruits and chocolate Kimberley mallow cakes. I made bread-and-butter pudding and fruit trifle, trying to do it the same way Mammy used to.

'A bit more sherry, next time,' Georgina would tell me, licking her lips.

At five o'clock each afternoon, I would pour her out a glass of Bailey's. 'Go on, try a bit,' she insisted. I had never tasted anything so delicious. This tipple became our daily ritual.

It took a while, though, for us to start talking about Michael.

'I hope he's being kind to you,' she had said. And when I pretended not to understand what she was implying she just raised her eyebrows. I felt myself go red.

'I may be dying, but I'm not blind or deaf,' she said.

And it was a relief – to be able to admit it, to talk freely about it all. Not so much about me and Michael, but about Máire.

'What do you suppose your sister's doing?' Georgina asked, taking another sip from her glass of Bailey's.

'I don't know. She hasn't been replying to my letters.'

'And you're hurt that she hasn't?'

'I guess.'

'People need to go away and find themselves. That doesn't mean she's forgotten about you, or that she doesn't care. I've had to remind Michael of that, too.'

'Maybe she has another boyfriend,' I said, ready to reel off all the reasons I had thought through in my head that would explain why Máire hadn't replied to my letters. 'Maybe she's too busy going to fancy New York parties, and she doesn't even have the chance to think about boring old Burtonport.'

'I don't know,' Georgina said. 'Your sister's a very deep

person, always been a bit distant. I can't really imagine her becoming a socialite. I'm sad I won't get to see her become a famous artist, though. I'd have liked that. But you – you shouldn't stay here, you know. Not on my account. Not on your mother's. And not on Michael's, either. There's a life for you outside of boring Burtonport too, you know. Not just for your sister. All those books you read. Michael says you're going to become a writer. You could travel the world and write about it.'

'Oh, I don't know. I'm not adventurous like Máire. And Mammy—'

'Don't let your mother's choices dictate your own, my dear,' she said, suddenly serious. 'She's the one who's chosen not to speak for all these years. It's cruel of her, really. I know you think that Máire's been the selfish one, leaving like she did, not being in touch much. I know Michael feels that way. But it was the best thing for her. I encouraged her to go, you know?'

'You did?'

'A person has to be selfish to really feel alive. Without that we're just wasting time, and that eats away at us. Children are supposed to leave. I keep telling Michael that he should. But I think he was holding out a candle in the hope that Máire would come back, even if just for a visit. And now, well – he won't go till I'm gone. He's a good boy. But I worry about you, little Ró. You shouldn't pin your life to somebody else's choices. You deserve so much more than that. You want my advice: be the one who leaves first.'

· · ·

'Will we watch the telly?' Michael asks, when the people have finally all left, as if watching the telly is something we do together all the time.

'All right,' I say. 'I'll bring your supper through. You must be starving.'

He shrugs.

'I have to take food through to Mammy, in any case. I'll be back.'

'You're all right,' he says.

While I'm reheating the stew, I'm wondering when would be the right time to tell Michael what I know about his father – what Georgina told me. I'm not sure I should tell him at all. Georgina told me not to, at the time. But I can't stop thinking about the story. One of the things I am worried about is not being able to do it justice, not being able to tell it with the energy she had. She kept that spirit till the end, or almost the end. We were still drinking Bailey's and talking until just a week or so ago.

. . .

I suppose that's what dying does. You don't have long left to tell your stories, so secrets don't hold the power they once did. Or perhaps it's because they hold so much power? Maybe she needed to tell someone, after years of holding on to the memory alone. Maybe it was just because she was on her third glass of Bailey's.

'I didn't even know his name,' Georgina said, a nervous laugh escaping from her mouth that made her seem much younger, like there was still so much life inside her. 'I ran away from home when I was sixteen. My father, he was a violent man, a drunk. And my mother never stood up for me when I stood up for myself. I'd hardly been in Belfast a month. It was that stage of summer where it hardly gets dark at night. One evening I was walking back from the factory, looking up at the sky. There wasn't a cloud in sight, you see. And there were no windows in the factory. I couldn't get enough of the sky when I got out. And I bumped right into him. This man, whose skin was darker than anyone's I'd seen before. He apologized and I just stood there with my mouth open. I thought he was so beautiful. It's strange, but right away I just knew I had to have him. I wasn't ashamed of the feeling, either. So I closed my mouth, and opened it again to ask if he was looking for company. Some of the girls I was living with were doing it. I knew how it worked. He didn't have much English, but when he understood what I was offering he reached into his pocket. I could see he didn't have much money but I let him hand me a couple of coins. I asked if there was a place we could go and we went down to the docks. Round the back of this timber shed, would you believe it? He was gentle with me, kind. He was able to make me laugh, without saying much at all. And I came alive. It was the first time that I really felt good at something, without even having to try. It was easy. We did it over and over again, behind that shed, lying on his jacket. I knew that he had paid for it, that he probably didn't feel anything for me at all. But that night was the best of my life. Only I never saw him again. I thought for sure that we'd bump into each other. He wouldn't be hard to spot. For a while, I'd actually run after other coloured men on the street, thinking they might be him. I couldn't leave Belfast, because I was still hoping he'd turn up – all the time I was pregnant. I thought maybe he worked on a boat, but that he'd be back. Every day I wished that he'd return, that I'd tell him about the baby and we'd become a family. I don't know how I got through that time, to be honest with you. Hope, I suppose. I lost my job at the factory when they realized I was pregnant. I would have ended up at a mother and baby home, or in a brothel, but the landlady at my lodgings, she took pity on me. Her husband had died and she'd never had a child, you see. But as soon as I gave birth and she saw the colour of Michael she kicked me out. It was terrible. Anyway, I won't dwell on that. It wasn't bad work, most of the time – being with men. I preferred it to being in the factory. The first thing I asked every man after that was what his name was. I'm sure most of the time they told me a fake name, but not knowing the name of Michael's father is one of the only things I really regret. So I always asked, after that. And every time, with every man, I'd close my eyes and pretend that it was Michael's father. And sometimes I'd believe it, even if just for a moment. Of course, I was always careful after that, as well. I don't regret not being, that time with him, though, because it gave me Michael. But I didn't want to wind up having children with any of the others. I wanted him to be the only one who had done that. Are you careful, with Michael?'

I had been so taken in by her story that it took me a moment to realize that she'd asked me something so directly. For I had been there, in Belfast, behind the timber shed. I had been her. It had made me think about how sometimes – often even – I would imagine I was Máire when I was with Michael. It shamed me to think about it. My ears were burning.

Georgina was looking at me, expectantly.

'Of course,' I said.

I didn't say that it plays on my mind, exactly how careful Michael always is.

. . .

After I've taken Mammy's tray up, I carry the pot of stew next door, serve up two bowls and bring them through to the living room. Michael is watching the television. There are two empty beer bottles on the table. The bottle in his hand is nearly empty, too.

'They've discovered a new element,' Michael says. 'And the Prince of Wales is getting married.'

I sit down next to him. 'To Lady Diana?' I ask, looking at the television. I watch the video footage of them on the screen. 'She looks a bit like Máire, don't you think?' I ask, regretting it immediately. It's easy, talking to each other about Máire, because she's the thing we share, but it doesn't solve anything.

'Obviously,' Michael says.

He doesn't touch his food. He doesn't look at me. I tell myself it's OK, that it's been a difficult day. But I can't focus on the telly, am willing him to say something to me, waiting. But I'm weak.

'Are you going to eat?' I ask.

'Would you leave it?' he snaps, slamming his empty bottle on the table and going to the kitchen to fetch another.

When he gets back, I lean my head on his shoulder, hoping he will move to put his arm around me. But he doesn't. I place a hand down on his knee.

'Jaysus, Ró,' he says, in disgust. 'Would you ever let up? Did you forget my mother's body's in the next room?'

I focus hard on keeping my eyes dry.

. . .

When we go to bed, I let myself remember how it happened – the first time. I think about it while I'm lying in the dark, looking up at the ceiling.

It was around the time Georgina got sick. Máire had been gone for a year and the Screamers had left to go and live on the island. I was giving Michael some lessons on Sundays so he could re-sit his Leaving Cert when I was going to be taking mine. He had done fine in the maths and science parts, but he needed to get more points in English if he was ever going to go to college. After the lessons we would often take a walk – either to the beach or along the abandoned railway line. We memorized scenes from *Romeo and Juliet*, the Shakespeare we were studying. We played the alphabet game. We tried not to talk about Máire, but every conversation we had was somehow about her anyway.

Eventually we'd circle back to Atlan, and he'd say goodbye to me like he was Romeo: 'Parting is such sweet sorrow / That I shall say good night till it be morrow.'

I knew that he was going to leave Burtonport, when he got his Leaving Cert. He had mentioned going to college in Limerick or Cork, maybe even in London, but we didn't talk about this much because he knew that I wouldn't be going to college right away. I had Mammy to think about.

For his twentieth birthday, I had baked an apple cake. At

the end of his English lesson, I pretended I was thirsty so I could get it from the kitchen.

'You're the best, Ró,' he said, after he blew out the candles.

'Did you make a wish?'

'You can have it.'

'It doesn't work like that. Go on, now.'

We didn't go for a walk after the lesson. Rain was coming down in buckets. I asked if he had anything else planned to celebrate, and he said he was going to go to Casey's with some of the trawler lads.

I heard him get back after closing time that night. His steps were louder than they usually were – and not so regular. I could tell he hadn't taken off his boots. That's when it happened. He knocked on the wall, three times. What else was I to do but knock back twice, to get out of bed and go downstairs, sneak out of the house like Máire used to when she thought I was sleeping? And there he was, waiting for me underneath the street lamp, sort of swaying under it. The rain had stopped.

'Happy birthday to me,' he sang out, swinging on the lamp post now.

'You'll wake up the estate,' I whispered.

'The estate can feck right off,' he shouted.

I ran over to him, then, put my hand over his mouth. His eyes were shiny in the lamplight. He put his fingers round my wrist. I let my hand down.

'Will you take a walk with me?' he asked.

I followed him out of Atlan and along the road into the village. He wasn't walking in a straight line but his strides were long. I was nearly having to run to keep up. I could see the fencing that had been put up around the Screamers' house ahead. 'An eyesore,' people said about the fencing, the boarded-up windows, the paint on the outside of the house all peeling, the symbols of the zodiac fading away, the black letters painted on the steps running into each other, so you could hardly read what they once said: KEEP DONEGAL FREE OF RADIATION. DON'T LET THEM DESTROY THE EARTH!

But Michael didn't go as far as the house. He turned down the lane that runs along the side of it, thick with trees. Though the moon was full, bright enough to see by, his shape was quickly swallowed up as he went beneath the branches.

'Come on,' I heard him say. 'There's a gap through the fence here.'

I followed the sound of his voice, and sure enough the fencing had come down. There was a gap big enough for a person to fit through, into the Screamers' back garden.

I had never seen the house from that angle before. It was a surprise. I had thought so much about the house's front, never considering that it had other sides. From the back it wasn't symmetrical or striking. It had been extended. Rooms added to the ground floor over time, including a dilapidated glasshouse, which had dead and dying plants inside. There were wooden boards over most of the house's windows, but one of them had been removed. The window it had originally been covering was broken. I could see the moon reflected in what was left of the glass around the edges, so it looked as if it was made up of jagged pieces.

'Stay there,' Michael said, when we approached the window. He placed his hands on the crumbling ledge and pulled himself up. His pants caught on a shard of glass as he went inside.

'Are you all right?' I asked.

'It's fine. Don't come in this way. Just give me a minute.'

I waited while he disappeared into the room, then reappeared at a door which he opened from the inside. He was holding a torch. 'Come on then,' he said.

The rooms at the back were all awkwardly arranged. You could tell they weren't part of the original house, that they had been built on at some point. But the main part of the house was still striking. A big set of steps in the hall. A huge room on one side, two smaller ones on the other.

Michael started going up the stairs. It was obvious he had broken in before, or perhaps he'd been inside with Máire.

I followed him up. At the top of the stairs was a huge bathroom, straight ahead, then several doors coming off each side of the landing. One of these – the one closest to the bathroom – was open. There was another set of stairs inside this room. Less grand than the main ones. I followed him up again. The stairs led up to a long narrow room, with slightly sloping walls. There were only windows along one side. It was still dark, but enough moonlight was getting in to see things when you got close to them. I ran my finger along the deep window ledge, coating it with dust. I noticed all the books lined up on the floor. Expensive-looking, cloth-bound volumes that had expanded from the damp. I pulled one out at random. I could read the title when I held the book up to the window. *Songs of Innocence and Experience.*

'It's through here,' Michael said.

I turned around. He was lighting the way for me to follow. He moved the torch as I came closer, tracking my steps. When I got to where he was he turned the torch on to himself. He was sitting on the edge of a pink armchair. The chair was up against the wall, and on the wall was what looked like a cupboard door, about two feet off the floor.

Michael pushed the door open. It slid to the side, like the wall swallowed it up.

'I'll go first,' Michael said. 'There's nothing scary, I promise. It's just the attic.'

'I'm not scared,' I told him, though my heart was racing.

I watched as Michael used the arm of the chair to vault himself up into the crawlspace. It got suddenly darker. Then he was shining the torch back at me.

'Come on,' he said. 'Climb through.'

I stood on the chair and pulled myself through the hole. On the other side, I reached up to work out if I'd be able to stand without hitting my head. There were no windows. The only light was coming from Michael's torch. He was shining it at something. For a moment, I lost sense of all proportion, as I realized I was looking at the house that we were in. Only the colours were different. There were swirls of smoke coming out both sets of chimneys, forming the words *Scream School*. The front door had been turned into an open, screaming mouth. You could see right inside it, to the tonsils.

We stood there in silence, the light from the torch moving up and down slightly over what I'd realized must be a painting, stood up on an easel. What I could see moved in time with Michael's breathing.

'Can we take it?' I asked. 'I mean, it's clearly Máire's.'

'I don't know,' Michael said. 'Maybe she'll come back for it someday.'

'Maybe,' I said.

The torchlight turned away from the painting, down to Michael's legs. He must have been holding the end of the torch in his mouth while he hitched up one of his trouser legs. I could see the blood, the shine of it on his leg, his white sock stained red.

'That's bad,' I said. 'We have to clean that up.'

' 'Tis but a scratch.'

'Famous last words. Come on, there was a bathroom downstairs.'

We climbed back through the attic door, then went down the stairs again. In the bathroom, Michael lay the torch down in the sink, so it lit up the wall and ceiling. Miraculously, there was a bottle of surgical spirit in the cabinet. Nothing else.

'This will sting,' I said to Michael, who was sitting on the edge of the bath. I helped him to remove the shoe on his left foot, then his sock. I made him put his foot into the bath before I poured the surgical spirit on to the wound. He winced, squeezing my shoulder.

'You're lucky you've had so much to drink,' I said. 'I need to tie something on it to stop the bleeding.' I looked around, even though I knew there weren't any bandages in the bathroom.

'Use this,' Michael said, taking off his jumper, then unbuttoning his shirt.

I'd seen him without his top on, of course, when we went swimming. But it felt different in the torchlight, the shadow of his body moving with him, on the wall.

I pretended not to look as I took the shirt from him and tried to rip one of the sleeves so I could fashion it into a bandage. I couldn't tear the fabric; it just burnt my hands.

'Give it here,' Michael said, taking the shirt back from me again and ripping it easily.

I tied one of the shirt's arms around his leg, tightly, then inspected my hands, which were still stinging.

'Did you hurt yourself?' he asked.

'It's fine. Just a friction burn.'

He reached over and touched my hands. 'They're cold,' he said, using his own hands to envelop mine, then rubbing them together. He swung his body round on the lip of the bath, so his feet were out of it again. Still holding my hands, he began to stand up, but I could see he was dizzy from the drink. Then the both of us were falling to the floor. His bare chest on top of me. He moved himself up a little, like he was trying to keep space between our bodies, resting his weight on his arms. But then his face was coming lower. I could smell the whiskey on his breath before he kissed me. It was actually happening. His lips were soft and his tongue was wet. *The texture of tastebuds*, I remember thinking. But as soon as I was thinking this, and kissing back, I knew that he would stop and get up and leave and we'd pretend it had never happened and he'd go away from Burtonport and I'd never see him again. So I pulled him closer, feeling his teeth clink against mine, pushing my tongue into his mouth. Then his hands were going underneath my coat, tracing my body over my nightgown, then finding the hemline. His hands on my bare legs, pushing my nightgown up to my waist. I lay there, catching my breath, as he knelt to unbuckle his belt, unbutton his trousers. I pushed my hips up and pulled off my underwear, not thinking about how exposed I felt, naked from the waist down. Because so quickly after that he was over me again, between my legs, inside me. I held my breath. He held my hand. It hurt, but then it didn't. He was moving deeper, pushing my nightgown up so he could run his tongue over my breasts, then moving up to bite my earlobe, as if he'd done this many times before. Something about his breath, heavy in my ear, made me lift my leg to pull him deeper into me. But that was a mistake. Because then I could feel him pushing against my hip crease, coming out of me and kneeling up again. He had his penis in his hand. The end of it was shiny. I didn't want him to stop. It had been the best I'd ever felt. He bent over me. I didn't know what was going on. Then his mouth opened in an O, and like thunder following lightning the sound came out of it: 'Oh.' I knew that it was over, even before I felt and saw the glistening on my stomach, as he reached for what was left of his shirt on the floor to wipe it off me.

. . .

The phone wakes me up. It's still dark. Michael hasn't stirred yet. He looks so peaceful when he sleeps, his lips free of the tension that's in them when he's awake. I get out of bed and go downstairs to pick the phone up in the hall.

'Hello,' I say, into the receiver.

The silence has a volume to it, a long-distance hiss. I know who it is, without having to hear her speak.

'Máire,' I say, lowering my voice and looking back up the stairs. 'Is that you?'

I can hear her breathing, thinking. Then the line cuts off. I am left listening to the dialling tone, my hand tight around the receiver.

'Who was it?' Michael asks, his voice still heavy with sleep when I get back into bed.

'Wrong number,' I tell him.

'Come here then,' he says, holding his arm up, his eyes still closed.

I fold myself into the space under his arm, and when he pulls me closer I can feel that he is hard, behind me. He pulls up my nightdress, holds a hand over my stomach. Our legs are wrapped together and he slides inside me, easily.

'You feel so good,' he says softly, right into my ear, so I can feel the words as well as hear them. 'You're so wet.'

'Yes,' I breathe, rocking my hips, trying to hold on to how it was at the beginning, when we couldn't stop doing just this.

'Not yet.' He holds my body still with his hand, then starts to trace his fingers over my skin, stroking me softly.

'Please,' I beg.

. . .

After the first time, in the Screamers' house, I thought maybe Michael would never talk to me again, or he'd pretend it hadn't happened. But he caught me outside the house when I was on the way back from the shops the next morning, running over to help me with the bags, although I had managed carrying them myself just fine.

'Just let me,' he said, and I gave in, dropping the bags to the ground and letting him bend to pick them back up. 'I'm sorry about last night,' he said, standing up again, catching my eyes. 'That was your first time?'

I nodded, avoiding his gaze.

'Would you want to do it better, maybe, do it again like?'
His voice trailed off at the end. Now he seemed to be the
one who was embarrassed, shifting his eyes away from
mine as if wanting to delete the last thing he'd said.

'All right,' I said, willing him to look at me again.

'Now?' he asked, his eyes darting back to mine, excited.

I tried to look like the kind of girl who would say 'I don't
think it's such a good idea', to put up some notion of resistance. But honestly, I felt none. To say yes out loud would
seem too much, though, might make him change his mind.

'Have ye something better to do?' he said, holding open
the door, the bags down on the path. I thought about how
Mammy would be waiting for her tea, but bent down to
pass under his arm.

'Is Georgina in?' I asked, when he shut the door
behind us.

'No.'

There, in the hallway, he pushed me against the wall and
kissed me. He placed his knee between my legs. He said that
he was going to show me how it should be. He said that I
was going to like it. I quivered when he spoke such things.
Was he like this with my sister? He lifted me up, so my legs
were around his middle, and carried me up the stairs, into
his bedroom, where he dropped me on to the bed, the room
a mirror image of my own. The curtains were still drawn but
there was just enough light coming through for me to see
what he was doing. Retrieving a slim torch from underneath
the mattress. Putting it inside an empty water glass, on his
bedside table. Pulling off his vest and draping it over the
water glass, softening the torchlight. I couldn't believe the
thought that had presumably gone into that sequence, and

yet he seemed to have carried out the actions entirely without thinking.

His room didn't have a whole lot in it – a Beatles poster stuck to the wall over a desk, a radio alarm clock on the bedside table – but it delighted me to be there.

He kneeled down at the edge of the bed and pushed up my skirt. I lifted up my hips to help him peel my stockings down. As I did I could see the shadow of myself against the wall. He put his face between my legs. I could feel his hot breath through my knickers. I lifted my head so I could see him doing it, but it hurt my neck too much to keep on looking. I let my head go back. I imagined I was Máire, that he was doing it to her instead. It didn't feel like an insane thing to do. I just wanted to be wanted like that, like I was the only thing that mattered in the whole wild world. I wanted to empty myself out, so he could enter her instead.

. . .

'Don't stop,' I cry, because as soon as he does the world will press in on us again. But it's too late. I can feel him pull out, listen to him panting.

Sometimes, I get the sense that we are but tiny dots, lost and lonely on this spinning ball of water and dirt, getting dizzy. But it doesn't matter how small we are. We can't avoid what's coming for us. Sure as hell she's coming for us.

March 1981

The clocks change – spring forward. I'm thinking about how much Máire hated sharing, when we were kids, even things she no longer wanted, or had long since grown out of. She was irate when she had to hand anything down to me, especially clothes. She'd sooner ruin her things altogether, even if that meant spoiling them for herself, too. There were sweaters that disappeared, frocks ripped right up the middle, coats that came home with mysterious stains. Missing buttons, busted zips. Socks and mittens separated from their partners, the lonely leftovers a reminder of what I'd never have.

But if I ever decided to do anything without her, to claim some sort of sense of self? That would make her go berserk. She was the only one allowed to change. I was supposed to stay the same.

So it was crystal clear to me why Máire suddenly wanted Michael by her side, why I had been hearing the phone ringing next door at strange times in the middle of the night, ever since Georgina's wake. She had heard my voice through the phone, and couldn't bear the thought of me being there with Michael, even though she had been the one to leave him.

'Did you hear me?' Michael asks, a hand on the door, about to leave for work at dawn. 'I'm going to New York next week.'

'I did. Was there something you wanted me to say?'

'Don't you think we should talk? You're not looking at me.'

How can I when I'm still lying in his bed, naked, humiliated? But I make myself look up at him. It hurts, but I do it. 'What's there to talk about?' I say. 'We both knew this was coming. It was only a matter of time.'

. . .

I go with him, though, when he insists. One last walk along the railway line at sunset, the sky like flying-saucer sherbet, our shadows stretching out in front of us, longingly. I extend my fingers and run them through the weeds that have started shooting up. Cow parsley umbrellas that will flower in a few weeks. Máire told me once that Michael had told her that the boys at his school said that cow parsley flowers smelt like semen. I didn't know what semen was, then, when she told me. I thought that she meant men at sea. And somehow I am telling Michael this, while we're walking.

It surprises me that we are able to speak openly, easily. For so long Máire's been between us – always there, even half the world away. We'd tried pushing her out, ignoring the presence of her absence. But that was futile. I wonder if the reason we can talk so freely now is because we've stopped pretending otherwise. It almost feels like we are younger again, the two of us conspiring to get Máire to the Screamers.

'It was exciting,' Michael is saying, about that time, 'imagining this shiny life for her, feeling like we were the ones who were going to make sure she lived out her destiny. But I don't believe in that now.'

'In destiny?' I ask. 'Or the idea that people can live shiny lives?' And it hits me, then, that my life won't be shiny any more, without him. I want to cry my eyes out, throw myself at him. Something drastic, out of character.

'Both, I suppose,' he says.

'Do you have fags?' I ask, instead of doing any of the other things.

'You don't smoke.'

'Perhaps I'm starting. Will ye give me one or not?'

He pulls a Carrolls packet from his jacket pocket, takes out a cigarette and lights it for me.

'Thank you,' I say, sucking in, then coughing. 'I think you're wrong,' I tell him, when I've recovered. 'You wouldn't be going to her if you didn't believe in destiny. She's your shiny thing. Like a puzzle piece falling into place, remember?'

'A very difficult puzzle, with lots of pieces.'

I roll my eyes. 'Well, no one ever said that love was easy.'

'You don't understand,' he says, seriously, slowing his steps and turning to face me, just before the second bridge. I want to carry on walking, but he grabs my wrist, pulls me back. 'She's really not well, you know.'

'No, I don't know,' I say, looking up at the sky, as if hopeful for some kind of intervention. 'I don't know any-thing, because she never replies to my letters. She's only talking to you.'

'Well, I hope that will change, in the future, after she gets help.'

'Of course it's not going to change,' I snap. 'She's going to make sure we never talk again. Can't you see?'

'I have to go, Ró. I wouldn't forgive myself if . . . She needs me.'

'What if I need you?' I'm desperate now. And I can't understand his eyes, the way they narrow, then widen.

'You don't,' he says, eventually. 'You're stronger than she is.'

'That's the stupidest thing I've ever heard.'

'Well, it's true.'

I step towards him, tossing the fag end into the cow parsley before kissing him on the mouth.

'Ró,' he moans. I can't tell if it's resistance or defeat.

'Shhh,' I whisper before we tumble to the ground. I pin him down, my knees on the damp earth, his body between them, my fingers laced with his. He doesn't resist, not until I can tell he's nearly done, when he tries to free his hands and push me off him. But I hold on.

. . .

We stay there, lying on the ground, until I realize it's dark. I get up, put on my knickers, brush the dirt off my knees.

'You're shivering,' Michael says, standing up now, too. He takes off his jacket and places it over my shoulders.

'I'm fine,' I say, but I hold the jacket to me, still warm from his body.

We're silent then, for a while, walking back along the path. Our steps are slow and short, in time, like we're both walking towards some fate we don't want to face.

'I think perhaps we shouldn't have done that,' he says, finally.

'Why?' I ask, breaking, broken.

'I don't want to make this harder for you.'

'It would have made it harder if we hadn't,' I say, not sure if this is true.

'Maybe it's that it makes it harder for me.'

'She doesn't really love you,' I say, unable to stop myself, even though I know pleading with him in this way will spend what's left of my power. 'She only wants you now because she doesn't want you to be with me. She's selfish. She never properly shared herself with either of us. You know, it's funny how everyone always said Máire was so loud. But she was quiet, too. Secretive. She kept things from us. She likes to be unknowable. That's why she left us for the Screamers. That's why she left to go to New York.'

I get the sense, while I'm speaking, and after, in the silence, that Michael's trying hard to hold himself together, not letting his body react in any way. Though maybe he's just cold, without his coat.

'I know she could be cruel to you,' he says, keeping his voice even, understanding.

'And to you.'

'But I don't think she means to be that way.'

'That's what I mean. I never knew what she meant. She never let me in.'

He stops walking, then starts again, his foot only missing a single beat. 'Do you want to play the alphabet game?' he asks.

'Don't,' I say, plucking at the cow parsley umbrellas. 'It will make me too sad.' Really, I'm sad he's changed the subject. Though I think he might be right, that I'm making this harder for myself than it has to be. But with him so nearly absent there's a twisted pleasure in unpicking it all, undoing me more.

'What are you doing that for?' Michael asks.

'I don't know,' I say, stopping. We're nearly back at the start of the path. His semen slides out of me then, soaking my underwear. It's not a bit like when I get my period. It makes me miss him already, acutely.

'Can I stay with you tonight?' I ask.

He takes a long time to answer. First he takes my hand. 'I don't think so, Ró,' he says, squeezing it. 'I'm sorry.'

May 1981

I've taken to screaming, first thing in the morning. The
first time I did it was after finishing *The Bloody Chamber*.
That final story – Wolf-Alice licking the Duke's bloody
face and watching herself in the mirror. It made me feel
something again.

It's not like anyone can hear, with Michael's house empty
next door. No one except Mammy. I even hoped, at first,
that she might shout back to get me to stop. I do it when I
get out of bed – stand on the carpet with my feet hip-
width apart, take a deep breath in and let it all out. I try to
make the noise come from my stomach, not my throat, like
that visiting chorister tried to have us do once, at school,
until they found out she was a Protestant. I'm not sure it
makes me feel any better, but it does make me feel something other than the panic of not living my life right, the
fear that I might never.

. . .

'Bobby Sands died yesterday,' I say, handing Mammy her
breakfast tray before I pull open the curtains. Another day
of drizzle. 'Sixty-six days. He was only twenty-seven.'

She stares down at the eggs, the rashers. Sometimes I
want to smother her, my mother.

Downstairs, my schoolbooks are spread over the kitchen

251

table, exams just around the corner. But I haven't looked at the books in days. Instead I've been writing. Not this diary. A story, taking its own shape.

Studying is a process of remembering, trying to get information to stay in your head, holding it in. This story feels like the opposite, like squeezing a tube of toothpaste. It was easy at first, the voice in my head turning into ink on the paper, sentence after sentence. Now it's more difficult, my insides clenching so I have to tease myself open.

It's strange, writing about the house without Máire beside me, giving direction. But it feels important, like I might be more myself again if I can get it right, if I can make this story mine, if I can see inside the house again.

I was going to wait until after my exams, but something tells me this is the right time, that I won't be able to focus properly until it's done.

I shout up to tell Mammy I'm going for a walk. I take the old umbrella. But there's sunshine, rays that almost seem to stroke my skin.

Everyone still calls it the Screamers' house, even though they've long since left, and the house looks so different now. The O'Regan brothers were hired to take the fencing down. They removed the boards covering up the windows. They re-plastered the walls and painted the house a creamy magnolia. Outside the front, the grass was cut, borders planted, the broken gate replaced. The last job was to properly wash off the Screamers' final protest – the message they had written in big block capitals on the steps, about the uranium factory at Fintown. Gone now.

The new owner moved in on Good Friday. A woman. She was from England, people said. Unmarried, in her thirties. Possibly attractive, though it was hard to tell. She wore plain clothes, tied her hair back. Odd that she didn't introduce herself to the neighbours. Queer that she lived alone like that. But at least the Screamers were gone, everyone agreed. At least the house looked respectable again.

. . .

I stand there, holding the closed umbrella, outside the gate, remembering Máire screaming on those steps while Michael and I watched, speechless. It seems like for ever ago, that moment.

I open the gate and walk along the path towards the house. Some of the pansies from the border have been blown away, heads plastered on the path. I climb the steps and pull down on the bell. I can hear it ringing inside.

Nothing happens. I count to ten, then turn around. I'm on the fourth step down when I hear her shout, 'Wait!'

I turn around. The door's still shut.

'Up here.'

She's leaning out of one of the upstairs windows, her head and shoulders flung through the frame.

'I'll be down in just a minute,' she cries, her head disappearing back inside.

I climb back up the steps, start counting to ten, trying to see through the frosted glass at the top of the door. A silhouette, coming down the stairs, getting closer and closer until she's beneath the glass, behind the door. Then it's opening and she's standing there, smiling. Dimples on her cheeks. I've not seen her this close up before. Wisps of hair around her ears, escaped from the ponytail. Face free of make-up. Hard to gauge her age. Straight white teeth and thin pink lips. She's wearing loose corduroy pants and a plain T-shirt. I'm staring at her. She's staring at me.

'I'm Scarlett Marten,' she says, at last. She has an English accent.

'I'm Róisín. Róisín Dooley.'

'I've seen you, walking past. Róisín Dooley.'

Silence, again. Something about her is disarming. Maybe it's her eyes – grey and gold.

'Well, do you want to come in?' she asks.

She holds the door open. I follow her inside.

Where My Sister Went

A story, by Róisín Dooley

In spring the sky went dark. A volcano had erupted, on the other side of the world. Crops failed, disease spread. The world was ending, people said.

We were lucky, our stepfather liked to remind us — me and my sister — while our mother lay coughing up blood in bed. Our real father had died at sea. Not even my sister could remember him.

We were dying to get out. I remembered summers spent on the beach, before the darkness. My sister never wanted to paddle in the sea, or run up and down the dunes. She just wanted to draw the big house over in the village, with its two sets of chimneys and steps going up to the door. The house had always been a steady structure in her life. While everything around us changed, that house remained the same. Symmetrical and striking.

'Why do you always make it look like a person?' I asked her once, about the house she was drawing in the sand.

My sister shrugged.

'See.' I pointed at what she was doing. 'You put eyes in the windows. And that door looks like an open mouth.' I found it hard to believe she couldn't see.

Our mother wasted away, like the flowers that had tried to open up in spring. So many did.

At the funeral, our stepfather was drunk. He was always with a bottle, after that. Didn't try to hide it.

When he went out in the evenings, my sister lay awake. She must have thought that I was sleeping. When our stepfather arrived home, she'd creep out of the room we shared. She'd be gone for hours. When she returned, I often had to help get her back to bed. Once, I found her outside the door, in a heap – unconscious, half-undressed. We never spoke about it in the morning.

Around this time, a visitor arrived. They moved into the big house in the village, the one my sister used to draw in the sand. Nobody knew who this visitor was, where they had come from, what they were doing. It was hard to know, even, if the visitor was a man or a woman, for they had long grey hair and wore a long black cloak.

Then, there were more. They became 'the visitors'.

We had all become suspicious of each other, living in the dark. But rumours still spread fast. We could make out day and night, and the moon's cycles. The light was just dimmer. The visitors had been seen standing outside the house, running their hands up and down the walls at night, when there was a full moon.

When I spoke about these rumours to my sister, she acted like she wasn't interested. What did she care about that house? Our trips to the beach seemed so remote, our childhoods like another life, some other time.

Then our stepfather demanded my sister's hand in marriage. If she refused, the two of us would be sent to the workhouse.

That night, my sister took herself to the big house. She went up the steps. The door was open. It shut softly behind her.

Inside, in every room, the walls were plastered with scraps of paper, covered in writing.

The visitors said they had been waiting for her, my sister. The house contained a spirit which had found a way to make itself heard. The visitors had been called to the house, just like my sister. They wanted to set the spirit free.

The house had been confessing its secrets, and the visitors had been writing the secrets down. 'Taking note is part of our service,' the visitors explained. 'Would you like to meet the house? The house would very much like to meet you.'

My sister felt excitement surge through her. The sense that the house was ready for her, that she was wanted. She could hear the house's voice reverberate inside her body. There was a sensation to it, a presence.

They spoke for hours that first night. No one had ever understood my sister so well, or come close. It was like they were two halves of the same brain, finishing off each other's sentences, holding space for each other. My sister felt cradled, known.

The visitors had to put a stop to it. 'Quit talking,' one of them ordered. 'We can't sleep with all that jabbering.'

They shut her inside one of the bedrooms, but my sister was too excited to sleep. She lay there on the floor, stroking the carpet, rubbing herself into its fibres, taking off her clothes, crazed. By the morning she was rubbed raw.

That day, the house asked my sister if she wanted to go further.

'What do you mean?' my sister asked, her insides already pulsing at this suggestion. She imagined the house pressing itself down on her, making it hard for her to breathe.

'Let's tell each other our dreams,' the house burst out.

'OK,' my sister said.

'Tell me yours.'

My sister said her dream was to not be herself. It wasn't that she wanted to be another person entirely. More that she didn't want to be a person at all. A person had to live by all the rules of being a person. It was so tiring, having to rearrange her thoughts all the time into words. She just wanted to be, without all that. 'I've only ever felt myself around you,' my sister said.

The house was quiet. It seemed like it was holding its breath. 'Do you want to hear my dream?' the house said, finally, tentatively.

My sister nodded, her eyes already closed.

'I wish that I could be a girl like you,' the house said. 'A girl like you with my whole life ahead of me. I wish that I could walk on two legs and open my mouth and scream for real.'

'But you're real to me,' my sister said. She was sitting in the corner of the room, her legs open so they were touching the two walls, her hands stroking the wallpaper. 'More than real.'

'It's not enough,' the house whispered.

They came in then. The visitors, in their robes. They lifted my sister off the floor. She didn't know what was happening. They were holding her so tight. She told them to stop but they wouldn't look her in the eyes. She was screaming. She screamed and screamed, but the house stayed silent.

The house hadn't been her friend, it was clear now. The visitors had come to set the house free. And the house needed a body — a younger, stronger body than any of the visitors possessed. Besides, what if it went wrong? My sister would hardly be missed, they thought.

They took her to one of the twin fireplaces and stuffed her, screaming, up inside the chimney. She couldn't move her arms or legs. It was black, inside the chimney, and the soot made it difficult to breathe. She could hear the visitors chanting, their voices vibrating through the brickwork but also sounding far away, like an echo. When the full moon moved over the chimney top the bricks around my sister seemed to turn to flesh. It was the best thing she had ever felt, even in her fear. Suspension, surrender.

It wasn't my sister who came out of that house. Of that I'm sure. The soul inside my sister's body pretended to be her but I wasn't fooled. Her eyes were different.

She got married to our stepfather, barely a month later. My sister wouldn't have let that happen. She'd have been kicking and screaming all the way down the aisle.

When the skies brightened, people said it was almost worth the year without a summer, to see the light return again. The warmth of sun on skin. Flowers, shadows, shiny things.

The visitors had disappeared, leaving the house empty. Except for all the paper on the walls, the stories. I thought I might feel my sister's presence there. But the house had never been alive for me. I had only ever been able to see the person in my sister's drawings, trapped within.

June 1981

Last week the sign went up. Not a for-sale sign, but a hand-painted wooden board, easily visible from the road.

Miss Marten's Victorian Tea Room, it says.

It's not my first day of work, but the first day we're opening to the public. We've spent every second of the last month preparing, working it all out.

We arrived at the idea together. 'A light-bulb moment,' Scarlett called it. I didn't think she was serious about it, though, at the beginning. I still can't quite believe how quickly she set it all in motion. Ordering tables and chairs, uniforms for us to wear. Removing anything she deemed as 'modern' from the ground-floor rooms. Putting a notice in the Church of Ireland newsletter – BAKER NEEDED – because I said Protestants did the best cake sales. I helped her with the interviews, in the lounge. We couldn't believe how many women showed up, bearing their baked goods for us to sample.

And now the day has come. The opening.

. . .

I pin my hair back, put on my cap, fetch my apron from the hook behind the kitchen door. I like looking at myself, dressed like this, my reflection in the hall mirror. There's something different about me. I'm becoming a new person in this house, I can see. I stand taller, hold my shoulders back, chin up.

'Good morning, Róisín,' Mrs Boyle says, when I go into the kitchen. 'Would you help me hold the stove door open?'

Already there are scones cooling, laid out on the wire rack. I go over to the stove and hold the heavy door open. Mrs Boyle reaches in with gloves to remove a cake.

'Carrot, is it?' I ask.

'With a hint of ginger,' she tells me. 'Now so. You can help with the icing, after your breakfast.'

I hear the door open, turn to see Scarlett, still in her pyjamas – boys' ones. She yawns without holding a hand over her face. Mouth wide, eyes closed, cheeks rosy.

'Did you not sleep well?' Mrs Boyle asks. 'Too excited?'

'I got distracted,' Scarlett says. 'It smells amazing. And look at you, Ró.' She walks behind me, brushes her hand over my back, then straightens up my apron bow.

At the table, with a pot of coffee, Scarlett looks over the reservations log. I get going with the sandwiches – chopping cucumber, buttering bread, cutting off crusts – while Scarlett asks me questions.

It was difficult to talk at first, to respond to Scarlett's questions. I wasn't used to someone being so interested in me – examining my thoughts, my words. If I try to gloss things over she'll tell me to slow down. She'll make me add in details. And I'll remember it all differently, like looking at myself from another angle. It makes my head hurt, sometimes, but in a way that's pleasing. Often, when I get home, I'll still be thinking about something she'd asked me, earlier in the day.

'Do you really think that you don't have a personality, separate to observing other people? What is a personality, anyway? Aren't we all just different, depending on who we're with?'

. . .

We talk about the house. How it brought us together. That day when she invited me inside and Máire's painting was hung up in the lounge. I didn't say that it was Máire's. Not then. But Scarlett caught me with my mouth open, staring at the words formed out of the chimney smoke. *Scream School.* I hadn't seen it in the light before. It was so good it hurt a bit to look.

'I found that in the attic,' Scarlett said, setting down the tea tray. 'After I moved in. The Screamers must have left it here. It really captures something, don't you think? I know I should give it back but I like looking at it so much.'

'You know about the Screamers?' I asked, surprised.

'Of course,' she said. 'I found out everything I could about this house before I bought it.'

'Just because you were interested?'

'It's a long story,' she said.

'I like stories,' I told her.

'The short version is my parents were killed, and I in-herited a lot of money.'

'And the long version?'

She looked at me, then. Seriously, as if trying to work out from my face if I was someone she could trust with herself. I knew that I'd have to earn her trust.

Focus, I thought, maintaining eye contact.

She waved a hand in front of her face, then said, 'Well, what about you? What's your story?'

Suddenly, I was spilling – telling her about my mother, about Máire, about Michael. All of it. Almost.

. . .

I didn't know, then, that Scarlett had a habit of turning questions around, shifting the focus. It's as if she's keeping score, only revealing herself in parts, only after I've uncovered something of my own first. It's only now that I have something like a story. The shape of Scarlett Marten.

She grew up in London, in a grey-brick house overlooking Highbury Fields. Her parents had been psychiatrists. They both practised in the ground-floor rooms of the house. The doors were always closed, though she often pressed her ear against the keyholes. When they weren't working, her parents were fighting. These fights weren't loud or violent. They wielded words as weapons, trying to seize power from each other. When they weren't fighting, Scarlett's parents played games with her, like they were a family. Card games and board games. Her favourite was Cluedo. She always played as Miss Scarlett. Her parents were very good at the game. They never let her win, just because she was a child. The three of them all used little notepads to write down their theories. The games were always tense, fevered. Scarlett couldn't sleep after. She'd pretend that it was real. *Miss Scarlett, in the billiard room, with the lead piping.* She pictured herself in every scenario, being caught.

Her whole life, she'd known she was adopted, that

Scarlett was the name her real mother had given her before she'd bled out in childbirth. That scene was always in her head – all that blood, all of it her fault – but she didn't tell her parents that it gave her nightmares. They weren't affectionate. They were so busy working. She was used to dealing with her problems on her own.

The school report cards she brought home were always stamped with red A's beside each subject, top to bottom. They made her parents proud, these A's. Her favourite subject was English, although her parents said her constant reading of novels was 'indulgent'. Fine so long as she did well in maths and science. When she was doing her A levels, they studied *The Scarlet Letter*. She'd had a vague sense already that her name implied something unseemly, something sexual. She knew because of how Miss Scarlett looked on her Cluedo card – a woman with blonde hair, wearing a low-cut red dress and a ruby necklace. She'd imagined that her real mother might have looked like this. She inserted the idea of her mother into the novel, a red 'A' sewn to her dress. A scarlet woman.

It was funny, Scarlett thought, that the red A's on her report card were what got her into Cambridge to study medicine. The medics were mostly boys, self-assured chaps in cravats who all appeared to know each other. Scarlett was put in a group with three of these boys. For the entire first year, they dissected a cadaver, bit by bit, under bright overhead lamps in a cold lab. Mostly, they ignored her.

It was disorientating, coming out into the light. The spires of the city, punting on the river, candles at dinner. Her room overlooking the college gardens, wisteria climbing the walls. The girls at her college were always going on dates. She didn't know how they found the time. A girl-friend set her up, once, on one of these dates. Scarlett didn't want to be seen as frigid, but she felt it, the entire time, sitting on her hands, not knowing what she should say, if she was looking at him in the right way.

She wasn't close to her girlfriends either, the other students at her Victorian-era college, where boys were not allowed to stay overnight. This meant they talked about boys constantly, as if the only reason they had worked so hard to get into Cambridge was to find themselves husbands.

'Most of them are married now,' Scarlett had said, when she told me this part of the story. 'With babies. Children, I suppose they'd be now.'

Still, I can sense there are things she hasn't told me. I know so little, really, about the life she's led – a great blank between her graduation and her parents' death a decade later. A car crash where they were crushed, the fire engine too long to turn down the twisty country road.

She'd given up working as a doctor, after that. It was freeing, she said, no longer needing to impress her parents, thinking about what she might do with her life. But she felt untethered, too, like she might just disappear and if she did no one would notice.

That was when she started looking into where she'd come from. She found the papers in her parents' filing cabinets. SCARLETT written on the tab of the yellow divider, like she was one of their patients.

She'd been adopted from a mother and baby home, in Stranorlar, County Donegal, run by the Sisters of Mercy. It had been shut down, not long after she was born, but her parents had compiled notes about the place. 'Meticulous, they were,' Scarlett told me. Reports of how the women were put to work in the laundry, washing clothes for local businesses. The forms they were coerced into signing, agreeing to adoptions.

'They'd told the truth,' Scarlett told me. 'My mother really did die giving birth to me. I was a year old before I was adopted. I had to go and see the place.'

She took the ferry, drove all the way to Donegal and stood outside the big grey building, just outside Stranorlar, found the burial ground all overgrown. No knowing if her mother was there, along with all the babies that didn't make it out alive.

Afterwards, she drove around the county, taking the coastal roads. 'It was painfully beautiful,' she said, 'and I kept having this thought that I might somehow be able to feel her, if I got to the place where she'd been from. Then I saw this house, the for-sale sign. For some reason, it made me think about the Cluedo house, something about it being so symmetrical. It made me want to see inside.'

. . .

I put out the display cakes, inside the glass counter. I'm nervous about the guests arriving. Until now, the plan felt like a story we were telling each other, because it started out that way, the idea appearing seemingly from nowhere, then Scarlett making it all real. She's like that – good at making things happen, in a way that I am not.

She makes me feel like the things I have to say are important. What I knew about the history of the house, the stories I made up with Máire, the game we played at school.

She forced me to recall some of the stories, and I told her about my story.

'You should submit it somewhere,' Scarlett told me, after she made me read it out to her. 'Magazines.'

The idea of this fills me with something sickly like excitement. 'Putting yourself out there', Scarlett calls it. But she's the one with real stories to tell, I think.

I prepare the cake stands, lay out the silverware. Scarlett comes down in her costume – the same dress and apron as the one I'm wearing, but hers blue instead of black.

'We look like sisters,' she'd told me, when we first tried on the outfits. She hadn't told me she was getting them. I protested about the expense, but she told me she was rich. She said it like it was nothing. It had crossed my mind that maybe she'd come up with the idea of us wearing costumes because my own clothes were so tatty, compared to hers. 'We're not going to argue about money, OK?' she'd said, as I watched her put her arm around me in the mirror. 'You're doing this for me. You might find it fun to be a character, to play with people's expectations. People do love to make assumptions, and I'd rather misdirect than be transparent.'

'Are you playing a character now, with me?' I'd asked.

'In some ways. But, with you, I want you to work me out.'

I'm waiting for her to work out that she wants more from life than running a tea room in boring Burtonport. She must do, surely? But I don't want her to realize, either. I want to keep her here, selfishly.

Miss Scarlett, in the hall. What would her choice of weapon be?

. . .

The tea room is big and bright, with windows all along the side, looking out over the orchard. The tables are covered in white lace cloths. The sun is flooding through the windows, shining on the silverware.

Although we'll only really be busy in the summers, we're hopeful the tea room will become a popular venue throughout the year for communions, confirmations, engagements, graduations, even wakes. Scarlett has grander ideas already. She's set on turning the parlour into a private function room, where we would provide amusements popular in Victorian times – Tarot card readings and séances. It scares me a bit, how quick she is to race ahead. I worry I won't keep up, that I'll be left behind.

The doorbell rings. I can hear the first guests coming into the hall.

'I've always wanted to see inside.'

I recognize the voice, but struggle to place it. I've not looked at the reservations log, I think because I'd be more nervous if the names in it were people I know, which they are bound to be.

Laura Cotter comes through into the tea room with another girl, the two of them accompanied by the O'Regan brothers.

I watch them settle down at one of the tables in the corner before I go to take their order.

'I heard you were working here, Ró,' Laura says, warmly. 'And have you heard from Máire?'

'Not lately.'

'And your mother?'

Something about her voice sounds false. Different to how she used to be. She's wearing make-up, her hair set, a string of pearls around her neck. She doesn't look a bit like Máire any more. Though of course I don't know how different Máire might be now.

'Are you ready to order?'

'Have you that cake with the pink and yellow squares? I always wonder how it's done. You know the one I mean. What's it called?'

'Battenberg,' I say. 'We do have it.'

'That's it.'

Across the table, Kevin and Sean are still talking about the soccer, the Lotto.

Is this what I'm supposed to want – dates and Battenberg cake?

. . .

After the guests have gone, and Mrs Boyle, Scarlett catches me in the kitchen. My hand's behind my back, reaching to remove my apron. She pulls on the end of the bow, letting the strings loose.

'We did it,' she says, excitedly, into my ear. 'How do you feel?'

'Tired,' I tell her. 'But sort of energized, as well.'

'Me too. Stay a little later, to celebrate?'

'I have to get back to check on Mammy.'

'Just a little bit.'

'All right.'

July 1981

After I've finished putting away the plates, I go out into the garden with my book under my arm, walk over the lawn to the bench beyond the vegetable patch. We've fallen into a pattern. The tea room busy, everyone in the village wanting to see inside the Screamers' house. The weather holding as the days turned into weeks, evenings spent sat out in the garden with Scarlett. The sun setting a little earlier each day, like a premonition.

I've nearly finished *The Bell Jar*. I knew from the very first page that I would gobble it up. But there was this sense, also, that there would be parts I'd want to savour. Right away it made me full of longing, hungry for the lives I'll never lead. Maybe it's just the fact that it's set in New York. There's a shininess to the narrator's life, the experiences she exposes herself to. Still the same feeling, though, of being trapped, not knowing how to act.

It doesn't matter how many people you know, or where you go. You're left with yourself.

Except now Scarlett is walking across the lawn, making her way to me. Yesterday, after work, she told me that she never needed many friends. I liked the way she expressed this – it wasn't that she couldn't make friends, just that she didn't need them. I've never needed people either – Máire pushing me away so often forced me to harden. But I feel attached to Scarlett now, in a way that makes me almost anxious, like I wouldn't know how to exist without her. Probably lots of people have felt this way about her.

She's carrying the red plastic briefcase that contains her portable turntable. We've been listening to records, skipping forward from the Victorian era, catching up to the present. There's something pleasing about this – still in our costumes, listening to Talking Heads, Kate Bush, Prince.

Scarlett puts the briefcase on the grass and sits down cross-legged to undo its clasps.

'You have to hear this,' Scarlett says. 'I was up all last night, listening to it.'

She pulls a record from its sleeve and places it on the turntable, then moves the needle over the record. I shut *The Bell Jar* and the music starts to play. Scarlett sighs, her face turned to the sky.

Usually, she'll comment that the quality's not great on the turntable. But I'm not sure I notice things like that. Michael used to play me records sometimes, too. And it's the same feeling, watching Scarlett listening to something, working out how it makes her feel.

The song is upbeat, poppy, the singer's voice smooth and sweet. Scarlett reaches into her pocket and brings out a box of matches. She slides the box open and pulls out a rolled cigarette. She holds it in her mouth as she strikes a match against the side of the box. I watch her suck in and the end of the rollie glows orange. She shakes the match till it goes out. The smoke smells strange – sweet and earthy.

'It's pot,' she explains. 'We can share it, if you'd like.'

'I've never done that before.'

'It's not difficult. Here.' She passes it over to me, between

271

her thumb and forefinger. I take it. 'Just hold the smoke inside your lungs for longer, like you're taking an extra breath in.'

The smoke burns my chest. It makes my eyes water and I start to cough. I try to hand it back but Scarlett tells me to go again, and I manage better the second time.

I listen to the music then, the words filling up my head as Scarlett lies back in the grass, her head nearly touching my boots.

All the boys think she's a spy. She's got Bette Davis eyes.

'Michael's mother said that Máire looked like Bette Davis,' I say, the words coming out strange and slow in my mouth.

'Funny, I was thinking that the song makes me think of you.' She opens her eyes. They look more golden than grey, out here in the sun.

'Hardly,' I say.

Scarlett starts to sing along. 'She's precocious, and she *knows* just what it takes to make a pro blush.'

'It's funny that you think of me that way,' I say. 'No one else does.'

'Everyone else is wrong.'

She plays the song again, after it stops. I lift my feet up and lie down on the bench. We pass the joint between us until it's burnt down to the end.

Suddenly it seems I must remove my boots, feel the grass under my feet. And while I'm doing that, standing on my tiptoes, then flattening my feet again to feel the blades of grass tickle my soles, Scarlett starts to speak about a school. At first I think she's talking about my stories, developing one of them and making it her own. We do this often, stop whatever we have actually been speaking about in the real world and start talking about the house instead. But I can't make sense of what she's saying.

'You gave me the idea. We'll call it an "authentic Victorian experience for young ladies". There will be classes during the day. They'll stay here, in the house, for a week or two. Women only. A getaway from the demands of the modern world.'

I want this to go on for ever. The sun hitting my face, finally low enough in the sky to cast shadows. I can't work out if I want to close my eyes or keep them open.

'We need teachers,' Scarlett is saying.

'Yes,' I say. 'Of course.' But I'm too high to remember why, turning round in a circle, looking at the sky, until I get dizzy and fall down to the grass, right beside her.

'Well, I was hoping you'd be the English teacher,' she says, her face still spinning. 'With a proper salary, of course.'

'Me?' I ask. 'But I'm not a teacher.' I can hear myself giggle.

'You could be,' Scarlett says. 'I mean, you read so much. And anyway, it's not like a proper teacher. It's just an "experience". You'll basically have to read Victorian novels out loud to a class. You know, like *Pride and Prejudice*.'

'Well, *Pride and Prejudice* isn't Victorian,' I tell her, pleased with myself for knowing this.

'Exactly.' Her hand squeezes my wrist. It makes me shiver. 'See, that was your test. You passed. You're perfect.'

Her face is flushed and shiny. The gold flecks in her eyes so sparkly, coming closer. It doesn't take me by surprise. Somehow I knew that she was going to do it, that it was always going to happen. This kiss. Her lips soft, her chin smooth. Hot breath coming out of her nose. I kiss her back. She slides her tongue between my lips. A moan escapes my mouth. And even though my eyes are closed, it's as if I can see us, lying there in the grass, our dresses pressing together, black and blue.

The pleasure makes me panic and I pull away, feeling my heart thud, the weight of it.

'I have to go and check on my mother,' I manage to say, after a moment.

She doesn't say anything.

'But I'll be back tomorrow,' I assure her, wanting her to know that I couldn't bear it if things were awkward between us now. I can't lose her.

'Sure,' she says, plucking blades of grass between us, not looking at me.

I lift her chin up with my thumb. I bring my face to hers, nudge her nose with mine before I push myself up off the ground.

'Don't forget your boots,' Scarlett says. 'And your book.'

I don't put my socks and boots back on. I stuff the socks inside the boots and cradle them in my arms on the walk back home, pressed up against *The Bell Jar*. The tarmac is warm under my feet, that song stuck in my head.

If only they could see me now, I think.

August 1981

The surgical spirit is still in the bathroom cabinet, upstairs in the Screamers' house. I check whenever I am in here. I do this instead of actively remembering the time when I was in this room with Michael, my back on the floorboards.

Surgical spirit, pack of razors, cotton buds, box of tampons.

I take one out of the box. The non-applicator kind. Then I put it back and close the cabinet.

. . .

My schoolmistress uniform's arrived. Scarlett has hung the clothes in her room, ready for me to try on. A white blouse with puff sleeves and a high collar. A high-waisted moss green skirt with decorative pleats and a velvet belt. My measurements were sent to a tailor in London who specializes in period dress – they make costumes for films and West End shows.

I didn't think that she was actually serious about the school when she first brought up the idea, before we kissed. I thought it was just because we were high, all of it.

We didn't talk about the kiss, but it was there, in the air. It seemed like she was using the school to cover up the kiss, focus our attention on a new idea. But I thought we were pretending, fantasizing, as she started to make a floor plan of the house, the rooms on its three storeys. Labelling each room with what it would turn into, like on a Cluedo board.

Classroom, study, dormitory, infirmary.

By the time I realized she was actually going to do it I felt powerless to stop it happening, swept up in it all.

. . .

The first time I came up here was barely a week after the kiss, the same evening that Scarlett first showed me her floor plan. She'd already started moving furniture around, ordering things in. She needed to get my measurements, for my new uniform, she'd explained. 'There's a full-length mirror upstairs.'

Until then, upstairs had been off limits. She'd never said as much, but it felt like an unspoken rule.

The bathroom was waiting where I'd left it, at the top of the main stairs. Scarlett's room was off the landing to the left. It was dark inside. She hadn't opened the curtains. It took my eyes a while to adjust, coming in from the landing. She shut the door behind us, and started apologizing for the state of the place. 'I haven't made my bed,' she was saying. 'I'm awful in the mornings. Such a slob, really. Give me a minute.'

That was when I noticed the greenish light over in the corner. I was trying to work out what it was when Scarlett pulled open the curtain. The green light stopped being so luminous, though I could now see better what it was coming from. Some sort of machine, standing on a wooden desk. Was it an electric typewriter?

It was still glowing, even as the room got brighter. It looked like something from the future. I felt myself being drawn towards it, till I was close enough to read the words, lit up on the screen.

YOU ARE ANOTHER VICTIM OF THE MAZE. DO YOU WANT TO PLAY ANOTHER GAME? (Y OR N?)

'That's better,' Scarlett said.

When I turned around I could see that she had made the bed. The sheets were peach-coloured. Lots of pillows. Above the bed was Máire's painting. She noticed me staring.

'I moved it in here. I hope you don't mind, just while we work out where everything's going to go.'

I didn't mind, but it was still strange, seeing it hanging there, like it was looking at us.

'Let me just turn this off,' Scarlett said, walking up to me. She leant down over the desk, in front of the machine with the words on it. 'Should have exited it earlier but it was driving me stir crazy.'

'What is it?' I asked.

'A game,' she said, looking back at me over her shoulder. 'It's called *Labyrinth*. I keep getting slaughtered by the Minotaur.'

'A computer game?'

'Don't act so surprised,' Scarlett said, coolly. 'I'm very forward thinking, and good at working things out. Besides, it's all about storytelling. I can get a bit obsessive though. It's a vice.'

The things I thought I knew about Scarlett were re-arranging in my head, making room for this new quirk.

'So this is what you do – for fun, like?'

'Amongst other things.'

'How does it work?'

'I'll show you. Another time. Maybe you can help me stay alive.' She turned back to the machine and pressed a series of buttons in the typewriter bit. 'No escaping from the labyrinth now though.' The words disappeared, the light went out. I hadn't realized the machine was making a noise until it stopped. Scarlett had stood back up. She stepped towards me. I could hear both of us breathing.

We kissed then, as if to cover up the silence. Scarlett pushed me up on to the desk and stood between my legs. We both struggled with our skirts.

'Now this is what I call a labyrinth,' Scarlett said, breathless, smiling.

It felt so good to be wanted.

. . .

I've uncovered more of Scarlett's secrets. The tattoo below the nape of her neck – the red counter piece from Cluedo. The Casio wristwatch she wears when she's playing on her computer – so she doesn't lose track of time. The science-fiction paperbacks she whips through, at least a new one every week. The fact that she hardly seems to need to sleep. The way she likes to be touched, in the glow of the orange lava lamp, when we're in her bed – soft at first, then harder, harder.

I helped her to escape the labyrinth. She had to kill the Minotaur. When it was done, I pulled her over to the bed.

'My Minotaur,' she calls me.

'Why am I the Minotaur?' I asked, the first time.

'Because I won't be able to escape you.'

I've learnt how she likes it, how to pull back and play with her. Afterwards, though, she always wants to talk about the school again. The desks that will need to be ordered, the sign that will have to be repainted. Her spending seemingly endless. Until I join back in it's like we're worlds away.

. . .

'Take off your dress,' Scarlett says when I get back from the bathroom. 'I can't wait to see you in a corset.'

It hurts, though, when she tries to tighten it. And I can't get the skirt up, over my hips, or the blouse over my breasts. I start to cry then, the tears rolling down my face. I can't remember ever crying like this. Not when Daddy died. Not after Michael left.

'Baby Minotaur,' Scarlett calls me. 'Don't be upset. You've just put on a bit of weight. It'll be all Mrs Boyle's cakes.'

'It's – not – that,' I splutter, out of breath, trying to get back out of the clothes, to loosen the corset. I can't. I'm stuck.

'Let me help,' Scarlett says. 'Stay still.'

I stop struggling then. I lie back on the bed, while Scarlett pulls the skirt over my legs. 'My period,' I say to the cornicing in the ceiling.

'Oh, well that makes sense,' she tells me, now loosening my corset. 'I always get bloated and upset before—'

'It's not that,' I interrupt. 'It's late.'

279

I can feel her thinking, can hear the hurt before she speaks. 'How late?' she asks, and I can tell she's trying to keep her tone neutral.

'From before,' I say. 'Before Michael left. Just before. I hadn't realized, or I hadn't let myself think about it. I couldn't . . .'

I don't know how much time passes. I almost don't want Scarlett to say anything, for time to simply stop. But it won't do that. Not for anyone.

'It's OK,' Scarlett says, at last. But her voice sounds cold and distant.

'How is it going to be OK? I can't have a baby.'

'You don't have to.'

She gets up from the bed, walks over to the door. I'm sure she's going to leave me. Then I hear her walk back over, in the dark. She turns on the lava lamp, the wax inside it cold and hard, but the light still golden.

'Get in under the covers,' she tells me. We both get into the bed. 'You know the stories about St Brigid, right?' she says.

'What's that got to do with anything?'

'Just listen. When I went to Stranorlar, I climbed over the chained-up gate. I wanted to get inside the house of horrors, see the place my mother had ended up, where I'd been born. I broke a window to get in. It was empty. Not a thing inside, except this cross hung on a nail in the wall, in one of the upstairs rooms.'

She points over to her bedroom door. It's too dark to see, but I know what she means. I've noticed it before. A St Brigid's cross, like the ones I used to make with Mammy and Máire.

'I didn't know what it was, at first. But I carried it around with me, when I started driving round the coast. I had it hanging from the dashboard mirror. It didn't take long for me to find out what it was. I read about her, then, St Brigid, in the library. I'm assuming you know her life story. The Irish love their patron saints.'

'St Brigid's cool,' I say, remembering some of the stories. One where she gets the king to agree to give as much land as her cloak can cover to the poor, and her cloak expands to cover the whole province.

'Did you hear the story about the nun who became pregnant?' Scarlett asks.

I nod my head on the pillow, remembering. Scarlett reaches for my hand under the covers.

'The nun went to St Brigid,' Scarlett says. 'Brigid put her hand on the nun's belly, and the bump disappeared – without birth. The nun went back to being a nun.'

I don't know what she means, exactly. But my hand is sweating. Scarlett's still speaking.

'I couldn't believe it. I mean, she's the original abortionist, the patron saint of Ireland! How ironic is that? All this time and Ireland could have been following in her example, instead of sending girls away in shame, forcing them to give up their babies, preventing women from having any kind of choice over their bodies, even now.'

Her voice sounds very far away. It's as if I'm somehow not there at all, like I'm watching myself get out of bed, following her through the door and into the room where the stairs to the next floor are, to the room at the top where the books used to be. They're no longer there. Neither's the chair. Instead, Scarlett is showing me the operating bed, the instruments. Mostly, I'm wondering. *When did they get here? Were they here the whole time?*

'Think of it as the opposite of a mother and baby home,' Scarlett is saying.

I think about the floor plan.

Miss Scarlett, in the infirmary . . .

'I know it's a lot to take in,' Scarlett is saying. 'But you're in the right place. I'm a doctor. This was always the real plan.'

I turn away from the instruments, try to force myself back inside my body. 'When were you going to tell me?' I ask, still dizzy.

'I wanted to protect you.'

'And now?'

'I wanted to tell you. I've hated not being able to tell you. Maybe it was supposed to happen like this. I can make it go away. But it's your choice. You don't have to decide right now.'

So why does it feel like I've become part of someone else's story?

The Classroom

YOU LEARN LATIN AND GRAMMAR, SOMETIMES
GEOGRAPHY AND HISTORY.

YOU HAVE TO SIT IN SILENCE IN THE CLASSROOM.
IF ANYBODY MISBEHAVES THEY'LL GET THE RULER.

THIS MORNING THERE'S ANOTHER EMPTY DESK.
YOUR SISTER'S.

'WHERE'S MAGNOLIA?' YOU ASK THE HEAD-
MISTRESS.

FOR THIS YOU GET A WHITE MARK NEXT TO
YOUR NAME ON THE BLACKBOARD, A FLICK OF
THE RULER OVER YOUR WRISTS.

YOU FEEL YOUR ENERGY DRAIN.

IF YOU GET THREE MARKS YOU WILL BE SENT
TO THE HEADMISTRESS'S STUDY.

DO YOU ASK ANOTHER QUESTION OR STAY QUIET
FOR THE REST OF THE LESSON?

(A OR B?)

Lyca Brady

Burtonport

2018

I

When I found Sanjeet on Facebook, in 2016, he wasn't using a photo for his profile picture. He wasn't using a photo at all, just plain text on a white background: *Where did the ducks go?* I knew it was him, even before I clicked on his About tab. I could see that he attended Harrow School. His home town was Croydon, London. He was an atheist. No evidence that he had spent the first years of his life in Burtonport.

I googled the line. It was a quote from a novel called *The Catcher in the Rye.*

'Cora,' I shouted from the upstairs landing. I never called her Mam or anything like that.

'What is it?' she shouted back.

I walked across the landing and pushed open the door to her room. She was sitting at her own computer, watching a video on YouTube. She turned her head when she heard me coming in.

'Have you read *The Catcher in the Rye?*' I asked.

'Why?'

'Well, have you?'

'I read it while I was pregnant with you,' she told me, but I didn't care about hearing a whole story about it.

'So, have you a copy?'

'Well, it wasn't mine, but it was in the house, so it could be anywhere. Why are you so interested in it, all of a sudden?'

'Book club,' I lied. 'I'm in one at school.'

'Book club.' She raised one eyebrow, the way I couldn't. 'Wouldn't Gaga be proud?'

She would, if it were true, I thought, for Gaga had loved reading. She wasn't able to read, though, any more. The lines slipped all over the page, going out of order before she was able to catch them and put them back in place.

'Do you want me to see if I can find you a second-hand copy, online?' Cora asked, for I was still standing there.

'No,' I told her. 'Don't worry, I'll look around the house.'

There were books in practically every room. Piles of them leaning against walls, lines of them stood up on shelves. I started the search in the tea room, and by the time I had worked my way through to the kitchen my eyes were aching. I had no reference for the book's size and shape, the colour of its spine. I suppose I could have googled different covers, and found out the book's length, so I'd know roughly what I was looking for, but that would have felt like cheating. So I made my eyes run over every book spine in turn as the autumn light dwindled. I wouldn't rest till I had found it. I was sure it must be in the house.

I went up to the bathroom. It probably didn't used to be a bathroom – was just turned into one at some point during the Victorian era. The toilet is one of those old-fashioned ones, with the cistern up by the ceiling and the flush attached to a chain. It's a big room. The toilet and sink and bath are all a fair distance from each other, standing awkwardly like strangers at a party. So Gaga had put lots of shelves up to make the room look more 'lived in'. There was also a big wicker chair with a high curved back so when you're sitting in it it's like you're inside it. I could remember Gaga sitting in that chair while I played in the bath when

I was little. The scratchiness of the towel as she dried me in her lap, the nursery rhymes she would start to sing with me sitting there, the way she untangled my hair.

The shelves in the bathroom were mostly all high up, which meant I hadn't examined them much when I was younger. I pushed the chair over to where the shelves were and stood up on it, aware that the wicker was weak in places. It creaked under my weight as I leant across to see the titles further down the shelf. Many of the spines had been bleached by the sun or had bloated out of shape. But there it was. *The Catcher in the Rye*, by J. D. Salinger, the spine so slender that I could easily have missed it. I pulled the book down from the shelf and opened it up, expecting to see Gaga's name inside the cover, or my mother's. They both did this thing where they wrote their names inside every book they read, I guess in case they ever needed to separate their stuff. To my surprise, though, the message inside was to my dead grandmother.

To Máire,

Happy 17th birthday, pet. This is the best book there is about New York, in my opinion.

Love, Nell

. . .

I liked reading well enough, but I hadn't sat down like that and read a book from cover to cover in years. Not since I was just reading kids' books. I'd always get distracted and end up checking my phone. But my phone was back in my room and I stayed there in the bathroom reading, not even looking up until Cora came in to use the toilet. By that point I was about halfway through. I hadn't found out where the ducks all went in winter yet.

'What are you doing in here? And why is the chair over there?' Cora asked. She had unbuttoned her jeans and was sitting on the toilet. I hadn't even noticed her coming in.

'Reading,' I said simply, pretending to look back down at the book.

'In the bathroom?'

'Why not?'

'Sure, why not?' She had a hand between her legs. She pulled out her menstrual cup and poured the blood into the toilet bowl.

'Couldn't you have gone downstairs to do that?' I asked.

'I didn't know you were in here.' She flushed the toilet and waddled over to the sink with her jeans around her knees to rinse the cup. 'Besides,' she said, turning to look at me while reinserting the cup at the same time, 'It's perfectly natural. You shouldn't be ashamed of your own bodily functions.'

'I'm not,' I said. 'But you don't have to do it in front of me.'

'You're the one sitting in the middle of the bathroom.' She turned back to the sink to wash her hands. 'You found it then, the book? Enjoying it?'

'I'm at the bit where he talks to the nuns at Grand Central Station.'

'You know that was *the* book I read before I had you.' She was looking at me through the mirror now. 'Only I read it in the armchair by the stove.'

'I thought *the* book you read was *Songs of Innocence and Experience*?'

'Well, yes,' she admitted. 'But that had lots of pictures in it. *The Catcher in the Rye* was the first *novel* I read after I came here.'

'It was your mother's,' I told her.

'I know.' She pulled her jeans back up and turned to look at me properly, her head angled slightly to the side. I averted my eyes, returned to Grand Central Station.

. . .

I studied that book like I'd never studied anything else before. When I finished reading, I consulted Google. I read essays and study guides and scrolled through online forums. I spent three whole days putting off actually sending a friend request. What if it wasn't even him? What if he didn't even remember me? Was I absolutely sure that it's never revealed in the book where the ducks went? I wanted to make sure I would have something interesting to say.

I added him in the evening, after school on a Friday. All weekend my computer was on standby. I had my Facebook notifications set to come through on my phone – but I wasn't sure if you got notified when someone accepted your friend request.

I made myself do things away from my computer. I went to visit Gaga at St Brigid's – I took the book with me and read her the first chapter. Back home, I did my homework downstairs in the kitchen.

After each task I'd set myself I ran up to my computer. I entered in my password and refreshed the browser.

Nothing. Perhaps it wasn't him. Perhaps he was away for the weekend. Perhaps he was one of those people who never went on Facebook. He was probably playing soccer (though he had never been into soccer). He was probably at the kind of party I struggled even to imagine – ones with alcohol and drinking games in houses where the parents are always absent.

It came through on Sunday evening – a notification on my phone saying that Sanjeet Khan had accepted my friend request. 'Say hi,' Facebook suggested.

I finished loading the dishwasher, putting things in that didn't even need washing like the soap dish and the toast rack. Without its dish to lie in, the bar of soap wouldn't stay still, so I left it in the sink. It slid towards the plughole. I turned off all the lights and went upstairs to my computer. I was pretending to be calm.

There were hardly any photos on Sanjeet's profile. He didn't have any albums of his own, but he had been tagged in a few photos by other people. The one I was most interested in was a bit difficult to make out. It was a photo of another photo, I realized, after staring at it for a while. HARROW, it said on the front, in fancy lettering. The photo was of three boys passing through two red-brick pillars, about to walk down a set of stone steps. They were all wearing straw boater hats. I only knew what straw boater hats were because of Gaga's Enid Blyton books. The other two boys had their heads turned, so you couldn't see their faces. Sanjeet looked like he was in the middle of saying something, his mouth pouting as if to sound out a word beginning with P. He was looking straight into the camera, as if he had just noticed I was there, staring at him.

The face of Harrow, the caption to the picture read. A few boys had left comments underneath. 'Scholarship Sanjeet represents,' someone had put. And: 'Course they choose the photo where you can't see George and Charlie's ugly mugs.' The photo had over twenty likes.

How long had it been? I counted on my fingers. Six years.

I could see Sanjeet was online. He'd be able to see that I was, too. I clicked on to his name, which opened up a chat window. I sat there, I don't know how long for. I waited for him to message. I typed in the word 'Hi', then deleted it.

I did this over and over, making up imaginary conversations in my head. But I didn't send a message.

2

Sanjeet and I were best friends for a couple of years in primary school.

When I first started school, I felt briefly popular. The girls in my class invited me over to their houses, and I invited them to mine in return. They never came on their own. There were always two or three of them, maybe even four, climbing the steps to the front door. Climbing them slowly, often holding each other's hands. I'd get inside and turn around, so I was looking out at them through the door frame. And there'd be these three or four or five open mouths. OOOOO.

When I invited these girls over again, they came up with excuses. They wouldn't partner with me for activities. 'It's not personal,' I can remember one of them telling me when I cornered her. 'It's because your house is haunted. We've heard the stories.'

Then they started playing this game, at lunch. Babykiller, it was called. If I wanted to join in, I had to be the baby. This involved zipping me into my coat with my arms by my sides, rather than inside the sleeves. I was supposed to tuck my legs up to my chest, too, so I looked curled up like a baby. My 'crib' was the top of one of the picnic benches, on the far side of the playground. The game would start out friendly, with the girls cooing and fussing over me. I was supposed to make baby noises or pretend to cry if

I wanted their attention. Sometimes they would feed me snacks from their lunchboxes. Strawberry-flavoured fruit flakes, a green grape, a broken-off bit of a rice cake. If I protested, to any of it, they'd say I was a 'bad baby'. It always got worse. They held my nose shut to make my mouth open. The bitter stem of a dandelion, sliding back into my throat, the yellow flower coming out of my lips. 'Suck on that, baby,' they'd say. 'No crying.' They filled my mouth with earth, with gravel, with stones. Once, all of them spat into a plastic water bottle, as much as they could before they got bored. They forced me to drink it. 'Mama's milk' they called it. Then they'd start singing 'Rock-a-bye baby'. They'd kneel on both sides of the bench, with me still swaddled on the table. The rocks were gentle, at first. But they got harder as they sang the song. It hurt the most along my spine, but I didn't mind the rocking as much as the rest. By then I knew that it was almost over.

> Rock-a-bye baby, on the tree top,
> When the wind blows the cradle will rock.
> When the bough breaks the cradle will fall,
> And down will come baby, cradle and all.

At least there weren't any trees in the playground. At least the ground was woodchip where I landed.

But if I told anyone, they threatened, they'd kill me for real.

. . .

I knew our house stood out, compared to the others in the village. It was big and old – grand-looking, but shabby at the same time, dated. The ceilings were high and the windows all single pane. Sash windows that rattled in the wind. Some of the ropes inside the frames had rotted away so they wouldn't stay open in the summer unless you jammed something inside. You could feel the floorboards move under your feet, and they seemed to creak even when no one was standing on them. Sometimes I could hear squeaking through the walls. Mice, probably.

Of course I wondered if the girls were right, if my house was haunted. But when I asked Gaga about the stories, she assured me that the girls were just 'telling tales'. The only part of the house I was really scared of was the hatch.

The hatch was in Gaga's sewing room, right at the top of the house. I knew it was just the entrance to the attic, but something about the way the hatch slid open made it seem sinister. I'd have never gone in there were it not for Sanjeet.

. . .

Sanjeet wasn't scared of my house like the girls had been. He didn't know about the stories. His mouth opened wide, too, when he came through the front door, but I could tell it was in wonder.

Sanjeet's parents had moved to Ireland from India before he was born. His father was an X-ray technician and his mother was a nurse. Good jobs. But they lived in a tiny house on the Atlan estate.

I only went over there after school once. I could tell he was embarrassed, because he had so much less space than

I did. There wasn't room for us to play like we did at my house, so instead we did our homework at the table, while Sanjeet's parents asked me endless questions. What did I want to be when I grew up? What was my favourite subject at school? What did my parents do? What about my father? They wanted to know more about my mother's job (which I didn't know much about at the time). They said it was wonderful that I lived with my grandmother and asked about my grandfather.

'He died before I was born,' I told them. 'In 9/11.'

'How terrible!' Sanjeet's mother said. 'Your poor grandmother.'

I didn't correct her about the fact that Gaga wasn't actually my grandmother. It made a change from people thinking that she was my mother. Besides, I already knew, at six, that explaining would lead to further questions that I wouldn't know how to answer.

'I remember watching it on television in the hospital,' Sanjeet's mother was saying. 'We'd only just moved to Ireland. I couldn't believe it. Just terrible. I was pregnant and, you know, that was the first time I felt Sanjeet kick. It was like he could see what I was seeing, like he felt for those poor people, falling. I knew then that Sanjeet was going to be a very smart boy.'

Whenever I told anyone that my grandfather had died in 9/11 they would tell me where they had been when it happened, unprompted. I was used to this. I never knew what to say back to them, though.

The meal was spicy, but I finished everything on my plate, and thanked Sanjeet's mother for the food – just like Gaga had reminded me to in the car on the way to school.

I offered to help with the dishes. When my mother came to pick me up (she must have just got back from a trip), I thanked Sanjeet's parents for having me. I hoped they wouldn't bring up 9/11 as I put on my shoes.

. . .

Though I only went to Sanjeet's house that one time, he was always over at mine. When Sanjeet's father came to pick him up (it was never Sanjeet's mother) he always refused Gaga's offer to come in for a cup of tea. He would wait on the bottom step, which meant he was actually quite far away from the front door.

Once, from the upstairs landing window, I saw him approach the house. He opened and shut the front gate so carefully that it can't have made a sound. He looked over his shoulder as he tiptoed up the seven steps to the door, as if worried someone would see him. He pulled on the doorbell, then raced back down the steps and turned around again, still up on his toes. He must have thought it would be terrible for Gaga to get to the door before he was back down the steps. Did he expect her to think that he had somehow reached the bell from the bottom?

Sometimes, Sanjeet's father would be waiting there for ages, at the bottom of the steps, while Gaga called out for me and Sanjeet. Sometimes we'd be hiding, because we wanted to carry on being together for ever, and Gaga would have to come looking for us. Sanjeet would often be returned to his father with his uniform askew, missing a button or two.

We played mostly in the garden, climbing the apple trees

and shooting at each other with potato guns. But, when the weather was bad, Sanjeet loved to explore the house and look at all the things in it. We'd get Gaga to play hide-and-seek with us, or we'd go into the tea room and climb over the old bits of furniture, pretending that the floor was a shark-infested sea.

'Let's go up to Gaga's sewing room,' Sanjeet said, one day when it was raining. I knew immediately what he was really suggesting, because of how he bit down on his bottom lip after he'd finished speaking. He wanted to go through the hatch.

I told him that I wasn't allowed in there. I said it was dangerous, that the floor might give way. I reminded him of the stories whispered about at school, the ones neither of us knew. But nothing would deter him.

The thing that made the hatch so creepy was that, from Gaga's sewing room, it looked like it could just be a cupboard, built into the wall. But I knew it wasn't just a cupboard. In my head it was a portal to another place, a black hole in outer space.

'Let's pretend we're explorers,' Sanjeet said, putting on a serious voice. 'We must press on, into the depths, so we can record what no one has ever seen before. Have no fear, Sanjeet and Lyca are here.'

He pulled a chair over to the wall beneath the hatch. I stood on it so I could slide the hatch open, then climbed through the hole so Sanjeet couldn't accuse me of being a coward. I knew there was a light switch, just out of reach on the wall inside, and I wanted to turn it on as quickly as possible. I was scared of touching spiders' webs or worse, imagined something damp and anomalous putting its mouth around my fingers, like the attic might be full of those deep-sea creatures on that nature programme I watched with Gaga – terrifying, blobby things that have never seen the light of day. 'Bottom feeders' Gaga called them, which would make us both laugh throughout the rest of the programme. Thinking of this gave me the courage to find the light switch, and the warm light that filled the attic also filled me with relief, as I felt Sanjeet crawling through the hatch behind me.

'Wow,' he said, his voice full of wonder.

We stayed there, like that, not moving or speaking for a bit, just letting our eyes adjust to the relative darkness of the attic. When I turned around, the light through the hatch – where we had just come from – looked blindingly bright, almost as if it was now the unchartered land, ice white like Antarctica.

'Come on,' Sanjeet whispered, pushing me forward, further into the attic. The roof got higher as we went in, so we were soon able to stand up. The space was full of old bits of furniture and cardboard boxes. Really, not so different to some of the other rooms in the house. But the attic didn't have any windows, and there was something unsettling about the fluffy roof insulation. It made me feel like we were up high in the clouds, and if I were to take a wrong step I'd find myself falling through the sky, not down to Earth but out into space.

I walked on my tiptoes, the way that Sanjeet's father approached our front door. There were lampshades with fringed bottoms, old canvases and art materials on top of what looked like a hospital examination table. A glass cabinet with strange-looking instruments in it. Everything was covered with a fibrous layer of dust.

It felt like the space went on for ever, but that was probably because we were only small then, and the light was so dim that it didn't reach the far end of the attic. I was sticking to the middle, where the light bulb was, running my fingers over the different objects and bits of furniture. There was an orange lava lamp that looked like it had been frozen in time, standing on a dumb waiter on top of an ottoman. I picked up the lamp to see if the hardened wax inside would move, but it was petrified. I looked around to see if there was a plug socket up there. I wanted to see if the lamp still worked, to bring it back to life and watch the lava bubbling inside. It bothered me that it had been left there, dormant. That was when I noticed an old tin, sort of wedged into a gap between the floor and sloping wall. I could see the word USA on the side. These were the biscuits we always had at Christmas – the ones which Cora said she'd never even heard of, growing up in America. But the box looked different to the kind I was used to – blue instead of red. I could tell it was ancient when I pulled it out because the edges were all rusty, even though the corner of the lid claimed the tin contained a 'new improved assortment'. I wasn't expecting it to still contain biscuits, but I could tell it wasn't empty.

The lid made a grainy sound as it came loose. I could feel the rust on my fingers.

Inside were envelopes. They had all been opened, and they all had Gaga's name on them.

Róisín Dooley
Teach Simléir Dúbailte
Main Street

Burtonport
Co. Donegal
Ireland

I picked one of the envelopes up. The flap where the seal had once been opened like a mouth, inviting me to peek inside. The letter was printed on headed paper.

Cantor Fitzgerald
North Tower
World Trade Center

'Miss Brady,' I heard Sanjeet calling, in a strange, affected voice, like he was putting on an accent. I spun around to check for sure that it was him, my heart beating in my chest, the envelopes held behind my back.

Sanjeet was standing at the end of the attic. I could just about make out that he'd put some kind of old-fashioned hat on his head, and he was holding on to a frilly white umbrella.

'A pleasure to make your acquaintance,' he said, clearly trying to sound like a fancy lady. He curtseyed, for effect. He must have lost his footing because the next thing I knew he had disappeared from view. I could hear that he had fallen, grabbing hold of something as he went down.

'Sanjeet,' I cried, though still somehow whispering, worried that he might have dropped into the cloud-like insulation and would now be suffocating in its depths.

'I'm OK,' came his voice.

I shoved the letters back into the tin and put the lid on, then pushed the tin into the gap where I'd found it.

By the time I'd made my way over to where Sanjeet had fallen he was standing up again, holding something shiny up to the light.

'Look at these,' Sanjeet said, handing a small plastic object over to me, about the size of a pack of playing cards. 'There's a whole box of them.'

'What is it?' I asked, turning it over in my hand. There was a picture of a man holding a bloody knife. A title written in a font made to look like dripping blood. *Jack the Ripper.*

'They're games,' Sanjeet said, excited. 'Old ones. Cassettes, they're called.' He was kneeling on the ground now, burrowing into a cardboard box. 'Some of these might be collectible.'

'I don't know,' I said. I knew nothing about computer games and was already feeling left out by the fact that Sanjeet knew more about the items in this box than I did. I knew it was a mistake, coming into the attic. I wanted to go back through the hatch where things felt safe, even when we were pretending to be heroes battling through grave danger.

'I could ask my dad,' Sanjeet was saying. 'Are they Cora's, do you think?'

'I don't know,' I said, again. 'I suppose so.'

Sanjeet seemed light years away from me, with his head inside that box. He was still wearing the bonnet, and it felt like he'd become a different person. I wanted my friend back.

He pulled out another tape. His mouth opened wide.

'Look,' he said, holding the tape out to me. 'Isn't that—?'

I took the tape, and finished off his sentence. 'My house.'

For he was right. There it was. A black-and-white drawing of the house we were inside. Unmistakable. I counted the steps up to the door to be sure. There were seven.

Scream School, the game was called, the words written in the smoke coming out of the two chimneys.

'Well, Gaga did have a life before you came along, you know,' Cora said, when we showed her the tape. 'Before I came along, as well.'

She was packing to leave for El Salvador. There was a wide-brimmed straw hat lying on her bed.

I still didn't understand. Was Cora saying that Gaga used to play video games? How did that explain why there was a picture of our house on the front of some of them?

Sanjeet (who had the best marks in our class) seemed to have understood something I hadn't. 'No way!' he said, with that look on his face that meant he'd just worked out the answer to a problem.

'Well then, smarty-pants?' my mother said to Sanjeet, after zipping up her suitcase.

'Gaga was a video game creator,' Sanjeet said, looking at me, then looking down again at the cassette tape in his hand. He was so excited.

'Not quite,' Cora said. 'That really would be something, seeing as Gaga's sworn off ever owning a computer. You're warm though.'

'What then?' Sanjeet said, deflated.

'Why don't you two go along and ask her about it,' she suggested. 'My taxi will be here in . . .' She lifted up her wrist to look at the time on her watch. 'Any minute now. I'll be back a week on Tuesday. All right, Lyca?' She got up to her feet and was holding out her arms to hug me when she noticed the sun hat, still splayed out on the bed. 'Damn,' she said, reaching for the hat, then bending to unzip her bag again.

'Lyca, come on,' Sanjeet said, pulling on my hand. We ran like that, together, to the kitchen.

. . .

'Oh, you found the tapes, did you?' Gaga said, as if it was only ever going to be a matter of time before we did. She'd hardly looked up from her knitting.

'Why does this one have our house on it?' I asked.

Gaga finished making a couple more stitches before putting down the sock she was working on. 'Let me see that,' she said to Sanjeet, holding out her hand for the tape. He handed it over. 'I haven't looked at this in years,' she said, smiling. 'Not since before you were born, Lyca. You should have seen your poor mother's face when I first brought her back here. Her mouth wide open when she got out of the car. She had a copy of this game, you see, growing up in New York. And I'd forgotten to mention, when she came here, that I lived in the house that was on the cover.' She put the cassette down on top of the sock, and closed her eyes to better remember the story. 'I was never certain she'd actually received the game, you see. And we'd had a rough journey back from Dublin – what with your mother losing her luggage and her being sick on the side of the road outside Cavan. An infected tattoo, on top of being pregnant.'

This story I knew already. Gaga loved to tell it. I must

have heard it a hundred times. 'We know all that, Gaga,' I said, impatiently. But what do the games in the attic have to do with you?'

'I wrote them, of course,' she said, looking back down at the cassette again. 'Well, the stories, anyway, and the writing on the inserts. This was actually the first one. And you know who did that picture on the front?' She turned it round so we were faced with the picture of the house we were standing in again.

'Who?' Sanjeet and I chorused, together.

'Your grandmother,' Gaga said. 'My sister, Máire.' She traced a finger over the picture on the cover.

'So you made the game together?' I asked.

'No. I made them with Scarlett. Remember, I've told you about her before? She's the one who's in prison.'

'In prison?' Sanjeet cried, in disbelief.

'The one you used to wear the funny clothes with?' I asked, for I had been shown a photo of Gaga and Scarlett, once, standing in front of the house, wearing old-fashioned dresses. I remember thinking they looked happy.

'She's the one,' Gaga said.

'And why is she in prison?' Sanjeet asked. 'What did she do?'

'She was trying to help people, but the law didn't see it that way.'

'Will she ever get out?' Sanjeet asked. 'Or is she there for life?'

'My my, what a lot of questions you two have today. Will we have our supper, so? Sausages for Sanjeet.'

She got up from the chair, leaving the half-finished sock there. 'Do you not like sausages any more?' she asked.

I knew Sanjeet wasn't supposed to eat meat, but he always failed to mention this to Gaga. He ate her sausages with great pleasure. But that day, he seemed distracted. He wouldn't stop asking Gaga questions, even with sausages on his plate.

'But how did it happen?' he asked, his brow furrowed. 'Writing the video games, I mean. Did you always know that was what you wanted to do?'

'Not at all,' Gaga said. 'I wouldn't have even known there was such a thing as a video game writer.'

'So how?' Sanjeet pressed.

'Well, it's rather a long story.' Gaga had her back to us now, fetching the butter dish from the counter.

'I like long stories,' Sanjeet said. 'I've read all the Harry Potters.' Sanjeet was the best at reading in our class. I was only on *Harry Potter and the Chamber of Secrets*.

'Have you now?' Gaga said. 'Why doesn't that surprise me? Well, it's not as interesting as all that. No magic involved, I'm afraid. And I wasn't the one who had the idea – that was Scarlett. She'd have been the one interested in video games. That was how I got involved, because she knew that I was good with words. But it was an odd thing to be doing, here in Burtonport, sure enough.'

'Tell us the story,' Sanjeet said. 'Please.'

'Go on and eat your greens,' Gaga told us, finally taking her place at the table.

Sanjeet and I quickly shovelled peas on to our forks, most of them falling back on to our plates before they reached our mouths.

'I've always been interested in stories, you see. Always written things down. Journals and notebooks and such.

But I was at a time in my life where I got to thinking more about people's choices – how everything would be different if just the slightest decision changed. Like if Lyca had gone to St Anne's, for instance, instead of the Gaelscoil. Then the two of you might never have met.'

St Anne's was the Catholic primary school. I watched Sanjeet consider what Gaga had said, his empty fork held in the air.

'You know,' Gaga continued. 'The thing about life is you don't get an undo button. You can't go back or start over. And even when you're reading a book or watching a film, you don't get to change anything. There's just the one way it'll go.' She paused, cut a sausage in half and popped it in her mouth. We waited for her to chew and swallow. 'The thing I liked about video game writing was that you got to think through other scenarios, imagine how things might have ended up if certain things had gone a different way.'

'You know that's not really a story, Gaga,' Sanjeet said. 'That was just *why* you liked being a video game writer, not *what* actually happened.'

'Well,' she said, after a brief pause. 'I suppose what actually happened was that we entered a competition where you had to come up with an idea for a video game. I didn't think we would actually win. It meant we were able to get in front of the right people at exactly the right time. We did well out of the games, for a time. The first few were reviewed in magazines. *Jack the Ripper* sold surprisingly well. Not at all surprising, now I think about it. But it quickly became clear we couldn't keep up with the big companies. We didn't want to play their games, metaphorically speaking, didn't want to sell out, though we had some offers.'

'What does "sell out" mean?' Sanjeet asked.

'It means to go against your values for material gain.' I loved it when Gaga explained things like that, not making them any simpler. 'And, Sanjeet,' Gaga added, looking at him, 'maybe all stories are more to do with the why than the what. Ever think of that?'

Sanjeet sat there, thinking about that. I suppose he must have conceded Gaga's point, or he would have said something else.

'I can show you the manuscript, if you'd like. It's in the tea room.'

. . .

It was always freezing in the tea room. Gaga had her slippers on, but Sanjeet and I were just in socks. We ran around on the wooden floor, racing each other along the length of the room. It was nearly as big as the dining hall at school, but full of scattered bits of furniture, which made the racing all the more fun. Gaga went over to an old wooden dresser standing at the edge of the room. It had three long drawers at the bottom, all of them crammed full with papers.

'Aha,' she said, finally, when she opened up the bottom drawer. 'Here it is.'

Gaga had pulled out what looked like a stack of A3 sheets. 'I think the best way to do this would be to lay it all out on the floor,' she said. 'We may have to move a few things around to make space.'

Sanjeet and I set about pushing one of the old sofas over the floorboards, towards the edge of the room.

'Now then,' Gaga said. 'Would the two of you be able to open this up very carefully and lay it out?'

We put the pile of papers down on the floor and began carefully to open them. The bits had been stuck together with sticky tape, so the whole thing opened up like a map, about the size of a big Persian rug. The words on the paper weren't even typed. It was all in Gaga's handwriting, in pencil. The manuscript was fragile, like some kind of historical arte-fact, a pirate map that would lead to hidden treasure. There were arrows connecting all the bits of text together, plotting out every choice a player might make in the game.

'Wow,' Sanjeet said, on his knees, crawling round the edges of the paper. 'Did they teach you this at school?'

Gaga laughed, looking down at us on the floor. 'Oh no,' she said. 'I got a book out of the library, about writing Choose Your Own Adventure stories.'

'They have books like that?' Sanjeet asked.

'They did. I suspect it's all on line now.'

She always said it like that. Like it was two words – on line.

Gaga explained that Scarlett had been a gamer, but she herself had never got her head around computers. So she wrote everything out by hand. Then she'd post the first draft of the manuscript to Dublin where the programmer who designed the games worked. After the initial version of the game had been designed, Gaga and Scarlett would travel to Dublin to see how it was taking shape.

'Scarlett would want to talk to the programmer about all the technical elements, but I would just sit there in front of the programmer's computer, reading through the text on every frame of the game. I wanted to make sure it had all been typed up correctly. I used to have nightmares about there being spelling mistakes when the game came out, because they'd be there for ever.'

There was something beautiful about the manuscript. You could see where bits had been rubbed out and rewritten. It bothered me, though, that the writing was all in pencil. She had held on to the manuscript for all these years, but the pencil would surely fade – was already fading.

'I regret sending off my sister's painting, for the cover design,' Gaga was saying. 'It got lost on the way back to us in the post. I never found it.'

I was staring at the connected bits of paper as if staring into space. I heard Gaga saying 'Come on then,' but it seemed to take a while for the words to reach me, like there was a delay.

. . .

Next Monday, at school, Sanjeet unzipped his backpack to give me a peek of the Commodore 64. He had sneaked it out of his father's study so we could play *Scream School* together, at my house.

'It's from the eighties,' he explained.

It looked just like an old-fashioned keyboard to me – grubby cream-coloured plastic with clunky brown keys on it – but I knew nothing about computers, then. Luckily, Sanjeet had used the Commodore before, to play *Bubble Bobble* and *Laser Squad*. I knew that Sanjeet played old computer games with his father, but until the day we found the tapes up in the attic he hadn't talked about this much.

Back at my house after school, we went up to Cora's

room. That was where the only computer we had at the time was. I knew that she used it for work, to talk to people from all over the world. She was still in El Salvador. I told Sanjeet I didn't know the password. But he said it didn't matter. All he needed was the monitor.

Sanjeet got the Commodore 64 out of his bag while I cleared space on the desk, nearly knocking over the framed photo of Cora as a little girl, pressed between her parents. For a few minutes, Sanjeet played around with different cables, plugging and unplugging things into Cora's computer monitor. I watched as he did this – he had a habit of sticking his tongue out when he was concentrating. Then I saw his face relax, and I turned to see the game loading on the screen.

'Yes,' Sanjeet said, satisfied. 'It's working.' He grabbed hold of my hand while we waited to play.

Text appeared on the screen. Not all at once, but word by word, like somebody was there, typing it in.

A HUNDRED YEARS BEFORE THE EASTER RISING, IRELAND . . .

A VOLCANO ERUPTS ON THE OTHER SIDE OF THE WORLD.

THE SKY GOES DARK. IT IS THE YEAR WITHOUT A SUMMER, THE SUN PALE IN THE ASHEN SKY.

Sanjeet was faster at reading than I was. I hadn't taken it all in before he pressed something on the keyboard and the text disappeared.

'So it's a basic Choose Your Own Adventure game,'

Sanjeet explained, jabbing at the Commodore, which he had pulled down to his lap so he could reach the keys more easily. 'There are different routes through the game, but you have to type in the right kind of command to progress.'

Typing in the right kind of command turned out to be frustrating, but we persisted playing the game for a time. When we got stuck, we tried asking Gaga for help, but she was adamant that we work it out for ourselves. She wouldn't even give us any clues.

The story followed two sisters who had been sent away to boarding school. Strange things were happening at the school, and the player had to find out what was going on and stop the students from disappearing.

It wasn't a bad concept, but to say the game graphics were basic would have been an understatement. From the cassette cover, Sanjeet and I had imagined the game would involve walking around my house, being able to explore it in as much detail as we did in real life, but back when it had been a school in the Victorian times. In that respect, the game was disappointing. You could tell the Scream School was based on the house we were inside, but it was lacking any detail.

'No offence to Gaga, but it's not a very good game,' Sanjeet said, when we had exhausted our patience with it. 'It's nothing to do with the story, though,' he added, consolingly. 'It's beyond cool that Gaga did this. The programming's just really clunky.'

He packed the Commodore away then. We didn't find out the school's secret, or save the students in it.

4

It wasn't a connection I made at the time, but my friend-ship with Sanjeet collapsed around the same time as the economy in Ireland did, when the Celtic Tiger was finally wiped out.

Until people started talking about it in the past tense, I had just assumed the Celtic Tiger was a real tiger. It was con-fusing to find out that the tiger wasn't real, and that it was extinct now, anyway. I hadn't been old enough to enjoy the things it symbolized. I was a crash child, really, everything falling down around me in our big old house, which I knew that Gaga owned outright, so we wouldn't have to emigrate to Australia like lots of other families were doing, but that wouldn't be enough to stop everything from changing.

The holidays were approaching – the summer before we would be going into third class. Sanjeet was going to India for six weeks to see his grandparents. He had never met them before, though he spoke to them every week on Skype. He dreaded these calls, and was nervous about going to India. I didn't want him to go either. Six weeks was an eternity.

My mother was in Kuala Lumpur. I'd asked Gaga if Sanjeet could come for a sleepover after the last day of school, when we were allowed to go home at lunchtime. We were going to put a tent up in the garden and tell each other spooky stories. We'd have a campfire and toast marshmallows on sticks. But Sanjeet was quiet on the last day of school. It felt like he was avoiding me. He wouldn't look at me properly. Finally, I had the chance to talk to him, when we were both put on door duty for the leavers' assembly. Looking at his shoes Sanjeet said he was sorry, but he wasn't allowed to come to my house any more.

'So you're not coming to the sleepover?' I asked, getting upset – eyes brimming, bottom lip beginning to wobble, my face hot and hopeless.

'I'm sorry, Lyca,' Sanjeet said, again.

'Why?' I asked.

'Because you're a girl,' he said, the word smarting. 'It's not proper.'

Somehow, I just about managed to hold the tears back, all through the assembly. They started to leak out, though, as I ran across the playground, after, straight to Gaga's car.

Seeing that I was in floods of tears, Gaga pulled me over the gearstick, on to her knee. I cried until I noticed the steering wheel was pressing into my back. My tears had left a wet patch on the shoulder of Gaga's cotton top. But those were only moments of being present. I was still inconsolable, as I started to explain, struggling to get the words out. After I did, Gaga tried to comfort me, explaining that Sanjeet's ma and pa were from a different culture. I knew culture was something to be respected. This was pressed on us at school, where we were taught in Irish to preserve the language, and parents often came in to give talks about their heritage. But I didn't care about culture.

'It's – not – fair,' I spluttered, between breaths. 'Lots of people in my class have sleepovers. Why can't we?'

Gaga told me she would give Sanjeet's parents a call

when we got home, to see if she could persuade them. But I knew already that it wouldn't work, that this was the end.

Sanjeet went off to India for the summer. When we both returned for the new school year things were different. Sanjeet seemed distant, though I suppose it wasn't just him. It was as if an unspoken rule had been introduced, that boys and girls could no longer be friends, could no longer play together. Sometimes I watched Sanjeet from across the classroom, waiting for him to look over at me. If he did, I told myself, it would all be OK. I'd pluck up the courage to invite him over again, and everything would go back to how it was before.

Then it was announced. Sanjeet had been awarded a scholarship to go to a fancy school in England.

5

In my bedroom there's a framed print of 'The Little Girl Lost' by William Blake. It's a poem about a little girl (called Lyca) who gets lost in the wilderness and is abducted by wild animals – lions, leopards and tigers. I asked Cora, once, why she had wanted to name me after this quite disturbing poem. She said the book the poem was in – *Songs of Innocence and Experience* – reminded her of her mother, and that Lyca was the only girl in it who had a name. So Lyca I became.

I never felt lost, though, until I lost Sanjeet.

There were other children who left my school as well, but Sanjeet was the only one whose parents left because of him, not the other way around. It was celebrated, Sanjeet's scholarship. He was given a prize in assembly. It was clear to me, sitting cross-legged on the floor, that Sanjeet was going to be something. For the rest of us, stuck in Donegal, our dreams got dimmer with each winter.

I formed a few half-hearted friendships with the girls in my class. I didn't invite them over to my house and I wasn't friends with any of them individually. But I existed on the fringes of their groups. It was easy enough to listen and pretend, to talk the same as they did. But I didn't feel connected to them.

. . .

I can remember Erin Rogers's twelfth birthday party – a sleepover at her house. It was just before we were going to be starting secondary school. She was the richest girl in our class, and she made sure we all knew it. Her father worked as a car manufacturer abroad – in Germany, I think – so they'd survived the recession practically unscathed. They still went on all-inclusive holidays to Lanzarote or Tenerife and they got a new Mercedes every other year. Erin wasn't the prettiest or the funniest or the nicest girl in our class, but she had that specific kind of confidence that came from having everything she'd ever wanted.

For her birthday, Erin received a MacBook Air. We watched as she unboxed it, then gasped in unison as she held the laptop up in the palm of her hand to demonstrate how light it was. There was an opalescent hologram of a feather on the discarded box. It was slightly raised, I realized, as I ran my fingers over it. This made me shiver.

After the masses left the daytime portion of the party (where there had been a bouncy castle which we all felt too old for but nonetheless were drawn to, particularly at the end when the air was being let out and we let it collapse around us), the girls who had been chosen to attend the sleepover went up to Erin's bedroom with slices of birthday cake on paper plates. We lounged on Erin's double bed while she turned on the MacBook Air. The noise it made when it came to life sounded like something I had heard before, though I wasn't sure I had. It took just seconds for the screen to light up with the Apple logo, then to a display that prompted Erin to create a profile name and password. It should have been boring, watching Erin use her laptop for the first time, but we were all mesmerized, or perhaps just knocked out after so much icing.

Erin was obviously familiar with the operating system. She connected to the Wi-Fi and opened up the App centre. She searched for *Sims 3* and, when asked for payment information, entered in a card number and security code by heart. The conversation was stilted, anxious, as we all waited for the game to download. Erin's eyes were glued to the screen, watching the progress bar inch closer to being full. I felt excitement swelling in my chest when it finished loading. Seconds later, Erin was creating herself on the screen.

Erin wanted her sim to look as much like she did as possible, albeit in a more adult way. 'You can't do as much if you're just a teen sim,' she explained. Her sim was slender and perky with a tiny waist. The figure moved around a bit while its features and clothes changed, waving at us every now and then, or looking down at its sim hand as if checking to see if there was dirt under its sim nails. Erin asked for our opinion on certain hairstyles or outfits, but really she just wanted us to affirm her choices and say how much the avatar on screen matched the real her.

I was transfixed.

. . .

I begged for a computer for my birthday, and cleaned the house each weekend in the two months running up to it. I told Cora and Gaga that it didn't have to be an expensive laptop like Erin's, just one I could do my homework on now I was at secondary school. Gaga said

I couldn't have a computer in my bedroom, so the Dell went in the playroom, which quickly became known as the computer room.

I downloaded *Sims 3*. It took a lot longer than it had done on Erin's MacBook Air, with her fibre-optic broadband. I had to be patient when I played. Often, the game crashed, or it went really slow. But the main thing was that I had it.

First I made myself a teenager. I made versions of Gaga and Cora, too. I entered in a cheat code so I had enough money to build an approximation of our house. I made Sanjeet's family and moved them in next door. I put them in the cheapest house that came ready-built. When sim Sanjeet walked past our sim house, I had sim Lyca go over and say hi. We talked and joked and teased and played. We officially became friends and hugged and got into the swimming pool that I had built.

But Erin had been right. You can't do much if you're just a teen sim. Sanjeet and I flirted and held hands and had our first kisses with each other. We started 'going steady'. We made out on every sofa in the tea room. But there was one thing we could not do, and that was to WooHoo.

It would have taken for ever to wait for us to grow up in the game, so I remade us as adults and we lost our sim virginity to each other in a hot tub behind the greenhouse. Then we went inside and did it in my bed. I watched us do it over and over, even though you couldn't see through the water or underneath the covers, and the game pixelated our sim bodies anyway. I watched with my heart thudding in my chest, my hand perspiring on the mouse. My limbs were restless. I lifted a foot up on to the chair as if to sit cross-legged. I pressed my heel between my legs and sat there, rocking, almost crying with pleasure.

Afterwards, ashamed, I evicted us from the house where we'd done such things and bulldozed the plot. I swore I'd never watch us WooHoo again. But I was weak.

6

I would create my father sometimes, too, imagining what he might look like. I'd have him seduce my sim mother and they'd WooHoo in a changing room at the shopping mall.

But if my sim mother got pregnant, I'd drag her to the trashcan.

. . .

When I was younger, Cora had been able to field the questions I had about my father fairly successfully. She had the perfect excuse. She simply didn't know where he was or how to find him.

I found it hard to imagine a world where people weren't contactable, traceable. But Cora's answers always sounded so reasonable.

'He didn't have a cell phone,' she explained. 'I never knew where he lived. He wouldn't even tell me his surname.'

After I got my Dell computer, I googled about people finding lost parents, sure the information I wanted would be online somewhere, under my fingertips – because that was what the internet was: everything.

I found out about genotyping services and read all the stories on all the websites about people finding out they were sperm donor babies, or realizing they were adopted, or that they had siblings on the other side of the world. I wanted to believe that he would have wanted to know me, if he had known that I existed.

I went to Cora and asked if I could have my DNA sampled, to see if I could find my father that way, but I could tell as I told her about the site that she already had an answer that wouldn't be the one I was looking for.

'I'm not stopping you from doing this DNA whatever it is,' she said, surprising me. 'Though I'm sure they probably have age requirements for it. I'm not trying to hide anything from you, Lyca, I just don't want you to be disappointed when you don't find anything.'

'*If* I don't find anything,' I said, steadying myself.

'I'm not sure about this DNA thingy,' Gaga said. Usually she was silent when the subject of my father came up. 'I wouldn't be after giving your genetic information to a database. Who knows what they're actually doing with it all.'

'You sound like him,' Cora said, to Gaga. 'That's exactly the sort of thing he used to worry about. That's why he didn't have a phone. He wasn't the sort of person who wanted to be found. He was basically a conspiracy theorist. He probably thinks 9/11 didn't really happen and that the Earth is flat.'

I was stunned.

Gaga took a breath. 'Well, maybe he was right. Ever think of that?'

'You're not serious.'

'I just mean about the DNA thingummy.'

The conversation had changed direction, but I had come away with something of value. I went back up to the computer room, trying to hold on to the details my mother had just revealed about my father's personality.

. . .

Cora was right – I was too young to get my DNA sampled, and I couldn't have afforded it anyway. But I carried on trawling the internet. I learnt the hard way that googling for answers doesn't just give you them; it leads you into a hall of mirrors, down infinite rabbit holes, leaving you with can upon can of worms.

I shut myself away in that computer room, creating my own worlds on the Sims and putting up walls between myself and my mother. I went into chat rooms and spoke to other people who couldn't find their place in the world – the misfits and the misanthropes. I was able to express to people I would never meet that I was bitter towards my mother because she knew who her father was. He was dead, but still a part of her story, a story she had built a life out of.

. . .

I knew Cora's job was about choices – giving them to women. Some of my earliest memories are of attending marches in Dublin. There's a photo of me as a toddler, sitting on Cora's shoulders, wearing a T-shirt that says 'I should have been a choice'. I never quite understood this statement, but I liked the idea behind it. Who didn't like having choices?

The word 'abortion' came up so much – in the conversations between Cora and Gaga, or when Cora had her 'sisters' over (women who weren't actually her sisters) – that I didn't really take any notice of it until I was older. I did take notice of the letters we sometimes received, though. Ones where the sender had cut up words from newspapers or magazines and stuck them back together to form a message. Was it some kind of game? Why did Cora always throw them in the fire? I soon forgot about these letters, though, as they didn't come that often. Until the day one came when Cora was away. It was hateful.

Burn in hell you MuRdErEr, it said – each letter cut out individually to make the final word.

It felt strange, typing *Cora Brady* into Google. I had been so focused on finding my father, that I'd never thought to check what her name might bring up.

I was astonished when photos came up at the top of the search results. The feeling was similar to when I first clicked on a pop-up that opened up a porn site – my whole sense of the world rearranging.

There were endless articles about her. She was 'The woman who will not stop until abortion is legal in Ireland', an 'infamous pro-choice activist'. Some people thought she was a hero. Others wanted her dead. At the bottom of one of the articles was a link to a video of Cora giving a speech at a conference. It was strange, watching her walk up on to a stage and stand in front of a lectern. But mostly I was in awe of how good she was at it, how polished her story seemed, but in a way that seemed like she was talking to each member of the audience as a friend.

I knew the basic facts, of course. She had got pregnant with me when she was sixteen. Her father had died in 9/11, leaving her an orphan. This part of her story was so familiar that it was like I couldn't hear it. I kept zoning in and out of what she was saying, not able to follow it properly.

I had access to some strong prescription medication . . . So I was taking these pills, lots of them, every day . . . life had just been turned upside down . . . actually losing weight . . . lots of girls don't have regular periods . . . I wouldn't have been able to tell apart yesterday from a month ago . . . withdrawals . . . the panic . . . didn't realize abortion wasn't legal in Ireland . . . The dire situations women in Ireland, and across the world, have had to put themselves through . . . And I knew I wouldn't rest until it was possible for someone like me to have made a different choice.

There it was: proof that my mother had never wanted me. Something I had suspected when I felt particularly bitter about how absent she was, whenever I let myself think about how different she was to other mothers. But it still smarted, hearing it aloud.

7

I kept my sims healthy, making sure their energy, fun and social levels were topped up. Meanwhile, I let myself dim. My eyes ached, sometimes throbbing along with my heartbeat. If I'd looked in the mirror (which I didn't really do) they would have been bloodshot. I stayed up all night and fell asleep at school. I couldn't focus. My grades began to slip. I got into arguments with Cora, whenever she was at home. I told her that I wished I'd never been born, that she should have had an abortion. I even shouted at Gaga, who didn't know what she was supposed to do with me.

I lost so much time, then wished I could go back. But real life doesn't let you go back. You have to do it wrong, to live with your mistakes and go on.

. . .

There were signs, of course. When I cracked the shell of my boiled egg only to find that it was raw inside. When I poured myself a cup of tea from the pot and all that came out of the spout was hot water. When Gaga left orange peel cooking on the stove all day so when I came home from school there was a rancid smell and smoke was billowing from the pan.

But I didn't say anything, even then. Cora wasn't there to tell, and even when she was I hardly saw her. I wanted her to be the one to spot the signs, to pay attention to what was going on at home, rather than taking on the plight of women she didn't even know, often on the other side of the world.

We kept having the same argument.

'It can't be good for you,' Cora would say, about the Sims. 'You need to be in the real world, Lyca, with friends.'

'You're saying you'd rather I was out drinking and taking drugs and getting pregnant?'

A big part of Cora's personality revolved around her understanding of herself as an addict. When she was at home, she went to AA or NA meetings several times a week. She had taken me to Al-Anon a few times when I was younger. I think she'd hoped I might make friends there. I listened to the other children talking about how awful it was when their parent had been drinking, and the parent next to them would burst into tears. I never spoke at the meetings. I had never seen my mother drink. I didn't see her much as it was. And whenever she was around she just wanted to go to these meetings, which to me seemed full of misery. They were always in cold, damp, windowless rooms where the paint was peeling and there were stains on the carpet. I hated going.

But Cora was right. I didn't have any friends, and I wasn't living in the real world.

Then I found Gaga on the floor, her face all wrong.

. . .

I googled furiously about strokes, then about Lewy Body dementia, after Gaga got her diagnosis. Her symptoms had presented at a very early age, the doctor told us. But it wasn't unheard of in people in their fifties. I burrowed my way inside the internet like an ostrich burying its head in the sand. But it was hopeless. There was no cure.

We had to move her into a nursing home, St Brigid's Lodge. Her speech was slurred and she got confused. She had dizzy spells where it was like she could see things that weren't there. It was upsetting, and I believed it was my fault. How long had she been lying there, alone?

The doctor had said, when he was explaining the diagnosis, that Gaga might find remembering past events, from when she was much younger, easier than recalling short-term memories. It was likely there'd be moments where she might feel trapped in an earlier time, and not recognize people, places or things she'd come to know at later points in her life. It was likely she'd forget us both – me and Cora.

. . .

If I went to see Gaga every day, after school, she might get better, I told myself. I could help her remember.

Half the time when I arrived, she was sleeping. She seemed decades older. The carers set up a table and chair in Gaga's room so I could do my homework there. They all assumed she was my grandmother. It was easier to pretend than to explain. Easier not to say when they kept dressing her in other people's clothes, even though we'd gone to the effort of getting all hers labelled. The same kind of name labels she'd sewn into my school uniform. I tried to remind her who I was by showing her the back of my tie.

'See,' I'd say, holding the tie out to her. 'Lyca Brady.'

But there was a fog behind her eyes, like she was under water.

It was the same when I showed her photos from my camera roll. She couldn't understand that what she was supposed to be looking at was *inside* the phone, not the phone itself. It was just an object to her.

The most upsetting thing was watching her try to speak. The words wouldn't come out. When they did they were slurred. The speech therapist I met one time told me I should encourage her to talk as much as possible. Mostly she just said 'yes' or 'no'.

Sometimes I could work out what she was trying to say. Sometimes she even seemed to make sense.

'You can see them?' she asked me, once. 'In there?'

'Who?' I asked. I had been looking at Sanjeet's Facebook profile, on my phone. I thought maybe she might remember him, and had tried to show her. 'It's Sanjeet,' I said. 'Remember, he used to play with me when I was little, before he moved to England?'

'He wrote to me, you know,' Gaga said.

'Sanjeet did?' I was excited, then. Was it possible he might have written, and Gaga hadn't told me?

'No.' Gaga waved her hand in front of her, swiping at my phone. It fell down on to the carpet.

It was hard, watching her struggle. Easier to speak for her, then see if she'd say 'yes' or 'no'. Like we were playing Animal, Vegetable, Mineral.

. . .

I probably wouldn't have remembered Gaga's diaries were it not for the fact that I was carrying my own notebook around. I was determined to keep a record, still hopeful Gaga's speech would get better, that she might tell me things.

Of course, it didn't work like that. But I kept getting out the notebook at St Brigid's, writing down the date, the weather.

I'd write about something else, then. Something that had nothing to do with being there at St Brigid's, or anything that had happened that day at school. I'd remember the calendar Gaga had made for me when I was small. She'd sewn it out of fabric. It had Velcro attachments so I could change the date each day. All the bits were kept in labelled pockets – the days of the week, the months, the seasons, the numbers 1 to 31, the phases of the moon, even options for the weather. *Cloudy, rainy, foggy, sunny, snowy.*

What had happened to that calendar? When we forget things, where do they go?

. . .

Gaga's diaries were in a cabinet in her room – at the house, not at St Brigid's. I'd always known about the diaries. She'd never tried to keep them secret. Still, I didn't tell Cora that I'd thought of them. Probably I was worried she'd say I had no right to read them.

She would have been right.

I knew that. But knowing it was wrong didn't stop me. The cabinet wasn't even locked. All the diaries were lined up in order, sticky labels stuck to their spines, dates written on them, like they were supposed to be read. Perhaps Gaga had somehow known what was going to happen to her? Why else would a person record their whole life, arrange it so meticulously?

The earliest volumes were on the left side of the cabinet. Visually, they were more distinct than the later diaries, which were all written in the same black leather notebooks.

I started at the beginning, removing only the first volume, so its absence wouldn't be noticed. At St Brigid's, I placed the diary in Gaga's hands, to see if it would spark anything, light up her eyes. I asked if she wanted me to read it to her.

'Yes,' she said, though that didn't mean she understood the question.

. . .

The way Gaga wrote reminded me of a kaleidoscope, even in those first diaries, when she was only nine or ten. She would start on one thing, then end up in another place entirely. It was like she lived that way, as if at any moment she could slip back into a memory.

I had wanted to help her remember who she was. But most of the time she didn't even seem to hear me, let alone recognize that the words were hers.

Part of the problem, I thought, was that I was reading to her about a time so remote. Though it was interesting, reading about Gaga as a child – about Máire and Michael and the Screamers' house, which I quickly realized was our house – I thought it might be easier for her to remember stuff that wasn't so far in the past. Maybe I should try a different diary, one from when I was little. So I went back to the cabinet, put the first diary back in its place, scanned the sticky labels until I found one of the black notebooks that had 2002 written on the spine.

But inside were just the same old stories. I checked every single diary, and they were all the same. Not exactly, but the same stories, rewritten slightly differently. About Máire and Michael. Sometimes about Scarlett.

I knew about Máire, my grandmother. And Michael, my grandfather. I knew about Scarlett, too. But before the diaries, my impressions of these people had been hazy. Máire and Michael had always been dead. Scarlett had always been in prison. The diaries didn't make them seem real to me exactly. They were more like fictional characters, their stories already decided, but them not knowing that.

The house started to feel different under my feet. I couldn't go into any of the rooms without wondering what it had been like, before. I looked up the Screamers online. Then I looked up Scarlett. I knew pretty much what I would find. The Burtonport Babykiller.

All the headlines called her that. The stories were mostly from 1992. Scarlett had been running a covert abortion clinic for ten years, behind the front of a 'Victorian school experience'. She had confessed, and was insisting that the people she'd employed to run the Victorian school experience had no knowledge of what was really going on. The article made it known, though, that it was unlikely the defendant had really worked alone.

There was no mention of Gaga in the article. There was

a photo of our house, though. Bird's-eye view, taken from a helicopter, I assume. It made me feel sick. Not the content of the article, what Scarlett (and presumably Gaga) had done. But seeing our house from above like that. It gave me the sense that I was being watched, even though I was the one watching the picture of the house on the computer screen. The aerial viewpoint reminded me of the Sims. All the versions of the house I'd built. All the versions of myself I'd created.

Gaga's diaries were the same, I thought. Different versions of the same thing.

8

Cora had been home more, since the stroke, but most of the time it felt like we were opposing magnets, not able to get close. And she was preoccupied. The Taoiseach had announced there would be a referendum on repealing the eighth amendment.

Often when I got back from visiting Gaga the house would be full of Cora's activist friends. I hated talking to them after seeing Gaga. They spoke so quickly and articulately. I couldn't keep up with the things they were saying, the questions they bombarded me with about what I was going to do with my life, the way they looked at me as if they were trying to crack me open. Occasionally I caught a glimpse of disappointment when they realized that I didn't measure up to my mother, that I was just an awkward teenager who didn't care that much about the referendum.

Other times the house would feel oppressively empty when I opened the front door, even if Cora was there. The kitchen felt wrong without Gaga in it, and I couldn't stop seeing the image of her there where I had found her, on the floor. We ate at odd times and both stared at our separate screens. We were like zombies, sharing this big old creaky house, barely speaking.

When we did try to talk, we couldn't put aside our resentments. We would argue about the fact that I didn't seem to care much about abortion. Couldn't I see that she was doing this for me? Why didn't I want to go with her to the rallies? I would argue back, 'When was the last time you saw Gaga? You're always talking about how she saved your life but you don't care about hers one bit.' She said, once, that there was no point in me going to see Gaga, but she never said it again. I knew she was grateful someone was seeing Gaga every day. It meant she didn't have to feel guilty about not going. And she didn't have to worry about me either, if that was how I was spending my time.

. . .

After the referendum result, my mother held a party at our house. I was offered a glass of champagne by one of her friends. Then another. I loved the way it made me feel – bubbly, like the drink itself. Everyone was happy and it felt like the wrongs of the world could be righted, like prog- ress could be made. I felt confident, wearing a black dress that belonged to my mother, which had belonged to her mother. I suppose it was a bit old-fashioned, but in a fash- ionable way. All of a sudden, it seemed, I'd grown a new body, like a child turning into a teen on the Sims.

I was sixteen, about to start my Junior Cert exams. I thought I might even do quite well in them. Since Gaga had been at St Brigid's, I'd been getting all my homework done there. I preferred sitting next to her – at my desk in her room, or in the residents' living room where the heating was turned up too high and the TV always on – than going home to the cold empty house, or to Cora. It was a peaceful place. Sure, the residents would occasionally get distressed, when it was like they suddenly regained awareness of what was happening to them, but most of the time they seemed serene. They were probably all on loads of drugs, but I wondered whether it might not be such a bad thing to forget things. If it weren't for the fact that they were all old (Gaga was the youngest resident there by far), and that the place clearly looked like a nursing home, you might think you'd stumbled across some kind of meditation group. They were so good at it. Sitting there, quietly, staring into space.

For some reason I was thinking about this at the party. Perhaps the champagne was wearing off and I was starting to find the energy of my mother's friends oppressive. I was thinking about how Gaga and I had always been what she called 'partners in crime' at any kind of event. This was funny because Gaga was always very sensible. She didn't like being the centre of attention, or even on the outskirts of it. Neither did I. If my mother was having people over, Gaga and I would retreat to the kitchen, sharing a mutual understanding that didn't need to be put into words.

I had stopped reading Gaga's diaries. Stopped reading them to her, at least. I still looked at them from time to time. But reading them always left me feeling disorientated, like nothing I knew was really solid. Particularly our house. Sometimes I was sure the ceilings had got lower, that the walls were pressing in.

My champagne flute was empty, and I needed to pee. The downstairs toilet was occupied, so I went upstairs to use the main bathroom. When I sat down on the toilet I felt the alcohol wash over me, whooshing straight to my head. I felt dizzy and elated. I think I might even have blacked out for a second, seen stars behind my eyelids.

When I recovered from the dizzy spell, I noticed my phone was resting on the edge of the sink. I must have left it there after I'd finished borrowing my mother's make-up. Just mascara and eyeshadow and a bit of lipstick. I stood up and flushed the toilet, then walked over to the sink and picked my phone up. I had a notification. It was a Facebook message from Sanjeet.

I closed my eyes then opened them again. I pressed the side button on my phone to make the screen go black, then brought it back to life again. The notification was still there. My heart was thudding as I looked into the mirror. I looked right into my eyes. They were brimming with excitement. I looked like a different Lyca. This Lyca wasn't lost or lonely. She was exactly who she was meant to be, and she was me.

This is what you've been waiting for, I mouthed into the mirror. Then I watched the other Lyca draw in a deep breath. I watched her rise up, two inches taller. She opened her mouth wide and let out a silent, primal scream.

9

I'd never liked any of Sanjeet's photos, or wished him happy birthday by writing on his wall. I did look through his photos, though, and read the things other people wrote on his wall. He rarely changed his profile picture, but it was no longer that quote from *The Catcher in the Rye*. It had been replaced by a photo of him crouching down next to a dog, some sort of terrier. I couldn't imagine him with a dog, even though there he was with one, in this photo. He was wearing thick-rimmed glasses, the kind that were in fashion. They made him look intelligent and interesting. He was still skinny, still smiley, his teeth showing more often than not in the photos he was tagged in. Most of his friends had double-barrelled surnames and their profile pictures showed them playing some kind of sport – hockey or rugby, sometimes even polo, on horses. Every few weeks, Sanjeet would be tagged in a new photo. The caption usually alluded to some kind of private joke that I wasn't able to make sense of. Recently, there had been a couple of photos posted where he had his arm around a girl. She looked like the kind of girl I knew boys fancied. Petite, with long blonde hair, almost down to her waist. She had an energetic smile. Very pink lips and pearly straight teeth. She was wearing a tiny T-shirt that was tight around her breasts and stopped above her belly button. Her name was Lucy Parker-Smith.

When I first saw the photos of Lucy with Sanjeet I zoomed in on her face until the picture became pixels. I shut down the tab and went next door to my bedroom, closing the door behind me. I lay down on the bed and unzipped my jeans. As I touched myself, I imagined I was Lucy, taking off that tiny top. I imagined how Sanjeet's face might look when she did that. I imagined him touching Lucy the way that I was touching myself, him wanting that. I came quickly, then cried when I returned to my body, staring at the ceiling.

. . .

But I wasn't thinking of Lucy when I walked from the bathroom to my bedroom, upstairs at the party. I felt light on my feet, like I belonged inside myself. I hadn't looked at the message yet. I was waiting, I don't know what for. I suppose I thought that if I put off looking, even just for a couple of minutes, then the message would become exactly what I wanted it to be. But what did I want it to be? The only reason I could think that he might be contacting me now, after we had already been friends on Facebook for years, was because of the referendum. He must have heard the news in England. Perhaps he even remembered what it was my mother did. I figured he'd be messaging to say something like congratulations – even though the vote had nothing to do with me.

I lay down on my bed with my shoes still on and put my phone, screen down, on my chest. I watched it rise and fall as I took some deep breaths, then counted to a hundred, as slowly as I could bear. My body started to tingle. I was still drunk, I suppose. There was something almost holy about lying there not looking at my phone. I felt saint-like, serene. I almost didn't want to get to one hundred. But I did.

I picked up the phone, unlocked it with my thumbprint, and opened up the Facebook Messenger app.

Lyca, long time no speak. I hope you're doing good – Gaga and Cora too. Are you still in the house in Burtonport? I loved it there – we always had so much fun. Anyway, I was just thinking of you. I mean, something happened that made me think of you. Hope you don't think that's weird.

He was still online, I could see. I could reach him, instantly.

L: Sanjeet!
S: Lyca!
L: Wild to hear from you. It's been a while. I remember those times too.
S: So you're doing well? I've looked at your profile from time to time, not going to lie. You look good. Weird we're not kids any more.
L: Yeah it's been nice seeing how you're doing too. Though I'm afraid there's not much to report from boring Burtonport.

I waited for him to reply. Seconds dragged like they were minutes. I couldn't bear the thought that the conversation might fizzle out and we'd never talk to each other again. I wouldn't let that happen.

L: So, what was the thing that happened?

S: It's a weird one . . .

L: OK. Go on.

S: Do you remember that photo, of Cora with her parents when she was a child? It was on her desk, next to the computer.

L: Yes, it's still there.

S: So I was on YouTube, down a bit of a rabbit hole about 9/11. As you do.

L: As you do.

S: I'm going to stay with my friend in New York just after Christmas, so I've been getting a bit obsessed reading about the city, googling stuff. Anyway, I was watching videos about 9/11 and there was this video about the posters people put up after. Like when someone's lost their dog or cat, but for people. They were all over the city for months. Do you know what I'm talking about?

L: I think so.

S: So now's the weird thing . . .

L: Go on.

S: So I think your grandfather was in one of the posters, in the video. You can only see it for like a second, but I'm sure it's from the same photo. He died in 9/11, didn't he? I didn't make that up?

L: You didn't make that up.

S: So if it is from that photo then I'm guessing Cora must have made a poster? The whole point of the video is that there's going to be a documentary about the posters, so the production team is looking for anyone

*who might be associated with the posters. So I wanted
to let Cora know. I'll send you the video link. One sec.
L: Thanks. I'll show it to Cora. She loves being featured
in things.
S: It's only a really quick glimpse, so I might be wrong,
or just going crazy haha.
L: Haha.
S: Here's the link. G2G but it's been great catching up.
Talk again soon.*

. . .

Sanjeet sent through the link but I didn't open the video
right away. I felt disorientated, like I'd just got off a fair-
ground ride. Already I was insecure about the fact that he'd
only got in touch because of something to do with Cora,
not something to do with me. But I was also exhilarated.
Adrenaline or alcohol was surging through my body. We
had just had a whole conversation. It didn't matter *why* he
had messaged, what mattered was he had.

I would show Cora the video in the morning, after all
the party guests had left. Instead of going back downstairs,
I scrolled back to the beginning of my Facebook conversation with Sanjeet and read it all again. Then again. And
again.

IO

When I showed Cora the video the next morning, she pressed pause as soon as it got to the bit that showed her father's face. I watched her look over at the photo on the desk, then back at the computer. She pressed play, as if hoping the picture in the video might turn into a movie.

There wasn't another shot that showed the poster in more detail. The footage was shaky, and the sun was shining behind the poster, messing with the exposure. The poster was wrapped around some metal bars, in such a way that you couldn't really make out the writing at the top of the poster. But it was definitely the same photo. Cora's father, cut out of it.

Cora and I watched the rest of the video together. The final frame showed a wall covered with posters, all the people in them missing. We were silent. I reached for the mouse to stop the next recommended video from playing.

'There were so many of them,' Cora said.

'Posters?' I asked.

'Well, yes. But specifically for people who worked at Cantor Fitzgerald. The company my dad worked for. Every time I saw one of the Cantor Fitzgerald posters I wondered if they had been with my father when it happened. They might have been the last person he spoke to. And I thought about the families, too, the people who made the posters. How we probably all relied on being able to get things printed out at the office. Because no one who had an office printer available every day would have a printer at home. But now the office was destroyed, and the people we loved who usually got things printed for us were all gone. I just kept thinking that everyone would have had this moment where they'd have realized they'd have to find another way to get their posters printed. Until then I don't think it had sunk in at all.'

'And you never heard from the families of other victims?' I asked. 'They never called?'

She laughed. 'No. At some point I realized I hadn't put my phone number on the poster. I didn't even have an email address. I just didn't think about it at the time. And I knew everyone at Cantor Fitzgerald was dead. The posters were all pointless.'

Cora read out the description beneath the video which outlined how to get in touch with the documentary production team. I could tell she was excited.

'I didn't know you were in touch with Sanjeet,' she said when I was about to leave. 'I liked him almost as much as you did.' She didn't wink but it was almost like she did, like I could see her thinking about doing it.

'Well, we're not really,' I said. 'It was just because of the video.'

I turned on my feet and was overly aware of my body walking to the door. I didn't want her to be able to infer that I had any feelings.

. . .

Back in my room I woke up my computer. Sanjeet wasn't
online, but I sent him a message: 'You were right.'

I opened up a new tab and searched for Cantor Fitzgerald.
There was a thumbnail image of the company logo in the
sidebar – CANTOR in block capitals, *Fitzgerald* like fancy
joined-up writing, the two words slightly overlapping.

*Founded in 1945, Cantor Fitzgerald specializes in
institutional equity, fixed income sales and trading.*

I added 9/11 to the search bar and felt the internet pulling me in as I opened up new tabs. That was the first time
I learnt about the conspiracy theories, and saw how many
people believed them. I read about why helicopters weren't
able to help. I looked at photographs of people jumping
and others of those who managed to get out, running
from the towers before they fell, covered in ash.

I did that for hours, until Cora asked if I would look
over the email she had written to the documentary production team.

'I haven't sent it yet,' she told me, peering in around my
bedroom door. 'I just need someone to check it all reads OK.'

The request made her seem vulnerable. This made me
uncomfortable.

'I can come and look now,' I told her, about to get up.

'No. I'll email it to you in a minute.'

The email came through quarter of an hour later. I
opened it on my phone and read Cora's message. It was
absolutely fine.

'It's great. Send it,' I wrote back in an email.

It didn't feel strange that we were communicating like this when we were in the same house, even though we wouldn't usually be sending each other emails.

'Have you heard of any of her films?' Cora emailed back. She had included a link. It went through to the IMDb page for Emily Baume, the director.

I hadn't. The films sounded arty, understated, about specific moments in cultural history, mostly set in New York. They had names like *Cardboard City*, *Coney Island Baby* and *Guardian Angels of the Subway*. The page said that she was working on a new project about the 9/11 missing-people posters.

I got another email: 'Sent it!'

'Well done,' I shouted out loud.

'I'm going for a run,' she shouted back.

. . .

Cora was a serious runner. She had run the Dublin marathon once in two hours fifty-nine minutes. Gaga and I had been there to watch her cross the finish line. I must have been seven or eight. Sometimes, when I was around that age, we'd cheer her on at cross-country or track races, too, all around Donegal. Gaga would pack cheese and cucumber sandwiches with the cucumber skin and bread crusts cut off. I'd grind salt and pepper over the cucumbers before the second layer of cheese went on. In the winter, we brought a flask of hot chocolate. In the summer, there'd often be the same ice cream van at the athletics track. *Casper's Ices*, the van was called. It had several slogans written on the side. *Never say BOO to an ice cream*, I can recall, as well as *I scream, you scream, we all scream for ice cream!* Gaga would get a lemonade lolly. I would get a Mr Whippy with a flake, the ice cream sometimes dipped in hundreds and thousands. It always melted so fast, dripping down over the serviette wrapped around the cone. Then on to my hand, and along my arm. 'The state of you,' Gaga would say, retrieving a tissue from up her sleeve. We'd scream from the side of the track, when Cora ran past. But she was always so focused, not once turning her head to acknowledge that we were there.

Running helped to clear her head, she said. I'd always struggled to understand the appeal of this. Wasn't the whole point of being human to have things in your head?

'You need to move more,' she would tell me, when I was a teenager. 'Don't you go crazy, sitting in the house all day?'

I resented her when she said things like this. Just because she was an addict who got pregnant at sixteen and had to talk about it all the time, didn't mean she knew everything. She should be grateful that I wasn't like her, that I didn't need to be occupying myself endlessly.

But of course I was occupying myself endlessly in other ways. And she wasn't wrong, about the head stuff. Needing to clear it. I just didn't believe it yet.

I checked my Facebook. I had no new notifications. Sanjeet wasn't online.

I closed down all the tabs I'd opened when searching about Cantor Fitzgerald. I exited programmes I never usually shut, then ran the software update I'd been avoiding for months.

I sat there, watching the percentage bar slowly fill: 4 per cent, 8 per cent, 9 per cent.

My door wasn't properly shut, but Cora knocked on it before opening it further. She had changed into her running gear. Shorts and a vest top.

'I've just thought,' she said, using her thumb to rewind a podcast on her phone. She was constantly re-listening to old episodes of what she referred to as her 'sex girls' – two comedians in New York, talking openly about sex. They answered emails sent in by listeners and interviewed guests. Often their friends, or people they'd slept with. But also sex workers and porn stars and people involved in movements like Reclaim the Night. They were fiercely feminist, pro-choice and anti slut-shaming. It would be a dream come true for Cora to be featured in an episode. All of this, of course, made me uncomfortable, especially when Cora put the sex girls on in the car and they inevitably started talking about blow jobs and butt plugs.

'Just thought what?' I reminded Cora, who seemed to have forgotten why she had come in.

'Oh.' She looked up at me. 'I had this camera. A Pentax. I was carrying it around New York with me, after the attacks. I was taking photos of the posters, every time I saw a new one. I'd totally forgotten. Do you think they might be helpful to the director, the photos?'

'Do you have them?' I asked, since Cora seemed incapable of thinking clearly for herself.

'Well, I suppose the camera would be in the attic, if it made it back with the rest of my stuff. God knows if I'd be able to find it, though. I can't imagine all the junk there is up there.'

I focused hard on staying very still, keeping my face blank while Cora carried on speaking. But my head was racing. I hadn't been inside the attic in years, not since that time with Sanjeet.

'I didn't want to go through it all, at the time,' Cora was saying. 'Even though it was years later when I finally got round to selling the apartment and shipping everything over. I'll have to look for it when I get back.' She looked down at her watch. 'I'm going to try and make it to the seven o'clock meeting, after my run.'

'I can go up there for you,' I said, quickly. 'I don't mind.'

'But you *hate* the hatch, honey.'

'Only when I was little.'

'Maybe wait. We can look together. I don't know how safe it is up there, to be honest. Order takeout, if you want.'

I looked back at my computer: 50 per cent. I hated just knowing the percentage, not how long the update would actually take. Something told me I should wait, that the update was a test. Not a voice, more a feeling. But if I waited for the bar to fill up completely, would I have enough time to go through the hatch and find the USA biscuit tin before Cora got back? 55 per cent. Would she be going directly on to the meeting, or would she be coming home first to shower? Still 55 per cent.

I closed my eyes, hoping the percentage bar might fill faster if I didn't look at it. That was when the phone rang. The landline. When I opened my eyes, the update was still at 55 per cent.

Sometimes I still wonder. If I'd sat there and waited the update out, not gone to answer the phone. Might that have stopped it from happening?

The Study

IN THE CORNER IS A GRANDFATHER CLOCK. STILL
QUARTER OF AN HOUR UNTIL THE END OF CLASS.

YOU TAKE IN THE REST OF THE ROOM.

THE CABINET, SUPPOSEDLY FULL OF FILES
ABOUT EVERY STUDENT, PAST AND PRESENT. AN
OPEN LETTER LYING ON THE DESK.

WHAT DO YOU WANT TO READ?

LETTER

YOU SIT DOWN IN THE HEADMISTRESS'S CHAIR
AND READ THE HANDWRITTEN NOTE.

*I AM WRITING THIS BECAUSE I AM SCARED OF
THIS SCHOOL. I AM CLOSE TO FINDING OUT ITS
SECRETS AND THEY ARE WORSE THAN I FEARED.
FINDING OUT THE TRUTH IS A GREAT BURDEN ON
MY SOUL, BUT I CANNOT CONFIDE IN ANY OF MY
FELLOW STUDENTS, NOT EVEN MY SISTER. TO DO
SO WOULD BE PUTTING THEM IN DANGER. I WILL
REPORT BACK AFTER I'VE BEEN INTO THE ATTIC.*

MAGNOLIA

Michael Brady

New York

1992–2001

February 1992

Dear Róisín,

A letter, as promised. Don't expect it to be any good, mind.

Máire is still at the psychiatric centre. It's in this huge building on an island just outside the city. Quite creepy, but it's meant to be the best. I'm not allowed to visit for the next couple of weeks, while she's being observed on the new medication. The psych doctor says she's more stable, though, which is good. They have to run a few more tests, but they think it's schizophrenia. I feel bad about not figuring it out sooner. Maybe I was too close to her to see. Maybe she just got good at hiding it. But hopefully now she can get the help she needs and she'll get better.

I'm writing this from the office, on my computer. My handwriting hasn't got any better since we were kids. If anything, it's got worse. So I'll print this off and put it in the company post before I leave. Can I ask you to send any reply to this address, rather than to the apartment? I feel bad about asking, but I haven't told Máire that I contacted you after it happened. I will. I just don't think she'd handle it well right now, when her emotional state is obviously very fragile.

Honestly I didn't think I'd get through to you. I can't believe the landline number still works. Please thank your neighbour for letting you come over to use their phone, especially given the time of night.

It feels a bit bad, writing to you now. But I do think you have a right to know what's going on. And – honestly – I don't know who

357

else to talk to. There's no one else who knows Máire the way that we do, who understands what she's like.

I'm hopeful that the situation might be different in the future. I'll talk to Máire about it when she's better. I know that Cora could use an aunt. Everyone always says that time flies so quickly when you have a child. It's corny, but it's true. It's like I blinked and Cora was six and things were so bad with Máire – bad again, I mean – and I could hardly remember why you weren't in our lives. How did we mess everything up so badly?

I worry about how this is all going to affect Cora. She's so perceptive, but also scarily adaptable. I've told her that her mammy's sick and needs to stay in hospital for a while so she can get better. Cora hasn't asked many questions about it and she seems surprisingly fine. But I still worry. I wanted her to have a more stable childhood than I had. And in lots of ways I'm sure she will. But, in trying to do things differently, you make other mistakes that you didn't anticipate. So then you just have to hope that they'll be OK, despite all the things that will hurt them, that you can't protect them from. I don't know what Cora will remember, how much of it she'll carry around in the future. Maybe it depends on whether she picks up on my anxiety. It's stressful. And I probably shouldn't be thinking about it so much.

Sorry for how all over the place this letter is. I'm not much of a writer. They say it helps, though, doesn't it, writing things down? Maybe that's why you've always seemed so grounded.

I'm sorry also that it took Máire trying to hurt herself for me to get in touch. I should have done before, and I'm sorry. I want you to know, Ró, that I still feel bad about everything that happened, with us I mean. I'm not looking to excuse myself, but I felt so conflicted and guilty when I left Burtonport to come and be with Máire here. For years I told myself that I wouldn't know *what to say to you, and convinced myself that you wouldn't want to hear from me. And it was easy, not talking to you, because I knew that Máire didn't want me to. For so long, I just had to focus on her, on trying to make her better. But I should have tried to do more to make things right between the two of you. Between me and you, too.*

I know that you and Máire have been in touch on occasion. I've seen your Christmas cards, so she must have told you when we've changed address. But I don't know if the two of you've really talked since your mother died. I'm so sorry you had to go through that alone, Ró. I wanted to come back to Burtonport for the funeral, but Máire was so anxious about the pregnancy, and worried that she wouldn't be let back into the US again afterwards. Mostly, though, I think she was full of fear that if I saw you again I might think I'd made a mistake. That was the real reason, I'm sure.

What I'm trying to say is, please don't blame her too much for how things are. I know that people always thought that Máire was so bold, but that was always just a front for how frightened she really was. Whereas you've always been so entirely yourself.

If this is rock bottom, then the situation can only get better. If Máire gets the right help and medication, if she's able to see things as they are again, then I'm hopeful she'll want you to be a part of her life again. And Cora's.

I don't think I've ever written something this long, except maybe in my Leaving Cert exams. I should probably read it over and edit bits out, but I have to go and pick Cora up from the childminder now. So I'll print this off before it gets any longer.

I'm sure we learnt at school how to finish off a letter. Something to do with how well you know the person you're writing to. I can't remember. I'm sure you do.

I don't expect you to reply, especially with a letter as long as this one, but I would love to hear about your life. I always loved anything you wrote. I still have some of the stories you gave me when we were little. Do you still write? I hope so.

Bye for now,
Michael

March 1992

Dear Róisín,

Thank you for sending the card and game for Cora's birthday.
I still can't believe it — that you write the stories for video games.
I mean, I always knew you were going to write, but this was
unexpected. I had no idea you knew anything about video games.
I thought for some reason you were working as a teacher.

I still haven't got round to buying whatever it is you need to play
it on. But I'm sure Cora will love it. And of course I recognize the
cover! How did you get the painting back? What's going on at the
Screamers' house these days? Will there ever just be a normal
family living there?

Máire's doing better, but she's not leaving the apartment much.
The doctor's said that part of recovery from mania is needing your
world to be smaller. She has a new agent, though, who wants to run
a small show to relaunch her as an artist. So that's taking up a lot
of her time. She won't show me anything she's working on. But I
can tell she's motivated. This whole time reminds me of after Cora
was born and Máire got badly depressed and did nothing for about
six months. But after that she did those birth drawings that got
picked up by Gracie Mansion and things kind of took off for her.
But it worries me that this might happen all over again sometime
in the future. I keep reminding myself we know what's really
wrong now. We have the right medication. I just have to make sure
she keeps on taking it.

Anyway, I took Cora out for her birthday without Máire because she didn't want to go into the city. We went to the zoo, which Cora didn't like much. She said she didn't think it was right for them to have a polar bear in New York City. It was still pretty much a winter day here, but she was worrying about it being much too hot for him in the summer. I know everyone thinks their kids are smarter than other kids, but I really think she is for just seven! She read the sign in front of his cage and noticed that the polar bear was the same age as she is. So now she wants us to come back on every birthday to see how he's doing.

She reminds me so much of what Máire was like when we were younger. Brilliant, but in a way that was always heavy. So it worries me whenever Cora seems brilliant. Is that terrible, to wish that she wouldn't be so brilliant, to want her to be normal?

Do you ever think that we shouldn't have sent Máire's drawings to the Screamers, that if we hadn't she might have been happier? I used to think that art would be the thing that saved her, but maybe it's just screwed her up? She didn't ask for us to do what we did. Maybe she'd have given up drawing if she hadn't won the residency, and overall that would have been better. Maybe she'd have just done some other job and been good at that instead. But then I think that it's nothing to do with art and just to do with the kind of person Máire is – that whatever she did she'd be the same.

When I first got to New York, she looked like a totally different person. So gaunt and thin. Left arm covered in tattoos. Puzzle pieces. I knew, then, that I was right to have come, awful as it was leaving you. Then I noticed the crook of her elbow. The puncture marks. I wanted to talk to you then, so much. But I didn't want you to know, either. How bad it was. It was scary. I wanted to protect you from that. And it felt like it was all my fault, my problem to solve. For years, really, there was so much to do, to create a life for her that would be safe and stable. I never could have done it if I wasn't able to convince myself that the point of my life was to hold Máire together. But I doubted it sometimes. Often, even. It wasn't easy. Then, when Cora came along, it made more sense. Having this safe, reliable job. Because, if I didn't, Cora's life would be all chaos. Then again, I'd probably have been like this anyway. It suits me, the work I do. I like that it's boring and normal. I like not having to think about myself. I like being high up in the sky, dealing with numbers. It makes me realize that we're all so small. I find that comforting, somehow.

Yet here I am at work, writing you this letter. All these words. And all about me!

I want to know more about you. Tell me everything. It brought me back, seeing the house again, on the tape. I try not to think about that time too much, to be honest. You must know that Burtonport never really felt like home to me. I didn't fit in, obviously. Your father accepted me, but I stuck out like a sore thumb. I couldn't believe it when I arrived here and all of a sudden I was invisible. Which sounds bad but when you've always felt like the boy everyone's staring at all the time, it was such a relief! People are always surprised when I tell them I'm Irish. It's like they don't even notice my accent because I don't look like I would be from Ireland. And I guess that half of me isn't. Sometimes I wonder whether my father might actually have been American. I find myself looking into the eyes of black men who seem the right sort of age on the street, on the subway. Trying to catch a glimpse of myself. I know that's mad. Other times I see black families and wonder what my life would have been like if I hadn't always been the only one. But at least I don't feel like I stand out all the time here. And Cora – hopefully she'll feel normal. There are loads of families here where the kids look different to the parents, mixed *families. Anyway, Cora takes more after Máire. I guess because Máire is so pale. I've enclosed a photo that was pinned over my desk here. I should have thought about sending it sooner. Don't you think she looks like Máire did when she was a kid? She smiles a lot more than your sister though, that's for sure.*

Yours sincerely (thanks for the lesson),
Michael

May 1992

Dear Róisín,

I'm sorry it's taken me a while to reply. I was quite shocked, and a bit hurt you hadn't told me what my mother had told you sooner.

But I've thought about it some more, and I'm thankful that you wrote it down, that I have it written as a story now. I'm also glad my mother felt able to tell you before she died, that she didn't go to the grave not telling anyone.

It's good to know that I was born out of something positive. As I got older I became convinced that either my mother hadn't told me about my father because she was having sex with all kinds of men for money, so didn't know who he was, or I thought I must have been the result of rape. I would think about the fact that she must have begged for me not to be black when she was pregnant, knowing there must have been a chance I would be. But now I know she wanted my father, I can believe she wanted me as well.

Of course I still want to talk to you. I just needed a bit of time.

We're all OK here. The show for Máire's new paintings opens next week, and it'll be her birthday. And writing that has made me realize that I missed your birthday. I'm sorry I didn't send a card or anything. I should have remembered, especially as it's the same month as Cora's. Did you do something fun to celebrate?

I don't have much else to report which must be a good sign. I hope all's well with you too. I'm sorry also to hear you lost Máire's painting of the house, but I'm glad it made it into one of your games.

Michael

PS I've included the flyer for Máire's show. Did you already know about her artist name? A lot of artists were using fake names when she first started getting into the art scene, for visa reasons. That's no longer an issue since Reagan legalized the aliens (one good thing he did!), but Máire's therapist said it would be wise for her to keep using the name, to protect herself more generally. I don't think she'd cope that well being recognized by people. And apparently people are talking about the new paintings. At least that's what her agent says.

The paintings are a lot more abstract than her previous stuff. I mean, her art's always been dark, but it seems impenetrable to me now. I don't understand it, to be honest, but I have to trust that she is working through some stuff, and that this is a good outlet. I'm sure you'd be able to see more in them than I do. I've never been good at figuring out hidden meanings. But I'm told they're there.

August 1992

Dear Ró,

I don't know how to start this. Thank you for telling me, first of all. You've been carrying around such a big thing. There isn't much about the story I can find over here, so I only really know what you have told me. I want to ask if it is true, about Scarlett, why she's been arrested. I want to ask how much you knew, but it's probably dangerous for you to say, so don't write anything that might be incriminating (not that I'm accusing you of anything). Thank you, though, for telling me about your relationship. I'll admit, I was surprised, but I was also pleased to know you found someone, there in Burtonport, that you haven't been on your own. And thank God you still have the Atlan house so you can hide away there a bit.

I'm worried for you, though. Is your lawyer good? Do you have people you can talk to? That house – you know I don't go in for anything people used to say about it, but weird stuff always happens there. Maybe we'd all have been better off if we'd stayed away from it. Maybe you could move away from Burtonport, sell up and try someplace new, where there might be more people like you? Why don't you go to college? Lots of people go as mature students. I bet you'd love it – you'd be smarter than all of them. Maybe this is all for the best.

I'm doing OK. Work's the same. I've got obsessed with the upcoming election. Don't know how I'll cope if Bush is re-elected, so I've been throwing myself into volunteering for the Clinton

367

campaign. It's been great meeting like-minded people, to feel a part of something, trying to create change.

As for Máire, things have been up and down. She's got really into going to mass and insists on taking Cora with her. I'm not totally against this, but I do think there are better things Cora could be doing on Sunday mornings. We've argued about it — because Cora's taking her first communion this year and I can't believe how cracked it all seems to me now as an adult. Seven-year-olds confessing their sins, dressed up like miniature brides. The girls have been told they're not to take the wine on the actual day in case they spill it down their dresses. I mean, what's the point in the whole fecking thing if they're not even going to be imbued with the blood of Christ? It makes me think that so much of growing up in Ireland was messed up, and how much of Ireland has been messed up by religion. And yet it's the one thing Máire seems really insistent on, that Cora goes to mass.

Máire has a new studio space over in Astoria so she's been spending a lot of time there, working. She's forgotten to pick Cora up from school on a few occasions. Other days she gets migraines and has to stay in bed all day with the lights off. Then there are the strange compulsive things she does which she tries to hide but I notice and I'm sure Cora has picked up on too. Sometimes Máire tries to turn these things into a game with Cora, like 'Don't step on the cracks'. But I want my child to step on the bleeding cracks. I don't want her looking down her whole life, fearful of things.

The city's a bit of a mess to be honest. The Aids thing has been just terrible, though they say now that people are living for longer. At least here people are trying to fight it. I was so mad when I found out about the Church in Ireland trying to deny it — though not surprised. I tried to use this to argue that Máire shouldn't be taking Cora to mass, but that didn't go down well. Máire knows more people than I do who have it or who have died from it – most of them people she was friends with before I came here, when she was living with a group of other artists in the Bronx. She could have got it so easily then. I dread to think. There was a time when Máire was going to funerals a lot, but she would never tell me when she was going to one or talk to me about how she knew the person. She'd just come home wearing this creepy black veil thing like she was one of those old Irish widows. God knows where she got it from. I heard her talking to Cora about Aids a while back – last year maybe – and at first I wanted to tell her to stop, that Cora was too young and didn't need to know. But she explained it in a really simple and compassionate way and it made me realize we should be telling our kids about this, not hiding it. Sometimes, when I'm most concerned Máire's going to say or do something that will mess Cora up, the thing she actually says is perfect, and I remember she's a good mother, that we're both just trying to do our best.

Máire's show went well. Obviously I was just so proud of her. I wanted to go back in time and tell the kid versions of ourselves about it. Watching her, though, from across the gallery, I had the sense that she'd become this other person – a version of herself that, for all our history, I would never be able to understand.

Some of her pieces are being auctioned off to buyers or galleries. I'm not really clear on how it works, but I'm glad other people are seeing that she's brilliant. And it will be good to actually get some money for all the work she's done. It means we can probably send Cora to a private middle school. Máire seems set on her going to a Catholic one, though, which I'm not sure about.

Do you ever think you might just get a phone so we could talk properly? I'm worried about you, with the arrest and all. Letters make you seem somehow even further away than when we just *weren't talking. Hey, that reminds me, did you hear about that married couple who are in space together, right now? They hid that they were married, to NASA! You must know, you always loved space stuff in the paper. What I'm saying is, when I heard your voice through the phone, it felt like everything else just disappeared. We could have been in space together. It felt like home.*

Michael

February 1993

Dear Ró,

I'm fine. I tried calling your neighbour afterwards but the call wouldn't go through. Please get a phone, Ró.

Everyone's saying it's amazing more people weren't killed. One of the victims was pregnant, though, which is too awful to think about. I didn't know any of the people who died – 50,000 people work in the towers and I was about as far away from the bomb as possible. But it was scary. We knew something bad had happened because the electricity went out right away. It was crazy how dark it went even though it was the middle of the day. It was snowing outside, so the sun wasn't getting through the clouds much. The evacuation alarm went on. They tell us when they're doing drills, because it causes so much disruption to the day, so we knew something had actually happened. The fire guy on our floor came round shouting at everyone to get out and take the stairs. People started grabbing their stuff, and we started going down. ALL THE WAY DOWN. In the dark with no emergency lights. The first few flights everyone kept falling over because the handrail stopped before the steps did. I guess that gave us all something to focus on, counting the steps so we'd know where the handrail would stop so we wouldn't fall. After a couple of dozen flights I guess my legs were able to remember for themselves how many steps there were between the flat bits. Because instead of counting the steps I was thinking about Cora, how I needed to get back to her. I was

371

thinking about how I overheard her telling her friends after school not so long ago that her dad worked at the World Train Center. And I didn't correct her, because I love the things that kids mishear, how it can change their whole understanding of the world.

I tell you, I never want to walk down a flight of steps again. It felt like I was in some kind of nightmare where the steps would never end. At points the smoke was pretty bad and we didn't know if it was just going to get worse, if going down was even the right thing to do. It took over four hours. I could hardly stand by the time we got out, loads of people were collapsed in the plaza, emergency services people everywhere, flashing lights and sirens. But mostly all I could think was how good the fresh air was. I turned around and it was so surreal, almost like the towers weren't there, not a single light in the windows. I didn't have my coat and it was snowing but I walked all the way home over the Brooklyn Bridge. It was freezing. I knew that Máire would be frantic, but it didn't cross my mind to stop at a phone box. I just had to get home.

Poor Cora. I could tell that she could tell that something bad had happened. She was just standing there, in the hall. 'You're so cold,' she said when she ran over to hug me. 'You smell like smoke. Did something go wrong with the trains?'

'Clearly must have done for it to take your daddy so long to get home,' Máire said. She was referring to the subway but I knew what Cora had really meant. I crouched down and kissed her on the nose, then looked up at Máire whose face was pale and cold. I was pissed off at her then, for not being simply happy I was home safe.

They're trying to find us some emergency office space as no one is allowed to go back into the towers until they're confirmed as safe – and apparently that might be months. On the plus side, they'll probably be the safest buildings in the city after the investigation.

I'll let you know when I have a new address for you to send letters to. It feels strange, writing from the apartment. It's Sunday. Máire and Cora are at mass. I spent all of yesterday kind of in shock. My legs are still like lead. When I put Cora to bed I explained that my job wasn't actually to do with trains, that where I work is called the World Trade Center. I asked if she knew what trade meant and she said, 'Yeah, it's like when you want a different smelly gel pen and you swap it with someone else at school.'

'Exactly,' I said. 'So that's kind of what my work is like, but with money. I'm just an accountant though.'

'What's an accountant?' she asked.

'I sort of keep track of the trades, and make sure that the money goes to the right people.'

'Ah,' she said, kind of disappointed-looking. 'So it's nothing to do with trains?'

'Nothing to do with trains.'

I'm sure that wasn't exactly what we both said. It's different, trying to remember actual conversations rather than just your own thoughts about something. But I enjoy it so much when you do it.

Take care of yourself. I hope you're coping OK with the trial preparation and that you're finding time to do things for yourself. It makes me smile to think of you still swimming. I should start going to the pool. It's not the same as the sea, though. I do miss it. And you.

Michael

April 1993

Dear Ró,

We're back in the tower! This morning we all had 'Welcome Back' mugs and torches on our desks, and we get 10 per cent off in the mall all month. I should really bring Cora to the Borders. They have this talking tree in the kids' section she would love. You would, too.

Máire was concerned about me going back to work in the towers. She's been more nervy than usual since the bombing. Not leaving the apartment much. She came with us to Central Park for Cora's birthday back before the bombing but even then it was like she couldn't even pretend to be happy. She said the zoo was 'grotesque'. Then when we walked to the Alice in Wonderland statue so Cora could sit in Alice's lap, Máire said the whole thing was 'tacky' which made Cora not even want to climb on it any more. I don't think we've done anything as a family since.

I'm sorry I missed your birthday again. I realize it must have been your thirtieth. I can't believe it, that it's been so long since we last saw each other, when you were still in school. I can't imagine you being thirty, though you always did seem grown up somehow, wiser than the rest of us.

It's no excuse, but everything's been pretty crazy for us since the bombing. Having to commute to Queens and trying to look after Máire and make sure Cora gets picked up from school. But I don't mean to just complain. It's great to be back up here. I get into the elevator and leave everything else behind on the ground floor.

How does Scarlett seem when you see her? That's a good thing she did for you. Having the house under your name, as well. How much are the legal costs likely to be?

I'm so relieved you're no longer under any suspicion. Don't let yourself be held back by all this though, Ró. It's not your job to stick by her. She did what she did. You have your own life to live.

Michael

June 1993

Dear Ró,

I keep thinking about you in that house. I imagine I'm standing out the front, waiting for you to appear through one of the windows. Then I remember when we were in there together, on the bathroom floor, our bodies casting shadows on the wall. I was drunk, but I remember realizing it was going to happen. And the next moment, it had. It was so easy. Sometimes I wish I could go back and have stayed instead. I want to know what that would have looked like. But I can't think like that. Things had to be how they happened because I have Cora.

I know it's not fair, me saying that I think about how it might have been different. Not fair to anyone. But I had to say it, Ró. And, I don't know, you being there in that house – maybe I'm just sad because I know your memories of the place are probably all to do with Scarlett.

When I first started writing to you, I was scared that maybe you hadn't moved on. But I found out that you had. And I don't know where that leaves me, because sometimes it feels like I've not moved on at all.

Michael

August 1993

Dear Ró,

I know you said that we should stop with the letters unless I was going to tell Máire. But I need to talk to someone. Not just someone — you. Sorry that this is coming out of nowhere but I'm just going to write it all down.

Last week Máire told me that one of her professors from when she was at NYU had died. I could tell she was really affected by it even though she'd never said anything about this professor before. She said she was going to go to the funeral. I offered to go with her, but she told me the funeral was in Vermont. This surprised me, as Máire never leaves the city. But she booked flights and packed up her funeral outfit — the veil and everything — and off she went. Then she came back two days later, clearly not well. She looked like she hadn't slept and the things she was saying weren't making much sense. I asked if she'd forgotten to take her meds, and she started shouting at me about how I'm always trying to control her and make her something she's not. Which is the fight we always have. It was the middle of the night and she was shouting, practically screaming, about how she should have tried to stop it, about how it was too late, like she thought it was the end of the world or something. She said she was being punished, that all of it was her being punished. Then she started yelling that the walls were closing in on her.

That was when I noticed Cora was there, her head peeking out from the hall. 'Daddy, make it better,' she said, when she realized

I had seen her. But Máire was just screaming. She wouldn't stop. It was like she couldn't even see that Cora was there, that her daughter was terrified.

I managed to get Cora back into bed. I said her mammy had had a bad dream and that I needed to help her understand she wasn't dreaming any more. I asked her to stay in her room and promised I'd come and check on her later. I told her to play the alphabet game in her head.

I went into the bathroom and got Máire's pills. I was surprised she didn't fight me, when I said that she needed to take them. She took them calmly, then lay down on the floor with her eyes closed. I got down beside her. She opened her eyes. I thought she was going to start screaming again but she just said really calmly, 'Promise me you won't abandon her, that you'll always look after her.'

'Of course I won't abandon her,' I said. 'Why would you even ask that?'

'I just couldn't tell you. I couldn't lose you. I needed you for Cora.'

'Tell me what?'

She turned over on to her side and looked right at me, about an inch from my face. 'You must know,' she said. 'It's obvious she's not yours.'

And you know what? I wasn't even shocked. I felt deadly calm.

She must have felt relieved, to have finally told me, for it to have come out. And I let her talk. She told me that she'd had an affair, when she was at NYU, with the professor who had died. He called it off and moved back to Vermont. She dropped out of school and got into drugs. She told me about the drugs part, after I got here. I guess I didn't ask too much about what had happened before. I was just focused on her getting better.

I built a life for us together. Got my accountancy qualification and got my job. Things were OK. Then Máire had her contraceptive coil taken out. She only told me about it afterwards. She said it wasn't a big deal, that it was due to be removed anyway. It made her periods heavier, and she didn't want to have to deal with that any more. Which is fair enough. So we were using condoms. I didn't think we were ready to have a child. We argued about that, more and more. She would say she didn't think I'd ever be ready. And she was right, really. Even though I knew I did want to be a father, I was scared about her being a mother, the way that she was. But I couldn't admit that to her, couldn't put it like that at least. Whenever I implied that she might be the one who wasn't ready, she'd argue that having a baby might be the thing that would fix her.

That must have been around the time that she met up with him again, the professor. He came to one of her shows, apparently. I can even remember the night it must have been, because we got into a big fight when she got home. It was five in the morning. I was confused because she didn't seem drunk or high – but she did seem out of it. And she was vague when I asked her why she was back so late and who she had been with. I guess I was suspicious. I'd seen her flirting with people before, when she was with her art friends. That was why I stopped going to events with her. She'd always leave me on my own and I didn't fit in with her friends. She'd act like a different person around them. It makes more sense to me, now. But I found it hard to understand, then, why she was always seeking attention, especially from men. It was like she wasn't able to resist other people taking an interest in her – even with me right there in the room. So I stopped going with her to parties. She often got back very late, very drunk. Of course I suspected that she might have cheated on me. But I turned a blind eye to it, because she always came home.

She still needed me, and that was just enough for me to still think
what we had was worth it. No one else had known her as long as
I had (except you, of course). But I was resentful, sure. Knowing
that she showed this shiny side of herself to other people, while I got
the version that would stay in bed all day crying, who would make
me promise not to leave her.

Anyway, that night, after we argued, we had sex without a
condom. I thought I would be able to pull out, like I used to.
I can't believe how reckless I was before, with you too. I guess I was
better at it then. It had been years since I'd had to think about
controlling it.

When she told me she was pregnant, I was the one suddenly
believing what she'd told me. That maybe it would fix it, fix us.
She was so worried about it, which oddly made me calmer.
I convinced myself that it was a good thing she was anxious,
because it meant she was taking it seriously. We did all the right
things. I got the books and read up everything about pregnancy
and parenting. We stopped drinking, we gave up smoking, we
went to classes. Cora was born and, yeah, her skin was fairly pale,
but she was darker than Máire and lighter than I was. I guess
I didn't want to even contemplate the possibility that she wasn't
mine, because I loved that little bawling baby so damn much.

I'm probably still in shock, but the main thought I have right
now is that it doesn't really change anything. I still feel like it's my
job to stop Máire from spiralling, like I can't be outraged or act
out. I can't just leave — even for a few days to clear my head —
because I'm worried about Máire, leaving Cora alone with her.
I know she'd never hurt Cora, but she's a danger to herself, and
Cora needs stability. She needs me.

But I'm realizing my life has never been my own. Máire's
always had this power over me. It's not like I was happier without

her, back in Burtonport, after she left. You know I was a mess then. I don't know what would have happened if she hadn't started calling. It pulled me out of this deep depression I was stuck in, a darkness that was hurting those around me, hurting you.

Still, I can't stop thinking about how uncomplicated it felt, being with you, besides the complication of Máire. I guess I was too young to see that perhaps the thing that drew me to Máire was her chaos – because it meant I didn't have to think about myself. But I liked thinking about myself with you, Ró. All the conversations we had, every direction they went in. And you were always kind, never cruel. I've never been able to talk to Máire like this.

I don't know, maybe now's the time to tell her we've been talking. Maybe the only way through all this is for there to be no more secrets. Because if I know one thing, it's that I don't want to lose you again. I've hated not being able to write to you. Every day at work I check my mail and hope you might have changed your mind, that you'll have written after all. I feel high each morning, getting to the office. Then, when I don't see your handwriting in my in-tray – I don't know how to explain it other than this falling feeling.

I know you probably won't reply to this either, until I've told you that I've told Máire. I think I will, because I don't know if I can continue to carry this on my own. Too much has gone wrong. More than anything I want you to know Cora, for her to know her Aunt Ró, the amazing woman who writes video games and has read more books than anyone I know. I want you to see New York. Damn it, I want you here, Ró. Please say you'll come. We need you. I need you.

Michael

September 1993

Róisín,

Máire is missing. She left your letter open on our bed. And now she's gone. I know I told you I would tell her, but you don't know what it's been like. I thought you understood how fragile she was, but you were clearly just thinking about yourself. How could you write those things, about how she should leave me? Why didn't you tell me about the baby? How could you do that without telling me? How could you still not have told me, not in any of your letters, after everything I've told you? Having to read about it like that.

    I'm trying not to feel angry with you. I know I am to blame as well. But I am angry. Did you never trust me at all?

Michael

. . .

Róisín,

She was found in Flushing Creek. They knew it was her, from the tattoos, but I made them uncover more of her, to be sure, when I went to identify the body. They're saying she must have jumped, or fallen, from one of the bridges.

I've told Cora. She took the news very calmly, which made me cry, so she was the one comforting me. 'Don't worry, Daddy,' she said. 'She's in heaven now.'

I don't believe in heaven, but I know that Máire did. For the first time, I'm glad she took Cora to mass, so she can believe in heaven too.

I don't think I can bear to hear from you again, even though I know she did this so that I could be with you. She must have seen it as a way to be right with God again, to give herself up so me and you and Cora could be a family. But I know in my heart that it wouldn't fix things. How could it come to any good? We'd be living in the past, trying to fix it rather than moving on. If her death gives us anything, it will be the freedom to start again – to live our lives, not together, but apart.

I know I said I wanted you to know Cora, but I wouldn't be able to live with that now, not when we're the reason her mother's dead. I have to go forward, for Cora, make sure she isn't tainted by all this. I could drag her back into the past, or I can give her a future free from it.

We shouldn't have done what we did when we did it. We knew it was wrong, back then. Máire was right – we had to stay away from you. I need my life now to be away from you, too.

Please don't write to me again.

August 2001

Dear Róisín,

I can't count how many times I have started writing this and not been able to finish, deleted everything I wrote and got on with my life. But it always comes back, the thought that I should write to you.

After I sent my last letter, I deleted the folder where the rest of them were saved. I didn't want to be reminded of what I'd said. Though I still have yours, and read them more often than I'd like to admit.

I can't remember exactly what I wrote, after Máire died, but I know it was hateful. I regret what I said about how we should never speak again. I wanted to believe it because I thought it would be easier. But it hasn't been easy. Nearly eight years, and it doesn't feel any easier.

I don't know if you still live in the Screamers' house, but somehow it feels right that this letter will end up there — back where it all started. I still think about the time I took you there, how you cleaned my leg with such care. It stung so much, being cared for like that.

I imagine you there, but part of me hopes you have left, that you won't ever read this because you're happy someplace else. That you've been able to move on, at least.

You were right — what you said in your letter to Máire. I have it here in the office because I can't bear the thought of Cora ever finding it. But at the same time I keep wondering whether it might

384

be time to tell her, for her to know everything. 'We're only as sick as our secrets,' you wrote. I regret cutting you out when all you did was tell the truth. I was the coward.

I've found myself feeling anxious lately, about what would happen to Cora if something happened to me. I don't know why. After Máire died, all I focused on was simply getting through each day. That was all that mattered. But recently something's changed in my head. At night I lie awake for hours, not able to stop my thoughts from racing. Then, whenever I do get to the point where I'm falling asleep, my body jolts me awake again, and my heart starts thudding really hard in my chest. Then I'm worrying about that as well as not being able to sleep.

The thoughts are to do with Cora. She hardly eats, and sometimes she seems out of it in a way that reminds me of what Máire was like when she was Cora's age. I spent so long just trying to keep the two of us going, that I didn't stop to think where we were going. Now I worry that we've been going nowhere, that we never really dealt with Máire's death. And maybe it's catching up with us. Maybe that's why I'm writing to you now.

I want more, Róisín. More for all of us. I want Cora to know you. I want to know that she would be OK if anything ever happened to me, that you'd be there for her. But I know that is a lot to ask. She's sixteen and she seems . . . lost. Maybe it's normal, but I worry. I worry and worry about her but I don't know what to do about it. And I feel so guilty, all the time.

The truth is I wasn't honest with you. It was my fault that Máire did what she did. It wasn't just your letter. I knew she hadn't been taking her pills, you see, so I'd been crushing them up and putting them in her drinks, to make sure she always took them. I did it for the first time that night when she told me I wasn't Cora's father. I lied in my letter to you, said she was calm when

385

I came back from putting Cora into bed. But she wasn't. I had to get her to drink a cup of tea and I'd crushed pills into it, benzos. It calmed her down enough to sleep, so I just kept doing it, giving her more. I was always in charge of her medication anyway, because a lot of the time she didn't want to take it. I went to the doctor and pretended I wasn't sleeping – well, I didn't really have to pretend. But I didn't take the pills myself. I gave them to her. I just knew they made things easier. I should have taken her back to the doctor, but she didn't want to see any more doctors.

On that day – the day she got your letter – I had already crushed up four pills and put them in her tea. But I didn't tell the cops this, when I went down to the station to report that she was missing. They said that there was nothing they could do, given that Máire was an adult and she had the freedom to go wherever she wanted. They advised me to go home, and I did. I had left Cora with the neighbour. After I got her to bed I took a shower and found myself staring at the medicine cabinet door, the mirror all steamed up. I don't know if I opened it because I thought maybe I would take something to help me sleep or if it was because I sensed something was up. I opened the cabinet. The worst thing was I couldn't tell if there were fewer pills than there should have been. I couldn't be sure.

The drugs came up in the autopsy, of course. But my lawyer pointed out the obvious. Máire had access to the medicine cabinet at home, didn't she? And hadn't she previously tried to take her life? The cops might have thought I was negligent for letting her have access to all the pills, but they didn't suspect that I had been drugging her. I got away with it.

I didn't ever really blame you, Ró. I blamed myself. I was the one who had never been honest. I don't know if I even knew how to be honest. It was only afterwards that I started reading about how dangerous taking too many of those pills could be.

I just wanted it to stop, Ró. I wanted her to be better. Or really, I didn't want to have to deal with it any more. I didn't expect you to send her a letter, and that was an easy thing to be angry about. But even if you hadn't written the letter, it would have ended badly. As much as I had said that I was going to tell Máire about us, I don't know if I would have done. I became addicted to it, I guess, trying to control the situation.

Of course, at times I've told myself that it could have been even worse if I hadn't been doing what I was doing. Maybe she would have done worse if she'd been unmedicated when she got your letter. Maybe she'd have taken Cora with her. I let myself believe that for years, though I knew she'd never have hurt Cora. The only difference would have been that we'd have fought about it. She'd have confronted me with the letter and all hell would have broken loose. But at least that would have had me face up to what I had been doing, writing to you. Instead she must have been calm leaving the apartment. Perhaps there's a small bit of mercy in that. But I can't believe it. She died alone, and my actions meant I didn't get the chance to try and stop her, to try and make things right again. You were the one trying to do that.

I've typed out and deleted too many versions of this letter now. This time I will send it, in the hope that I might one day hear your voice again, see your face again. I want to start living, Ró. Not living in the past. Living in the present, with you.

Michael

The Attic

You light the way forward with your stolen lamp. The walls appear to shrink back as you pass, retreating from the light. You get to the bottom of the forbidden staircase. The steps creak, as if shrieking in pain. You tread, softly as you can, along a narrow passageway.

At the end of the passage is a small door, halfway up the wall. The door is locked.

You think of the keys the headmistress carries always on her person. You wonder where she keeps them when she's sleeping.

Knock, knock, knock.

It's your secret code. Your sister.

Your energy is low. Do you start searching the school for the keys, in the cover of night, or recharge so you can use your power?

(A or B?)

Lyca Brady

New York and Burtonport

2018

I

The letters were in my hand luggage, on the plane. Luggage in the hold could easily get lost. I knew this from the story my mother told the world about herself.

It was after Christmas, but before New Year – that period that stretches while you're in it, then shrinks impossibly after it has passed. We were flying business class, Dublin to JFK, but the relative luxury of this was lost on me, since I'd never been on a plane before. Besides, the plane had Wi-Fi, so I was mostly elsewhere while we were actually in the air.

. . .

Exactly seven months had passed since the phone call from St Brigid's. I can remember dropping the phone after, how it seemed to fall for ever before the cord went taut. It swung back and forth, just above the skirting board.

A nurse was waiting at the entrance to St Brigid's. I didn't have to sign in at reception. 'I'm sorry for your loss,' the nurse said, kindly. I probably knew her by name, but I couldn't tell you who it was.

Gaga was laid out on the bed, on top of the covers. Her mouth was open. I wondered if that was just what happened to bodies, when they were dead, if the undertaker then used a special trick or technique to get the mouth to close again, after. Or had she died like that, looking terrified? I wanted to know, and I didn't want to know at all.

I hadn't noticed that Cora was already there. They must have reached her on her mobile, while she was running. She was sitting in the chair next to the bed. She appeared to be crying, and she was holding one of Gaga's dead white hands, whispering things to the body. I didn't know what to do, so I just stood there, staring.

I was numb, I guess. It didn't feel real.

It didn't feel real, either, the next day, when I went to get the letters. I have no memory of actually going through the hatch, but I know that I emerged with the USA biscuit tin, Cora's old Pentax and a copy of *Scream School*, the cassette still wrapped in cellophane.

Cora was out, meeting the funeral director. In my room, I took the letters out of the tin and used a screwdriver to remove a panel from my old Dell computer. I hid the letters in there.

The Pentax was black plastic with red accents – red shutter button, tiny red print that said AUTO FOCUS, a black-and-red striped strap so you could hold the camera round your neck. It had textured bumps on the side, to make it easier to hold on to with one hand. I couldn't turn it on, though. The batteries had probably corroded inside, the internet informed me.

When Cora got home, I brought the camera to her. I showed her the empty tin, too. 'It must be really old,' I said. 'Do you remember the tins ever being like that?' But she was trying to figure out how to open up the camera.

'Hopefully the film hasn't been ruined,' she said.

'You can take videos on that thing?' I asked.

'My digital baby,' Cora said. I didn't realize she meant me, not the camera.

. . .

After I read the letters, I hid them back inside my Dell computer. I had searched for everything I wanted to know on that computer. The Dell had given me answers, even if they weren't always the ones I was looking for. I slept with the screwdriver under my mattress, like a character in a book.

What the letters revealed – that Michael wasn't Cora's biological father, and that he had played a part in her mother's death – felt explosive. Of course I thought about giving them to Cora. If anyone had a right to read the letters, it was her. But Gaga hadn't ever told her. She'd hidden the letters instead. But wouldn't she have destroyed them, if she hadn't wanted the letters to be found? My head went round and round in circles like a carousel.

Cora had thrown herself into the funeral arrangements. She wouldn't let me help, because I was supposed to be revising. But I wasn't revising. I wasn't really sleeping or speaking or eating, either. I felt like a ghost.

. . .

The day was beautiful for the funeral. Fuchsia in the hedgerows on the walk to the church, the flowers mostly closed. I wanted to pop the ones that hadn't opened, expose the purple petals hidden inside, like I had done as a child. Cora was explaining that she'd been trying to arrange compassionate bail for Scarlett, but her request had been denied, since Gaga and Scarlett hadn't been married.

I'd not really been listening, but my ears pricked when Cora mentioned Scarlett, sending signals to my brain that made my whole face flush. Had Cora previously been in contact with Scarlett? I tried to remember how much I was supposed to know about her. Not the character in Gaga's diaries. Not the villain on the internet. The actual person who was still alive. She'd be grieving, like we were.

'But they couldn't have been married,' I said, suddenly angry. 'Gay marriage only became legal three years ago.'

We followed our lengthy shadows on the tarmac. I saw Cora's shadow arm reaching out before I felt her grab my hand. She'd stopped walking, which made my body twist to face her when I tried to take another step.

'Lyca Brady,' Cora said, her face full of surprise. 'Is that injustice I see blazing in your eyes? You really are my daughter, after all.'

She rarely saw herself in me. I allowed her the moment.

. . .

Cora gave the eulogy. I haven't a clue what she said. It was like I was watching the service through a screen, with the volume down low.

In the letters, Michael had said that Róisín had written 'we're only as sick as our secrets' in her letter to Máire. This was something both Cora and Gaga had said to me, throughout my childhood. Secrets could eat a person up. That much

I knew. It was better to have things out in the open. But we didn't do that as a family. Not really.

There were the things you presented to people – your stories. Then there were the things you never confessed to a soul – your secrets. That was how we existed, how we knew ourselves at all.

The days went by, and it was always easier not to tell. Cora was busy. She had found a way to have the photos from her Pentax developed and digitized. She was talking to the director of the documentary quite often at night, on Skype. They were on first-name terms.

Emily wanted Cora to come to New York, so she could film an interview. 'She seems very interested in my story,' Cora told me. 'She said it's helpful that I already have a public profile.'

The more Cora talked about the documentary, the more I held on to the letters, keeping them from her. Michael's voice was often in my head, this man we shared a surname with whose voice I'd never heard, who wasn't actually related to me or Cora. I held on to the idea of him, though. He had stuck with Cora even when he discovered that he wasn't her real father. This made him the kind of father that I had always wanted. I wanted to keep him for myself.

. . .

Not long after, Cora started going through Gaga's diaries.

'They might be a way to help Scarlett,' she explained, as justification. Now Gaga was gone, it wouldn't matter if it came out that she'd been an accomplice. It might help reduce Scarlett's sentence. 'Anyway,' Cora added, 'it's not like she kept them a secret.'

How could I explain that the shock on my face had nothing to do with principle, with privacy? I was just afraid of being found out, fearful that the diaries would somehow tell Cora that I'd already read them.

I was more likely to betray myself, though. 'You might not find what you're looking for in them,' I said to Cora, about the diaries. My mouth felt like a loaded gun. Whenever I opened it, something strange would come out, like I'd been possessed by a spirit.

I was realizing, I think, that Gaga might have stopped writing anything new in the diaries precisely because she wanted to protect Scarlett. There wouldn't be anything in them about the trial. She didn't want her words to be turned into evidence.

I waited for Cora to realize the truth about the diaries. What had taken me weeks to figure out, she understood in under an hour. She must have skipped right over the plot, straight to the point.

'This is insane,' I heard her shout from Gaga's room, next door.

The diaries were all fanned out around her on the floor. She was still flipping through one of them.

'What?' I asked, willing my face to be blank.

'There's nothing after 1981,' she said. 'Nothing.'

'But lots of the dates are later than that,' I said. 'Aren't they?' Even playing dumb made me seem to know too much.

'They're all just the same stories. Nothing new. She just kept writing about what had already happened.'

'Aren't all diaries about what's already happened?' I asked.

'All right, smart-arse.' She used her hands to push herself up off the floor. 'Read them if you want,' she told me. 'Don't expect to see anything about yourself in there, though. We're not in it.'

She was like a hurt child who thought the whole world revolved around them, dismissing Gaga's story because she didn't feature in it. She wasn't mature enough for the letters, I was now sure. I didn't want them to be turned into evidence, for Róisín and Michael to become the accused, responsible for blowing up everything Cora thought she knew about herself.

2

We crossed the Atlantic Ocean, suspended in the sky. The whole time I felt high.

Cora was asleep, or pretending to be – her seat reclined, neck supported by one of those doughnut travel pillows. I was too wired to even close my eyes, my thoughts wound up like swirls inside a marble.

. . .

Not long after Gaga's funeral, I'd searched on eBay for a Commodore 64, and negotiated my way through a bidding war. I waited for it to arrive from England, and finally got it working after getting help from a man in Mongolia who'd replied to the troubleshooting question I'd posted on an online forum.

I'd thought about telling Sanjeet what I was doing. I wondered whether he might even still have the original tape we played, if it was still inside his father's Commodore 64. I thought of us playing it together in our separate bedrooms, messaging each other on our phones at the same time. But I was scared he might not remember us finding the cassettes in the attic, though I could remember him saying the game wasn't good, when we played it. Perhaps that was part of it. He hadn't cared about the game and I didn't want to admit that I was still searching for something. Completing the game, getting to the ending, was something I had to do alone.

The problem was, I was no better at guessing the commands, now I was older. I tried my best to think how Gaga would have thought, but I wasn't able to. How much had I known about her, really? I would get stuck and it would drive me crazy. Then I'd read the letters, hoping there would be some clue hidden in them. Gaga had sent a copy of the game to Cora in New York, via Michael. I could just ask Cora if she had played it. Maybe she'd be able to help me. But I didn't want Cora to know what I was doing in my room. The game felt connected to the letters, which felt connected to Gaga's diaries. Companion pieces. I didn't want to share any of them with her.

I was obsessed, like I had been in my Sims years. But this obsession was more frustrating. In the Sims, I was God. I could pause time or speed it up. I could design and delete. In Gaga's game, I was powerless. She was the creator. Time would only pass if I was able to understand what she wanted me to do.

For the first time, when Cora spoke about her 'higher power' it didn't make me roll my eyes. I had always thought this vague kind of faith just made coping easier when life didn't work out the way you wanted it to. 'Everything happens for a reason,' Cora would say, whenever anything bad happened to me when I was younger. I had never found the sentiment comforting.

But when I found myself really stuck, I closed my eyes and asked Gaga for guidance. I remembered the manuscript.

I waited for Cora to go to AA, watching from the window

on the upstairs landing as her car disappeared from view. I ran downstairs and turned the lights on in the tea room. I went over to the cabinet and opened the bottom drawer. I was worried Cora might have done something with it – she'd started going through more of Gaga's things – but it was still there. I lifted the manuscript out of the drawer, holding it carefully. I took it up to my room and made space for it on the floor. The pencil marks were faded, but I could still make out the writing, just about, if I shone my phone torch at the paper. I remembered how the pages had looked like a treasure map to me, before. All I had to do was use it to help me get to the end of the game.

But as Gaga had said to me and Sanjeet once, video games weren't the same as novels or films. There wasn't just a single storyline. It was up to the player to decide which way to go. I still had to make my own decisions, choose my own adventure.

I made my way through the game. It seemed like there would be a happy ending. The sisters, after being estranged for a while, eventually work together, using their powers to uncover the school's secret: the headmistress has been cursing the students, sacrificing their bodies in exchange for her own eternal youth. With the headmistress in exile, the school is facing closure. The sisters don't know where they will end up. They stand there, at the top of the steps, holding hands. The front door closes behind them and the final question appears on the screen.

THERE'S JUST ONE CHOICE LEFT TO MAKE. COM-BINE YOUR POWERS TO DESTROY THE SCHOOL FOR

GOOD AND IN DOING SO BECOME MERE MORTALS,
OR KEEP YOUR POWERS AND RISK THE SCHOOL
BEING FOR EVER HAUNTED.

(A or B?)

I sat staring at the screen for what felt like a very long time. Obviously, the right thing to do would be to sacrifice the powers and destroy the school. The sisters wouldn't need their powers any more. They had served their purpose. But I didn't want the school to be destroyed. It was my home.

'A' was the right answer. But my finger was hovering over the 'B' on the keyboard.

I knew exactly what would happen, before I even pressed the button. The school would remain in the background, and the sisters would let go of each other. They would go their separate ways, disappearing off the edges of the screen.

I almost couldn't watch it happen, even though that had been what had happened, in real life.

The game had never really been for Cora. It was for Máire. That's why Róisín used her sister's painting for the cover. It was Róisín's way of saying that she hoped they might be together again, in the future. They had the choice to make things right. *A or B*. But Máire hadn't found the game, and Róisín had stayed here in this house, haunted by its secrets.

3

I opened up my chat with Sanjeet, for probably the fourth or fifth time during the flight. *G2G*, was his last message – got to go. He often went offline suddenly like this, and I wouldn't know when he'd be back.

Whenever he came online it was like every bit of me lit up. After I messaged him to say Gaga had died, he said he wished he could be there to give me a hug. That sent a tingle through my body. It made me twist my wrists around, as if all this extra energy had just been created inside me and I had to find a way to get rid of the excess.

Mostly, when we messaged, we talked about nothing much, in the way that everyone does. He had finished his exams and needed to decide on his A levels. He thought he would do Latin, and English Literature of course, but he didn't know what else to take. I asked if he remembered any Irish and teased him when he started trying to remember basic phrases. I told him about Cora talking to the director, Emily. He told me again that he was going to be in New York after Christmas, staying with a school friend who was 'crazy rich'.

L: Cora's been saying we should go out there for the documentary.
S: And you'd come too?

L: Yeah, on holiday.
S: Wouldn't it be cool if we ended up being there at the same time?
L: Can you imagine?
S: I can, funnily enough.
L: Me too, weirdly.
S: It kinda wouldn't even be weird though.
L: Yeah, I know.

I had already started writing these conversations down, into the same notebook I used to bring with me to St Brigid's. There was this whole section in it of things Sanjeet had helped me to remember about Gaga. The section had subsections. *Meals she made. Things she said. Games we played.*

Sanjeet's memories mixed up with mine. Sometimes we played Alphabet I Spy. When I used 'wall' as my answer, I told him Gaga used to knock between our rooms before I went to sleep each night. Our own secret code. Three knocks from her, then two from me, then a final one from her. At the end of this conversation, when we finally agreed that we should go to sleep, he sent me this message.

S: Knock knock knock
L: Knock knock
S: Knock
Now I'm just thinking knock doesn't even look like a real word.
L: It really doesn't.
S: I like talking to you, Lyca. Goodnight now.

That was my favourite conversation, but I wrote down every one of them. It seemed likely that Cora and I were going to come to New York at some point for the documentary. Sanjeet and I talked about what I might say to persuade Cora to plan the trip for just after Christmas. When I told him the good news I scribbled down our shared excitement. I wanted to jump forward, to the future. At the same time I was hungry for each second, soaking it all up like a sponge.

. . .

The leaves fell, and it was soon dark outside by the time I got home from school. Inside the house, the windows all looked like turned-off screens. Sometimes I had to convince myself that they were really windows. I'd put my head up against the glass until I could see there was another side. The rotting apples on the lawn, beyond the greenhouse. I preferred sitting with the lights off. That made the windows look more real. So I'd be there in the dark, my face lit up by my computer screen. Cora hated that.

There were several tabs that I kept open on my browser. I surveyed them when Sanjeet wasn't online, waiting for him to reappear. I couldn't stop myself from searching, the screen shining light into my eyes, late into the night.

. . .

One of the tabs was a blog post about an exhibition called Plague Time. I'd found it after typing Máire's artist name into Google.

The flyer Michael had mentioned in one of the letters

was still there in the envelope. It was very minimal. It didn't show any of the paintings, and the bio was short: *Mag Noland is an artist living in Manhattan.* Inside were strange shapes and repeating patterns, printed in red on the creamy card. There was a bit that looked like arms twisting, hands holding on to each other. I licked my finger and rubbed it on part of the pattern. The shapes smudged.

There wasn't much information on Mag Noland's Wikipedia page. Just two paragraphs of text, none of it telling me more than I already knew.

I only found the picture of the painting by looking through the references. One linked through to a blog post from 1998, about an exhibition. I had to scroll down to basically the bottom of the post before I saw Mag Noland's name.

> The mysterious Mag Noland appears to be enjoying a posthumous moment of resurgence, here employing mathematical principles to explore repeating patterns.

I hated the writing. How could somebody who was dead enjoy anything at all?

At the bottom of the blog post, though, were photographs of some of the pieces mentioned, including the painting by Mag Noland. I opened the photo up in a new tab and tried to make it bigger. I saved it as a file and zoomed in on different bits of it. But I couldn't work out what the painting was supposed to be showing. I couldn't find it anywhere else online, or any other paintings by Mag Noland. Still, I set the grainy photo as my desktop background and stared at it whenever I felt stuck.

. . .

The other tab I kept open was the Wikipedia page for the Dóchas Centre: *a closed, medium security prison, for females aged 18 years and over, located in Mountjoy Prison in Dublin, Ireland.*

It hadn't taken me long to find out Scarlett was in there. The page included a list of 'high profile inmates'. I looked up these other inmates, found out what they had done. The best story was about the so-called 'Scissor Sisters', who had murdered their mother's abusive boyfriend. One of them had stabbed him with a Stanley knife. The other struck him with a hammer. After he was dead, they chopped him up, even slicing off his penis.

I imagined Scarlett with these sisters, in this centre. Maybe they were friends. *Dóchas*, I knew, meant 'hope'. The building was designed to be 'campus style'. Prisoners lived in houses and did their own cooking and cleaning. They had their own keys to their own rooms. They could wear their own clothes.

I knew the address by heart, but I didn't know where I should start.

4

We arrived late in the evening. It should have been easy for us to go to sleep since we had spent all day travelling and it was the middle of the night back in Ireland, but I had been re-energized by all the lights blinking through the window in the cab, the cars around us honking.

Our hotel room was on the tenth floor. I couldn't remember a single time when Cora and I had shared a room before. Cora was audibly relieved when she opened the door with the key card and saw the two queen-sized beds.

Cora had all kinds of fancy travel accessories – an eye mask and noise-cancelling Bluetooth earbuds. But she stayed up for almost an hour looking at her phone while I was rereading *The Catcher in the Rye*. I had read most of it again on the plane.

'I don't know how you can read in that light,' Cora said at one point.

The bedside lamps had different settings. I had mine on the dimmest one. I wanted to tell her that I could see just fine, and that it was probably worse for her eyes to be looking at a lit screen in the dark. But I said nothing. I wasn't sure I was right about the light, I suppose. And Cora hated it whenever I so much as suggested that she was more addicted to screens than I was.

I had forgotten how good the ending was. It made me want to go back to the beginning. Instead I shut the book and placed it on the bedside table. 'Goodnight,' I said to Cora before I turned off the light.

I could tell she couldn't sleep. Neither could I. Perhaps because I was too tuned into her movements and breathing. Perhaps because I was overly excited.

'Cora,' I said, half an hour, or an hour, or perhaps hours after I had turned off the light.

She didn't answer, and I remembered about her earbuds.

I don't know what I was going to ask her. There were so many things we didn't talk about, not properly. I wanted to know if waiting to see my father had ever made her too excited to sleep. I wanted to tell her how I felt about Sanjeet.

Most of all, I wanted to know whether she would want to know about the letters. Would the truth, written out like that, be worth her knowing?

'I don't know what to do, Gaga,' I said to the ceiling.

I wanted to read the letters. Each time I did it was with the hope that they'd reveal some kind of clue, tell me what to do. But I couldn't risk going into the bathroom and reading them there. So instead I tried remembering what was in each one. I must have fallen asleep doing this because the next thing I knew the digital display on the clock on my bedside table said it was six in the morning and Cora was awake, unzipping her suitcase.

'I'm going for a run,' she whispered when she saw me looking, as if there might be someone else in the room who would wake up if she spoke any louder.

. . .

The weather app on my phone said it would be raining, but when I opened the curtains the sky was clear and cloudless. I could tell our window was facing east, because I could see the sun, creeping higher over the buildings. *Like an apricot*, I thought. *Like a peach*. I remembered New York was where James's giant peach ended up, speared on top of the Empire State Building. I remembered the ending to *King Kong*, the giant ape holding the tiny woman in his hand. I wanted to be held like that.

I couldn't see the Empire State Building, or any others that I might have recognized. But I could see a lot, from that window. More than I'd ever seen before, really. I pressed my forehead and nose against the glass and let the pane steam over from my breath. I stood there until Cora came back.

'How was your run?' I asked, wiping the glass clean with the sleeve of my pyjama top.

'Heaven. Central Park is magic.' She kicked off her runners and pulled the long-sleeve thermal top up over her head, then reached behind her back to unclasp her sports bra. Steam was rising from her skin. 'Time to get a move on,' she said, turning round, topless.

'You take longer to get ready than I do.'

'I do not.'

'You do.'

. . .

All the clothes in my suitcase looked unappealing now I was in New York. Items which I had coveted, before, now looked worn and out of fashion. Cora had hung her clothes up the night before. Smart chinos with a white blouse and a cashmere sweater. Her statement piece was her woven wool coat which was red and yellow and green and brown and went with everything. The only thing I liked that I had brought with me were my oxblood-red Doc Martens which I had got for Christmas. I pulled on my stretchy ribbed black trousers which flared out at the ends. I pushed my head and arms inside a cream polo neck. I layered a black jumper over the top, then looked about the room to see where I'd discarded my leather jacket, the one I'd found in a charity shop in Sligo in the summer.

At breakfast, I could sense both of us trying to be cheery and light.

'Have you seen there are five different types of milk?' I asked, sitting down with my bowl of fruit salad and yoghurt.

'Let me guess,' Cora said. 'Cow.'

'Obviously.'

'Soya, oat, almond and . . .' She paused. I had nodded after each of her previous guesses. 'Coconut?'

'How are you so good at that?'

'I've been to lots of hotels. It was a toss-off between coconut and hazelnut though.'

'Cora, it's toss-up. Not toss-off. How many times?'

'I know. I know. You were the one who said it the first time.'

'I was six!'

'You seem energized.'

'Must have slept well,' I said, shrugging off her observation. In truth, I had never felt so buzzy. Everything felt hyper-real, yet also like I had somehow imagined it. All the milks. The sunshine pattern, repeating in the carpet. The way the toilets were different in Ireland – lower down, with more water in them. All this before we'd even left the hotel.

5

The plan was that we would dedicate time to both our fathers in New York. Cora had been more open to the idea of me trying to find mine, since we'd started planning the trip. She'd even told me his name: Kyle. But she'd been sure to warn me that it might have been a fake name and that there weren't many places she could actually take me that she associated with Kyle. I believed her when she said she didn't know where he had been living, in 2001. But she said she'd try her best to tell me stories about the two of them. I think part of me thought we might just bump into him. I imagined this man, Kyle, recognizing my mother from across the street, then there'd be this big reunion. But I knew that wasn't going to happen.

Outside, the air was biting, so much drier than the atmosphere in Donegal. It made my eyes water while my mother tried to hail a taxi, her scarf blowing as the cars sped past. She looked like she was important in that coat, like she belonged in New York, sparkling in the sunlight. It didn't take long for one of the yellow cabs to pull up beside her.

'Ground Zero,' she said when we were inside.

The driver and Cora told each other their stories, extraordinarily efficiently. He looked at Cora through the mirror. His eyes lit up when she spoke. Her voice sounded more American, talking to him, as she told him that she'd left New York for Ireland after her father was killed in 9/11. The driver said he had a friend, a firefighter, who had died of cancer earlier in the year. 'From all the ash after,' he explained. 'Didn't know what they were getting themselves into.' I could tell the driver didn't want the conversation to end. 'My family are originally from Ireland, you know?' he said. When he found out I was Cora's daughter he said, 'I thought you must be sisters.' I could sense Cora blushing. She loved it when people said that.

The letters were in my backpack, down by my feet. It dawned on me that I was bringing them back to the site where they had been written. I thought about the fact that Róisín's letters had been up there, on the 104th floor, in one of Michael's office drawers. I imagined him working late and opening the drawer up, reading and rereading Róisín's letters. I wished that I could somehow read them, though I knew they'd become dust.

. . .

'Are you sure you don't mind hanging around on your own a bit this afternoon?' Cora asked, before we got out of the cab. After the meeting at Ground Zero, Emily was going to discuss the documentary with Cora, maybe even start some of the filming.

'Absolutely,' I said, trying not to sound overly enthusiastic.

'So have you planned on meeting up with Sanjeet while we're here?' She was trying to sound casual, I could tell.

I'd told her Sanjeet was going to be in New York at the same time as we were, but it made me embarrassed, somehow, admitting that we'd arranged to meet up.

'Actually,' I said, looking at my phone, 'I'm going to meet him today, after this.'

'That's exciting,' Cora said, enthusiastically. 'Where are you meeting?'

'I don't know.'

Sanjeet had been the last one to message. *I'll let you know,* he had said, after I'd asked where would be good for us to meet. But that had been the day before, and he still hadn't said where.

'Tell him to come and meet us here. I'd love to see him.'

'Cora,' I said. I was desperate to get out of the cab.

'I won't embarrass you, I promise.'

I looked at her. It was like I was the parent and she was the child. 'OK, OK. I'll message him.'

Do you want to meet a bit earlier? Cora wants to say hi.

. . .

I noticed Emily before Cora did. She was on the other side of one of the memorial pools, water falling into the big black hole between us. I could tell she was going to be the exact same height as Cora long before we actually got close enough for me to be proved right. She looked a lot friendlier in real life than she did in the photos I'd seen online, where her eyes seemed almost impossibly blue.

The water was deafening, blocking out the noise of the city. I couldn't hear anything Cora and Emily were saying to each other, after they'd hugged. We were all awkward around each other, looking for Michael's name which was etched into the bronze parapet of the North Tower pool.

After we'd found it, we walked around the museum. I was thinking that there must be something wrong with me, because I wasn't able to focus on the exhibits at all. The steel column, the staircase, the fire truck.

My phone buzzed, and before I even looked at the message I heard Cora starting to explain to Emily about Sanjeet.

I was embarrassed. I didn't think the conversation was appropriate for where we were. It seemed disrespectful, somehow.

'She doesn't like it when I bring him up,' I heard her say.

I opened up the message from Sanjeet.

Sorry L, something's come up with Eugene's family. I'm not going to be able to meet now till a bit later. Hope that's still OK? I have tickets to an exhibition if you fancied that?

'Everything OK, Lyca?' Cora asked.

I felt dizzy, looking up at her. 'Sanjeet's not going to be free until later in the afternoon,' I told her, trying to hide my disappointment.

'What time?'

'I don't know yet,' I snapped.

There was a fractured silence. Emily opened her mouth. 'How about we all go back to my apartment for a drink, something to eat? We have a ton of stuff from Christmas still.'

'Oh, you don't need to—' I started to protest.

'That's very kind of you,' Cora said, cutting me off.

6

Emily's apartment was on the Upper East Side, facing east. The apartments on the west side of the building were more desirable, Emily had explained in the elevator, but she liked the view they had, of Randalls and Wards.

The main room in the apartment was open plan – the kitchen leading to the dining area leading to the living area, which was a couple of steps lower down. After introductions, Emily's husband, Jason, opened up the fridge. It had an ice dispenser built into the door. He called out all the drinks that were inside. The Coca-Cola was in one of those giant bottles. He asked if I wanted a wedge of lemon or lime.

'Just ice is fine,' I told him.

I sat down next to their son, Bobby, on the big cream corner sofa in front of the floor-to-ceiling windows. He was drinking Coke, too, through a straw. There were cork coasters on the glass coffee table. From the window I could see across the river. Lots of green space, and a big old building, in the distance.

'Do you know about the islands?' Bobby asked me. He was twelve, Emily had told me. A real nerd.

When I said, 'Not much,' Bobby drew my attention to a map, framed inside the coffee table like it was a work of art.

'That's what it was like, in the late 1800s,' Bobby said. 'The islands were separate then.'

'They're not any more?'

'The channel between the two islands was filled up with construction rubble, from when the skyscrapers were built.'

Bobby looked excited, telling me this. When we'd met, he'd kept his mouth as closed as possible. It was because he was wearing braces. I'd been the same when I had mine. But now he seemed to have forgotten the train tracks on his teeth.

'Mom's the one who knows all the stuff about the islands,' he admitted. 'Some of it's pretty cool. She wants to make a documentary about them some day.'

'Try telling me what you know,' I said.

'Really?' he asked.

I nodded.

'Well, they used to be known as the islands of undesirables.'

'Who were the undesirables?' I asked.

'You can get a good idea from the map,' Bobby said, pointing down at the table. 'See, it tells you what the different institutions were.'

I leant over the table, trying to read the writing on the map without putting my hands down on the glass.

Emigrant Refuge & Hosp, Inebriate Asylum, Negro Point.
Foundling Asylum, House of Refuge, Idiot Asylum.

Bobby continued speaking: 'Most people don't know that before the opening of Ellis Island, Ward Island used to be an immigration station. The building you can see, out the window, it was the biggest hospital in the world at the time.'

I looked up and out through the window. The building was wide instead of tall, like it had wings.

'It's supposed to look like a bat,' Bobby explained. 'Oh, and "inebriate" means drunk,' he explained, pointing to that bit on the map. Then he added, embarrassed, 'If you didn't know.'

'I didn't,' I said.

Bobby moved his finger so it was pointing to the other island on the map. 'The Foundling Asylum was where unwanted babies were born. And the Idiot Asylum was where they put people who didn't fit in – the neurodivergent.'

He looked pleased with the big word.

'And the House of Refuge?' I asked.

'Mom and Dad used to joke that that's where I'd be sent to if I misbehaved. But it doesn't exist any more – I checked. It was basically a workhouse. Most of the boys who ended up there were Irish, actually. Ones who had escaped the Famine and survived the crossing, only to be rounded up off the streets in the city, declared delinquents.'

'You know your history,' I said. 'I'm impressed.'

'It's just from Wikipedia, mostly,' he told me, shrugging his shoulders.

My phone buzzed in my pocket. I took it out. I had a message from Sanjeet.

Whitney Museum. 4pm. Looking forward to it. X.

. . .

It was decided that instead of a proper lunch, we'd eat Christmas leftovers. I helped Bobby lay the table, and Emily passed us things to put on it. Half a ham wrapped in tin foil. Small bowls that contained dips. Hummus, olive oil with a blob of balsamic vinegar, that pink one with the long name that made me throw up once when Cora told me it was made from fish eggs. Jason had just returned with fresh bread rolls from a bakery called Doh.

'What's the name of that bridge?' Cora asked, standing over by the windows.

'That's the Ward Island Bridge,' Bobby informed Cora. 'It was designed by the same engineer as the Golden Gate Bridge, in San Francisco.'

'My dad called it the Guillotine Bridge,' Cora said, turning round and coming back up the steps to where the dining table was.

'You know it?' Emily asked, walking over to the table with a pair of wooden salad hands.

'Yes,' Cora said. 'My father and I once walked over all the bridges round Manhattan Island.' This was news to me.

'That's some walk!' Bobby said.

'I can remember it, because it was the only bridge that was just for pedestrians. And my dad had to explain to me what a guillotine was, after he called it that. For years, I thought all the executions during the French Revolution were performed on bridges.'

Bobby laughed, though not unkindly.

We all sat down and took turns to hand our plates to Jason who was carving the ham.

'You know,' Bobby said. 'People say the bridge is haunted, and the bat building. The bridge only used to be open during daylight hours. Because people actually did escape from the psychiatric centre. The river's known as Hell's Gate.'

'The islands have always had a bad rep,' Emily said. 'But it's mostly scaremongering.'

'Mom's part of this Facebook group for the islands.'

'It's not just a Facebook group,' Emily said. 'The islands facilitate a lot of community work. Most of the city's homeless shelters are there, for example. It's really transformed since I was little, when I was told it was where all the crazies lived. It's mostly parkland and sports grounds now. And a huge firefighter training facility. We took Bobby there lots when he was little. He loves it there.'

'Used to,' Bobby corrected.

'He doesn't want to be a firefighter any more,' Jason explained. 'What is it these days?'

There was a heavy silence. I could sense Bobby tensing up from the scrutiny.

'Help yourself to salad,' Emily said. She turned to Cora. 'Walking over all the bridges in Manhattan. I'd have loved to have done stuff like that with my father. Whenever I came with him to New York we just went to galleries. Nothing wrong with galleries. I just have bad associations.'

Under the table, I took out my phone to look up how long it would take for me to get to the Whitney Museum. Forty-five minutes on the subway. I was going to have to leave right after the meal. Cora must have noticed. When she kicked me I looked up again.

'Emily was just saying that her father is an art dealer,' Cora said.

'He was,' Emily corrected. 'He died when I was thirteen. So I didn't really get to know him, at least not as an adult. And the stuff I have found out about him hasn't exactly been favourable.'

'Oh?' Cora said, questioning. Then she said she was sorry, retracting the question mark.

'It's OK,' Emily said. 'I was asking to find out, I suppose. Coming here for college, looking for something, you know.' She finished putting salad on her plate. 'Just affairs,' she finished, as if she was worried we might have thought it was something worse. 'Probably in this apartment,' she added. 'I hated having to move my mother here when she got sick last year. But it was that or a nursing home. We couldn't move to Vermont.'

'Emily's mother died, just last month,' Jason explained.

'I had no idea,' Cora said. 'If I'd known . . .'

'Don't be silly,' Emily said. 'It's good for me to be getting on with my work again. Anyway, the real shock wasn't the death itself – we knew that was coming. It was what she said to me, before it happened.'

Jason was holding Emily's hand over the table. Only Bobby was eating.

'What did she say?' I asked.

Cora kicked me under the table again. 'You don't have to tell us,' she said to Emily.

But she must have wanted to.

'It was right at the end,' Emily said. 'The priest was on his way. I didn't think she'd talk again but she told me she had something to confess. I'm not sure she fully knew who I was. Possibly she thought I was the priest, and I thought it wouldn't matter if she thought I was. I didn't know how long she was going to last, whether the priest would get to her in time. I don't believe in all that, but I do think it's important for a person to have a good death. If there is a heaven and hell, I think it's about the mental state you're in when you die. So the Catholic thing makes sense to me in lots of ways. The idea that you can be forgiven at the final moment – that must bring people huge relief when they're dying.

'So I told her she could tell me. I even said something about how her sins would be forgiven. I don't know what I was expecting to hear. I just wanted her to feel better. It was hard to make out what she was saying. She had to take a breath practically between each word, and her voice was raw and raspy. But she told me—' Emily's voice was breaking. 'She told me that she wasn't my real mother. She told me that she'd done an awful thing. That she'd taken a young woman's baby. She was saying other things, too, things I couldn't make sense of at all. But what she said about the baby, I couldn't stop thinking about it, because I knew she had meant me.'

'And do you know if that's true?' Cora asked. 'What a shock. I'm sorry.'

'After she died, I sent a saliva sample off to the lab,' Emily explained. 'I'm still waiting to get the results back. But it feels like I already know, like I always knew . . . something.' She picked up her wine glass, but didn't drink from it. I was thinking about whether I could ask her about the testing, how it worked, what company she was using. But the moment where I might have done so passed.

'You know the funniest thing?' Emily said. 'I think I might have met her. My birth mother, I mean. At my father's funeral, and before.'

'You did?' Cora asked.

'It's a long story. I'll tell you later. It actually relates a bit to the posters.'

'What about you, Lyca?' Jason said, changing the subject. 'How are you liking New York?'

He gave me some recommendations for things I could do with Sanjeet. I took out my phone to make note of them, then noticed the time. 'I'm actually going to have to go,' I said. 'Sorry. And thank you for the food. Sorry I didn't have time to finish. Sorry.'

'Stop saying sorry,' Emily said. 'Go. Have fun. I'm going to steal your mother for the rest of the day and after you can come back here and tell us all about your date. Bring the boy, too.'

'It's not a date,' I said, my cheeks going red.

7

The Whitney Museum of American Art spanned 200,000 square feet and was home to the city's largest column-free art spaces. I looked it up online using the museum Wi-Fi while I waited for Sanjeet. He wasn't late, but I was early.

Then there he was, crossing the street in a puffy black jacket, blue jeans, a red beanie hat. From the top of the steps, I watched him get closer. At the bottom of the steps he turned his head to the left and the right before looking up. I waited for him to see me. He smiled and waved. Then we were both taking the steps to meet in the middle. Him coming up, me going down.

He was still one step below me, so I couldn't quite gauge his height. Obviously he was much taller than he had been when we'd been friends at school. Back then he had been smaller than I was, and slighter. My bones were bigger than his, I remembered. Thicker wrists which he'd try to get his thumb and forefinger around. When he did this, he couldn't make them meet. I remembered also how we used to squeeze each other's chins. Cherry or bum.

When he said my name, it was like something out of a dream. The same but different.

He held out his arm. I didn't realize he had meant to hug me until I'd jabbed him in the chest.

'Ow,' Sanjeet said. But he was laughing, and I could see

the boy that he had been, even as I noticed the stubble on his cherry chin.

. . .

We'd just missed one of the exhibition time slots. The man behind the information desk told us to come back in an hour. Sanjeet asked the man if he knew of any nearby diners. I didn't say that I'd just eaten and I couldn't pay attention to any of the directions because I felt stupid for not anticipating Sanjeet's English accent.

The diner was just like in the movies. We sat in a booth, opposite each other. The red leather seating was slippy. I had to steady myself with my hands so I didn't slide down on to the floor. I put my elbows on the table, and could hear Gaga's voice in my head, telling me to take them off.

The shiny surface of the table had a geometric pattern, the kind you could get lost in. A waiter wearing a red-and-white chequered apron came over and placed laminated menus down in front of us. That was when we really started talking. The same waiter came over three times before we were finally ready to order.

Sanjeet ordered a hamburger and a Coke.

'I kind of already ate,' I admitted. 'But I'll have a vanilla milkshake, and you can dip your fries in it.'

'I thought they only did that in movies,' Sanjeet said.

'Is that everything?' the waiter asked, tapping her pencil on the pad.

After she had gone, I reminded Sanjeet about Gaga's 'sausages for Sanjeet', and asked if it was only pork he would eat, or other meat.

He chuckled. 'A hamburger's not pork. I forget you don't even have McDonald's.'

'I think there's one in Derry,' I said. 'And don't forget Supermac's, in Donegal town.'

'Supermac's!' Sanjeet said. 'How could I forget? Anyway, the burger will be beef, which I'm definitely not supposed to eat. But what my parents don't know won't hurt them.'

We chatted, like people do. About Trump and #MeToo. About Brexit and climate change. I told him about Ground Zero, and Emily's apartment. He told me about his friend Eugene, his huge apartment in Tribeca. We talked about Gaga, about my house. I asked him questions about England, about his school.

He said he no longer knew what he wanted, that coming to New York had made him feel confused. It was like he'd known this was going to happen, months before, waiting for the trip to change something essential about him.

The plan before had been to continue with school and apply to Oxford. But now he wasn't sure. Maybe he would just work. He didn't think he saw the point of getting a degree. But all his parents had ever wanted was for him to go to Oxford.

Whenever he spoke for more than a couple of minutes, he'd stop to ask me a question. I was never ready for them. Like when he asked what I had been reading but I would have felt too embarrassed saying *The Catcher in the Rye*, so instead I mumbled something about being between books at the moment, and managed to turn the question back on him. He told me he was reading *Infinite Jest*, that it was the best novel he'd ever read. I had never even heard of it, but I pretended that I had.

Our orders arrived, and we both dipped fries into my milkshake. I loved that I was introducing him to something new, watching his face as he experienced the flavour combination for the first time. Salty and sweet.

We stayed talking in the booth for a long time after we had finished eating. Once our table had been cleared, though, I felt very aware of myself, particularly the fact that my hands would not stop sweating.

Sanjeet was interesting and interested. He looked me in the eyes. But I hated when he asked about me, because I didn't feel like I had anything to say. I didn't know what I wanted to do with my life. I hadn't been anywhere exciting, or done anything of note. I'd not even read the right things. Whereas so much had changed for him since leaving Burtonport. He had this whole other life I wasn't part of.

I had this burning desire to tell him about the letters, to bring him in on the discovery, so we could explore together, the way we used to. But I didn't. We were playing a different kind of game now, pretending to be adults. To participate, I had to know what kind of person I was, to project a personality.

The waiter came and cleared our table and I told Sanjeet I needed to use the bathroom. At the sinks, I tried to summon the other Lyca I had seen through the bathroom mirror, back in Burtonport. She wouldn't appear.

8

Back in the museum, I was already nervous about what I would have to say about the exhibition, afterwards. The man at the information desk handed over our tickets and directed us to the elevators.

I couldn't stop my mouth from opening when we stepped into the one that had arrived. A window had been painted on the wall, and when I turned around the sliding doors transformed into a front door, like we were inside a house. Sanjeet smiled and pressed the button for the sixth floor.

Outside the exhibition entrance, an attendant asked if either of us had epilepsy. We shook our heads and stepped into the pitch black. It was like going through the hatch.

I wanted to reach out for Sanjeet's hand, to tether him to me, but I couldn't. Then I could see lights flickering, and Sanjeet walking away from me towards them. I followed.

Round the corner there were hundreds of old TVs, stacked on top of each other like bricks. The screens were sort of all showing different things, flashing on and off, but sometimes a single image would be shown across multiple screens, like they were all connected. Loud music started playing. An old pop song I thought I knew, but it had been distorted – stopping and starting, looping back and jumping forward.

I looked over at Sanjeet. He was standing so still. I could

see all the screens reflected in his glasses. He had put them on before we went in. Barely noticeable tortoiseshell on the frames. It felt like the world was about to fold in on itself. Everything inside me was racing, though I was stuck there on the spot.

Perhaps I did have epilepsy, I was thinking, blinking. Everything was flashing behind my eyelids. I couldn't work out what was real.

With great effort I moved my feet and walked with my arms stretched out in front of me until I stumbled into the next part of the exhibition where the lights were on. Sanjeet wasn't with me. To ground myself I focused on the writing printed on the wall.

Ideas as form, employing mathematical principles, creating thought diagrams, or establishing rules for variations of color and/or patterns.

The words made no sense to me at all, but I found myself reading them, over and over, in my head, like they were some kind of incantation. I let them burn into my retinas, and as I did I had this crazy sense that I was going to turn around and see Mag Noland's painting, the one featured in the Plague Time blog post.

I turned around, just as I heard Sanjeet calling my name. He had appeared in front of the blank wall, where the painting was supposed to be. I was trying to look through him, to focus my eyes in some special way so I could see what I was sure was somehow there. I still wanted to believe the painting would reveal itself to me.

Sanjeet was waving a hand in front of my face. 'Are you OK?' he asked. 'Those lights were kind of trippy.'

'Yes. No. I mean, sort of.' I didn't know what I meant, but I knew I couldn't be there any more.

'Here, have some water.' He'd taken a canteen from his tote bag. He unscrewed the lid and passed me the metal bottle. It was cold in my hand.

'You want to get out of here?'

I was drinking from the bottle when I nodded. The metal rim clinked against my teeth.

. . .

Outside, it was almost dark. The cold was so sweet on my cheeks. Sanjeet asked me what I wanted to do. I told him I was totally fine, that he could go back into the exhibition if he wanted and I could wait for him.

'Nah,' he said. 'You cool with walking for a bit?'

I nodded.

'You know about the High Line?'

I didn't know what he was talking about.

'You'll love it,' he said. 'Starts right here. Have you got Spotify on your phone?'

I nodded again.

'Can I borrow it a second?'

I got my phone out of my pocket and unlocked it for him. I watched him tether my phone to his hotspot. He had to keep sniffing, to stop his nose from dripping.

'You have headphones, right?' he asked.

I reached inside my bag. I had used my headphones on the subway but I was worried they might have somehow disappeared in the interim. I was reassured when my fingers felt their coated wire.

When I pulled them out Sanjeet was taking his AirPods out from their little container. I never understood how people could spend so much money on these when it would be so easy to lose one. I liked the fact that my earpieces were attached to each other. And I liked the fact that when I was listening to something I could always find my phone, connected to the other end. They reminded me of how Gaga used to sew my mittens together with a strand of wool and thread them inside my coat sleeves so I couldn't lose them.

I wanted to tell Sanjeet all this, but he was talking.

'I've downloaded an album to your phone. *Koyaanisqatsi* by Philip Glass. We're going to listen to it at the exact same time as we walk along the High Line, OK?'

I had basically no idea what he was talking about but I nodded and plugged my headphones into the bottom of my phone, then followed Sanjeet up a set of steps that didn't look like they would lead to anywhere.

We walked along the old railway line, and I couldn't help but think of the abandoned railway line in Burtonport. I wondered if Sanjeet remembered it too, if this was why he had brought me here, but whenever I opened my mouth to ask him something I would be reminded of the music and it would take over all my thoughts. It felt like I was inside that music and it was carrying us along. I could tell that we were hearing exactly the same thing at the same time. Every now and then, we'd look at each other and beam. I wanted to dance, even though it wasn't that kind of music. I wondered if we looked mad. We had slowed right down. It was like we were moving as slowly as we possibly could while still moving forward. Then, as the music darkened, reflecting the evening sky, I found myself wondering whether the reason Sanjeet had suggested this activity – listening to the music at the same time – was because it would mean we wouldn't have to talk. What if he didn't want to talk to me, if this was a convenient way of passing time? Then the next track would start and I'd feel buoyant once more, like I was flying through the city, between the skyscrapers and churches, above the traffic, all the twinkling lights. Like a bird, like a bat. I remembered the bat building, over on Ward Island. I thought about the letters. Where had Michael said that Máire had been in hospital? Didn't he say it was on an island?

The High Line was coming to an end. We didn't seem so high up any more. Everything was wider. I could see a subway car depot, water beyond it. But I didn't know if it was the Hudson River or the East River. Then suddenly we were on a normal street, and Sanjeet was taking out his AirPods, smiling at me. I removed my earphones, too, and it was like silence and sound all at once – deafening and mundane.

'That was great,' I told him. 'Thanks.'

'I stole the idea from Eugene,' Sanjeet said. 'The music was my choice though.'

'The music felt so right.'

'I'm glad you thought so.'

We were looking at each other in the eyes. For a moment – only a second, really – I thought that he was going to kiss me.

'I should probably be getting back to Eugene's,' he said, instead. 'Let you get back to Cora.'

I wanted to ask him to come with me. It should have been so easy.

'You know where you're going?' he asked.

'I'll figure it out,' I said, tapping where my phone was in my jacket.

'And—' He looked a bit sheepish now. 'This has been all right, hasn't it, Lyca?'

'It's been really nice.'

We hugged, then. I wanted to hold on to him for ever. But I couldn't bear it, either. The pressure.

'Did you ever find out where the ducks go?' I whispered into his ear, the words escaping from my mouth.

'What?' He sounded genuinely confused.

I'd spent so long thinking about the ducks, trying to close the space between us. Now I was pulling back, turning away. Though we were both here in New York City, in winter, the ducks had never been a thing we'd shared.

9

In the months leading up to the trip I had spent entire days in Burtonport exploring New York City on Street View. I picked up the little man and dropped him where I wanted to go. The Statue of Liberty, Times Square, Grand Central Station. In Central Park I found the Alice in Wonderland statue and walked around the zoo. I inspected every bit of water, and couldn't see a single duck in any of the panoramic pictures taken during winter months. But I had been looking forward to verifying this myself. I'd imagined Sanjeet and I holding hands, shuffling through snow, quacking.

Recalling this projection was painful. I had turned the entire city into a fantasy land. It had spoilt it all.

My boots were rubbing against my heels. I hadn't realized the whole time, walking along the High Line. I stopped outside a café to see if it had Wi-Fi. The password was written on a chalkboard above the counter. I took off my right glove, took out my phone and opened it with my thumbprint. I put in the Wi-Fi password and opened up the map app. Then I looked around to see if Sanjeet had followed me. If he had, I'd have told him everything, held on to his hand, taken him with me. I knew, though, deep within my soul, that I was supposed to be alone.

I typed my destination into the search bar. The most efficient route was highlighted in blue for me to follow.

It was a two-hour walk, mostly a straight line. Past the Empire State Building and the Rockefeller Center with its big Christmas tree and the Museum of Modern Art. I distracted myself from my feet, playing Alphabet I Spy.

Avenue, bus, Coca-Cola advert, drugstore.

I was walking along the edge of Central Park. On my map, Fifth Avenue was described as an 'iconic and elegant major thoroughfare'. There was a stall selling hot nuts. I stopped walking because the smell was so delicious. The man roasting the nuts smiled at me and raised his hat. I looked back down at my phone.

The map showed that I was close to the Alice in Wonderland statue, an 'iconic bronze sculpture in Central Park'. I wanted to take a detour but it was like my feet couldn't veer from the blue line marked on the map.

At East 96th Street, I turned right. I was sure my heels were bleeding, that there was blood seeping into my socks. But I didn't stop. My ears were numb and my nose felt like it was about to fall off.

I walked right past Emily's apartment block, towards the river. I crossed FDR Drive, over six lanes of traffic, on to the Bobby Wagner Walk, which went along the river. Hell's Gate, Bobby had called it. My feet hurt like hell.

Even in the dark, I could see the bridge up ahead. That was the thing about New York, compared to Burtonport. It was so light, even at night. No stars, though.

There was a ramp to get up to the bridge. It went back and forth like a zigzag. A green sign with a bicycle and an arrow on it saying *Randalls Island*, under a lamp. I followed the arrow.

There were more lamps lighting up the bridge. It was

narrow and abandoned. In the distance, I could see the bat building. All the lights in the windows, like little blinking eyes. Above the building, the light was an eerie blue. Really, none of it looked real. I could have been the only person in the world. That made me feel powerful, like I might be able to change the story.

I even knew what I wanted that story to be – one where Róisín flew to New York to meet her sister. It played out like a montage, in my head. Róisín calling out to Máire, on the bridge, holding out her hand. Like at the end of *Scream School*.

Of course, I didn't know if I was right – if this was the bridge Máire had jumped from. But it was possible. Maybe she'd been trying to take herself back to the bat building, to get better. Maybe all she had wanted to do was to look down at the water. The barriers weren't that high. It wouldn't be difficult, to climb up on to the handrail. I thought about doing it, just to see what it would feel like. But I was frightened of losing my footing, of falling.

At what seemed like the middle of the bridge, I put my backpack down on the ground and opened up the zip. It felt strange, holding the letters in my gloved hands, like I was a librarian looking at a rare artefact. Inside my gloves my fingers were numb, which made the letters seem already absent.

The blue light was getting brighter, over the bat building. It was white in the middle, like the opposite of a black hole. It didn't look real. I wanted to get out my phone to take a photo, but I couldn't with the letters in my hands. Probably it would be like trying to take a photo of the moon.

I removed the elastic band around the envelopes and held the letters up over the railing. I wanted to let go, to watch the letters swirl and scatter before being swallowed up by the choppy water, the paper getting wet, the ink starting to spread. But I wouldn't have been able to see any of that, even in the blue light.

. . .

Was it a UFO, a nuclear explosion, an alien invasion? I kept turning my head, on the walk back to Emily's, looking back at the blue light. I wasn't frightened, but if the world was ending, I wanted Cora to know about the letters, after all.

Only it wasn't ending. The world. We can't avoid what's coming for us.

Back in Emily's apartment, Bobby was standing in the dark with his head pressed against the window, looking out. Cora and Emily were still recording, Jason had informed me, at the door.

'What is it?' I asked, about the light.

'An electrical transformer in Astoria,' Jason said. 'At least, that's what people are saying on Twitter.'

'It blew up,' Bobby said, turning to face me. 'But don't worry. Nothing nuclear.'

I lay back on the sofa while Bobby spoke about charged particles in the atmosphere, excited atoms in the sky. 'Like a man-made Northern Lights,' he said. 'The Astoria Borealis.'

. . .

E: OK, so look at me, not at the camera.

C: Like this?

E: Exactly. Why don't you just start by telling me what you had for breakfast?

C: Oh, it was a hotel breakfast, so that might take a while. And it feels like it was a long time ago.

E: Go on.

C: Let me see. I'd been for a run, so I was starving. I had a croissant with raspberry jam. Then pancakes with bacon and maple syrup. In Ireland, they don't do pancakes like that. They're these big flat things you roll up. Oh, and there were lots of milks. Lyca had me guess all the kinds.
E: That's great. You're a natural.
C: Well, this isn't my first rodeo.
E: First question then. Start by telling me your name, and what your relationship was to the person in your poster.
C: My name is Cora Brady. I'm the daughter of Michael Brady. He worked for Cantor Fitzgerald, on the hundred and fourth floor of the North Tower.
E: Great. And can you describe your missing-people poster? Any memories you have – of making the posters, or putting them up.
C: I only decided to do it a whole month after the attacks. I'd spent weeks looking at all the posters, taking photos of them. But I hadn't made my own one. They all appeared so suddenly. But by that point it was already obvious that these people weren't alive. I knew my father was dead, so I didn't see the point of putting up a poster.
E: But then you did?
C: It was because I was going to Ireland, where my aunt lived. And I wanted to leave something behind. I'd driven myself crazy in the apartment, searching for a photo of my dad. I had a digital camera, but I was sixteen, so I wasn't just going round taking photos of him. So in the end I had to go through the actual family albums. I hadn't done that since before my mother had died. It felt strange, looking at this photo of the three of

us. I think I might have a photo of it, on my phone. I'll find it for you later. Looking at it, then, I couldn't work out if I was remembering a memory, or just remembering seeing the photo before. They looked just the same, you see. I was the one who'd changed.

Anyway, I took the photo to an internet café and paid to have it scanned in. I'm glad I didn't think to cut him out of the actual photo. Instead I used the eraser, on Paint, to rub me and my mother out of the scanned version. That photo means a lot to me, now. Sanjeet recognized my father on the poster in the video you put out, because he'd seen the real photo in our house. But I didn't do a very good job of the poster. I had to be quick about it because I only had thirty minutes on the computer. So I added my father's name, and where he'd worked. Said that he was missing because that's what all the posters said. I didn't realize till later that I'd forgotten to include any contact information.

E: Yours was unique in that way. After the attacks, I was spending a lot of time walking around the city, too. I saw a ton of posters, but I don't think I ever saw yours.

C: Why are the posters important to you, do you think?

E: I felt really lonely in the city at that time. It's a specific kind of sadness. Not feeling at home in New York, but knowing you wouldn't anywhere else, either. My relationship with my mother wasn't great at that time, and I was still processing a lot of stuff about my father.

I'd been obsessed with New York all my life. My dad used to bring me with him, sometimes, when he visited for work. From when I was really little. So, when it came to college, I only applied to schools in New York. I enrolled at Columbia in 1998. I was sure my life would start as soon as I got there. Only it didn't, or at least not in the way I expected it to. I felt lonely, and I kept thinking about my father, about our trips to the city. He never made a thing out of it, but often we'd see the same woman. Never for long. She just popped up from time to time. She had helped me choose a teddy bear from FAO Schwarz. She had been there when I had my first hot chocolate at MarieBelle. She was at his funeral, too, I was sure. By the time the service was over she had disappeared. But on the pew where she'd been sat was this tiny wristwatch with the Virgin Mary on the face. I took it.

I wanted to go to college in New York so I could return the watch and talk to her, this woman. But when I arrived in the city, it became clear that was never going to happen, that you couldn't just find people like that.

Then 9/11 happened, and I was certain that I'd see her in one of the posters, this woman. The thought of finding her filled me with hope again, though I was aware that if I did see her, in one of the posters, it would mean that she was dead. But it would mean that she had been real, too, not just a figment of my imagination.

C: And had she died in 9/11? Did you find her in one of the posters?

E: No. But something about looking at the posters did help me to snap out of the state I was in. The people in the posters were all missing, but it was the people who'd made them, I figured, who were experiencing the loss, the absence. Everyone's missing something, someone. The posters made me realize we're all just walking around with missing pieces. None of us is whole. The short answer is, they helped me see outside myself, made me feel less alone. We all have our stories. It made me want to be a documentarian.

C: What you said, about the missing pieces. You know how I said I wanted to leave something behind, and that's why I made my poster. Well, I wanted to take something with me, too. In the original photo, you can see my mother's tattoo. I hadn't thought about it in ages until I made the poster. Then I went to Coney Island, because I used to love going there with my dad. I was sticking up the posters in places that I associated with him. There was a tattoo parlour there. You know, one of the seafront ones which everyone says are really dodgy? My tattoo did actually get infected. I got it the day before I went to Ireland. My mother had a whole sleeve of them. Mine's just a piece.

. . .

The rest is difficult to transcribe. The shock, the silence, the sense that this might be some kind of elaborate hoax, a joke, for that would be easier to process.

But that came later – stopping and starting the video over and over, writing it all down.

At the time, I had been dreaming that the whole world had been turned into a bouncy ball, small enough for me to hold in my hands. It was very important that I didn't let go of this blue-green ball, but someone was shaking me, and I had somehow dropped it. The ball was ricocheting wildly off the edges of wherever the dream was taking place, waking me up.

It took a while for me to remember where I was: Emily's apartment. It was Cora, shaking my arm, telling me something had happened.

'I know, I know,' I said, remembering the blue light, my eyelids still heavy.

'Sit up,' said Cora. She seemed shaken, like she was trying to hold herself together.

I thought then she must have found the letters in my bag, while I was sleeping. But the words – which were falling out of Cora's mouth, all joined together – didn't seem connected to the letters.

That was when I noticed blood had seeped through my socks into the fabric of the sofa. I registered this, as if from a distance – like it wasn't my blood, like they weren't my feet. It didn't cause me any distress. In fact, I felt serene as Emily and Cora lifted me up, balancing my body between them. They made such a good team, carrying me through Emily's bedroom, putting me down on the toilet seat in Emily's ensuite. Cora started running the bathwater while Emily searched for antiseptic cream and bandages in the drawers below the sink. I thought perhaps I was still dreaming, because I didn't feel any pain.

I only saw it for a few seconds. I was simply stunned to see it, after so much searching. Máire's painting, hanging in Emily's bedroom, taking up an entire wall. What I'd never been able to make out in the photo online was obvious at once to the naked eye. To my naked eyes, at least – from their upside-down perspective. The pattern was made up of tiny figures, joined together like handwriting. The whole wild world.

The Hatch

THERE'S JUST ONE CHOICE LEFT TO MAKE. COM-
BINE YOUR POWERS TO DESTROY THE SCHOOL
FOR GOOD AND IN DOING SO BECOME MERE
MORTALS, OR KEEP YOUR POWERS AND RISK THE
SCHOOL BEING FOR EVER HAUNTED.

(A OR B?)

Lyca Brady

Burtonport

2023

The house is up for sale. I watch them put the sign up, two men trying to slide the stake into the lumpy earth.

I pick my phone up from the desk to message Cora. I can't think what to say, though. She doesn't think about the house like I do. It's not the only home she's known.

. . .

When the estate agent came to do the valuation, they said I shouldn't get my hopes up, because of the house's 'reputation'. I acted dumb, because I wanted to be told a story. 'I suppose you're probably too young to know,' the agent said. He seemed twitchy, like he wanted to be out of there quick. I told him there was quite a lot of space, up in the attic. I took him up to the hatch and slid it open. 'There's a light, just inside,' I said. The man was terrified, checking an imaginary wristwatch so he could say he'd best be going.

. . .

I suppose this is a haunted house. Full of stories, secrets. It felt that way to me for a while, when Cora and I got back from New York. The letters were eating me up. The revelation that Cora and Emily were half-sisters had ruptured what I'd meant to do. I'd told myself that I would wait till we were back in Burtonport. I'd put the letters back in the USA biscuit tin, pretend I'd just found them. It would be difficult, I knew. But it was the right thing to do.

After Emily got the results back from the DNA test she'd done, Cora and Emily both ordered 23andMe kits. I was still too young to get one for myself, though Cora said I could as soon as I was eighteen. The results revealed they shared 29 per cent of the same DNA. Then, through the app, Emily received a message from a woman called Franny, claiming to be her half-sister.

It was like that arcade game where no matter how hard you whack the mole down with the hammer, another one would pop up in its place.

It was confusing enough as it was, without throwing the letters into the mix. What good would it do for Cora to know that Michael hadn't been her father? How might Emily feel, if Cora told her that Harold had in fact been hers? It would mean dredging up the dead, casting Róisín and Michael as villains – the two people who had been there for Cora the most. I didn't want that, didn't want to witness the blowing up of Cora's story, the reconstruction that would follow. The butterfly effect.

I decided, then, that I'd destroy the letters. Throw them in a fire, feed them through a shredder, drown them in bleach. I thought about these endings all the time, but I didn't act them out.

Sometimes, I would question whether the letters were in my possession, or if they were in fact possessing me, pulling me back into the past.

I had them sealed back inside my Dell computer, out of

sight. But often in the middle of the night, I'd find myself checking to see if the screws were still twisted tight.

In a month or two, I knew, I'd hear them whispering my name. Before long, they'd be screaming to be let out.

. . .

It was only when I admitted everything to Scarlett that I was able to let go of any of it.

I'd booked myself on to campus tours at Trinity and UCD. Cora said that she would drive me but I told her that I'd take the bus, that I wanted to go to Dublin on my own. The driver blasted pop anthems through the speakers. Most of them older than I was, all of them awful. 'Who Let the Dogs Out?', 'My Heart Will Go On', 'Baby One More Time'.

From the outside, the Dóchas Centre looked not unlike some of the prospectus photos of college residences. There were posters of historically notable prisoners – mostly freedom fighters – displayed on the railings. One poster titled 'In Their Own Words', with excerpts from diary entries and letters prisoners had written.

So I sit and dream and build up a world of birds and butterflies and flowers from the sheen in a dew drop or the flash of a sea-gull's wing – Constance Markievicz, to her sister Eva (11 December 1920).

At reception, I had my bag and body searched, then put my phone into a combination locker. On the walls were displays like at a school – motivational quotes, acrostic poems, children's drawings. I followed a guard through a series of long corridors.

The visitors' lounge had lots of windows looking over an internal courtyard. A rectangle of well-kept grass.

Everyone was wearing their own clothes, so it was difficult to tell the prisoners and visitors apart. I'd expected Scarlett to be in one of those old dresses, looking like she did in the newspaper articles. Instead, she was wearing a two-piece velour tracksuit – maroon with orange accents. Adidas. She obviously looked older than in the photos I'd seen, but she had a youthful air about her. Long white hair and dimples in her cheeks.

There was a café at one end of the lounge. Scarlett ordered two teas and a Twix. When I offered to pay, she waved my hand away. 'But you can make a donation,' she said. 'It's a good cause.' There was a box by the till with a coin slot in the top. RELEASE, it said on the side.

The soft seating was upholstered in faux leather, ripped in places, the stuffing coming out like clouds. Scarlett tore open the gold Twix packet and handed me one of the bars. 'So,' she said. 'You look troubled.'

I hadn't even meant to tell her about the letters. The very fact of their existence could potentially be hurtful to her, I knew. But I blurted it all out, the words escaping from my mouth.

Scarlett didn't interrupt. While I was speaking, she dunked the Twix bar in her tea and sucked the chocolate off the biscuit before she bit into it, the caramel then stretching out from between her lips. Every time she did this she looked so satisfied, like a child.

By the time I'd finished speaking I felt empty, exhausted. The backs of my legs were sweaty on the chair. To fill the silence, I bit into my half of the Twix until the whole bar was in my mouth, the caramel stuck in my teeth. Scarlett frowned at me while I tried to swallow the paste down. I reached for my mug, took a glug of tepid tea and started coughing.

Finally Scarlett spoke: 'Why do you think you haven't destroyed them then, the letters?'

She seemed genuinely curious. I hadn't really asked myself why, before. I just knew that I hadn't, like my hands were tied.

'I don't know,' I said. 'Maybe just because Gaga didn't. Róisín, I mean.'

'Hmm,' she said, pulling at her earlobe. 'You know, I knew about the letters.'

'You did?'

'He must have sent them to the Atlan estate, her mother's house, you know. She didn't sell that until after I got sent down here. But I knew she was writing to him, that he was writing back.' Scarlett was looking past me, out the window. 'She had a spring in her step, a heaviness in her head.'

'You thought she was still in love with him?'

She looked back at me. 'I assume you've read the diaries by now, too?'

I nodded.

Scarlett spoke slowly, like she had all the time in the world. 'You know, she didn't write anything, after the abortion. Not a word. Not for ages. I was worried that I'd made a mistake. The only time I ever wondered whether what I did might have been wrong. I know we never talked enough about it, that's for sure. Not before. Not after.'

'You think she regretted it?' I asked.

'I thought she must have done. For a long time. I kept waiting for her to leave. But she didn't leave. She stayed. She knew what I was doing, and she stayed. She never said that I should stop. Then one day she was writing again. And I don't mean the video games. They were always more my thing. Except *Scream School*. I mean that writing to him made her write for herself again. She went back to her diaries. So what if all she wanted to do was rewrite those same stories. They were the stories she needed to tell. It was her art.'

She smiled, then. And I could see the woman Róisín had been drawn to. Scarlett had a way of looking at things, wanting to understand them.

'We were happy together,' she continued. 'He made her happier. But he hurt her, too. I could see that she was tormented by whatever was in his letters. In the end, we talked about them. What I'm trying to say is that the letters were never this big secret between us. We had a real relationship. Not saying it was always easy. But when everything blew up, she stood by me. I never asked for her to do that. In fact I told her to run. But she was here, pretty much every week. For years.'

'I'm sorry I'm not her,' I said.

'That's OK. You're you.'

'Do you think that I should give them to my mother, the letters?' I asked, just in case it could be that easy to find the answer.

'I can't answer that,' Scarlett said. 'What I will say, though, is that you're far too young, you know, to be thinking so much about everyone else. I don't mean this to sound flippant, but the letters, the diaries – they have nothing to do with you.' She looked me dead in the eyes. 'Tell me about you, Lyca. What do you want? What are your stories?'

. . .

I didn't think that I had any stories to tell. I was in my final year at school, about to turn eighteen. Suddenly the whole world was in crisis, but it felt like everything that happened to me was entirely unremarkable. My exams being cancelled, the email from the University of Galway saying that Freshers' Week events would still be going ahead virtually. When I did finally get to go, I couldn't bear talking to Cora on the phone. Cora, who had never been to college, because of me. She'd have loved it. Said yes to everything, joined countless groups and societies. Why wasn't I like that? Those years just blended together. Not seeing anyone's actual mouth for months, then the rare moments where it was as if the barriers between me and other people were lifted and I could really feel, when all I wanted was to dance in a club like that, to be held like that, to wake up like that. But mostly it felt like hard work, even when nothing was happening.

The next time I came home for the holidays, I unscrewed the panel on my Dell computer and took the letters out. There wasn't a moment when I decided to do it. It just felt good, holding them again in my hands. I typed them all up on my laptop, and saved the document in a folder titled Bits and Pieces. I did the same with Gaga's diaries. There was a process, then, of deciding which entries I would use. I began cutting and pasting, rearranging. It wasn't long before I was writing my own words, rendering my own worlds.

'It doesn't matter if it's not exactly true,' Scarlett assured me, when I visited her again at the Dóchas Centre. 'And write as though your mother will never read it.'

I knew that I had access to more of the story than anyone else. At times, I felt this as a great pressure, the weight of it keeping me up at night as I wrestled with the loose ends, trying to tie them all together. There were cracks I had to skirt around, holes I skipped right over.

At different points, I had to print the bits and pieces out and cut them up with scissors, arranging them on the floor, then sticking them on the wall with Blu Tack.

The process reminded me of Gaga's manuscript, how she wrote *Scream School* – connecting all the bits together like they were a map.

I remembered what Gaga had told me, once, when I showed her a story I had written when I was little. The story was a thinly veiled reimagining of my life, where a little lost girl is found by her father. Gaga must have seen straight through it. But when she finished reading it she turned to me and said, 'You're the real writer, Lyca.'

. . .

These words became my mantra. I wrote them on a Post-it note and stuck it to the lid of the USA biscuit tin. I read the note whenever I felt lost.

The tin is on the window ledge. Lined up next to it are all the novels Gaga mentioned in her diaries. I asked Cora, too, what books she had read when she was my age. I read them all, but wouldn't have been able to express, until very recently, which of these novels I personally liked, let alone why. *The Catcher in the Rye* is there, as well, next to *Infinite Jest*. The whole time, while I was reading that, I was trying to work out what Sanjeet saw in it. I told myself I wouldn't contact him till I had finished it. I was going to take notes, have something to say. But when I got to the end, all I could think was that I'd secretly been hoping he would contact me first, before I finished it. So I read through all the footnotes at the back, waiting for my phone to buzz, which didn't make a difference.

I reconnect the internet and type Sanjeet's name into Facebook. *Studies English at New College, Oxford.* I click on his profile picture, which hasn't changed in over a year now. I don't know why I keep on searching for him. Why do any of us hold on to things, and write them down, when it is surely easier to let go?

. . .

In the end, I didn't send my DNA off for screening. I don't quite know why. It wasn't that I was scared of what I might find. If anything, I was putting off the moment where it would become clear my mother had been right, that there was nothing there to find. For now, at least, I tell myself the truth doesn't much matter. More important is the quest to understand yourself.

The sun is sinking, shining a golden light over the desk. I reach over for the USA biscuit tin. It's where I hide my cigarettes, even though Cora's not here to find them. Right now, she's in Louisiana, with Emily. They're making a documentary together, about Roe vs Wade being overturned in America.

I think about Máire, chopping up her sister's paper-doll chains. I imagine Róisín, carefully and patiently sticking their hands back together. I think of all the women who have been here, inside this house. Screaming students, hippies holding hands, gutsy girls in petticoats and bonnets. All of them changed within these walls. What happened to them, later in their lives? I have to stop myself from wondering, trying to work everything out.

I open up the tin, take out the almost-empty pack of Camel Blues and my green Clipper lighter. Then I open up the window and look down at the for-sale sign, swaying slightly in the wind.

If the house sells, everything will have to be packed up into boxes. I'm sure a lot will be thrown out, let go of. I use my thumb to twist the wheel on the lighter, edge the end of the cigarette into the flame. And as I inhale, I realize what I will do. It's like I've always known.

When the cigarette has burnt down to the end, I flick it out the window, then peel the Post-it note off the lid of the tin. I go downstairs to retrieve the letters one last time, from inside my Dell computer. I put the envelopes inside the tin and slide the hatch open.

Maybe Cora will find them, when we're clearing out the house. Maybe she won't. Maybe someone else will, someday.

. . .

I did go back, to finish off the game. I played as Magnolia instead of Rosemary, and changed every single answer, using the manuscript to guide me along a different path to the one I'd taken before. The story changed somewhat. Different characters to encounter, different obstacles to overcome. It was interesting, to me, that there was no Michael in the game. No one really came between the sisters. Whatever way I played it, the question at the end remained the same. Gaga had meant for it to end this way, so every player would have to make the final decision.

The sisters, standing on the steps outside the school, holding hands. *A or B?*

I typed in A and watched the school crumble. The sisters kept their hands held as the words appeared above their heads.

THE END

Acknowledgements

This book would not have been possible were it not for the generosity of Anne and Sean, who welcomed me into their home in West Cork when I was a total stranger – a lost and broken one at that. I wrote most of *Confessions* in their box room, underneath the duvet in my single bed. I had come to Ireland knowing that I needed to make my world smaller. I look back on that year now as the richest of my life.

Anne, you are the most free-spirited, magnetic person I have ever known. I will be for ever grateful for the wisdom and stories you have shared with me. Each day I spent with you by my side made me less fearful of the world and of myself. I'm sure you would argue that I've always been bold, but I had never felt proud of my boldness until I had you to look up to.

Sean, thank you for lending me your old laptop after I arrived on my bike with practically no possessions. The first chapters of this novel were written on that laptop not long after, and I can still remember the password you created for my account: *Londonlass*. Thanks also for letting me use your printer, many times, so I could chop up bits and pieces and rearrange them on your carpet.

Writing a novel is a lonely process, and putting it out there is frankly terrifying. I am so lucky to have the support of my brilliant agents, John and Hillary, and my thoughtful editors, Isabel and Jessica. My first conversations with each of you meant the world to me. You spoke about my novel as if it was real, and made me feel like an actual author. *Confessions* is so much stronger because of your combined input and encouragement. Thanks also to Mary for such brilliant copy-editing – especially the small details about Ireland in the 1970s.

I would never have got here, though, without continued support from friends who have always believed in me, especially when I didn't believe in myself. Thank you, James, most of all, for seeing me first, and reminding me always to be my own best friend. Thank you, Pip, for teaching so much more than the school syllabus, even when it got you in trouble. Thanks also to Declan, who would have been so proud of me.

Finally, thank you to my family. Lizzie, for being my big sister more than I am yours. Alice, for being the first person to finish reading the first draft of this book. My mum, for your incredible eye for detail. And my dad, for the shelves you have built for our books over the years and for reading this one more time than you've read *The Old Man and the Sea*.